THE ENGLISH BOOKSHOP

JANIS WILDY

BLAKELEY PRESS

The English Bookshop by Janis Wildy published by Blakeley Press, 1143 Martin Luther King Jr. Way #96, Seattle, Washington 98122

ISBN:979-8-9854575–1-3

ISBN:979-8-9854575-06

Cover by Leah Jacobs-Gordon

For Rolf

---

*L*ucy lifted the page on her wall calendar and stood still for a minute, transported dreamily into the English countryside. The month of September showed a photo of an English country house. Clipped boxwoods lined a path in front of the home, while a rose stretched itself over the entrance portico. Inside, the rooms glowed with warm lamp light. She could almost smell the wood smoke rising from the chimney. She imagined herself there. It would be a wish come true to travel to England, in spite of everything.

Aaron appeared in her office doorway, gripping a packet of papers. "Hey, Lucy, are you free for a moment?"

Lucy immediately let the calendar page drop, feeling guilty at being caught daydreaming about impossible things. They weren't technically into September yet anyway. August's picture of a green field of corn settled back into place. She was definitely still in Seattle, standing beside her stepfather's old metal desk just off their showroom floor.

She looked up at her kid brother, who had stepped into the room and was now towering over her. "What's up?"

"It's time we had a meeting." He looked hesitant and paused.

"About?" Lucy prompted.

"Our future here."

Her heart sank. Had he found out something? The business she and her brother ran was centered around making and selling artisan mattresses. It had been in the family for decades. Yet, Aaron, who had recently graduated from college and never paid much attention to the business, was suddenly looking into everything.

"In fact," he continued, "I'm calling Mom in."

Lucy's stomach tightened in anxiety. "Well, we can't now. We have a photographer coming in to take our picture for the website, remember?"

"Why aren't you doing the photos?" He looked at her quizzically.

"I'm busy," she lied, "and besides, I've got a photography student at the UW to do them. For free."

The word "free" seemed to calm Aaron. "Good. So when will we be done with that?"

"She needs an hour to take the photos."

He nodded and backed off. "We'll have the meeting afterward then." He turned and waited for her response in the doorway of her office.

Lucy scrambled through her mind for some reason to put him off. Something to say that would distract him, but finally she sighed. "Okay, let's meet in the break room."

Before the photographer arrived, she went into the bathroom. In the mirror, she pressed her cold fingers against her face. It was time to face reality. She'd tried, she'd really tried to ignore the signs, but Aaron was right; their beloved family company was in financial trouble.

Fifteen minutes later, Lucy and Aaron were standing in the sunshine just outside of the Wellslept Mattress building with the photographer. She looked so young. Lucy wondered if she herself had looked like that when she was in college, only a few years ago.

At the moment, the student was having trouble stabilizing her tripod on the uneven sidewalk. She had been adjusting the legs for several minutes and she kept apologizing. Lucy walked over to peek at the setup. "Carla, I love this viewpoint. Why don't I help you move it into the grass? I bet the surface will be a lot more stable."

Carla looked up at her with a flushed face. "I should've realized that."

Aaron sighed with impatience but Lucy ignored him. "No worries, that kind of stuff just comes with experience. In fact, maybe you should zoom in on the shot of just us at the door? If you go too wide, I'm afraid the garbage cans will show."

Carla turned a deeper shade of red. "I'm sorry, I didn't even notice them."

"It's okay. You'll develop a garbage radar once you've done it a few times." Lucy laughed, hoping to put Carla at ease.

"How do you know all this? Are you a photographer?"

"Oh, no. Well, I haven't done it for a long time. I'm way out of practice." She didn't mention that she'd been in the photography program at the University of Washington herself before she had to drop out. She had absolutely loved going scouting for new shots with Paul, her stepfather. But that was ancient history now.

The young photographer bit her lip while hunching down on the sidewalk to get both them and the Wellslept sign into the photos. After several attempts, Aaron's arm had become stiff around Lucy's shoulders, and her own mouth was frozen into an expression that she hoped still looked something like a smile.

After a few more shots, Carla stopped for a moment. "I think maybe you two need to loosen up a little? Sometimes it helps to pretend that you're looking at a friend, you know, someone you care for, instead of a camera."

Lucy looked down at the camera and thought of Paul again. He would have had them all laughing. Her smile faltered and her throat started to hurt. Yes, five years had passed since he died, but she still missed him. She forced her smile even bigger.

"Okay, just a few more by this tree." The photographer led them over to the back entranceway from the parking lot. "I spotted it when I drove up."

Lucy shared a solemn look with Aaron. It was the maple tree they'd planted after Paul's funeral. The leaves were just turning a cheerful red at the tips, hinting that fall was around the corner.

The young photographer stared at them with a contemplative expression. "A serious portrait might work better for you two." She bent down on one knee and hoisted her camera to her shoulder. "Can you stare out into the future with a confident look?"

"More like the opposite of that," Aaron muttered, and his dry, dramatic tone somehow struck Lucy's funny bone. She burst out laughing, and then her brother did too. Carla's camera clicked furiously, and Lucy hoped she caught a few great images.

Once their photo session was over, Lucy hurried back to her office in order to find a way to make the facts about their declining sales seem less alarming to her mom. When she couldn't delay any longer, she made her way toward the break room. All was quiet on the showroom floor. They wouldn't be open to customers for another hour. The brass bed frames were dusted and shined up. The bed linens were freshly stacked on their shelves. Lucy just loved how welcoming and familiar it was. It had been the same way for years.

She climbed the carpeted stairs, straightened her shoulders, and walked into the break room.

Aaron was sitting by himself at the round table with a bunch of printed papers and his computer. He always sat nearest to the coffee machine. When Paul was alive they didn't need to have these kinds of meetings. But after he died, all three of them were involved in the big decisions.

"Where's Mom?"

Aaron shrugged. "I told her a few minutes ago to come in."

"Maybe we don't need to involve her." Lucy suddenly hoped that she could reason with Aaron. He often listened to her points if she could get him alone.

He snorted. "Oh yes, we do."

"Fine." Lucy walked back out to the hallway.

The walls were bathed in a pink glow as she approached the open door to the room where her mom did her creative work. Unlike her own office, Celia's office changed its colors frequently. Currently the walls were painted a bubblegum pink. Over by the window, a white slip-covered couch sat layered with what seemed like a thousand woven cushions of every color of the rainbow. Reams of fabric leaned against each of the corners of the room.

Perched on the edge of the cluttered desk was a crystal candy dish filled with Skittles—for the fabric suppliers, she claimed. The floor was covered with stacks of home magazines. The thing about her mother was that, whether it was a throw pillow or a sheet set design, she went all in to the process.

"Mom, we have a meeting now."

"Oh?" Mom pushed her red polka-dotted reader glasses up her nose and kept staring at her computer screen. "Just a minute."

Lucy knew better than to turn around. Her mom could get lost in her projects. Many times, when she was a kid, her mom had forgotten to make them dinner. Lucy had learned how to make a pretty good macaroni and cheese. She always added butter and Aaron always loved it.

As much as she didn't want to discuss their budget crisis, she knew Aaron wouldn't let her avoid it. She cleared her throat after silently counting to sixty. "Ready?"

Her mom got up slowly. She did a full yoga stretch of her arms before moving toward the door. They left the pink glow of her office and reentered the break room, a place that had escaped her mom's artistic energy and was still done in the dusty rose-brown color that was popular when her stepgrandparents began the business.

Her mom took her seat between them and looked up with a pained expression. "What are we discussing that's so urgent?"

Aaron passed their mom a spreadsheet with highlighted lines that dominated the page. He wore a serious look on his face. Lucy was surprised at his determined attitude. He gave one to Lucy too. "The blue lines are where Lucy has been supplementing our sales since January."

Lucy gulped. She had hoped to keep her "help" a secret. She'd slowly been draining her own savings account to boost the business account. She quickly passed around her own neat printouts. "This is a spreadsheet showing which months we historically make the most income."

Her mom pushed her polka-dotted reading glasses up her nose as she inspected the information. She looked up at Aaron. "I suspected sales had been flat, but what you're suggesting is that sales have been dropping?"

Aaron jumped in. "Not just dropping. Drying up. And then there are the bills."

Lucy cleared her throat but her words still came out in a whisper. "As you can see from my handout, we just need a few good sales on Labor Day and Christmas to get us back in the game. I also have a plan to show you where we need to make cutbacks." She held her breath after that. She knew how much her mom hated budgets.

Aaron gave her a deprecating look. "We're behind in paying the suppliers. We've refinanced as much as possible on our mortgage. But the deal breaker is that our taxes went up this year. By a lot. Where are we going to get twenty thousand dollars next year to pay for them? Cutbacks won't be enough."

Lucy snatched at the little piece of paper from the city office that her brother was brandishing. The property taxes had gone up? She saw the numbers and gasped. "What happened?"

"Development happened. You know how close we are to Lake Union."

The cute Eastlake neighborhood where they were located always seemed a step removed from the downtown area of Seattle. But now condos and apartment buildings were sprouting up all along the corridor that led to the tech-heavy businesses around the lake. Still, she wondered, had the city assessors even looked at their sixties building with its mushroom-shaped roof and stucco exterior? They were not a fancy place.

Aaron turned in his chair to face their mom. "I thought we'd have more time, but we must act now before we're looking at bankruptcy."

Lucy grumbled, "Oh, come on."

"Seriously, I think it's finally time to"—he paused, sending an apologetic look toward Lucy—"sell Wellslept."

Lucy's response got stuck in her throat.

Their mom looked thoughtful. "Sell or merge?"

"Merging is good. I mean, I want to stay in this field if I can. I think you both do too, right?"

"Yes, without a doubt. I've been wanting to expand my design work for years." She pointedly looked over the rim of her glasses at Lucy. It was a familiar argument. Mom always wanted to create more bedding designs and Lucy always had to keep her projects matched with their financial reality.

"Good. Then all we need to do is get acquired by one of the bigger names in the business."

"No!" Lucy exclaimed in shock, her voice finally catching up with her thoughts. "Never. How can you even suggest we abandon our family legacy to some other corporation? That's horrible."

"I'm not saying we abandon anything," Aaron said. "We can still be Wellslept Mattresses." He looked over at Lucy. "We become known as an eco-choice inside a national mattress company. We control our own brand."

Lucy was taken aback by the zeal in Aaron's eyes for expanding their business. She knew they needed to do something about the numbers, but he didn't seem to be understanding the problem: merging with another company would change Well-slept in ways Lucy couldn't bear. It would be the end of an era. A betrayal of Paul's wishes. Didn't he realize that?

Their mom nodded. "Makes sense to me. With more money, we could expand our brand to a bathroom line. I've always wanted to design bath towels."

"No," Lucy sputtered again. She couldn't take her mom talking about Aaron's idea as if it was as simple as choosing a new tooth-paste. Lucy didn't want to see her stepfather's trustworthy company name turned into a parody of itself. She knew that if she allowed it, Aaron would have them become a partner of Night Train or even worse, Sleepsy Fields, one of those cheap mattress producers.

The anger she felt galvanized her. She turned to address her mom. "This is going too fast. Our big Labor Day sale is coming up and we're going to make a bundle at it. We'll buy ads, put up flyers, and do a big Twitter campaign with giveaways. I know it's going to bring in the traffic. Then I'll go over the books to see where we can make some strategic budget cuts. We can scrape up the money to pay the taxes. Nothing needs to change here."

"Oh, Lucy." It was the dismissive tone of voice her mom used when Lucy proposed any new idea. "You need to evolve." She looked up, her eyes gone misty. "I don't want to lose who I am, Lucy. It took so long to get here."

"What? I don't understand," Lucy asked, feeling hurt by her mother's refusal to consider her plan.

As her mom folded her hands in front of her, her gemstone rings clacked against the table. "It's simple. If Aaron is right, and we do lose the business entirely, we will be out of work. How am

I going to get hired at my age? Without new projects I won't be invited to lunches or asked to be on panels or to participate in industry conferences. I have a career now and we must have money to keep those new products coming."

Her mom glanced significantly at the papers on the table, her voice raised. "I'm especially not going to go back to those days where we spent all our time eating ramen and stealing toilet paper. I won't ever go back to that kind of life."

The thought of ramen mixed with chicken broth for their dinner had not come up for Lucy in years. "We don't have to go back to those times. We're not going bankrupt. We can just cut the budget until after the Christmas sales."

Celia shook her head firmly. "Nope, at my age, I am not pushing pause ever again."

Lucy tried to control the anger that was rising up inside of her. Why couldn't her mom sacrifice just a little to save the business?

Her mom held up her hand. "Before you object again, Lucy, I want to say that I loved Paul. He did save us. He was a good father. To you both." She shifted in her seat and looked from Aaron to Lucy. "But I didn't marry Wellslept Mattresses. If it's time, if we have to sell to further our careers and get some security, I absolutely support that. I think he would too."

Her mom was wrong. Paul loved Wellslept. And what would Nana and Papa think if she let Wellslept go? She told herself to calm down and think fast. "Let's at least take a little time to think up some other solutions."

Aaron gave her a sad look. "I'm sorry, Luce. You know the numbers are telling the truth. You've been avoiding telling us and hoping you could make it better. I get it. But now we need to move on this. Delaying isn't going to work."

He pushed one final piece of paper across the table. "Let's look at which possible companies we want to get in bed with." He winked at their mom, who laughed like she always did at Aaron's mattress business jokes.

It was like they had already decided everything without her. She scanned the paper Aaron had given her. It was a list of national mattress and bedding companies. Despite what she thought about merging, closing the company forever would be truly awful. Lucy knew she had to offer something to give her the time she needed to think of a third solution.

She took a deep breath. "Okay, if the upcoming sale doesn't go well, I'll agree to a merger." Lucy forced herself to speak in a steady tone over the frantic pounding of her heart. "But let's wait until the Labor Day sales numbers are in before we do anything drastic. It's only two weeks away."

Aaron looked at her mom and they shared a glance. Celia cleared her throat. "Okay, Lucy. You can manage the sale. Let Aaron and me work on our plans. Just be open to the future, whatever it holds. You might be pleasantly surprised at where we end up."

Lucy knew exactly where she wanted to be and it was maintaining the company Paul had left to them. She was not confident about any plans that her mom might cook up. She knew her mom was very talented. She had a beautiful eye for design. But Lucy feared that in her quest for a bigger career she'd forget to value the security that Wellslept had always offered. Paul used to be the wise voice of restraint where her mom was concerned. Now with Aaron and her mom aligned, Lucy's only hope was the sale. "In two weeks we won't even need to be having this conversation."

She slid the list of possible company mergers back to Aaron as they all got up from the table.

He shook his head. "Nope, this is for you. Part of being open to the future."

Lucy heard smugness and excitement mixed in her brother's

voice. She put the list in her back pocket. It was heading straight to the recycle bin.

Once Lucy was back in her office, she slumped into her chair. The upcoming Labor Day sale had just become the most important one Wellslept would ever have. She felt wave after wave of anxiety rise up in her chest. What could she do? She had never been good at writing ads or pushing sales on people. It hadn't mattered so much before because they had always had a steady stream of customers. Her gaze fell to the framed photo that she'd taken one summer day she and Paul had had lunch together down by the lake. She managed to smile back at the picture. "Hey, at least it's not all bad news. The Apple style still sells well. The Hawthorn is doing okay, but as always it's the Linden that is doing the best."

"Who are you talking to?"

Lucy's cheeks colored. It was Aaron at the door again. "Nobody, just myself. What's up?"

"Got the mail." Aaron dropped a load of papers on her desk, a little harder than usual.

Lucy glanced at them as he made his way out the door. "Bills?"

"Exactly. Let's get them in the system right away," Aaron said in a bossy tone as he strolled down the hallway.

Lucy barely managed to not roll her eyes at that. She surveyed the pile of papers, noticing two glossy advertisements and several envelopes that looked like bills. As usual, Lucy didn't want to open them. However, now she had no choice but to look at every single one, so that she knew exactly where they stood. A very good sale result and fully paid bills would probably work to convince Aaron to shelve his merger idea.

One official-looking piece of mail with an unusual stamp caught her eye—probably a fake advertisement from some insurance company. She tried to see through the envelope to determine if it was a sales offer, but the paper was thick. She shrugged, slid her thumb into the back of the envelope, and ripped it open along the seam. As she unfolded the letter, one name stood out, as if it had been written in bright neon ink, which told her this was for real. She felt an inkling of curiosity. The letter's subject line said it was referencing Brian L. Baslow.

Brian Baslow was her biological father. The one who had left when she was four. The one who had never returned. The one who she blamed for all those ramen dinners. The one who had stopped communication with her after her seventh birthday. Would this be a plea for money? Was he finally in the dilapidated state that her mom had warned he would find himself in? She saw that the letter was from an attorney's office. She flattened the thick paper and let herself read the text. It was a letter concerning Brian L. Baslow's estate. "Oh," she said, as a feeling of dismay ran through her. "Oh no." The letter said her father had died.

Lucy closed her eyes and put her hands to her face, pressing them against her forehead. He was gone? She blinked and tried to read the letter again, but the words didn't make any sense in her brain. He was only—she paused to guess—in his late sixties. She was notified that her father had died very recently and that she was named as an inheritor in his estate. That first part she under-stood. It was the word "estate" that confused her. Because her father didn't have any money. Her mother had always said he was a loser, a failed nineties-era grunge music record album cover artist who had gone home to England. Someone they didn't want in their lives.

Lucy thought of the treasure box in her apartment, an old shoebox really, where she kept the things that had come from her biological father, and felt tears prick at her eyes. Inside the box there were glass marbles and a ceramic pin of red British phone box that she used to wear, a set of dried-up Japanese gel pens that her father had left behind, a famous Seattle band CD he had illustrated, and five charming self-drawn postcards from various places in Europe and England that he'd visited. Oh, she'd loved looking at them. He'd drawn mice at the Colosseum, a group of cats at the Eiffel Tower, and a scholarly owl perched on top of the Big Ben clock tower.

She'd been curious about the life he'd had away from her, but Lucy's mother wouldn't tolerate any mention of him. Though it made her feel guilty, her mom's opposition didn't stop Lucy's interest. She often wondered about her set of British grandparents, why she had freckles and her half brother did not, and why the heck she loved fruitcake so much when no one else did.

She turned the envelope over. How could there be an estate to leave? The address was from Bath, England. In the past, when she was a teenager, she'd pored over web pages that cited her father online, but had never tried to contact him. He'd never called her or sent her a drawing after second grade. Not even a late birthday card. So, she'd stayed silent too out of respect for her mom and respect for herself.

She swallowed and started reading the letter again. It referred to a property with a business. She was requested, by Sappworth & Higgins Solicitors LLP, to come to England and sign papers. She winced at the invitation. She couldn't leave now, not with the dismal business and big sale coming up. She thought about calling the lawyer's office, but realized that it was nighttime in England. She folded up the letter, took a deep breath, and rolled her shoulders slowly forward and back. This was insane. She almost expected the letter to disappear now that she had read it.

She glanced at the framed photo of her family: the Wellands. It was her stepfather who she constantly missed. She didn't know how to feel about Mr. Brian Baslow; he'd already been gone so long. Instead, she felt hollow anxiety, like she'd misplaced something but didn't know what.

She stood up, compelled to tell her mom. She would know what to do. Lucy made her way up the stairs. Her mom was talking on the phone when she walked in. She motioned for her to wait. Lucy moved a tray of candles off a chair so she could sit down.

After she hung up the phone, her mom smoothed back her curly blond hair. "What is it, Lucy? I'm not going to change my mind about what we discussed in the meeting."

That stung, the certainty in her mom's words, but she shook her head. "That's not what it is." Lucy's voice came out a little bit husky.

She handed over the official-looking paper and Celia started reading. Lucy watched as her mother sunk into her chair, the frown lines deepening around her mouth.

Without looking up, she started talking. Her voice was low. "So, is this true? He died? I wonder how?" She shook her head as if to clear it. "Probably smoking. Or something like liver failure. Or exposure to cold."

Lucy looked up, embarrassed by her harsh words. "Mom."

"Well, he worked in a pub for a while. He already drank a lot back then."

"I thought he was an artist."

"Yes. A self-centered *artiste*." She spat out the word as if it had left a bad taste in her mouth. "Hmm." Her mom patted the letter slowly. "This feels more odd than I expected it to. I almost never think of him and now I'm thrown back into the early nineties, when you were a newborn. Have you responded to this?"

"No. I only just got it."

"Good. Don't get involved."

"It says I'm named in a will. It's pretty clear I need to do something."

Celia pursed her lips. "Did you get an email as well?"

Lucy shook her head. "No."

Her mom turned the letter over. The only finger that didn't have a gemstone ring was the one wearing her diamond wedding ring. "This wasn't certified?"

Lucy shook her head no again.

"Then they don't know that you even got this. Listen, I don't want you named as a person needing to deal with his debts."

"But it said there was an estate."

Lucy's mother laughed bitterly. "That's just code for mortgage, bankruptcy and repossession. Believe me, nothing good ever came from Brian but you." She pushed up her glasses. "I've protected you all these years from him because he was selfish. You are not. You are the opposite. Too giving, too caring. I don't want you getting involved with all of this mess. Certainly not while we are in a crisis."

"I kind of thought this might be a way for me to find out about my family in Britain." Lucy put her hand out for the letter, feeling deeply disappointed with her mom's response.

"That's a terrible idea. If there is anyone, they'll think they can come to you for money. Especially now." Her mother shook her head. "Lucy, we need you here, focusing on the business. That's what you're good at. Really, I'm sure the attorneys can handle all the details that you wouldn't even know about, right?"

"I suppose so." Lucy accepted the letter back but didn't like letting it go. "I'm still curious."

"Have you been listening to me?" Her mother's voice had taken on a higher pitch.

Lucy fought to stay calm, but she was surprised at how close to tears she was becoming. Why couldn't she know about her father? "Yes, you said to not respond."

"Even in death, that bastard is reaching out to you and trying to turn you against me. Well, I say no, Lucy. We don't owe him anything." Her mom's eyes filled with tears and Lucy was shocked. She didn't expect her mom's reaction to be so strong. She didn't know what to do. Her mom's tearful eyes were staring right at her.

"Okay, I'll let it go," Lucy backed down.

Her mom quickly wiped away a tear, while giving her a tight

smile. "Good. Focus on your own life. There isn't anything to find out about Brian. He was a narcissistic man who thought his own genius was more important than us."

"Fine. I get it, Mom." This rambling insult was more her mom's style.

Afterward, as Lucy walked slowly back down the hall, she wrestled with the thought of not doing anything. It didn't feel right to ignore the letter. She didn't think Brian had tried to turn her against her mom. Admittedly the postcards had given her hope and a secret interest in England and Europe. She had always hoped Brian would send her more cards. But since he hadn't, she had accepted he didn't want her in his life. When her mom married Paul during the summer after fourth grade, Lucy finally gained the father she had always wanted.

Only, her longing to know her real dad had always been there, when someone said how much her brother, Aaron, was the very picture of Paul with their curly reddish-brown hair and warm brown eyes, when they then turned to her, frowning into her pale skin, blue eyes and dark brown hair and thick eyebrows and concluding she took after her mother. Lucy knew that her mom's looks, with her crazy blond curls, didn't support their comments. Those yearnings to know about her father might have faded, but now they were back.

---

2

*H*aving returned to her office, Lucy opened up her computer and typed in her father's name on the keyboard. It couldn't hurt to learn a little more about him. Unlike her previous teenage attempts, this time she also added in the location of Bath, England. Across the top of her screen one photo stood out. A single black-and-white of a smiling man with stylish glasses and woolly eyebrows. Was this him? With his graying whiskers and crinkles around his eyes, she figured it was a fairly recent photo. She zoomed in on it and stared. It had to be Brian. There was something about his eyes that she recognized. Afraid to start thinking too deeply about him, she quickly let the photo resize and scanned the rest of the images. There was a surprising number of sites showing children's book covers. A few more clicks revealed that her father was the illustrator of these books. A children's book illustrator. It was a direction she had never considered searching for. How had he gone from grunge music illustrator to children's book artist? Zooming in on the books, she scanned the brightly colored words and illustrations of penguins, cats, and children. Her heart leaped to her throat. She recognized the little animals from her own postcards. That made the lump in her throat grow.

Lucy minimized the page and tried to get back to focusing on Wellslept's finances, but the numbers on her computer screen swam in front of her eyes. Finally, she got up and grabbed the keys to the company van. She needed to talk to someone. Nina, the manager of production at their warehouse, was her closest friend. Together they might be able to come up with some kind of plan to save the company and figure out what she should do about Brian.

Lucy made sure that her mom would be around to cover the store if anyone did come in during the afternoon hours to buy a mattress, and then she headed south on the I-5 freeway. She felt so much clearer once she was out in the sunshine, driving along with the familiar Space Needle to the west and an astonishingly clear view of the glorious white-capped Mount Rainier to the south.

After a short drive, she took the exit ramp, made a sharp right, and in a few blocks pulled up to where several warehouse spaces shared a parking lot. This part of Seattle was a blend of industrial businesses, old buildings, and tall ancient trees. It was also extremely normal to hear the loud rumble of low-flying airplanes on their way to nearby Boeing Field. Next door to Wellslept's warehouse was a design shop for faucets, and down the street was an old building where kids practiced acrobatics and gymnastics.

Lucy parked the van under an impressively large maple tree, walked up the ramp, and entered the Wellslept workshop. As she did, she felt her heart calm down. She loved this place. The smells of varnish and fresh wood immediately took Lucy back to her childhood, when Paul would take her along with him for the day. Coming here with Paul meant she'd get to make her own hot chocolate from the vending machine in the workroom. There was always a can of whipping cream in the office refrigerator.

In the back of the open shop, she could see tall stacks of mattresses reaching up to the ceiling while the tools of the trade were neatly tucked into wooden workbenches. She'd spent many happy hours following her stepfather around as he showed her how the mattresses were constructed. Nina had been working for them even back then, as a young art student helping in production, and she was here now, walking toward the door with a grin on her face. "Lucy, come on in."

Nina's hair was pulled back in a ponytail and she wore tiny gold hoop earrings and blue Doc Martin boots. The women quickly hugged.

"Nina, how are you?"

"I'm doing great, but we've got a problem to talk about."

"Oh no, I thought I was bringing the problems," Lucy said.

"You need a cup of tea?" Nina had already turned toward the counter where the electric kettle was kept.

Lucy nodded. "Always." Tea had become a shared tradition, once Lucy had outgrown the hot chocolate.

Nina leaned against the counter while the kettle warmed up, a straightforward look on her face. "It's the Burke building across the street. It just sold."

Lucy frowned. "Ooh, I don't like the sound of that."

"Well, there's a bigger problem. Joe stopped by. He's going to raise the rent on the space here. Said he started thinking about selling once the Burke sold, but decided to raise our rent instead."

Lucy closed her eyes, just for a second, letting the latest news crash into her. "How much?"

Nina reached for the paper notice. "He's raising it by five hundred."

Lucy gasped. "A month? That's too much."

"I know. I told him that we'd been very good tenants for years. I offered him a free mattress to offset the cost for a few months." She looked guilty. "I hope that was okay."

"Of course." Lucy couldn't believe it. She put her head in her hands. "What can we do? I already need more money and now this?"

The kettle whistled and minutes later, Lucy was clutching a proper cup of black tea, a malty strong English breakfast blend that Nina always bought on her trips to nearby Victoria, British Columbia. They each put in milk, before carrying their cups from the office into the large open workshop. Nina also got out a Costco-sized tin of Walkers shortbread. As Lucy took a bite of the buttery cookie, beams of bright sunlight came in from the multiple skylights in the ceiling. Across the room, big rolls of fuzzy wool and squares of white latex peeked out from their shelves.

"What's wrong?" Nina asked after Lucy explained how Aaron had discovered that they weren't pulling in a profit anymore. "Aren't the college students and parents coming in?"

Lucy cradled the smooth china cup in her hands. "It's the competition. I counted twelve new places selling mattresses in Seattle and some of them call their products 'natural.' We aren't unique anymore. I mean, we *are* because of our quality and sustainability, but the public doesn't know not to trust some of those other guys. Aaron believes it's time to merge or sell, and Mom backs him up on it all the way. She wouldn't even consider my point of view." Her voice tightened as she spoke.

"After all these years, she wants out?"

"All she cares about is continuing her design career. And, like always, she doesn't think I should focus on anything but running the day-to-day business. Maybe my ideas could have turned us around earlier." Lucy sighed. "I mean Aaron only graduated from college a year ago and his ideas are golden, while I've been running the company for five. I don't get it. Stick to what I'm good at, she says. But the thing is, I'm not sure I'm really that good at running this company. I mean it's not..."

"It's not your zone of genius," Nina said, smiling. Like usual, she understood perfectly.

Lucy laughed. "Right. So what am I going to do?"

Nina put her hands on her lap. "Let's see how we can perk you up first."

Lucy nodded, thinking for a moment about the letter she had received. She hadn't even processed that yet.

Nina must have noticed something in her expression because she cocked her head and said, "Are you okay?"

"I'm okay." Lucy was suddenly aware that her eyes felt itchy, her shoulder-length hair was limp, and her tan pants were wrinkled. "On top of everything, I also got a strange letter today. I just learned that my biological father died. Brian Baslow."

"Oh, my gosh, I'm so sorry." Nina got up and gave her a big hug. "What a shock."

Lucy tried to stop them, but tears squeezed out of her eyes. Her nose started to run, and her throat constricted. She hadn't realized how much it mattered to have someone understand how affected she was. Having Nina acknowledge that it meant something that her biological father had died struck a chord in her. Maybe it mattered more because her mom had been so dismissive. In one day, it seemed she had lost her company's future and then lost a father, albeit a distant one. She tried to smile a little while wiping her eyes. "It's okay. He didn't matter to me. I mean, he did, but I'm not totally broken up about it, not like with Paul."

"It's different, but I'm sure a part of you will always belong to him too," Nina said.

"Mom thinks I should ignore the letter."

"What do you think?" Nina calmly asked while swirling the tea around in her cup.

Lucy leaned forward. "There is something exciting about it. Apparently, Brian owned a property that they're saying I'll inherit." She shook her head because she still didn't believe it. "It's in a little town west of London. London, England. The lawyers want me to sign the papers in person."

Nina's eyes opened wide. "Really? You could go to England?"

She clapped her hands together. "You've always been an anglophile, even as a kid. I remember the books you'd carry into the shop. *The Little Princess* and *The Secret Garden*…"

Nina was the only one who remembered stuff like this. "Yeah, but I get the impression that this isn't going to be like those books by Frances Hodgson Burnett. I could be walking into something a little more gritty."

"But it's England. Think of the opportunity to explore a place you've always been interested in, and to find out more about yourself. Like from whom you got those bright blue eyes." She smiled, her own hazel eyes wide with interest.

"Hold up. No, I'm not actually going. I can't. It's just too busy a time to go and Mom thinks that I'd be held responsible for whatever kind of financial trouble he might have been in. She's still really bitter. I was surprised at how angry she got when I brought it up."

Nina groaned out loud. "Lucy, he's dead for goodness' sake. Why would she be trying to control you over this? It's a dream trip and it would be good for you. When was the last time you had a vacation?"

"Actually…not since Paul died."

"Right. So go. Get inspired. Maybe you'll get a spark of creativity for your own work."

"At Wellslept?"

"Pfft." Nina laughed. "No, your photography."

Lucy felt a pang of annoyance. "Oh, that."

"You were very good, and if you hadn't had to quit college so early, you'd be working in that field, I know it."

"Maybe." Lucy crossed her legs. Since Paul died, Lucy hadn't felt the urge to take photos. The camera that Paul had bought her was gathering dust in her bedroom. Nina was a successful weaver and she never gave up on trying to get Lucy back to working on her school major in photography. Lucy shook her head. It was her duty to the family business that mattered most to her now.

22

"Promise me you won't say no to this chance. Find the time. Go after the sale is done. Give Aaron a chance to really step up instead of just thinking he can do it."

Lucy thought of Aaron's enthusiasm for change. "I'm half worried…" She paused. "No, honestly, I'm terrified that he'll sell the business if I go anywhere."

"What if you leave some strict rules not to make any changes? He can probably behave for a week or two," Nina said lightly.

"I could, but he is serious. Mom is serious too. And they're right that we can't go on like this. Something does have to change. My only hope is we make enough money at the Labor Day sale. Nina, is there anything we can do at this end?"

Lucy watched Nina's face. She knew that these efforts to save money would affect Nina's work as well. But Nina leaned forward without hesitation. "Have you considered closing out the Willow or the Poplar?"

Lucy tensed. Maybe she shouldn't have asked. "We haven't stopped production on anything for years."

"Sounds like it's time to be bold. The Linden and the Apple are the ones that consistently sell. The Willow doesn't."

"But the Willow is our best. And it won that award a few years back." Paul had been so proud of winning that award.

"That was eight years ago. Come look at our stock." Nina got up off the stool and started toward the storage area. The mattresses were stored in rows on pallets at the back of the large room.

"I've taken to storing the Willow back here." Nina hefted a mattress out from the stack. She was tall and strong with lean muscles. As she bent over the large mattress to wipe the dust off the plastic mattress sleeve, Lucy noticed a few gray strands in her ponytail and pushed away the thought that Nina was going to be forty soon. She hoped that Nina would never leave Wellslept. Together, they were a team. Without Nina she never would have made it through Paul's death.

Nina wiped her hands on her jeans. "They're getting covered with dust. It's been so long since one was purchased."

Lucy ran her hand underneath the thick opaque plastic wrapping to feel the padded layer below. She loved the color of the Willow, all proper in dark quilted brown with black piping.

"This one and the Poplar use the most expensive batting. We'd do better if I didn't have to order any more from Johnstone's. Their shipping fees alone are killing us."

Lucy knew she had to consider it. These answers were not going to be easy. She'd already made the easy changes back at the office. "How much could we save?"

"Over the year?" Nina considered. "A couple thousand dollars."

Nina moved toward the next row. "Over here is where I've been keeping the Hollys and the Oaks. I think we should retire them as well."

"Even the Oak?" Lucy's voice rose in shock. She wasn't prepared for this carnage. What would Paul think?

Nina spoke simply. "It hasn't been moving. If I cancel our latest order to Johnstone's now, we'll save money right away." Lucy patted the brown tufting and helped Nina push the mattress more securely into the stack.

Would she miss seeing the Willow? The Poplar had been her grandmother's favorite. And the Oak; it had been their flagship product forever. "Maybe we shouldn't rush this."

"It's okay to let them go, Lucy. They've done a great job for us, but maybe their run is complete if no one wants them anymore."

Lucy's heart was in her throat. "Someone might order one in the sale," she offered feebly.

"We have enough if that happens."

Lucy heard her own voice get wobbly. "I hate things changing." She immediately wished she could go back in time. Back even a few seconds before she had to kill the Willow.

Nina nodded slowly. "You've been through way too much of

that lately." She walked over to the calendar and flipped the page up. She had the same mattress manufacturers calendar, and underneath September's dreamy photo of the English house, Labor Day weekend was shaded in green. "Let's try to see what we can do to make that easier. I'll send you the numbers on how much closing out the product will impact the budget so you can have that to tell Aaron. I'll get the whole place clean and ready for pickups during the sale. Maybe we can turn this around by next week."

Nina paused abruptly, her voice cutting off.

Lucy looked up at her. Watched her come to some decision.

"But if you need to, it might be time to let me go too."

Lucy's face flushed. "What? No, never."

Lucy could see Nina's throat move as she swallowed. "At the least, you don't need me here full-time. And Jerry could be here during sales." Jerry was their part-time helper.

"I couldn't do it without you."

Nina's features softened. "Yes, you could. We aren't so busy that you need me here all the time."

"That could change, and then who would I turn to? Who could I trust to do it well enough?" It felt urgent she squash Nina's suggestion immediately.

"Thank you. But you know I produce all my weaving here in the downtime. I feel guilty about it. My side hustle is starting to do really well these days and I think I could transition to making it my full-time hustle." She sounded so inspired.

Lucy stood up straight. "I know. But I still need you here. And we aren't that desperate yet. I hope we won't ever be."

"Okay, Lucy, I'm not leaving anytime soon." Her voice was reassuring. "This is the coziest workshop on the west coast after all."

Lucy felt her shoulders relax a little. She walked over to the bench where they had left the teapot, intending to have a second cup, when her phone rang. She fumbled to answer it, concerned something else had gone wrong. Aaron's voice blared out of the phone speaker. "Lucy, where are you?"

"Everything okay?"

"Quit worrying. Are you coming back soon?"

"I'm just leaving the warehouse." She glanced at Nina while mouthing the name "Aaron." She nodded in response.

"We'll see you here. We've got some happy news."

Hanging up, Lucy reached for the teacups. "Aaron needs me back for some reason. He says it's good, though."

"Maybe things aren't as bad as you think."

Lucy nodded as she dug in her bag for the keys. "Yeah, that would be a relief."

Nina leaned in to hug her and Lucy didn't want to let go. She didn't want to leave her friend and the comfort of the warehouse to go back into battle at the shop.

"Go get them, Lucy." Nina paused to smile as she stepped back. "It's hard to make changes like these, but I know you can turn this around. And then you must go to England." Nina dramatically waggled her finger to emphasize her point.

Lucy laughed. "Maybe. Thanks for the pep talk. I needed it today."

3

_____

*T*raffic was light going north, and Lucy made it back in about twenty minutes. She rushed in through the entrance hallway, eager to hear what Aaron considered good news. As she entered the showroom she spotted a bottle of sparkling cider on the counter and a bouquet of roses. Aaron and his girlfriend, Serena, were standing around the cash register. Lucy was hoping that there had been a big order on the mattresses and she wouldn't need to cancel production on anything after all. She strode up to them, impatient for the news, but Aaron told her she had to wait.

As her mom came down the stairs, Aaron opened the bottle of cider. Lucy accepted a glass from Aaron, and Serena handed one to her mom. Serena had been Aaron's girlfriend for two years now, and Lucy liked her. She was fun and full of energy, but also dedicated to finishing her studies and becoming an optometrist. Lucy was pretty sure that Serena was the reason that Aaron had bought a used but nice BMW last year. Lucy suspected that he had wanted to impress her. There was something about Serena that seemed to bring out a new, more mature Aaron. Right now, Serena's dark brown eyes were glistening and her cheeks were flushed. Aaron turned to her, drew her close, and exclaimed to Lucy and her mom, "We have some big news. We're getting married!"

"What? Oh, wow, that's so awesome," Lucy sputtered, letting out the breath she'd been holding. As she tried to get her head around news that had nothing to do with mattresses, she laughed and gave Aaron and Serena hugs. Why hadn't her brother mentioned it earlier? What had happened between the morning meeting and now?

"So, let me see it!" Celia reached for Serena's hand.

Serena blushed all the way up to the roots of her dark brown hair. "It has all happened so quickly I don't have a ring yet."

"Oh, that's okay," Lucy's mom gushed. "I'm so happy for you both. There will be so many fun decisions to make for your wedding."

As her mom became increasingly excited about color palettes and wedding food, Lucy thought of Paul. She wished that he could have been here in the showroom with them. Another thing he had missed. Another thing his illness had taken away from them.

Then her mom sidled up to Aaron to give him a hug. "So, have you set a date?"

"We want to do it pretty soon, now that we've decided." He glanced at Serena with a shy smile.

Serena nodded. "The last day in September."

Lucy's eyebrows rose. "That is soon."

Serena shrugged slightly. "I know. It's because my uncle is here visiting, and my mother will insist he be at the wedding before he returns home to the Philippines."

Celia grinned happily at Aaron and gave Serena another hug. "We can do a lot in a month. This is just the happy boost I needed today. I love weddings." Her eyes flickered over to Lucy and Lucy wondered what that look was supposed to mean. Was she referring to the news about Brian? Or was she supposed to have provided her mom with a wedding first? Just because she was older?

Mom continued, "I'll host a grand party to celebrate the engagement."

"My parents will want to help. I'm sure they'll want to have a big dinner with a bunch of traditional Filipino food. They'll want to meet you."

"That sounds wonderful. We can have a combined party. Let's schedule it for next weekend."

Lucy objected, the words squeaking out. "You mean Labor Day weekend?"

Serena nodded. "That sounds perfect."

"No." She couldn't believe it. "I mean, we're having the big sale here next weekend, so we're going to need all hands on deck."

Her mom's voice became petulant. "Oh, Lucy, we don't all have to be here for that. And the celebration can be in the evening, of course."

She was already turning back to Serena. Lucy recognized the familiar feeling of becoming invisible and moved around to face her. "I'm planning on extended hours for the sale. We'll be open until 7 p.m. all weekend to maximize the sales."

"Darling, let's not talk business right now."

"But—" Lucy protested.

Celia gave her a dark look. "It's up to what Serena and Aaron want."

Serena appeared apologetic. "Labor Day will be so festive. Since Aaron and I have set the date for late September, we might as well do this party as soon as possible."

It was like a punch to the gut. Lucy had expected them all to work the sale together, like in the old days. But her mom was now more committed to this wedding than she was to the sale. It was obvious.

Surely Aaron would get it? He would know that they couldn't cut short the last day of the sale, if they were really serious about giving the store a chance. She waited while the happy couple talked about venues with her mom, before moving on to talk about floral arrangements and dresses.

When Lucy finally got a chance to interrupt, she waved at Aaron to get his attention. That's when she saw he was looking at Serena with such soft eyes, that she was certain that he couldn't hear or see anything else. She felt a pang in her heart—a strange mix of jealousy and love for her brother that kept her from redirecting his focus.

It was fine, Lucy decided. Those last few hours of the sale she could staff the place by herself. If the sale was going well enough, it might be a little crazy, but she could do it. She tuned back into the conversation between her mom and Serena when a shiny metallic food truck pulled up outside in front of the store. As the truck backed up into the sunlit parking spot outside their windows, a rainbow reflection lit up the entire showroom. Aaron suddenly looked up and met her eyes. Paul had loved rainbows.

Lucy promised herself she would not let Wellslept change. Somehow, she had to find a way to keep Wellslept and her family secure.

After a flurry of frantic days preparing for the Labor Day sale, the long summer weekend finally arrived. The weather app on her phone featured a fortuitous row of sunshine icons. Lucy showed up to work extra early wearing her formal navy blue blazer, blue button-up shirt, black trousers, and black comfort flats. She'd been to the balloon store, and with a Starbucks latte cup balanced in her hand, she tied a raft of red balloons to the wooden sign announcing the sale. She stood back and took a deep breath. *Let the games begin*, she told herself, if only to help banish the fear that had dogged her all week.

I'm ready as I'll ever be, she added to calm herself down, and considered running through all the other sayings she'd looked up on the web to help her feel positive. She went into their store and dropped by her office to check on her online advertising. On the days running up to the sale, Lucy had unleashed her final push of advertisements. She'd spent hours designing them in Canva using photos of their mattresses. Then hours more trying to get the words right. She'd had to use her own money to buy them, but if you read local newspapers or logged onto social media, you would know about the sale.

The Facebook ads were up and running. Everything looked good. Just before she left her office, Lucy reached for the calendar. September first was finally here. A niggling thought about England filtered into her mind as she put the new month's page into place, but she pushed it away. The only thing she would focus on today was the sale.

Out in the showroom she put on some music from the independent radio station to keep the good energy going. The college student they'd hired arrived right on time at 9 a.m. Lucy called out to her as she walked in, "Happy Labor Day sale!"

Ashley smiled. "Look, I'm wearing my best dancing sneakers." They were soft pink with a big white chunky sole.

"Those are perfect," Lucy said while going to grab the wearable sandwich board that displayed the words "Big Sale."

Lucy used to wear it as a teenager, then Aaron did it for a few years, and now Ashley. They'd hired her for last year's sale as well, so she knew what was expected. It was totally cheesy, but Lucy knew it would get the attention of the people driving by. Ashley pulled it carefully over her head, popped in her earbuds, and ran to the curb outside the store to start her dancing-on-the-sidewalk routine. Lucy caught a glimpse of Ashley with her magenta hair pulled back into ponytails dancing happily and felt a glow of appreciation for her.

Lucy set up right behind the cash register. Every time she saw someone walk by on the sidewalk outside, she looked to see if they'd be coming in, but the door remained shut. After a while she turned to straighten the bedding on the shelves behind her. At 10 a.m., her mother and Aaron walked in.

Aaron frowned. "You look like you're going to a convention. Why are you so dressed up?"

"I want to look professional."

He grimaced. "People are going to be intimidated by you and your blazer. And those stodgy shoes."

She looked at his jeans and T-shirt. His khaki jacket had an obvious coffee spill on the collar. She sighed and pulled off her blazer. "Better?"

"Yes." He ran up the stairs and was back in a few minutes. "Here, tie this around your neck."

It was one of her mother's fabric samples. Her brother had folded the soft pink and gold fabric into a bandana shape. She tied it on.

Aaron stood back. "Yes. That's much better. You'll at least look friendly if anyone comes in now."

"Fine," she said sternly, but then softened it with a smile. He was probably right. Aaron often had a better sense of what looked good with what. Lucy thought of it as a talent that he shared with their mom but had skipped her.

Even though Ashley was out there doing her best, no one came in over lunch. Lucy told herself it was okay; it was only Friday. At two in the afternoon, she called Aaron to watch the floor and decided to grab a late lunch at the deli a short bike ride away.

As she peddled up the street, brightly colored signs advertising a new mattress store began to appear on the sidewalk and power poles. She felt a burst of irritation. Why had some business picked this weekend to officially open? She decided to check the place out. It was across from the grocery store and of course it would look just like all the other cheap mattress places in the area. She parked her bike outside the grocery store and walked over.

She expected to see ugly overhead lighting, blank white walls, and scary salespeople; the usual all-around bad experience that drove people to choose Wellslept instead. In the shop window, the standard red sale signs shouting "50 percent off Labor Day Sale," promised just that, but as she peered inside, she saw that this store didn't have bad lighting like the mall mattress stores did. And it wasn't empty.

Inside, plenty of students and their parents were milling about. The sight of so many customers made her heart squeeze in worry. Lucy didn't feel any better when she saw the shop was advertising an eco-mattress. She had to see what this was about.

She walked in. The shop had four eco-mattresses on display, but as she got closer, she saw each one was actually the same mattress in four different sizes.

A muscular young guy came up to her wearing a bright blue polo shirt. "Welcome to Sleep Bold, where sleep is your first quick win of the day."

She cleared her throat. This was awkward. "I, um, I'm looking for a mattress?"

"Great, we have memory foam, euro top, pillow top, pocketed spring, coil, and hybrid. Today we have special savings on everything." He smiled at her with exceptionally white teeth.

"Just a twin."

"Under ninety-nine bucks or over?"

"Under?" She was terrified that that low price was even a choice.

"Super, I've got these three. Everyone is getting this one for college. It's fifty-nine bucks."

"It says this is eco?" Lucy's worry increased. An eco-mattress for fifty-nine dollars was an amazing price.

"On this one"—he paused to read the tag—"we use a natural cover and recyclable materials."

Lucy leaned down to read the tag for herself. It revealed that the quilted cover was made of fire-retardant polyester. In tiny type it read that fire-retardant was known to cause cancer in California. The internal latex was made from a chemical bonding process that used a plastic composite. It would outgas the same as any of the others. A deep sniff made her wrinkle her nose. The only thing that qualified this bed to be called "eco" were the coils. The coils were recyclable. She wanted to throw up her hands in frustration. This wasn't eco, this was marketing.

She saw a family looking at the fake eco-mattress next to her. The man pointed at a sign with a cute sheep in a green circle. "This what you want? A healthy one?"

The daughter bounced on the side of the queen-size. From a few feet away, Lucy could smell the patchouli she was wearing. "Yes, I told you, Dad."

Lucy listened to the sales guy talk up the earth-friendly features. She felt the urge to butt in and tell the truth about the kind of latex they were claiming to be natural. Maybe it was natural at one point, but the layer on top wouldn't break down in a hundred years. If they really cared about the quality, these customers should have been filling the showroom at Wellslept, instead of being duped into false advertising. She left to angrily walk around the deli, but found she wasn't hungry anymore. Instead she went next door to the drugstore, and got as many brightly colored signs as she could that said "sale." They were meant for yard sales, but she was in a panic now. She would put up signs for the Wellslept sale here, at night. There had to be some way she could redirect the customers to her store.

When she got back to the showroom at Wellslept, she was relieved to see it wasn't totally empty. At 5:30 p.m., Lucy did make a sale. One queen mattress sold to a conscientious couple of graduate students who had done their research and knew exactly what they wanted. She didn't have to launch into the difference between Sleep Bold and Wellslept because they already knew. They'd pick it up themselves from the warehouse the next day.

That night, she filled out ten plastic sale signs and took a big stapler in the basket of her bike. She stuck them to the wooden telephone poles on each corner surrounding the Sleep Bold mattress store. She rode her bike home in a slightly better mood.

Over the weekend the sales added up. Sunday had brought them in the most, with eight mattresses sold. But it wasn't enough, and Lucy knew it.

By Monday afternoon of the long weekend, she was in a panic. She'd told herself just this morning that things could still turn around, that things would pick up as soon as the breakfast hours were done. That things would pick up near lunch, as the people who had procrastinated would eventually come in. When Ashley was on break, Lucy actually took the sandwich board and went out onto the sidewalk to wave at customers herself. Shortly afterward, two families came in. She pitched to them with a smile. She explained the quality that the kids would love. They smiled back but soon left. She wanted to scream at them, *School starts soon! You need a good mattress!*

When a woman in her twenties came in at 6:30 p.m., Lucy had already given up. Aaron and her mom had gone to prepare for the party. The families had planned to meet at a grassy park on the lake just a few blocks away. Still, she put on her happy face. "Hi, welcome to Wellslept."

The woman nodded and walked right over to the Linden. There was something about her golden hair that made Lucy look at her twice—and then she recognized her. It was Amanda Alba Grouse. The star of the art department back when Lucy was at college. At one time, they had been friends.

Lucy hoped Amanda wouldn't recognize her. She watched as she started digging around in her bag, then pulled out a flyer. Just not their flyer.

"I'm looking for the fifty-nine-dollar mattress?" Yep, it was Amanda. She still had a soft Southern accent.

Lucy glanced again at the flyer from Sleep Bold. "We don't—" She paused. Was she going to lose this sale to those creeps? No way. She rearranged her face and smiled. "Super. I'll show you what we have."

"My sister wants an eco-friendly mattress for school. She's going to stay in the new dorms."

"Does she want a twin-size or full?"

Amanda laughed. "She probably doesn't know what she wants. But I'll get her a twin."

Lucy considered how to pitch their more expensive mattresses. "This one is a very high-quality eco-mattress. It has a soft organic cotton cream cover." Lucy often sold these because they looked pretty, had a good price, and were still natural. "Our Linden doesn't have latex. Instead we use coils and natural wool batting to give it durability. It is *really* comfy."

Amanda peered at the tag then coughed. "It says five hundred dollars."

Lucy thought fast. "Let me show you all the options."

"What's this one?" Amanda wandered over to the Apple. It was an eye-catcher with its delicate swirl pattern embroidered in pale green over the cream fabric. Her mom had designed it with spring in mind.

"That is our Apple. We start with the naturally woven cover, add soft cotton batting, and layer it generously over the coil interior. You get a great firm sleep. Some people say it makes a big improvement in the way their backs feel."

Amanda patted the bed and sat down on it. She rested her Louis Vuitton bag on the brass bedpost. "As long as it's good for the planet." She chuckled then looked up slyly. "Hey, you're Lucy, right? At the UW, art major?"

"Yeah, that's me. Good to see you."

"How are you? Still doing photography? I remember you were really good with those black-and-whites."

"Not anymore."

"Struck out on art, huh?" She shrugged and looked around the room. "Not everyone can make it."

Lucy felt heat rise to her cheeks. "I run our family business now."

"Oh, really? This is a local shop?"

"Yes. We make the mattresses here in Seattle."

"That's cool."

"Want to see one more?" Lucy did not want to talk about her college days. She brought Amanda over to the last mattress on the row. Never bring customers closer to the door was a rule her stepfather had taught her.

"Say hello to the Oak. It's covered with plush organic cotton quilting for comfort and has a natural botanical latex interior. All of our mattresses are made in our local warehouse so there are no carbon costs from shipping." Lucy paused, then added, "And we can deliver to her dorm."

Amanda nodded her head slowly. "I like the pattern on the other one. Let's get it."

Lucy felt a sense of relief. "Great. She'll love the Apple."

"Say, I've got a show coming up. You should come."

Lucy smiled, thinking she'd go anywhere if she could make a sale. "Sure, where?"

"Richard William Gallery."

Lucy stared at her. Richard William was the biggest gallery in Seattle. Lucy had spent many hours there during her college days, dreaming of a future in which she had her own show displayed on those very walls. Lucy looked into Amanda's eyes to see if she was joking. But she returned her gaze with no impish grin.

"Wow, the RW. That's amazing."

"Yep, things are going really well these days. Rewards come to those who persevere, you know."

Was she insulting her? "I'm glad you're having such success." Lucy hoped she sounded more sincere than she actually felt.

"Illustrative art is selling really well. All those tech workers' condo walls need filling. Sometimes I don't know if it's my art or just that it's the right shape to go next to someone's fig tree." This time she did laugh, a throaty, scratchy laugh. Lucy almost forgave her.

Amanda wandered into the back behind the counter. "What's all this stuff?"

"We have our own signature bedding lines. My mom designs them."

"I absolutely love this one." She picked up a teal coverlet with white lace overlay.

"It comes in a twin size."

"No, not for my sister. This one would be for me. My sister can scrounge up her own blanket."

She carried it over the counter. "Ring this up for me too, will you?"

"Sure." Lucy hesitated. "So the Apple is $399."

Amanda smiled sweetly. "Is that the sale price? I came in with the sales flyer and this is a lot more than the one advertised." She gazed at Lucy and then looked outside as if she was considering leaving.

Lucy was annoyed at Amanda's blatant bargaining—after all, she was the one having a show at a major gallery—but she just had to make this sale. "Okay, if you're buying the coverlet, then I'll put you on the friends-and-family discount. It's $320 for the mattress, fifty for the coverlet."

Amanda smiled even more broadly. "Perfect. Now we're both happy." She signed the receipt. "Love your scarf. Do you sell those here too?"

Lucy absentmindedly touched the fabric Aaron had tied

around her neck. She had taken to wearing it. "These are in development."

Amanda picked up a business card from the shop. "Do you mind if I take a few pictures of your linens? I want this for my Instagram."

"Sure, knock yourself out," Lucy said. She noted Amanda's perfect skin and peach lip gloss. She was probably always ready for a selfie.

Amanda walked back down to the coverlet section. "These colors are just so exquisite."

"That's my mother's eye. She's the creative of the family." Lucy felt a surprising jab of bitterness at her own words.

"Fantastic." She snapped a few pics and headed toward the door.

"Oh, and Lucy, do come downtown to my opening next month. I'll introduce you around as my long-lost college friend from my formative years."

Lucy imagined the way she'd feel after an evening witnessing Amanda's success in the world of art. As she smiled and nodded at Amanda, she decided that, no, she wouldn't be going.

Lucy glanced up at the clock as the door closed behind Amanda. The clock said 7 p.m. Aaron's engagement party was halfway over. She thought about closing up, but decided not to, in case another person from her past showed up. Besides, it was impossible to resist taking a peek online at Amanda's art. It turned out Amanda produced illustrations of women, capturing their movements with a few brilliant strokes. Lucy pushed down her feelings of envy. It was stupid to feel jealous. After all, it had been her own choice to give up photography.

Finally, at 7:30 p.m., Lucy walked slowly to the door to pull down the sale sign. She stood in the silent entranceway and felt light-headed. The sale was officially a disaster. Lucy wandered into her office and sat down.

She picked up the framed picture of Paul, recalling the

promise she'd made to him, when he was sick. She had gone into his room, when he was home with hospice. He had taken her hand in his bony one and asked her to watch out for her brother and mother. She had promised to him that she would, and that she'd protect everything he had worked for. She had whispered it to Paul, and he managed a smile in response. "I know you will take care of everything, my sweet daughter." Her throat had choked up at that. He knew how important it was to her that he had formally adopted her.

She blinked away the tears. She couldn't let Wellslept go. As long as she was at Wellslept, Paul wasn't gone. He was just around the corner. No one else could provide that comfort for her. Not her mom and not Aaron. She looked at the picture of Paul again. Tears flooded her eyes. She'd been here before. The dull feeling of grief was always there. But this time she had completely let him down.

Her phone rang. It was her mom. "Lucy, where are you? Surely the sale is done now. We're getting ready to officially toast the couple and everybody is waiting for you."

Lucy looked at the clock, blinked rapidly, cleared her throat, and tried to sound upbeat. "Okay, I'll be there in five minutes."

"Good, and bring the flowers from my office. I forgot to put them in the car earlier."

"Okay."

Lucy changed into her flat oxford shoes and tossed on a windbreaker jacket. It was hot outside, but whizzing along on her bike would be a little breezier. She grabbed the flowers from the office, noticing that her mom had spared no expense. She leaned in to sniff the multicolored tight-budded roses, mixed with sprays of green Bells of Ireland, but they had no scent. These were not from the natural foods grocery or garden, but from a real florist.

She put them in the basket of her bike, secured them with a bungee cord, and pulled on her helmet. Before she rode away, she glanced back at the mushroom-shaped building. Wellslept wasn't the prettiest, but it was homey. A good place to buy a mattress. Tears filled her eyes and became one horrible sob. She shoved off and rode her bike down to the lake.

Despite her wet eyes and running eyeliner, she knew she made a pretty picture as soon as she caught people smiling at her. It was the roses leaning heavily in her bike basket, and probably something about her upright bike and her oxfords and the scarf tied jauntily at her neck.

She circled down to the little park by the water where the party was being held. She could do this. She patted her face, swiped on some lip gloss, and blew her nose into a napkin in her bag. There were kids running through the grass, picnic tables were covered with pretty blue tablecloths, and older people gathered together on lawn chairs. She wished Nina had been able to join them but her teaching schedule kept her from attending. Lucy prepared herself to not know anyone except her family and Serena. As she was locking her bike and repeating her worries to herself, a cute guy wearing khaki pants and a blue plaid shirt came over to her.

"Looks like you need a hand with those flowers."

She was pulling the lock through her bike tire but looked up immediately at the sound of his familiar voice. "Bruce?"

"Hey, Lucy."

She looked more closely. That impudent smile and those bright blue eyes used to be topped with long surfer hair. "Bruce. It *is* you. Oh, wow. I didn't know you were in town." He was still handsome, but pulled together now with short hair and the look of a former athlete.

He leaned in and gave her a hug and kiss on the cheek while holding the flowers to the side. "Just moved back a few weeks ago. You look great, Lucy."

She felt her face flush. Another blast from the past. This time an old boyfriend. They'd been at high school together and had dated for a while in her first year of college. He'd left to enter a business program in Nashville, and she hadn't seen him for about five years. Aaron must have invited him. Bruce had been a good friend of his too.

"Everyone is down toward the water," he said, helpfully carrying the flowers, while leading her along a paved path lined with white birch trees. Lucy was excited to meet Serena's family. She had never been to a Filipino family gathering. Most of the adults were gathered around two picnic tables set up next to each other. Lucy greeted Serena's parents, shook hands with aunties and uncles, and tried to remember the name of each kid as they darted by. Serena and Aaron's friends, including Bruce, added to the total number as well. After getting a plate full of Serena's family's special grilled barbeque pork on a stick, rice, and a scoop of sinful macaroni salad that came from a Welland family recipe, Lucy wandered over to say hi to her mom, who was sitting in the shade and looking at her phone with Serena's aunt.

"Lucy, you're here. Can't you smile a bit? You look like a grump."

"We didn't meet our sales goal." It had slipped out of her mouth. She waited for her mom's reaction.

Her mom looked at her over the top of her red polka-dotted glasses and gave Lucy a distracted smile. "Oh, that's too bad. Tina and I are talking about these flowers for the wedding. Aren't they gorgeous?"

Lucy limply accepted the cell phone and looked at the image of white roses. How could her mom act so blasé? Lucy desperately tried to think of new options for the business. Renting the space out as an Airbnb? Letting her apartment go and moving into Wellslept? There had to be a way to keep Wellslept safe.

Aaron walked up and took a glance at the flower pictures at their mom's urging. "I like them. And, this took a long time, but I think Serena and I have also come to an agreement about the after-party. We're thinking of renting a yacht."

Lucy tried to control the frustration in her voice. "Can we afford that?" She hoped that Serena's aunt wasn't listening too closely.

Mom stretched out her arms and a bunch of bangles slid down to her wrists. Her voice was terse. "Lucy, I don't want to hear that tone, today of all days. I know you've had a hard time with the sale. I know you want to stick to Paul's strategies, and we all respect that."

Lucy started to sweat. She interrupted her mother. "I wasn't just using Paul's strategies. I used my own. Our competitors are lying and undercutting us, so it didn't work."

Aaron looked to Lucy. He spoke in a gentle voice. "I take it the numbers didn't improve today."

"Not enough."

Her mom pressed her lips together. "We did it your way, and now it's our turn."

"We can refinance again..." Her desperate-sounding voice trailed off.

"Don't think the bank would go for that, sis."

Serena walked up, paused, and then tapped Aaron on his shoulder. She looked with concern at each one of their faces. "I'm sorry to interrupt, but it's time for the champagne toast and cake."

He glanced at their mom, who followed the couple over to the picnic table. Lucy walked up at a distance behind them, passing Bruce, who looked with curiosity at her and Aaron. She didn't want to have to explain it all to him, too, so she quickly wiped the worry from her face and stepped up to him with a smile. "Ready for some cake?"

Serena's parents raised a toast, as her elementary-age cousins crowded very close to the big white frosted cake that read "Happy Engagement" in bright blue gel lettering.

. . .

After meeting all the relatives and getting lined up for many family photos, Lucy slid her hand into her purse to check her phone for the time. She was ready to get out of the awkwardness of smiling at people she didn't really know. She began to help an older lady clean up the table and pack crackers and cheese into plastic bags when Bruce appeared.

"Lucy, you aren't thinking of leaving, are you?"

"I've had an exceptionally long day."

He looked concerned. His earlier smile had gone away and now he was looking at her carefully. "Want to get a drink? I know it's been a while, but we used to go to Pizza Planet across the bridge and it's still there. Aaron and Serena are coming too."

Lucy remembered going to that bar back in college. They'd order pitchers to drink and there was always a pool game or darts to play.

He smiled. "You used to be a good shot at darts."

She looked up at him, grinning. "You remember my dart-playing abilities?"

"I remember lots of things," he said quietly, following her over to the recycle bins and helping dump several empty plastic trays. "Since I've been back I've been hoping to see you and Aaron, but it's been busy. I haven't got a chance to get over to this side of Seattle until now. Most of the time I've been setting up our new offices in Bellevue. When Aaron told me the good news, I was psyched to reconnect with you guys." His glance seemed to linger on her eyes a little too long.

She looked away, flattered and confused all at once. "What's your new location all about?"

"I'm the cofounder of an incubator-style business." He laughed at her puzzled expression. "We're an investment group that funds start-ups."

"Oh, I get it." Lucy thought that explained the fresh haircut and his business casual look.

"So, will you come? I've really missed the old days, you know.

Aaron and Serena want to play a game of pool and I'm going to need a partner."

She was going to say no, but the idea of going back in time, to the Pizza Planet, sounded better than figuring out what she could possibly do to stop Aaron from going crazy with a merger in the future. She looked up to the new-old Bruce. "Okay, let's go."

he old pizza place was comfortably familiar with its collection of local beer signs showing Mount Rainier rising above a Rainier Beer bottle claiming "It's Mountain Fresh" and the simple Olympia Beer sign claiming it was "In the Water," but there were changes as well.

The wooden tables that they had gathered around in the past were gone, replaced with new metal-topped tables and leather chairs. The graffiti carved into the booths had gone too. The bar remained largely the same, and Bruce ordered them all an honorary pizza with what he and Aaron used to get on top: Canadian bacon and pineapple with extra garlic. Bruce was as fun to be around as she remembered, convincing her to play several games of pool and taking extra care to coach her on her shots. Aaron and Serena left after that first game, but she and Bruce stayed to play another few rounds. She had laughed more in one evening than she had in months. It was easy to slip into their old roles. It made her feel light and flirty and stress-free.

Bruce suddenly became serious as he walked her out to the parking lot. "I had a great evening."

"I did too," Lucy said, and she was amazed that it was true. The heavy feeling in her heart had lifted a bit.

He looked around. While the street hadn't changed that much, all the college dorms in the area had been remodeled. "I've been gone for too long. The last time I was here was probably six years ago."

She sighed, looking past the parking lot toward Lake Union. The water reflected the sky in a shade of orange sherbert tinged with blue shadows. It was nearly ten, but the light lingered long after the sun had set in the Seattle summer. "So much has changed."

"Tell me about it. You are running Wellslept now. I'm really impressed, Lucy. I'm sorry that it's been rough lately. Aaron told me you've had some stiff competition."

She frowned. She didn't want to talk about business. This night had been to forget all that.

He looked at her closely and suddenly smiled. "I guess some things have changed since you and I were taking trips to Vancouver to enjoy underage drinking."

Normally, she would be backing away. Her life was complicated and he would be a distraction, she told herself. Not to mention, he was now her brother's friend more than hers. But tonight the fun of the evening kept her close. Once she left this parking lot, the rest of her life would come crashing in on her. She tipped her head up to look at him. He was smart, with a broad chest and those hazy blue eyes. Definitely not a skinny teen anymore. Would it hurt to flirt with him a little longer? She smiled. "Those were the most fun times. The lowered drinking age didn't hurt one bit."

"Yeah. We were crazy up there in Canada." He laughed and she was swept into his positive energy. "And now I have clients in Vancouver, in New York, LA. I miss those uncomplicated days."

"You went away to get your master's, right?"

"It was a solid program. After that, I went through an online course that really changed my life. From there, I met my cofounder, David. It's been an amazing time."

"And now you're back."

"I missed Seattle. I missed being home and near my family. And what better place to connect with so many great tech companies? It wasn't hard to convince David and our staff to relocate."

Lucy didn't know how to respond. "I've been here the whole time, while you've been out adventuring."

"I'm glad you've been here, Lucy." He moved closer to her.

A car beeped as the driver unlocked the car next to them. The dark sky made her realize she needed to get home. She reached for her keys to unlock her bike and jangled them a bit. "This has been super fun, but I should get going."

He tilted his head toward her bike. "You need a ride? It's pretty dark."

She shook her head. "My place is a five-minute ride from here."

"Okay. I'll stay until I see you geared up and ready to go."

They walked over to the bike rack where she had left her bike hours ago. She pulled on the helmet, knowing that it would feel a lot colder to ride home in the cooler night air. Maybe she should accept his offer. Aaron had told her that he was going to ask Bruce to be his best man. With the wedding coming up in a few weeks, they would be spending plenty of time together. She didn't want to think about the future or what would happen after the wedding. "Actually, I could use a ride home. Can we fit my bike in your car?" She unlocked her bike, pulled her purse across her back, and looked up at him.

He stepped back and smiled. "Sure there's room. You are a very sexy bicyclist, you know. I couldn't believe it when I saw you riding up with that big bouquet of flowers."

"Thanks," she said a little shyly. It had been a long time since anyone had complimented her like that. He didn't know how boring she'd become.

Bruce opened the back of his SUV and lifted her bike inside. She directed him down Eastlake and up two blocks. Out the window, she could see the Wellslept building coming up on her right. The windows still proclaimed they were having a sale. She quickly looked away and focused on directing Bruce. Right before they passed the local middle school, she had him turn into an alley. There was a big open parking garage underneath her building. He pulled into a spot. After lifting out her bike, he immediately started walking it toward the elevator. "Do you keep it down here or in your apartment?"

Her throat felt a little dry as she replied, "In the apartment."

He smiled and pushed the button to call the elevator. They talked about bike paths around the city as they rode up. Totally innocent stuff, but she knew this wasn't about bicycles. It didn't matter. She recognized she didn't want the day to end.

They rolled the bike down to her door on the fourth floor.

"Do you have a view of the lake from up here?"

"Yes, it's one of the perks of the apartment."

"Can you see Gasworks too? Remember when we used to hang out there and watch the sailboats go by? Remember when Aaron hopped the security fence and climbed to the top?"

She nodded, not having thought of those days in forever. Bruce was a surprise. His familiarity made her feel safe. She sensed he was missing something. Despite his move to Seattle and successful career, he seemed as eager as her to recapture something from their past.

He paused, then quickly leaned down to kiss her on the lips. He had the comforting smell of minty clean soap and beer. She thought one more moment about the problems that could come from starting things up with your old boyfriend. After a few more kisses, she fumbled for her key and asked him in.

. . .

There were dark bags under Lucy's eyes the next day. She didn't need a sleep app to tell her how little she had slept. There was also a gigantic feeling of awkwardness lodged in her chest. Bruce hadn't stayed the night or anything. But after he left, she couldn't get to sleep. She tossed and turned until the clock said 5 a.m. After that she allowed herself to get up, get a shower, and simply get going. As she walked through her apartment, she remembered showing Bruce the view over Lake Union toward the old Gasworks plant. It was now a grassy park with space to fly kites and look at the city. He had slipped his warm hands around her waist as they gazed out at the twinkling lights shining from the Queen Anne neighborhood houses tucked up high on the hill.

After leaving her balcony, they moved into her living room. She poured him a drink in her nana's old gold-rimmed china teacups. He commented that she didn't have much furniture except for bookcases. Even her walls were blank. She had laughed, and later had brought him back through the hallway to the door, where another small bookshelf sat. The comfort she had felt in the pages of books had become so important in the past few years that she liked to have books around her. She had become a permanent resident of several mythical towns in the many mystery series she liked to read. Lucy tried to avoid reading the most current book in a series, so she could save it for the next hard time. It looked like she'd have to buy another whole round of books to survive the next few days. Even though she had tried to keep it at bay, the day after the sale had come anyway.

After a quick breakfast, she rode her bike into the office parking lot at 8 a.m. She felt if she could just sit in her office, a solution would come. Strangely, there were already cars in the parking lot, including Aaron's. Maybe he was going to help her come up with a solution. As she entered the hallway from the parking lot, she heard another man's voice coming from the coffee room upstairs. Then she heard Aaron's answer. "You really think so?"

Lucy couldn't make the other voice out. Could it be Bruce? She brushed her hair back behind her ears and felt for her lip gloss. She crept closer to the bottom of the stairs but stayed out of view.

Aaron continued. "So you're looking for the same integrity of these mattresses, but they would be sold in your stores? Like an imprint?"

"Yes, more and more customers are demanding we carry several green mattress options." Not Bruce. She didn't recognize the voice. Who was Aaron talking to?

"I can never get Lucy to consider changing anything on these classics."

"I can see why—you guys have a unique market, but if we were absorbing your line, we'd want to tweak them a bit. Their weight alone is a problem for our manufacturing plants."

She fumed. Tweaking? No one would be *tweaking* the mattresses. She would find out who this guy was, or she would pry it out of Aaron later. Why was he even talking to this person? Had Aaron assumed the sale would fail and called this guy in advance? She clenched her fists.

"Mattresses are only a part of what we envision for the future. What would be the process to develop Wellslept bedding and sleepwear lines with Sleep Bold? My mother and I want to continue to develop our bedding brand, of course."

Lucy heard herself gasp. Aaron was talking with their competitor? The eco-fraud people? And about a buyout?

"Including a bedding line could be a great way to market the beds." The guy cleared his throat. "So, is it just you, or are your mother and sister also making the decisions for Wellslept?"

"All of us."

"You mentioned your sister might be reluctant to join strategies."

Aaron's voice lowered. "She grew up with the business and she wants to see that the legacy is preserved. She's our detail gal. Makes sure everything is running like a machine. She's great with the operational aspect of running the company."

Gee, Aaron, thanks, Lucy thought.

"And your mother?"

"My mom will back me in this. She's our creative and visionary leader."

A visionary? She admired Aaron's gift of gab. But he wasn't qualified to negotiate with Sleep Bold without her. They were the biggest mattress distributor in the region. She didn't think they cared at all about the value that Wellslept brought. It was more likely they wanted to get their family's business off the market.

The voices moved toward the stairway. If they glanced her way, they'd see her, so she backed up to the far corner of the bedding display area.

Lucy stood still, pressed against the down pillows, but her thoughts were racing around her head. She waited a second and then went back to her office. Shut the door. Shut off the lights. Fell into her chair and clutched her arms to her chest. Hot tears crowded into her eyes. Only one day after the sale and he was already beginning to negotiate a sale to a competitor. It had her so infuriated.

Then she heard the main door to the shop floor open again. She peeked through the blinds into the parking lot. Her mother's car had just pulled in. At 8:30 in the morning. Mom never arrived this early.

She roughly brushed away her tears. When did her mother and Aaron get so impatient? She clicked on her contact screen and frantically looked up their attorney. Her heart was beating and there was a hollow feeling in her gut. She looked at the picture of her stepgrandparents on the wall. "This is not going to happen," she told them.

Lucy hid in her office. At nine, she made a quiet call to their family attorney and got an appointment for the afternoon. At nine fifteen, she heard the Sleep Bold executive leave. At ten, she opened her door and made a lot of noise, like she had just walked in. In the office bathroom, she pressed her fingers into her face to get more color into her cheeks. She felt weirdly floaty, yet filled with purpose, a sense of steel inside. On the outside, she was all smiles, as she walked upstairs to make a big fresh pot of coffee. She'd keep it together until she got to the attorney's office, Lucy told herself. She couldn't seem to hold any other thoughts in her mind but panic, and the need to clarify if she could legally block her mom and brother's plans.

"Darling, you're just the person I want to talk to." Her mom walked into the break room, dumped her book of fabric samples on the small table, and reached for her enormous black mug from the open cabinet. Lucy froze, hoping this wasn't going to be about the secret meeting she'd overheard; she needed to talk with the attorney first. "What's up?"

"Let's discuss your role in Aaron and Serena's wedding. She'll want you to be one of her bridesmaids. And I want us to cohost a prewedding luncheon. I just love her family. Then we'll have everyone come over to breakfast on Sunday after the ceremony too, so we can offer them congratulations. What do you think I should serve? Prosecco or champagne?"

"What?" Lucy had zoned out at the word "wedding" and was thinking about whether she should walk or cycle to the attorney's office.

"Drinks for my...our party?"

"Maybe prosecco."

"I'll have it catered by the Warren Café, of course."

Lucy turned to stare at her mother. "Can't you make up a frittata or something yourself?"

"But they have such nice baked goods."

"It would be less expensive to go homemade."

Her mother wrinkled her nose. "I don't want homemade for a wedding."

Lucy felt all her calm dissolving. "Don't you get that we're trying to save money right now?"

"You keep harping on this. We already discussed this. I expect to be coming into new funds." Her mother looked happy at the prospect of the merger. "Besides, this is about making a memory."

Lucy took a deep breath. "What about the memories we already have? What about our family's company?"

Her mom's blue eyes coldly stared at her. "I can see you don't want to talk about weddings."

"You're right," Lucy snapped back and got out of the break room before she said anything worse. She flung on her linen jacket before heading outside.

Their family attorney's office was in a small building several blocks south of Wellslept on Eastlake Avenue. Lucy passed a school, a Starbucks, and a shop selling marijuana before she arrived at her attorney's parking lot.

In the office, Lucy was glad to be ushered into the familiar brown-toned room with wooden chairs, faux-suede cushions, and grass wallpaper. Phil Dunlap had traveled to Africa once in the seventies and apparently the trip inspired his décor still. They had been in the office a lot in the months following Paul's death. Even those times felt comforting compared to her emotions today.

"So good to see you, Lucy. What is on your mind?" Mr. Dunlap looked the same except for a little less hair on his head.

Lucy considered how to say it without being so blunt, but then gave up. "I need to talk to you about how much legal power I hold over the direction of Wellslept."

His forehead immediately wrinkled. "In what kind of situation?"

"I'm worried about"—her voice suddenly didn't want to work —"about the possibility of maybe merging with another company. I want to know if I can stop it against the interest of my mother and brother."

Mr. Dunlap pulled out a file and opened it. He ran his hand over the pages until he found the section he was searching for. "The short answer is a majority vote determines the direction of the company."

He looked up at her with a concerned expression. "There might be a way to fight that, if you could prove that you're the one with the most invested in the company, but that would be very messy and expensive."

She held his gaze and slowly nodded. "So, you're saying majority rules."

He nodded kindly. "You are all equal partners in the business. Your stepdad wanted it that way."

"Thank you, Mr. Dunlap." She knew she didn't have to explain, but the look of concern hadn't left his face. She sighed. "We've come to a crossroads about the direction of the company. I hoped I could keep the company as it always has been, you know."

"I remember meeting your stepdad for the first time over thirty years ago, Lucy. I hope your family can come to some understanding. Businesses like yours are rare these days."

She stood up and shook his hand. "We will do our best."

He patted her on the shoulder and walked her out toward the door. The receptionist looked up as she entered the main room. "Will you need a follow-up?"

Lucy glanced at Mr. Dunlap and shook her head. She put on a brave smile. "I hope not. There won't be any good reason for another appointment."

.　.　.

Back at Wellslept, Lucy went directly to her office. She didn't want to see anyone. Or talk about the sales figures. Instead, she opened up her computer, planning to do some desperate Google searching for an idea that would magically help her save the business when she saw a notification whiz into her email inbox. It said "sale" and was from one of their competitors. She moved her mouse to delete it but paused. What did the Dream Depot have planned? She stopped to read the ad. They were promising online delivery. More things Wellslept didn't do. She shook her head.

Right below it there was another email, this one from Sappworth & Higgins. The British attorneys. They had found her. She hesitated, then muttered, "This day is just getting worse and worse."

After clicking on the email, she found another forwarded email, from a name she didn't recognize.

Dear Lucia,

I've been told that you may not have heard that your father had died. I am very sorry for your loss, indeed it is my loss too. Your father and I married many years ago. As you and I are both named in the will, it is imperative that we initiate contact. I am certain we can conduct business over FaceTime or Skype, but the attorneys have told me that ideally you would come to Wakeby and we could quickly finish together all that needs to be decided regarding the sale and proceeds of his business and property.

Warmly,

Maura Hersh Baslow

Lucy, who had never been called Lucia, was hit with many thoughts all at once. Like a geode cracking open, she suddenly saw a different picture. This letter felt legitimate. There really was an estate. Her father had a business and it was to be sold.

There was a property to be divided. There was money to be shared. Would it be enough to inject significant money into Wellslept?

Her mother had warned her not to get involved. On the other hand, what if this property and business was worth something? This Maura woman seemed to think so. Seemed to think it was worth reaching out to someone who she had never contacted before, not even to tell her that her father was dying. Lucy felt tension in her stomach, almost a pain. Her hands were sweaty. But if there was money, Lucy could use it to protect Wellslept. And wouldn't that be poetic? Her biological father's money saving a business for the man who stepped in to father Lucy in his absence. Her hand wavered over the phone. Getting involved would make her mother very angry, and she would have to trust her brother not to make things worse with the business in the meantime, but how could she not find out?

Think of Wellslept, she told herself and reached for her phone.

It was late in the afternoon in England according to her phone's world clock, but perhaps they were still in the office.

"Sappworth & Higgins Solicitors office."

"Hello, I'm Lucy Welland, I mean, Lucia Baslow," she corrected herself, thinking how odd it was for her to refer to herself with such a floral name. "I'm calling about the…"

"Baslow, did you say Baslow?"

"Yes, Lucia Baslow."

"Just one moment." She was abruptly put on hold.

An older man answered. "Miss Baslow, it is good to hear from you. Let me extend my condolences. I'm Mr. Higgins, your father's solicitor."

"Thank you. Could you tell me more about"—she laughed a little, suddenly nervous—"everything."

"Yes, certainly." He took a breath.

"Your father died unexpectedly three weeks ago. We are currently running the estate through our version of probate. One of the first things to do is to make sure there aren't any outstanding financial obligations, so we've taken out ads in the newspapers and run a few notices online."

"Is there any evidence that there would be?" Lucy couldn't control the squeak in her voice. Had she made a mistake?

"No, this action is purely customary. Mr. Baslow's business was self-sufficient, I understand, and was making a modest profit."

A modest profit. Those words gave her such a feeling of relief she sunk into her chair, not even realizing how tense she had been. "I just received an email from Maura Baslow. She said we could take care of things over Skype."

The solicitor made a tsking sound. "That would not be ideal."

Now Lucy sighed in frustration. "Maybe we had better back up a bit. What was Mr...." She blinked rapidly, wondering just how she should refer to Brian. Lucy adjusted her words. "What is the extent of my father's estate?"

"Simply put, he owned a building located in the village of Wakeby, a couple of hours or so outside of London."

Lucy spoke quietly. "And what was his business?"

There was a hint of surprise in Mr. Higgins's voice. "Your father ran a bookshop."

Lucy wasn't sure she'd heard right. "A bookstore?"

"Yes, that's correct. Baslow's Books. Forgive me, but you didn't know about it?"

"No. I had no idea." She could not even wrap her mind around it now that she did know.

"Well, it is a bit of a specialty bookshop. Your father illustrated many children's books and he sold them there as well as other popular books. His art studio is also on the property."

So those children's books the Google search had shown up were truly his. How quickly the vision of her father as a down-and-out person had changed. A business owner? A bookstore owner? An illustrator of children's books? It was all confirmed.

Surely her mom had no idea of what kind of person he was now. Lucy felt a sharp twinge of anger. Why hadn't she known this?

"It brings a fair amount of interest. You'll be able to see it when you come. It's quite charming and the village there is of good size."

"It's called Wakeby? I'll take a look online." An image of a village with paved stone roadways and flowers in windows eagerly leaped into her mind.

He made another tsking sound. "I highly recommend that you come to sign papers. I have found clients greatly benefit from an in-person meeting. A few days would be enough."

Lucy's voice wavered. "It's...well, I'm not sure I have the money to travel to London."

"Ah. A minute, please."

Lucy was suddenly put on hold again.

"Miss Baslow?"

"Yes." She wondered if she should correct him. She was more of a Ms.

"There is a provision for your travel expenses."

Looking around her office, Lucy's eyes settled on the picture of the English house on the calendar. "Wouldn't a last-minute flight to London be very expensive?"

"The provision seems to reflect that expectation." When she didn't respond, he continued, "We can arrange a flight and accommodation for you, if you wish. It is important to proceed as soon as possible with these legal documents. We will arrange it later for this week or next."

"So soon?" She gulped.

"We'll get a few documents ready, and then send an email to review the travel arrangements with you."

Lucy felt her breathing become rapid. Hearing all the details, she felt like putting the brakes on, backing up as fast as she could. "Wait, Mr. Higgins, I hope you understand this comes as a big shock. I wasn't in touch with my father. I didn't know anything about him.

Before I make a trip, I need to understand a little more. I'm not sure I've thought this all through. From what you are saying, there is a business and property that needs to be gone through."

"Correct."

"And that business and property, if sold, could bring a profit."

"Yes."

In the silence while he waited for a response, she looked at the picture of her family. She knew what would happen if she didn't get more money for Wellslept. "Okay…please book my flight."

Mr. Higgins cleared his throat and reconfirmed that he had her correct information. He was intent on sending her paperwork. She would be hearing from his assistant. Her passport was current, he hoped. She said yes to everything.

Lucy hung up the phone and ran up the stairs two at a time to her mom's office. She was there with Aaron.

"Oh, good, I'm glad you're both here. I've got a solution to our problems." She was out of breath.

Aaron raised his eyebrows. "A magic hat?"

"No, a magical inheritance."

Her mom looked up immediately.

"What are you talking about?" Aaron said.

"My biological father died a few weeks ago." Lucy swallowed and looked at her mom. "Brian Baslow wasn't poor like you thought. He owned a thriving business and a property. He left the proceeds to me and his wife." She watched for some sign of shock from her mother, but her mother sat like a stone, only her eyes had changed, taking on a skeptical squint. Lucy continued. "She wants to sell. That means all that money can go directly into our business. It's ironic, right? My biological father finally steps in to help. We take his money for our business. And then you guys design an amazing line that makes us even more money." She was talking so fast she ended up gulping for air. She hadn't meant to say as much as she had.

Her mom pushed up her glasses. "I don't want you going there. His money isn't worth it."

Lucy shrugged, feeling triumphant. "This is better than getting in bed with Sleep Bold," she said curtly.

Her mom shared a guilty glance with Aaron. "Aaron and I are only entertaining an offer they made."

"An offer?" Her heart dropped. This was further along than Lucy had even realized. Lucy took a deep breath to calm her rapidly beating heart. "Would you and Aaron please give me the chance to get the money before moving any closer to a place like Sleep Bold?"

"This is big news, Lucy. How much time do you think you'll need?" Aaron asked. If he was impatient with her, he didn't show it.

"A week should be enough."

"I don't understand this compulsion to go there. Why on earth can't you conduct this business over the internet?" Her mom's voice had become tense.

"Because I want to go." As soon as it was out of Lucy's mouth, she realized how true it was.

"Going is a mistake. There is nothing there for you. You're not going to find anything that I can't tell you."

"But you don't answer me when I ask. Did you know he ran a bookstore? I don't know anything about my father or if I have other family there. I have to go."

Her mouth tightened. "We're in a crisis and we need you here to answer questions. You are not going."

Aaron was standing there silently, staring at the floor in deep concentration, apparently having decided that it was better not to interfere.

Lucy saw her mother's point. She knew she could help them

write up letters of inquiry and meet with different companies if she stayed. But could she give up hope so easily?

No, she couldn't. She swallowed wrong in her haste to reply and then started coughing. Once she could speak again she said, "Sorry, but I fly to London probably next week to settle the estate. There may already be a buyer. I just have to sign the papers."

Her mother turned to stare at her. "This trip is just another chance for you to avoid reality. Stop running away from what we need to do."

"I'm going for Wellslept," she said, hurting from her mom's words, but standing firm. "It's about getting us money." She decided to leave out the part about learning more about her biological father.

"So how can you afford to fly to London?" Aaron asked after an awkward few seconds had passed.

"The lawyer said there are funds for that." Lucy cleared her throat. She sensed that her brother had accepted her declaration. Her shoulders lowered in relief. "I'll need your word that you'll wait to bargain for a merger while I'm gone. And if you are going to look at buyers, could you at least try to find a company that has a little more integrity than Sleep Bold?"

He looked reflective. "If you give me a list of worthy companies, I'll contact them."

She didn't want one more thing to do, but she'd do anything to stall the process. She looked over her mom's head to meet his eyes. "I'll do it right away."

ith all the arrangements to be made, Lucy didn't leave Seattle for another week. It was the third Saturday of September when Nina's car pulled into the long line dropping off passengers at SeaTac airport. Lucy's mom hadn't spoken to her since she'd announced the dates of her trip. Conversely, when Nina heard Lucy was going to England, she had immediately offered to drop her off at SeaTac and chatted happily with her about all the details.

Lucy found herself swinging between joy and terror. The hours and days before the trip were a blur. After consulting Pinterest and Aaron, she had ordered and pulled together a wardrobe of clothes to wear. She then packed her bags three times, according to different reports on Wakeby weather. Wakeby. From the internet it looked like a quiet, small village. Lucy was fairly certain that she had memorized the email detailing which train she was to take after arriving at Heathrow and what B&B she had been booked into. That didn't stop her from repeatedly checking that she had put her printout of the email in the front pocket of her purse.

Once they got a temporary parking spot near the British

Airways sign, Nina turned to Lucy and smiled. "Well, you look ready. You've got your new trench coat and I love your ankle boots." She pointed at Lucy's neck. "That's a pretty necklace you're wearing too."

Lucy touched the gold charm in the soft shape of a rose. "It's really a brooch but I thought it would travel better strung onto my necklace." She had brought another pin with her as well. But that one was packed away in her suitcase. "Paul gave it to me. I'm wearing it for good luck."

"Oh, that is so nice." Nina reached over to hug her. "You can take my hug for good luck too."

Lucy felt her friend's warm arms around her. She stalled for a moment, safe in the car.

"Nina? Can I ask you something before I go?"

She paused with her hand on the door frame. "Of course."

Lucy's voice was super quiet. "Would you mind just letting me know how things are going while I'm away? Maybe go up to the office once during the week?"

Nina nodded. "Sure. I could send you an email or call with updates. What should I look for?"

"I'd like to know if Aaron has any meetings with more of our competitors. But you don't have to be a spy or anything."

Nina laughed. "But I want to be a spy. That sounds fun." She paused, and the tone of her voice changed. "Don't worry about the business, you still have time." She patted Lucy's knee. "This is so exciting. How are you feeling about going there really?"

Lucy stared out at the line of cars moving slowly past them. "I wanted to go to England and meet my father so badly when I was a kid. And now…I don't know. I just feel terrified."

"It's a big trip." Nina smiled encouragingly. "A big, amazing trip."

Lucy nodded. "I think it's the getting there that's scaring me. Once I'm there, Brian's wife will be there to show me around."

"Great. And don't worry about calling me at any hour if you

want to talk. Remember that it isn't all about the property and financials but also about connecting with your family history and that beautiful country."

"My family," Lucy echoed, feeling another zing of fear and wonderment shoot through her body.

"Did you bring your camera?" Nina asked in a nonchalant tone of voice, while looking straight ahead.

"No."

"I really want to see some photos."

"I know. I've got my phone so I'll take a few photos for you." Lucy reached over to hug Nina once more. "Thanks, Nina, you're the best."

"You're the best too. Just be yourself and you'll get everything done."

Lucy sat back, dropped her shoulders, and reached for the door handle. "Be myself. Okay. Here I go." She stepped out and got her luggage from the back seat.

Nina rolled down the window and yelled out, "Don't forget to smell the roses and buy lots of treats to bring home."

"Don't worry. I wouldn't dare return without several bags of candy." Lucy laughed, waved, and stepped determinedly through the sliding glass doors into the airport.

At the Seattle airport, Lucy moved along with the other people in the security line as if it was a normal occurrence for her to be traveling to a foreign place. It wasn't. She'd barely been out of the country, not counting the day trips to Canada she'd taken with Nina. She found herself shaking a little, from what she suspected was either a lack of food or sleep and not wanting to admit how frightened she was to travel alone, to an entirely new place, and learn about her father's real life. Finally she made it to the departing terminal and, after a long wait, onto the plane itself.

Right before they took off, she texted Bruce. *See you when I get back*. Since the night of the party, they'd been on two more dates. He was so eager to hang out in Seattle again and try all the new places he'd been reading about in the press. They had a beautiful dinner at a very fancy restaurant on Puget Sound with a view of million-dollar luxury boats. The night before last, Bruce had invited her to a big corporate restaurant in Pioneer Square. It was fun and dazzling to be out on the town, but she had secretly hoped he would have picked a place with a cozier atmosphere. Over dinner, she told him more about her reason for going to England, trying to put into words how she felt, but in between courses it became obvious that Bruce was more interested in which airline she was taking and the level of leg room, rather than the actual destination.

After nine hours of flight, during which she dozed upright but didn't really sleep, she found by her final meal that her fear of traveling was dulled by exhaustion. As soon as the plane landed, the people around her were up and gathering their things. She shared a smile with a couple getting their carry-on luggage out of the bin next to her.

The woman glanced out the tiny window. It was hard to see through as rain was pelting at the glass and streaking down the sides. "Can't believe we left a sunny day in Seattle and got a rainy day in London."

Lucy cleared her throat—after all, she hadn't spoken to anyone but the flight attendant for nine hours. "Yes, but how great to be here in England." Her voice sounded funny, and higher than usual. She forced herself to ask, "Have you been to Heathrow before? I'm looking for the bus to the railroad station?"

"Sorry, honey. I don't know where that is. We're taking a taxi into London for our anniversary trip." She touched her husband's hand. "How about you?"

"I'm traveling to the countryside."

"Well, you are brave to be going alone. I find Heathrow to be quite confusing. I'd never find the way out if I didn't have George

66

with me." She gazed up lovingly at a cute balding man with big ears and a tidy beard.

Lucy smiled at them. She wished she had her own George.

After the plane unloaded, she followed the couple to customs where she clutched at her passport and said that she was going to Wakeby. The official frowned, but let her through. Once out in the main area, she did her best to follow signs to the baggage area.

She felt a little better when she spotted the couple again at a large turnstile and then panicked when they got their luggage before she did. She watched as they went toward the open doorway and left her completely alone in a sea of strangers.

"I can do this," she told herself sternly. First she would find the bus. She had to ask more than once, which generated deeper and deeper embarrassment, but eventually she found what she thought was the right place to catch it. Rain was coming down very hard and, occasionally, the rain whipped off of the awning and sprayed the waiting area. No one was waiting there with her, which made her anxious, but she just kept looking at her phone and hoping she was doing the right thing. Once the coach came, she sat upright in a purple fabric chair, clutching at her damp bag. After an hour she disembarked and entered the drippy open train station. An attendant suggested she'd have the time to walk around the local streets while she waited for the train but at that point she couldn't bear to leave. She pulled her wet luggage behind her until she found a counter that sold sandwiches.

After officially going through a turnstile, she claimed a seat on an empty bench and unwrapped an egg salad sandwich. It was homey and delicious, but her feet were squishy and cold from stepping in a puddle. As the train boarded, Lucy wandered down a few cars filled with busy people and finally found a chair in the back of the last car.

Once they were moving, she smiled. This was it. The last leg of her journey. As backyards started nudging up next to the tracks, she could see rows of cheerful brick houses. Later, the yards were gone and through the fogged-up window she could make out vast green fields and wooded valleys. She felt her shoulders relax as the peaceful views slid by. Slowly but surely the train drew ever closer to the little dot on her phone that marked the Wakeby train station.

Once they were only thirty minutes away, Lucy went to use the little bathroom on the train. She looked at the reflection of herself and tried to brighten up her face with a swipe of her lipstick. It was a lot to ask, to expect the lipstick would take away so many hours of traveling. Even her ponytail looked droopy, so she untied it and brushed it out before styling it back into her hair tie. Her raincoat remained tied around her waist, valiantly holding her together ever since she had put it on early that morning in the dark. Feeling much better, she smiled at herself.

By 3:30 p.m. the train approached the village of Wakeby. Overhead the clouds were dark and little droplets of rain filled the window so she couldn't get a clear view. She was expecting a good-sized town to appear but all she saw were fields of grass and small outcroppings of trees. She was ready with her bags as soon as she saw the Wakeby sign and train platform. She stepped down to a cement walkway and entered a small brick building with a gently sloping ramp. There was only one little office here with a glass window and a sign that read, "Will be back." As the train pulled away, she realized she was quite alone. She pulled up the hood on her raincoat and stepped out toward the road. The rain was falling steadily and fat droplets clung to the sides of her trench coat before rolling down to ground. She looked around at a parking lot with more puddles than cars. The train station seemed to be all by itself except for the wet lush greenery. Far off in the distance, she could see the tall spire of a church. The town would be near there, she thought.

Lucy looked at her watch. The lawyer had told her she'd be picked up and taken to a nearby B&B where she would stay for the week. Maybe she ought to call and see if they had forgotten her? "Okay, Lucy, what should I do?" She wasn't above talking out loud to herself.

She was fumbling in her bag for the number of the B&B, called Hollyhock Cottage, when she spotted a small car driving up the road toward her. Was this the B&B people? She waited as the car came to a stop.

An elderly man rolled down his window. "Excuse me, would you be Lucia Baslow?"

"Yes. Hello," she answered to her given name in a weird, overly bright voice. It was very odd to be called Lucia Baslow.

He emerged from the car slowly wearing a tweed cap and a navy blue raincoat. "I thought so. You do resemble Brian. I'm Mr. Clive Emery from Hollyhock Cottage. Flora, my granddaughter, asked me to get you. I've got the car to take you and your luggage into town."

He was tall and had white hair under his cap. She refused to let him carry her heavy tote bag, but he seemed okay pulling her wheeled luggage along.

Lucy took another peek at Mr. Emery. She wondered how old he was. He might be in his early eighties by his hair and lined face but his eyes were bright and focused and he walked with a very straight posture. "Thank you. I so appreciate you coming to pick me up."

"I'm sorry we're having some late summer rain today. We had all hoped you would have the best weather. Don't worry though, sunshine is expected tomorrow."

His car had a sign on the side that reassuringly read "Holly-hock Cottage." He quickly opened what he called the boot. She worried he wouldn't be able to heft her luggage into the car, but he managed it in one sweeping motion. She went around to wait at the passenger door and was surprised again when he walked up to her. "If you're not planning on driving, you'll want the other side." He grinned and it was just possible that his eyes actually twinkled.

She shook her head and blushed. "Oh my goodness, I can't believe I forgot that."

They left the train platform on a misty country road that led straight into a green tunnel of trees arching toward each other. With the window wipers on full speed, they motored along with a field on one side and a few small houses on the other.

"If you like car racing, there's a famous racetrack nearby. But I suspect you'll probably be more interested in the gardens at the manor house, and of course your father's bookshop." She enjoyed listening to his lovely accent, while aware they were getting closer and closer to the village. She knew logically Brian wouldn't be there. But she still felt her chest tighten in anticipation.

She distracted herself by looking out the window. She caught glimpses of isolated cottages. Nowhere did she see any evidence of a thriving business community. "Is Wakeby very large?"

"No, not large, though it is the largest village for a few miles. Wakeby has a tea shop, a wine shop, and a greengrocer. Your father's bookshop is also a very popular place."

She couldn't see anything yet but tiny little roadways extending off into grassy fields.

"You won't see it coming, you know, with all these rolling hills. But when we get there it all opens up into our lovely village."

Lucy sank into the car seat, but somehow couldn't stop grasping nervously on to the handle of her tote bag. She was eager to see it now, the place where her father had lived. Where he had worked. Soon they saw more houses and as they turned a corner, shops suddenly filled each side of the narrow street.

From what she could tell the village was about three blocks long. As they passed through an intersection she spotted a post with metal signs pointing off in different directions. Each sign showed the names of nearby towns printed in blocky black letters. One mentioned a nearby castle. As she reminded herself with excitement, the signs as well as the castles around here really could be hundreds and hundreds of years old.

Lucy glimpsed a darling café with black-and-white stripes on its awning on the right hand side of the street. Perhaps she'd get her latte there. Then she saw a grocery mini-mart and a clothing shop. Everywhere late summer flowers bloomed in planters. At the next intersection, they drove around a roundabout with an ornate lamp post, passed an iconic red telephone box, and then suddenly Mr. Emery was parking in front of the last two buildings on the street.

Lucy shifted in her seat to look out past the window wipers. Hanging above a big bay window, an old sign read "Baslow's Books." At the store's entrance, a very large, out-of-control pink rosebush climbed up and around the doorway. The building was made of beige-gray stone, and there were two windows above the bookstore that she guessed were part of the upstairs apartment.

Through the window she spotted an armchair and a cheerful wall of books on display. She sat spellbound in the car, looking at the window, inexplicably expecting to see her father appear. It was stupid, she knew, but she couldn't help it.

Mr. Emery gently opened her door. The rain wasn't impossible now, just a light constant dripping. As she stepped out of the car, she caught a whiff of the rose. The scent was heady and lovely. She breathed in deeply.

Mr. Emery noticed her glance at the flowers. "Your dad was very fond of that rose. It's a David Austin."

She took a step forward. This was it. This street. Brian Baslow's life had been here. She exhaled. She wanted to go closer. The sound of Mr. Emery opening up the trunk of the car caught her attention and she spun herself away from the bookstore.

She moved quickly toward the back of the car, knowing how

heavy her suitcase was. "Mr. Emery, you don't have to carry it. I can get it from here."

"Nonsense, you needn't worry. I help Flora all the time. She'll have set up your room and I know she's made up a fresh batch of scones, if you're hungry."

Her eyes were drawn then to the cheerful building beside the bookstore. This was the B&B. It was set back from the road a few feet beyond a stone fence in a small garden filled with flowers. The B&B had a yellow door, planter boxes filled with pink geraniums, and a brass bracket holding a painted sign with loopy gold letters spelling out "Hollyhock Cottage."

Mr. Emery opened the gate, then handed her the umbrella and they both dashed up to the front step. Against the yellow door, a shiny brass lion's head was mounted as a knocker.

Mr. Emery opened the door without needing a key and called out for Flora. A college-age young woman with a big smile came out down the hallway wearing a peach-colored apron over a pretty blue dress. She had cornflower-blue eyes and wavy blond hair pulled back in a messy bun.

"You must be Lucia. I'm Flora." And before Lucy knew it, Flora had put her arms around her in a hug. "It's so good to have you here in Wakeby."

Lucy heard Flora's voice go throaty and she could see that she was blinking back tears. Lucy also had a fleeting impression that she smelled like butter and vanilla, before stepping back awkwardly.

"It's so nice to meet you, Flora. Please call me Lucy. Your B&B is gorgeous."

"Come on in and I'll show you around. Oh, you do look like your dad. We were all wondering if you would."

It was the strangest sensation, being told she looked like someone. It made Lucy feel as if she actually was a long-lost relative now come to visit.

. . .

Once in the door, Lucy gazed into a quiet living room. There were two matching blue-and-brown-plaid-patterned armchairs set next to a lit fireplace. Nearby a very well-stocked bar cart provided a glimpse of a variety of wine, gin, and whisky bottles. A worn blue velvet loveseat occupied a space that faced windows with a view of the colorful garden outside.

"This weather is dreadful for September so I've lit a fire if you need to warm up. Our breakfast room is down at the end of the hall," Flora told her as she turned to go up the stairs. "And the bedrooms are right up here."

The three of them walked up the carpeted stairs and entered a cream-colored hallway. Between the bedroom doors sat an antique bureau covered with rabbit figurines. Flora smiled when she saw Lucy looking at them. "Those were my granny's collection. She insisted they stay there, so they do."

They went into the room Lucy would be staying in. The bed had a light pink rose-patterned headboard and matching comforter cover. Soft gray curtains hung from the ceiling to the floor and made the whole room feel calm. In front of the window, a simple white desk gleamed in the light. Lucy wondered if Granny had had a hand in the décor, or if this area was all Flora's doing.

Flora directed her over to the tiny bathroom and showed her how to work the shower and the bath. "Feel free to use as many towels as you need." Then she walked back into the main room. "I know you'll be wanting to settle in. But I'd love to make you a proper cup of tea. There is a kettle here in the room if you'd rather do it yourself. Just push the button and it will heat up. If you come down into the kitchen, I can fix you up a snack too."

"Thank you. I might want to rest for just a little bit," Lucy said apologetically, exhausted and anxious to get out of her travel clothes.

Mr. Emery cleared his throat and glanced significantly at Flora.

Flora nodded at him. "Lucy, I hope you don't mind but we're having a small welcome dinner for you tonight. A few of your father's closest friends in the village are coming here, and Sam, of course. They'll be around about six. Everyone's been so eager to meet you."

Lucy wanted to protest. She couldn't imagine how she would have the energy to be interesting or even a good listener when it seemed any quickness of thought had faded away hours ago.

Instead she managed to ask, "Who is Sam?"

"Sam Burke? Oh, he runs the bookshop," Flora said.

"I thought my father ran the bookstore," Lucy said.

Flora looked at her grandfather. Mr. Emery replied, "Sam worked for your dad and he's the one who handles the daily operations."

"Oh. I hadn't thought of that. I'm sure there is a lot for me to learn here." Lucy was hoping she hadn't said the wrong thing already.

Mr. Emery walked to the door. "We'll let you settle in now."

Lucy let out an involuntary yawn. She quickly put her hand over her mouth. "Oh gosh, I'm sorry. I didn't sleep well on the plane."

Flora followed her grandfather over to the door. "I keep forgetting how far you've come. Is there anything else I can get you?"

Lucy shook her head and tried to ignore how dizzy she felt. "Everything is perfect. Thank you."

After the door clicked shut, Lucy finally let go of her tote bag. She took a seat on the fluffy bed covering and let herself sink down into that comfort, letting out a happy breath. She had arrived. Feeling dazed and a little stunned, she decided to close her eyes for just a minute.

.　.　.

Lucy woke on top of a strange bed. She could hear the light patter of rain outside. It took her a minute to remember where she was. Then she anxiously checked her watch. Five thirty. She blinked and tried to wake herself up. She would be cutting it close, but decided she had to have a quick shower. She went into the bathroom, turned on the water and stripped down. The relief she felt at washing her hair with a nice-smelling shampoo was amazing. She stepped out of the shower feeling renewed as she grabbed a plush white towel, wriggled into a fresh pair of pants, pulled on a white button-up work blouse, and topped it with a gray cotton sweater. For luck, she tied her brother's scarf around her neck and dried her hair as much as she could. Hopefully a damp ponytail wouldn't look too bad. Another few minutes went toward applying a squeeze of foundation to her face and a brush of mascara to her lashes. As the clock ticked toward six, she slipped on her ballerina shoes and swiped her lips with lipstick. With any luck she'd be able to beg Flora for that cup of tea.

Just as Lucy was descending the stairs she heard the door knocker tap twice against the wood. She paused as Flora dashed down the hall and opened the door. Two ladies stood on the doorstep. One was an older woman with a head of curly gray hair, a round face, and brown skin. The other was closer to Lucy's age. She carried a wicker basket filled with two bottles of wine.

Lucy stood still, hoping not to disturb them, while the second woman kissed Flora on both cheeks. The older woman offered Flora a hug and held on for a long time. Lucy realized that these women were sad, understanding in a flash that they were mourning her father. Lucy stood in place, not wanting to disturb them, but the creak of the stairway gave her hiding spot away.

Flora noticed her standing awkwardly on the stairs and broke into a smile. "Lucy! Come down. Let me introduce you to Beena and Evangeline. Beena runs our tea and cake shop and Evangeline is the owner of our local wine shop."

Evangeline laughed and stepped forward to kiss Lucy on both cheeks. She had lovely fine features, a big smile, delicate pierced earrings going up her ears, and light brown hair in the shape of a long bob. "It's a pleasure to meet you." Lucy thought she detected a faint French accent underneath the British one.

After Evangeline said hello, Beena reached forward to grasp Lucy's hands. She was staring at Lucy, her warm brown eyes filling with tears even as she continued to smile. "Oh, I see him. In your eyes and the shape of your face. It's wonderful." Beena's slight Indian accent blended softly with her British one as she spoke.

Flora nodded, her own eyes now looking watery. "I know."

Lucy felt shaken. Did she really look that much like her father? "Thank you," she said.

Flora put her arm around her and guided her toward the hallway. "We shouldn't overwhelm Lucy yet. She's only just got here. She hasn't even had the whole tour of the place yet. Or Wakeby. Not even the bookshop. But first, you must all come into the kitchen. I'm sure you're hungry."

Lucy followed the ladies into the large warm room at the end of the hall. This room had a gray brick floor and a tall open space with a mantel. Inside of it there was a woodstove. Lucy had never been in a kitchen with a fire in it like this before. It felt both ancient and modern at the same time. Industrial metal lamps hung from beams over a long wooden table. The cabinets were painted in a dove-gray color and above the windows, curtains patterned with rabbits hung in tidy pleats. More touches from Flora's granny, it seemed.

Evangeline moved into the kitchen and helped herself to several wineglasses out of the cupboards. Lucy saw that there would be six of them. Hopefully Maura would be coming—at least she'd spoken to her over email and would know one person there.

Beena slid onto a bench behind the table and patted the spot next to her with a wide smile. "Come sit down. I'm sure you've had a long day."

Lucy joined her, feeling relieved that they were all so friendly. There was something calming and fun about this older woman. Flora put a tray filled with three different kinds of cheeses and two dishes of chutney in front of them. Evangeline uncorked the wine. She brought the wine and some glasses over to the table. "Would you like a glass?"

Lucy nodded, hoping she wouldn't feel like sleeping right afterward.

"Now, Lucy, how was your trip?" Beena asked. She had a glass of sparkling water in front of her and took a sip.

Lucy reached for a glass and laughed. "I survived. It's so hard to believe I woke up yesterday morning in Seattle and now I'm here," she said, before tasting the refreshingly cold white wine. Evangeline was clearly a wine connoisseur.

"Traveling takes so much energy. I've only traveled out of the country a few times but Evangeline flies many times a year," Beena said.

Evangeline sighed. "My family is in Chartres. They expect me to visit frequently."

"But you live here?"

"Yes, I moved here a few years ago and I love it."

Beena patted her hand. "Evangeline was one of those people that helped bring our little village together."

Evangeline blinked. "Your father really did that."

"How?" Lucy asked. At last she would learn about her father.

Evangeline reached for the metal cheese shaver. "Brian started a little local business group and invited us to meet at the bookshop."

"Brian was generous that way, always offering us his place and keeping our meetings going," Beena added quietly.

Flora sat down at the table. "I don't know how he managed it, but we eventually became more of a group of friends than a business group."

They all became silent and the three women looked at Lucy.

Lucy wasn't sure what she should say. "Thank you for sharing your memories with me," she offered. "I'm so eager to learn about Brian."

At the front of the B&B, she heard the door knocker tap once again against the door.

"That must be Sam," Beena said softly.

Lucy heard Mr. Emery saying hello. And then footsteps down the hall. Flora hopped up to check the oven. Evangeline joined her and set her baguettes on the counter, ready to cut them into slices.

Beena smiled at Lucy. "Sam can always be relied upon to bring something sweet."

When a black dog emerged from the hall, with his tail waving like a flag, Lucy wondered briefly if she had somehow become confused and this dog was, in fact, Sam. But then a tall young man appeared a few paces behind wearing a nice blue button-up shirt over a pair of jeans and carrying a white cake box. He had wavy reddish hair and shadows under his eyes. He called to the dog in a tolerant tone of voice, "Barley, come back here."

Barley had made a beeline for Lucy. He jumped up, placing his big paws on her lap, and sniffed at her face and clothes before sitting right on her feet. Barley was some kind of Portuguese water dog, she guessed. His round eyes and cute face were almost eclipsed by a big curly mop of black fur.

As Sam looked from Barley to her, his skin seemed to pale. He glanced at Mr. Emery for some kind of confirmation before turning back to her.

A second later, Sam nodded. "Lucia. I've been wanting to meet you." She loved his strong British accent. "I'm Sam. I ran the bookshop with your father."

Like Barley, Sam also had big eyes; his were a gray-blue that matched the soft blue of his shirt. He gazed solemnly at her, waiting for her to say something.

"It's Lucy, really. Glad to meet you too." She extended her hand and he shook it quickly and firmly. Out of nowhere she felt her cheeks start to get warm. It was a silly reaction. She was just surprised because, somehow, she hadn't imagined a bookshop employee to be handsome or so close to her age. She had thought he'd be older, like her father.

Beena glanced at Barley. "He's sitting at your feet like he would with Brian. Look, do you see that?"

Flora came over to the table. "Barley, what are you doing? Do you know who this is?"

Lucy reached for her glass of wine and took a decent gulp this time. Could this dog recognize something in her?

Sam squatted down to pet Barley behind his ears. He looked into his face and then up at Lucy. He smiled, crinkle lines forming around his eyes. "I'd say he likes you."

Lucy set down the glass, her heart only beating a little faster at the nearness of this attractive guy, and reached out to pet Barley herself. At least with the dog here, she wouldn't be the only curiosity at the dinner. When Barley looked up at her, she introduced herself. "I'm Lucy."

Sam said, "Shake." Barley immediately raised his paw and she took it, which somehow broke the ice a little more.

"Wine, Sam?" Flora brought Sam and her grandfather the last glasses of wine and Lucy realized then that Maura wasn't coming.

Sam sat down on the chair opposite Lucy and offered her some bread.

Lucy carefully took a bite of the chutney-cheese-bread combination and its cinnamon apple flavor made her stomach growl for more. She was hungry. The egg salad sandwich was now a distant memory. Before she had time to load up on more bread, Flora brought out two steaming crockery dishes filled with shepherd's pie. Lucy hadn't ever had it, but took a good scoop of the potato and meat pie as the plate was handed to her. Along with the bread and a crisp pear and arugula salad, the meal was perfect.

"Everything is so delicious," Lucy said as soon as she'd had a mouthful.

Beena looked up. "Flora's a great cook. It's been so hot, but with the rain this week, it feels like autumn is right around the corner."

"Don't be wishing the summer away," Mr. Emery cautioned. "Once we reach this time of year, the summer days are not long for our area," he confided to Lucy.

"Oh, I won't," Beena said. "I definitely need the tourist season to last a little longer."

"So"—Evangeline looked thoughtful after they'd had a chance to tuck into the food and share compliments on each other's contributions—"you must tell us all about you, Lucy." She glanced at Flora. "We were all so excited when Flora told us you were coming."

Lucy glanced at Barley, now more interested in Sam's plate than entertaining the group. So much for that distraction. "Well," she cast about for something to say, "I'm from Seattle..."

They all seemed to know that by the nods. She launched into talking about work. "I help run my family's mattress business. Actually I'm president, now that my father, I mean, my stepdad, died a few years ago." She felt like she should stop talking but it was her habit to finish her spiel about Wellslept. "Our company makes eco-mattresses out of organic materials and we have a storefront close to the downtown area."

"Eastlake?" Flora asked.

Lucy was surprised and it must have shown, because Flora's eyes darted around. "Oops, sorry. I'm afraid that I looked you up online once I knew you were coming."

"Yes, Eastlake." Lucy smiled and turned to the others at the table. "I work there with my mom and brother."

Beena's eyebrows rose. Lucy realized they all might be confused. She interjected, "My half brother."

"You already run a family business," Sam said, his voice quiet.

"Yes. It's very important to me. The economy is changing so fast in Seattle and I've been very busy lately. I could barely get away. We have so many things to take care of there."

"So you won't be staying long," he added. Was he judging her somehow? She wasn't sure how to interpret his brief statements.

"Here? No, I can't. I hope I can get to all the details this week that need to be taken care of." Had he thought she would move here? Suddenly she felt super awkward. She didn't meet his eyes. She didn't want to meet any of their eyes—they might read there what she didn't want to say about her plans for the bookstore.

She swallowed quickly and continued, "Thank you for welcoming me here. Even though I never really knew Brian, I'm glad to have met all of you." She glanced up at Sam. He was still gazing at her with those gray-blue eyes, so she went on talking, hoping that it would get her out of the hot seat. "I saw it actually. The bookstore. I saw it when Mr. Emery drove us up. I understand that I've inherited it, along with Maura Baslow."

"Maura," Sam mumbled, like her name was just a little distasteful.

"Do you know her?"

"Yes." His short answer seemed to convey a low opinion of Maura.

Mr. Emery interceded. "Maura lives nearby in another village."

She turned to Sam. "I'd love to come tour the bookstore."

"It's the book*shop* to us," he said firmly. But then he softened his voice. "Come by tomorrow. Barley and I will be there." He met her eyes again briefly, before concentrating back on his plate.

Mr. Emery rubbed his stomach. "I think it must be time for cake."

Flora served the chocolate cake that Sam had brought with a side of local raspberries. The conversation was pleasant, but Lucy could tell a change had come over the group ever since she spoke about her own business in Seattle. Evangeline didn't seem to notice, though, and kept the conversation going by describing the village.

Between bites of the moist, rich cake, Lucy learned about a local parish councilor who was too bossy according to Evangeline. She learned about the famous gardens, where many local weddings were held and it was rumored that Jane Austen had visited.

Sam objected, "You can't tell that to Lucy." He leaned forward and offered her his opinion. "That's mainly what we tell outsiders. Jane Austen most likely didn't grace us with her presence." He paused and smiled at her. "The gardens don't need that legend anyway, because they have something better. Your dad's most popular children's story is set there. So you must go see it before you head home."

Beena nodded. "They have the finest collection of flowers and a walled garden in the area. Brian loved it there, I'm sure you will too."

It didn't take long before Lucy got the idea that they were all determined to get her to like Wakeby.

Flora lit candles as the cloudy night sky darkened outside the windows. "Brian found a secret entrance into the gardens and Sam and Barley sneak in there all the time. We even had Brian's birthday party up there last year in the little garden," she said, her blue eyes getting watery again, as she settled on the end of the bench.

"Oh yes, the parties Brian came up with were legendary," Beena said brightly. "Remember the one in the chicken coop?"

"That was for the school fundraiser. There was a big fire pit and signature cocktails from the White Hare. That's the pub up the street," Mr. Emery said. "Your father was extremely creative."

Flora clasped her hands together. "He had Sam wire the old shed with a chandelier and fairy lights and brought in a record player. It was the best party."

Lucy couldn't help but smile back at Flora, who was trying so hard to tell her about Brian. "It sounds like a fun time."

"Remember the Christmas parties?" Sam said in a wistful voice.

Lucy had been trying to be positive. She had been trying not to think about Brian having a full life in a negative way. But as they made his life sound better and better, a bitter thought grew. Where was the evidence that Brian had remembered he was her father? She felt her capacity to control her thoughts getting weaker. Suddenly she yawned. She brought her hand to her mouth. "Sorry about that."

"You must be tired. What time is it in Seattle now?" Flora asked.

Lucy counted on her fingers. "It's only two o'clock in the afternoon, but I feel I've been up for more than twenty-four hours since I didn't really sleep on the plane."

"Okay, I think we need to tuck Lucy into bed. She's been valiantly listening to us go on and on." Flora started picking up the plates. "Let me walk you to your room."

"Oh no, I'm fine. I don't want to stop the party. Please don't worry about me." As she said it, another yawn erupted out of her mouth. This one was even bigger.

Evangeline laughed. "It's okay. You should rest. I was just about to head home." She glanced at Beena.

Beena nodded. "You must come to the tea shop soon. Have you had afternoon tea before?"

"Yes, in Victoria, British Columbia, in Canada." She added all the place names, not sure if they would be familiar with the Pacific Northwest. "But never a true proper English one. I would love to experience that."

"Okay, my dear, you must come around to see me." Beena laughed and stood up. Lucy said a round of thank-yous as Evangeline and Beena told her how nice it had been to meet her. They put on their raincoats and hugged once more before going out into the evening.

Before he followed them out the door, Sam looked back to meet her eyes. "See you tomorrow, Lucy."

---

6

*H*er sleep was blissful, until she woke up in the dark. The clock by the bedside said 3 a.m., but for her it was eight hours earlier. Only 7:00 p.m. in Seattle. She wiggled her feet. She stared at the ceiling as all the visual inputs of the plane ride and train swirled around in her head. She thought of all the things that she would have to do to get the bookstore on the market. Her stomach tightened and she tossed and turned. She thought of Sam. Finally she told herself sternly to go to sleep. That she'd put her problems aside until the morning. Somehow she managed it, and when she opened her eyes again, it was light outside.

Lucy lay wrapped in the warm cocoon of the down comforter. She could hear birds happily chirping. In a moment, she got up and pushed the curtains aside. The sky was a soft peachy hue that promised sunshine. Beyond the window she could see the shops across the street. A man was out watering planters filled with flowers. Off to the left she caught a glimpse of the vast countryside rising slowly in green hills all around them. Mr. Emery had been right about the weather improving. She stretched out her arms, feeling rested. She was tempted to look at the brand of the mattress she had slept on. Instead she gazed out the window again and thought about all the people she had met the night before. She loved Flora's energy, was intrigued by Evangeline, and was eager to visit Beena at her tea shop. Sam was a surprise, a good one or a bad one, she wasn't sure yet.

Today would be important. Finally meeting Maura and then hearing the official reading of Brian's will would set everything in motion. She had packed one blazer to wear and this would be the day to wear it. She pulled on her cream blouse, black trousers, and ballerina flats and put her rose pin from Paul on her lapel. The other pin she had brought was in her purse. It was the one Brian had sent. A red telephone box pin. She sighed, and then tucked it back inside her bag. Its bright red color didn't seem appropriate. But she was glad she had brought it anyway. It was her own connection to Brian. Something that made it seem real, that it wasn't a dream that she was waking up in England. She slung the bag around her shoulder and headed down to the breakfast room. The grumbling from her stomach told her it wasn't on British time yet, either. In fact, she'd been hungry for several hours.

Lucy descended the stairs and walked through the wide hallway toward the kitchen. When she peeked her head in, she realized that she was in the wrong place. Flora looked up from the stove. "Oh, hi Lucy. Good morning. Let me show you our breakfast room."

Flora wiped her hands on her robin's-egg blue apron. "This way." She walked into a brightly lit dining room with a wallpaper of yellow flowers and green leaves against a warm taupe background. Little round tables covered with white tablecloths were each topped with a single creamy white dahlia in a glass jar.

There was only one other couple sitting drinking coffee on the other side of the room. Lucy shared a brief smile with the woman as she walked by them. Flora led her to a table near the window that had a view of the blooming garden that Lucy had spotted the night before. The dahlias must have come from the profusion of flowers out there.

"It is so beautiful here," Lucy exclaimed as she spotted a metal arbor arching over a stone bench beyond the back patio.

Flora set down a printed menu. "Thank you. Sunshine makes all the difference, right? Now, what would you like? I can make you a traditional English breakfast or anything else here."

Lucy glanced quickly at the list. She was hungry enough for a full English breakfast, including eggs, bacon, fried tomatoes, mushrooms, and something called blood pudding, and sweet beans, but she couldn't afford to lie about digesting it for the rest of the morning. "You know, I'd love the eggs and a piece of toast."

Flora put her hand to her mouth. Her eyes filled up entirely with tears and spilled over. "That was Brian's favorite too." She sniffed and wiped her eyes.

Lucy sat there silent, shocked at Flora's tears. She hadn't expected this. She didn't know how to respond to direct grief about Brian. She softly mumbled, "I'm sorry."

As soon as Flora left, Lucy angled her chair to face the garden. What was she going to do? It hadn't occurred to her that people would react this way. She didn't feel this particular grief they all shared. She didn't have moments to reminisce about or even knowledge of the way he smiled or the sound of his voice. It was as if she was on the outside looking in.

To center herself with thoughts of Seattle, she pulled out her phone and started checking emails from home. Lots of advertisements but nothing crucial. Bruce had sent her a text with a picture of a sad puppy, which made her smile. She wondered if it would be appropriate to bring her computer to breakfast the next day and get a start on the to-do list for the bookstore. As she scrolled through her phone, a group of birds caught her eye as they flew rapidly and playfully around the garden. She set down her phone next to the dahlia and acknowledged that this spot was way too pretty for computer work. An unexpected urge to take a photo of the garden for Nina pulled at her, but as she thought about picking her phone up again, Mr. Emery came out with a tray of food, asked how she slept, and set down her breakfast.

Lucy responded, "I slept wonderfully well, thank you."

Mr. Emery placed a bright blue teapot and a tiny striped cornishware jug for milk on the table beside her plate, and followed the tea setting with toast. The toast came in a silver tray made to hold each slice individually. Lucy wanted to clap with joy when saw the toast-porting device. It was so wonderfully English. Another plate held marmalade, blackcurrant jam, and strawberry-rhubarb jam, each in little jars. Finally, he set down a plate of eggs dotted with chives.

"Thank you. Everything looks delicious." Lucy's stomach grumbled loudly now as she tucked into the eggs with both fork and knife. The scrambled eggs were lightly salted and melted in her mouth. Lucy surprised herself by consuming three slices of toast, each with a different flavor of jam. They were all good but the mixing of blackcurrant and butter on the thick toast had her taste buds in paradise. At home she'd usually have an energy bar before hopping on her bike.

After devouring the meal, she checked her watch. Maura would be driving her to the attorney's office in the city of Bath soon. She was looking forward to meeting her and getting things rolling. Lucy was just putting her fork and knife down when Flora appeared. "Did you enjoy your meal?"

"I loved it. Those jams were divine." Lucy glanced at her watch again, fearful that she might be late to miss Maura's arrival outside.

Flora pulled out a chair and sat down. "Thank you. I made them this past summer." She smiled shyly. "I wanted to say all of us were so happy to meet you last night. Your father mentioned you sometimes. I know he would have been so happy to have you here."

Lucy hesitated in responding to that. Did Flora know that Brian had never contacted her?

Flora was still talking. "Once, when he knew I was struggling with the cooking, he ordered in the best cookbooks to his shop for me to look at. He did that sort of thing for everyone. You'll see it on Wednesday at the memorial."

"Oh, there's a memorial this week?"

Flora widened her eyes. "Yes, I thought you knew. We wanted you to be there of course, and so it's planned for Wednesday."

"Thank you. So, tell me, what will the memorial be like? I've never been to one in England."

Flora's eyes lit up. "It's more of a get-together at the book-shop. I'll make my special tea cakes that your dad really liked, Grandad is arranging music, Evangeline will bring the wine, Sam will do a reading—poor guy, it has been hard on him—and Ada, that's our grocer and parish councilor, she'll be officiating. Her husband is curating the photos from everyone to display. I think Ada will want to meet you beforehand to prep you."

Lucy frowned. "What for?"

"So you can make your speech."

Lucy sat upright, her heart beating hard in protest. She raised her hands and waved them in front of her face. "Oh no, no. I can't possibly do that. You know," she lowered her voice, "it's sort of weird to admit but I didn't even know Brian. I don't think I can talk about him." She reached for her bag. She really needed to get going.

Flora looked at her closely. "That's okay. I forgot that you might be overwhelmed by everything. Of course, this is all new to you." Flora reached out to pat Lucy's hand. "You don't have to worry about anything. Or do anything, except be there. You will come, right? We're just so happy that you're here."

Lucy inhaled deeply, touched by Flora's understanding. "Thank you, Flora. I appreciate you and your grandfather being so kind to me."

Flora still had a look of expectation on her face. Lucy smiled. "Yes, of course I'll come to the memorial. It sounds really nice. Just no speeches."

She felt her phone buzzing. She glanced down to see it was a text from Maura. "Looks like my ride's here. Thanks for everything. The breakfast was incredible."

Flora got up. "You're welcome. We'll see you for dinner?"

"Is dinner included? I don't want to inconvenience you."

"As long as I know in advance, I'd be delighted to have you here. Nothing fancy, really."

Lucy looked at her gratefully. "Thank you. And yes. I'd like that. But now I must get going. I'm on my way to Bath." She stood up.

"Going there on business?" Flora prompted.

"Yes, we are going to hear the will today." Lucy said softly.

Flora looked a bit sheepish with a hint of a blush on her cheeks. "I thought that might be happening today. Have a good time in the city. It's a stunning place."

Lucy said goodbye and hurried toward the door. She had barely any time to wonder what Maura would be like. Would she look like her own mother, for instance? She stood in front of the door for a second longer, and then briskly opened it. It was time to find out.

Out across the street, a woman in her midforties wearing enormous black sunglasses, very slim, very tan, with amazingly long blown-dry dark blond hair was sitting in an open-topped convertible car. "Lucia?" She opened the car door and got out to meet her. There was no traffic at all on the main road so Lucy crossed right away.

"Yes, are you Maura?" Could this younger woman be Brian's wife? Lucy had imagined Maura to be closer to sixty, not forty.

"Yes I am, welcome to England." Maura rushed up to her and quickly air-kissed her cheeks, enveloping Lucy in a cloud of perfume with a follow-up scent of cigarettes. Maura wore white jeans, a tan silk blouse with leopard-print heeled boots, and several gold bracelets on her arm. Lucy thought of Jennifer Aniston and California and suddenly wondered what brought Brian and this glamorous woman together.

Maura stepped back and looked at Lucy. "Lucia, it is good to finally meet you. You've come a long way, how are you feeling?"

"Fine, thank you. Call me Lucy." She smiled.

"Did you get breakfast?" Maura spoke in a crisp accent different to Flora's softer-sounding one.

"Yes, a very good one."

"Good. As you know, we're off on a drive to Bath today, where we'll meet with the attorneys and finally have a reading of the will." Maura gestured toward her car. "Come, let's get going. We can talk more in the car."

Lucy felt good about Maura as she went around to the left side of the car and got in. She seemed efficient and to the point. There were no tears so far and that had Lucy relieved. She did notice one shared trait with her own mother. Maura might be at least fifteen years younger than Celia but they both had a flair for dramatic dressing. Maura turned on the car and selected a radio station. "I always like having energetic music to listen to. Connects me to the outside world. This local community can be so dull." The radio station was playing an Ariana Grande pop song.

"Do you live here in Wakeby?" Lucy asked.

"I live in Shaftsbury now, but as soon as we sell, I'll move to London. I like the pace of life and attitudes so much better in a big city." She glanced over at Lucy and smiled. "This area probably seems so quaint to you. I'm sure you're on the cutting edge of new technology in Seattle."

"Well, we have our skyscrapers and amazing delivery services, but my personal business isn't so technological."

"It's a mattress business?"

Lucy tried not to flinch when people asked in that certain

tone of voice that implied that mattresses were not a worthy product.

"Artisan mattresses. We have our own warehouse where we build them and my brother and mother design them as well as a line of bedding."

Maura merged onto a busy road outside of the village. "And this is the business you could support with extra money?"

"Yes. We need money. It's the reason I'm here. I expect that the bookstore business and building will bring in a good amount? Even split between us, it ought to be enough to make a difference."

Maura brushed back a strand of her long hair while gazing forward. "Look, you should know that Brian was a terrible business owner. He concentrated mostly on his design work. He often gave books away for free, and donated too often to various causes. He absolutely overpaid his shopkeeper. Things like that. The bookshop could have been bigger, with more money-making potential, but he didn't care about that. He just wanted a village bookshop." She paused, shook her head. "That's all under the bridge now but I don't want you to have unreasonably high expectations about the value of the business."

Lucy nodded, but felt a sense of gloom come over her. Had she made a mistake in coming here? She had hoped her mom's opinions about Brian would be completely wrong. Maura seemed to back them up.

Maura glanced at her before focusing back on the road. "I do believe there is value in the building and property. Tomorrow I've set up appointments with estate agents. I'm confident we can sell it for a good price."

Lucy began breathing again. "Oh, thank goodness. All I want is to clear up this situation so I can get back to Seattle."

Maura rewarded her with a wide smile. "I'm glad we have the chance to discuss these things and know we both feel the same way before we're in front of the solicitor."

"Will it take a while to get there? I see there are fewer farms and it's becoming more hilly." For a while the land around them had reminded Lucy of driving in the rural areas of her own state of Washington, with hills covered with trees and grassy areas. The road itself was a narrow two-lane. Sometimes the view from the car was only of tall shrubbery layered with morning glory on top, an occasional stone fence, and trees providing a canopy overhead. Othertimes, the view opened up and she could see taller hills covered with trees. They had just emerged from a stretch of this wilderness, when suddenly one side of the road transformed into identical rows of neat light-colored stone houses each with their own garages. Soon the other side of the road had its own houses and driveways.

"We're making good time actually. But here's another warning. Don't get too excited about Bath. It isn't like I imagine Seattle must be with Microsoft, Amazon, and Starbucks."

"Seattle is a great city but there are some drawbacks, you know, with traffic and construction." It was surprisingly hard to conjure up the traffic in Seattle as they whizzed past gardens filled with pink anemones, purple buddleia, and yellow daisies.

"Unfortunately, we will likely run into some traffic around here too. There's a music festival in Bath today."

Lucy pictured a group of medieval musicians in a line. She suppressed a giggle.

Maura sighed. "Traveling to Bath is our big excitement around here. That's why I want to move to London. I'm completely ready to live where I can choose from hundreds of things to do every day."

They settled into a comfortable silence as the music played on the radio. Lucy watched as the homes began to cluster together in rows, attached to each other with their own neat front lawns. Bus stops appeared along with planted trees and sidewalks. They were now traveling through neighborhoods rather than villages. The hill in the distance was all homes, not fields. There was a bit of traffic and then they were sailing over a bridge and right into the downtown area. They had arrived in Bath. Street after street was lined with ancient honey-colored buildings. The effect was impressive and welcoming.

Maura confidently drove past rows of shops and zoomed right into a city parking lot near a large church. After getting out, Lucy stretched her arms and legs, feeling the warmth of the sun on her shoulders. Her blazer would be too much in a few hours.

Maura tucked a well-worn Chanel leather bag under her arm and led Lucy up a few narrow walkways before turning into a wider lane with cute shops on both sides. Lucy spotted a group of people setting up music stands in a square garden up ahead of them. "Is that the festival?"

"Yes, that's it. It's an annual event. All sorts of actors, musicians, and writers come to Bath that you wouldn't ever see in Wakeby."

Maura turned toward a navy blue doorway in a simple building with an iron railing. They went up a flight of stairs and through big wood doors with the words "Sappworth & Higgins" painted in tidy block letters. A receptionist waved them toward seats in a beige-toned room and from there they waited for the attorney.

Mr. Higgins appeared in less than a minute. He was a thin man with a long face and dark receding hair. He gave them a warm welcome into his office and offered them both a cup of tea, which they politely refused. Lucy was eager to get on with the proceedings and knew that Maura was too. There were three brown leather chairs facing Mr. Higgins's desk, and the women sat in two of them. The solicitor folded his hands on his desk and gazed at Lucy. "We've got one more person to go and then we'll proceed with the reading."

Maura frowned. "Who are we waiting for? I was under the impression that Lucy and I were the only inheritors."

There came a knock at the door. Lucy felt her mouth fall open as a freshly shaven Sam walked in wearing a modern cut navy jacket over a gray shirt. He brought a cool breeze into the room with him.

He sat down with a quick nod at Lucy and settled into his seat. Maura sat stiffly between them.

Maura crossed her arms in front of her. "What are you doing here?"

Mr. Higgins spoke up. "Mr. Burke is also mentioned in the will."

Maura's face began to look splotchy. Lucy watched this all with interest. It was clear that Maura didn't like Sam. Lucy assumed that he was the overpaid shopkeeper that Maura had already complained about.

Mr. Higgins cleared his throat. "Now that you are all here I'll go ahead and read the will. First let me say that Mr. Baslow's death is a great loss. We met about seven years ago and I admired his thoughtfulness and creative output."

He smiled gently at Lucy. "He was hopeful even then that you would come here."

Lucy smiled at him in return, while pushing aside some anguish that no one realized her father really hadn't cared if she came or not. She accepted a copy of the will and scanned it. It was true that all of their names were mentioned.

Mr. Higgins's jaw tightened a bit when he focused on Maura. "Here is your copy."

"Finally," Maura exhaled as she sank into the seat cushions.

"And to you, Sam."

The solicitor regarded them all. "You will see that each of you is to inherit one third of the business and property. To you, Lucy, a number of sketches and any residual royalties from your father's books will also be yours."

Maura cried out, "One third to Sam? This is extremely unfair. Sam doesn't deserve to be part of this."

Maura turned to face him. Sam's face had gone a shade of

white. Lucy guessed that he had no idea he would receive so much. Lucy felt a jolt of worry. Would one third of the property be enough to save Wellslept?

"Did you trick him into putting you in the will?"

"Now, Maura. Brian made it completely clear that he wanted it this way," Mr. Higgins firmly reminded her.

Maura stared at Sam, and when she spoke, her throat was choked up. "Brian wouldn't have done this if he were well."

Maura looked pleadingly at Mr. Higgins and held up the paper. She blinked a few times. "This document doesn't make the ownership of all the items very clear. How are we to divide the business? Or the property?"

"I believe Brian felt you'd be able to reach an agreement. I'd hate to see this go to the courts."

Lucy's stomach started to hurt. It was her Seattle problems all over again. This would not be done in a week if they were going to have to lawyer up. She would have to make sure they agreed with each other.

Sam seemed to find his voice, but it was a bit shaky. "Sorry, Maura. You and I will have to work together. On this at least."

Maura twisted in her seat to look directly at Sam, her voice suddenly cool. "Fine, I'll be emailing you a list of which items belong to me. I don't want you to walk off with anything without a chance for me and Lucy to discuss it."

"I wouldn't do that, Maura." His voice became quiet and low.

"Wouldn't you?" Maura raised her eyebrows, then reached for her purse and took out her phone. She quickly typed something into it.

Sam stood up. "Listen, I need to get back. I appreciate your time, Mr. Higgins."

The attorney quickly cleared his throat. "Wait, Sam, before you go, I need you to sign the documents that show the property will transfer into your names. All three of you will need to sign."

Mr. Higgins pointed out the places where he needed Sam's

signature. While still looking pale, Sam scrawled his name on the document. Lucy watched in case he looked her way, and after shaking hands with the attorney, he did shoot her a brief glance before walking out.

"Do you have any questions?" Mr. Higgins turned toward Lucy.

"Plenty," she chuckled nervously. She leaned forward. "So, as of now, we are all the owners?"

"Once you two sign these few papers it will be official."

Mr. Higgins gave his pen to Maura first. Lucy noted that it was a fancy kind of ballpoint with deep blue ink. Maura flipped her hair back and took the pen.

"Can you tell me what the rules are about selling a property with a business?"

"In general, if you sell the property, the business could relocate. If you sell both together, of course, that would be ideal. And if you close the bookshop entirely, the contents could be sold to another bookshop, I imagine, or donated to our libraries. I'm happy to facilitate any discussions or answer any questions."

"I'm confused about the artwork," Lucy asked. "Did my father work on contract with book publishers?"

"He sold his work as part of his publishing contracts. Perhaps Mr. Burke will have more information for you on that matter."

Lucy wondered fleetingly if she should refuse to sign until she really understood what she was getting herself into. But when Maura handed her the pen and leaned over to whisper, "Let's do this," she decided to go ahead.

Maura was right. She couldn't act like she normally would and research every detail. While she was here in England, she had to make things happen. Lucy grabbed the pen and signed her name everywhere Mr. Higgins requested. She was at least glad that she and Maura were working together and had the same ambitions. She had no idea how the addition of Sam was going to affect their plans.

When they were done, Maura and Lucy stepped back out into the street. For Lucy, it was a shock to think she was now officially the part-owner of a bookshop in England. She felt stunned as she quietly followed Maura along a street next to a park of tall leafy trees.

Brightly painted cafés filled the walkways below the cream-colored stone buildings and nearby a line had formed to enter what Lucy realized was the Jane Austen museum. She saw a woman in Georgian costume beckoning tourists in. She thought to ask Maura about it, but she had already moved way ahead of her.

Bath, England. Jane Austen actually had been here. Scenes from *Persuasion* and *Northanger Abbey* crowded into her mind. She slowed down a minute to drink it all in. She owned a bookshop, she was in England, and she was standing where Jane Austen had lived. It was like an amazing dream. She only wished she could actually have the chance to enjoy it.

Ahead of her, Maura wasn't looking for Jane Austen, but efficiently cutting through crowds of tourists. They passed by a shop selling maps. Lucy knew she could have spent hours in there too if she had the time. As she finally caught up with Maura's pace, Maura kicked a tiny piece of paper out of the way. "Dirty streets."

Lucy blinked. These streets and buildings were very clean, with fresh coats of paint around windows and friendly chalk signs imploring people to stop by for coffee or tea. The sounds of the outdoor orchestra reached her ears.

"Maura, have you always lived in this area?"

"Well, technically this is Somerset, and the bookshop is in Wiltshire, but in general yes. I went away for my studies, but when I met your father I was working at the grocery in Wakeby."

"What brought him to Wakeby?"

Maura turned to gaze at her, the question finally halting her quick gait. "You really don't know anything about him, do you?"

Lucy felt her cheeks flush in embarrassment. She thought of

the way her mom's face closed down and her mouth tightened whenever she tried to ask about him. "No. I really don't."

"Your great-aunt owned the building. She provided your dad the apartment upstairs to live in after he left London."

"I remember he left us to go to London." There was a bitterness in her voice, but she didn't have to hide it with Maura.

"That's where he initially made his name." Maura's voice took on a dreamy quality. "He did hundreds of record and magazine covers with his illustration work. He told me all about the rock stars he met and the glamorous parties he went to. I wish I had known him then. But after a while, the music industry moved on from his style. Grunge and punk were over. The money in his kind of work dried up. It wasn't until much later that he figured out he could get work illustrating for the children's books market. And he did, particularly from his most famous one, *The Gardener's Cat*. You know he was inspired by those little postcards he did for you."

Maura looked at Lucy expectantly.

"I loved those postcards. And I've heard of the book." Lucy didn't say that she'd only heard of it one night ago, when Sam mentioned it before dessert. "But I don't know it." She looked down at the pavement to hide her surprise. Maura had been around when Brian had drawn her postcards. Those cards had been her own private joy for so long. And here was another person who knew about them. Lucy was beginning to see that she was connected to Maura and to Wakeby.

Maura's eyes opened wide. "Well, *The Gardener's Cat* established your father as a children's book illustrator."

They reached Maura's car. "As more of his books came out, he ended up using the ground floor space in his aunt's building to start up a small bookshop. He mainly thought of selling his children's books but then when Sam got involved, it was turned into a regular bookshop."

"I hope we can find someone who wants a bookshop."

"Personally, I don't care who buys it, as long as they have the money for the building. Lots of money, now that we have to split it three ways." Maura groaned. "The problem will be selling it quickly enough. I'm sure Sam will want to keep it. Selling it would mean getting a real job. He won't want to let go of the easy life."

"Won't he have to realize that we both need to sell? He'll get money from that to start again."

"You don't know him. He can be a complete arsehole."

Lucy thought of Sam's quietness. He didn't seem like an arsehole, as Maura had put it. "What can I do to help?"

Maura shrugged. "We'll meet the estate agents tomorrow. We'll be miles ahead of him."

They left Bath and picked up speed as they drove back along the narrow roads, returning to the country. Far in the distance Lucy spotted some little white cottages nestled into a dip in the land.

"How did Sam come into the picture in the first place?"

Maura made a face. "Brian was the kind of guy who happily took in stray cats and dogs. Have you met the latest charity case, Barley?"

At Lucy's nod, she continued. "Sam's quite the same as Barley. A while ago, Sam was just a kid who needed a job. Brian suddenly decided he needed an assistant to make calls, do deliveries, and send his books to other sellers, and Sam was somehow the only one who could do that. At the time I was completing a year-long yoga training course. Sam saw an easy way to entrench himself, since I was so busy."

Lucy left Maura's comment about Sam alone. She wanted to know more about Brian anyway.

"Was Brian ever going to retire?"

"He used to promise me we would travel again as soon as he finished the last big project. That didn't happen."

It was the first time Lucy had noticed any sadness in her voice.

"Did you travel with my father a lot?"

Maura smiled. "When we married, we traveled as much as we could on our little budget. I'd never even been to London before, and there we were eating pasta in Italy and walking through fields of lavender in France. I wanted our trips to go on forever. We talked about everything together. He listened to me back then."

Maura slowed the car as they came to an intersection. The land had become flat again and they began to pass long stretches of farmland. "As soon as I came home from the honeymoon, I started my yoga training. We were both so enthusiastic about the future. I had big plans. Brian was very supportive. We were both dedicated to living a life of health. I thought that we would run the yoga studio out of the space where the bookshop is now located. Change the entire front space to a yoga studio. We talked about doing yoga retreats in Europe. There was so much potential. But by the time I'd qualified as an instructor, the bookshop was established. Brian refused to make any changes. He said it was good for the community." She paused. "I argued yoga was good for the community. He suggested that the little cramped storefront across the street could be our yoga studio. He thought I might enjoy the independence of my own space." She rolled her eyes. "No. It was too small. I settled for work at the community center and then finally started working for a new studio in Shaftesbury."

Maura frowned. "I mean, really, the community isn't even literary. For instance, that wine shop is flourishing, which tells you all you need to know about the people of Wakeby."

Lucy didn't think that a successful wine shop was a negative signifier of the people of Wakeby, but she didn't say anything. She was starting to think that Maura didn't like anything about Wakeby at all.

"Did you get to do more traveling?"

Maura shrugged. "Brian got caught up in deadlines for books. He encouraged me to travel alone. So I did. I went to amazing retreats in Morocco and Greece. We started going to Cornwall in the summers. That was blissful. But I became very busy with my studies. I wanted Brian to come with me. To establish a new base in Spain. He still wanted me to start my own studio here. He wanted me to stay home and bring people to the country for the retreats. I kept telling him it didn't work that way. People don't want to come to our little out-of-touch village. He kept warning me that I was becoming too obsessed with learning from famous teachers. No. I kept meeting the most amazing people at these retreats. They are my people. We disagreed about what made a healthy life. He spent his days in Wakeby, working with Sam. I spent my days in Shaftesbury. The bookshop and his work kept him grounded. Too grounded. One day I noticed that he was getting old. We weren't having those great conversations about our futures. It was constant arguing between us. That's why I finally moved out formally. That bookshop and his career drove a wedge between us, and that led to our separation."

"But you didn't divorce."

"I was gone on and off for six months. There wasn't time. I only recently returned from a course in India. The last time I spoke to him was in June."

They fell into an uneasy silence as they entered Wakeby. Lucy thought it looked even more quintessentially English in the sunshine. To her the village wasn't out-of-touch. It was nearly perfect in its size and beauty. She was eager to walk around and peek into the shop windows.

Maura pulled up to an alley a block beyond the bookshop. "I'll drop you off here. It's easier for me to turn around. But before you go, I want to tell you something." She waited until Lucy gave her her full attention. "Don't talk too much to Flora. She is known to gossip. I'm sure her family will be nice to you, but everything in this village gets around, and we don't need to tell everyone our plan is to sell. There are certain people who will get nosy and upset. I don't want Sam or Flora to turn the place against you. We can't afford to deal with anyone getting ideas on how to stop the sale when we need this to happen as soon as possible for the both of us."

Lucy remained unfazed on the outside, but she was surprised by Maura's warning. She thought about how she had been peppered with questions the night before over dinner. "It might be difficult to avoid mentioning my plans, if people ask."

Maura raised her perfectly arched eyebrows. "If they ask, just avoid answering directly. Say you are overwhelmed."

Lucy laughed. "That is actually true."

Before she got out Maura kissed her on the cheeks again. Lucy could smell Maura's perfume on her own hair.

"Remember, don't get too friendly with the villagers," Maura said just before she drove away.

After waving goodbye to Maura, Lucy moved slowly along the walkway. She looked around to orient herself. Just up the street she could see the corner of the bookshop. When she was directly across from the shop window she stood to admire it. Baslow's Books. She turned the words over in her mind. She couldn't quite believe it was her name right there on the building.

Lucy crossed the street to stand below the sign. A part of her was here somehow. Her father and her great-aunt had lived in this very building. A sense that she was connected to the place settled into her bones. The sun shone through the window and painted a stripe of sunlight onto the armchair just inside. She could almost smell the special scent of fresh new books and anticipate the feeling of the smooth covers in her hands.

A little chalkboard sign in the window front declared that the shop was open. She ducked under the rose growing around the doorway, but it caught on her navy blazer. As she carefully unhooked the thorn from her jacket, she got out her phone from her bag and made a note that the rose needed pruning. Standing on the worn tiled entrance, Lucy pushed at the brass handle and the door opened with a jingle of bells.

Inside, the ancient wood floorboards creaked a welcome. Barley padded out sleepily from behind the counter and then trotted up to her. She didn't see Sam but heard him call, "Welcome to Baslow's. I'll be right out."

For the moment she was alone. She gave Barley a quick pet and he sat down on her feet. Not by them, but, once again, on them. She looked around and was transfixed by the bookish room. The place wasn't big enough for aisles. Instead, solid wooden bookshelves lined all the walls of the bookstore and cheerful overhead lights lit the back of the store. Resting her hands on the table in front of her, she breathed in deeply. Like she anticipated, the room did smell deliciously rich with the scent of paper, which delighted her. But she also had a sense of… what? She struggled to define it. A sinking sense of doom, perhaps. Because this wasn't just an anonymous piece of property. This was clearly a wonderful, well-loved bookstore. Book*shop*. She had to get it in her mind that it was a bookshop. Before her were the books. On display tables, squeezed into bookcases along the wall, and stacked in a sturdy pile in the corner. It was a place that she would love visiting, if she lived here.

Stepping away from Barley, she resisted the urge to straighten and tidy a few novels that had taken to leaning on the shelves to her right. She turned away, her eyes drawn back to the display table in the middle of the room. The covers were shiny and new. She saw familiar titles by Jenny Colgan, Veronica Henry, Jasmine Guillory, Zadie Smith, and Nick Hornby, mixed up with a local authors section including Mark Dawson, Jane Austen, and Joanna Penn. She couldn't resist picking up an Austen. It was a copy of *Pride and Prejudice* with a floral cover she had never seen before. She held it lovingly. There was something about seeing an old friend in a place where she had thought she knew no one. It sent a little happy ringing through her body.

Sam strode into the room and spotted the book before she put it down. He had removed the blazer he'd been wearing that morning and had rolled up the sleeves on his shirt. She immediately straightened up her posture. He probably thought she was boring for having picked up such a predictable classic and would be disappointed in her choice.

Instead he seemed happy. "Are you a reader?"

"Oh, definitely. Lately, I've been trying to read even more."

"Who do you like to read?" He stood there, all attention on her. She was conscious that she wanted to say the right thing to impress him.

"I love authors who write mysteries set in England."

"Oh, like who?'

She thought of her bookshelves at home. "P. D. James, Alice K. Boatwright, Charles Finch, Will Thomas, Anna Sayburn Lane, Stephanie Barron." She looked down at the table, compelled to impress him. "I read other genres too. I love Fredrik Backman, Rosamunde Pilcher, and Diana Gabaldon. I see you have her books here too."

"Yes, they sell very well." He paused to pick one up. "I started ordering them a few years ago and now I can't keep them in stock."

That was promising, she thought. Maybe Maura was wrong about the financial health of the bookshop.

"Some of those you mentioned are historical mysteries set in England. You like that kind of story?"

At her nod, he smiled broadly. "That's good to hear." He hesitated, and then said, "Some of my favorites are historicals too."

She didn't know exactly why he seemed so pleased, but his smile warmed up his face. It overcame the sadness that seemed to shadow his eyes. Maybe it was just that she hadn't met a man who avidly read books. Or read books from different genres. She didn't discern a snobbery in him. She was drawn in by his enthusiasm by all the books in the shop and also that rich accent. He carefully patted a Jacqueline Winspear and then selected a Sir Arthur Conan Doyle to show her. "Anything Sherlock Holmes always does well. But I can also recommend some really good local authors, if you're interested?"

"I'd love that."

They both stood looking at the books. A quiet camaraderie grew between them until Sam spoke. "So, we're co-owners of this place."

She glanced up at him. "We've had an interesting morning."

He ran his hand through his wavy hair. "I didn't know he was going to do that. I'm still in shock that Brian would give me part ownership," he said with an abashed tone in his voice. He took a deep breath. "Seeing as we're going to be business partners, I should show you around. We have different sections according to topic," he said as he waved his arm to encompass the bookshop.

She followed his gesture. The cash register was toward the back by the windows. *Just as it ought to be*, she thought, *to draw the customers farther into the store*. On the counter there was a bouquet of flowers in a vase, a whisky bottle wrapped with ribbon, and a row of cards. These were sympathy cards about Brian. Tucked in against the very back corner of the bookshop was a children's section with a cheerful rug and stuffed animals in a basket. Above the low bookcases, painted against a yellow wall, was a sign done in multicolored letters. She read the words out loud: "Lucia's Book Corner."

She turned to look at Sam with a question in her voice. "Lucia's?"

Her name was on the wall? She noted the expectant look on Sam's face.

"He named it for you."

A wash of emotion rushed over her. Brian had put her name in the children's section, as if they had a loving relationship, for the whole town to believe. She felt the shock build. The cute corner mocked her. This was too much. This was asking too much of her. She became very still, and then she couldn't stay there a moment longer.

"That sign? That is all wrong." She turned and walked right out the door.

Once she got outside, she stopped. She didn't want to go toward the village and risk running into anyone while she felt so upset, so she turned to the right and kept walking until she reached a small stone bridge. She looked over the side. A few feet below a cool green waterway rushed along beneath her. Beyond the bridge, the sides of the road were thick with brambles and grass. She could hide away there from anyone's view in the village. She took a few more steps and stopped under a tree. She was angry.

Brian, who couldn't be bothered to call or write her a letter, who couldn't be bothered to send money to her or her mother, who couldn't be troubled enough to be a father, thought he could show off by making a kids' books section with her name? Maura was right. Her mom was right. Brian was a total hypocrite.

She stared out across the beautiful landscape, with breath-taking rolling fields and stone fences and a coppice of trees. None of it was real. This gorgeous village and bookshop and happy birdsong. She'd wanted to find herself here. Find a place that explained who she was, who her father was. But the answers had been in front of her all along.

He didn't care about Lucy the person. Just some idea of her, she guessed. She'd thought that she was over it, over the feeling of being rejected. But to see her name being used in that way? No. She couldn't accept that. She couldn't pretend that her real life didn't happen for these people. Because it did. She sighed.

This was just about math. She needed money. She would get the bookshop sold and its profit would fuel the thing that deserved it: the legacy that Paul, her real father, had left her.

She was so focused on this new thought in her head that at first she didn't notice when an older woman with short gray hair stopped in front of her with a waddling pug.

"Excuse me, are you Lucia Baslow?"

Lucy only heard the word "Baslow" and it took a moment to focus on the petite woman, who was wearing a shiny royal-blue raincoat with polka dots.

"I'm Lucy," she said quietly.

"Oh my goodness, this is spectacular." The woman turned to yell at a tall man a few feet down the road. "Gordy, this is Brian's daughter."

Lucy reached down to pet the pug, who wore a pink collar and had big sweet eyes. This dog didn't have an opinion about her or Brian. Lucy swallowed hard against the lump in her throat, wishing that everyone was as unbiased as dogs were.

Gordy lumbered up to them.

"Isn't she just the spitting image of Brian?" the woman exclaimed, her voice almost catching in her throat.

Lucy straightened up after petting the dog to meet a pair of friendly eyes.

"How do you do?" the man asked and held out his hand.

He seemed like a gentle old giant. "I'm doing well, thank you."

The woman spoke up. "I'm Ada Cowcroft. Gordy and I used to see your father every day. I'd ask him how he was, and he never mentioned that he was feeling ill. I'm so sorry for your loss."

Lucy felt a little more in control of her feelings. "Thank you, Mrs. Cowcroft."

"You should know I've been planning the memorial for your father. It's set for Wednesday night. We heard you were coming and of course we wanted you to be there. I hope Wednesday will work for you? You won't have to do a thing. We run the grocery in town, and we'll be providing the refreshments. I saw Flora at the checkout line earlier today and she mentioned that you were still adjusting to the village, as you should be. Speaking now as a key member of the parish council, the bookshop means a lot to us."

Lucy mustered up a gracious tone of voice. "That's very kind, thank you. Wednesday sounds great."

"You'll be the guest of honor, of course. We want to learn everything about you." Ada looked thoughtful. "Gordy and I were saying that we were a bit surprised that you hadn't visited before now, weren't we, Gordy?"

"We've known about you for years, you see," he offered in an apologetic tone.

"I was never invited before." It came out sharper than she had wanted, but she didn't know how to soften it. Telling the true story was going to be hard.

"Oh, indeed? I assume you are included in the will, of course," Ada said, leaning forward. Lucy hoped she wasn't going to fall over in her pursuit of the latest news.

"Yes," she conceded, "that was read today."

"We're delighted to have you here now," Mr. Cowcroft added tactfully.

Lucy wondered how much longer she'd have to talk about Brian, the very thing she had been trying to avoid. She rubbed her eyes. "Excuse me. I'm a little tired today."

Mr. Cowcroft nudged Ada. She started and then patted Lucy on the arm. "You must be jet-lagged, dear. How long will you be visiting?"

"I'm here until next Saturday."

Ada raised her eyebrows. "You must know what you're going to do with the shop then? Since you're only here so short of a time?"

Lucy froze. Ada was so direct. She thought of Maura's

warning about gossip. "No, I don't know yet. I'm a bit over-whelmed by it all."

"Now there, Ada, Lucy just arrived in Wakeby. She hasn't had time to decide much, has she?"

He looked into Lucy's eyes. His were a watery blue. "Wakeby is a wonderful place, you'll see."

"I can tell it is. It is really beautiful around here."

Gordy smiled. "It's a place that clears the mind, what with all this open country."

Lucy liked Gordy. He didn't have the sharp, interested eyes that Ada had.

Somehow, she felt a little better for being distracted. "I think I'll explore more on another day and head back into town now."

Gordy stepped aside. "You go on ahead. We don't move too fast, with old Daisy, our dog."

Lucy smiled and reached down to pet Daisy again, and then walked back toward the town, determined to keep calm this time and get things done.

As Lucy reapproached the bookshop, she paused to prepare herself for all sorts of awkwardness with Sam. She was still standing on the sidewalk when he opened the door.

"Lucy, I'm afraid we got off on the wrong foot."

He held the door open with confidence and she did the easy thing and followed him back into the store. Behind her, she noticed that Sam flipped the closed sign facing out. "I'm shutting the store early this afternoon. Tuesday is a bigger day for customers anyway."

The sun had now found its way in through the southwest-facing windows. Diamond patterns stretched along the floor. Lucy tried to ignore the back corner of the shop.

She crossed her arms. "Listen, there are things about all of this I did not expect. Like that children's area."

"You didn't expect it to be named after you?" he said in a curious voice. It made her wonder just what he knew about her.

She looked straight into his eyes. "I haven't heard from Brian since I was a little girl. I didn't know about this bookshop or anything else until only a few weeks ago. To be honest, I'm finding all of this overwhelming." There it was again. A very useful word.

Sam frowned. "That doesn't make sense. I know Brian's been sending a Christmas card to Seattle every year."

"I have never seen a Christmas card from him, not in the last ten years," Lucy said firmly.

His brow furrowed in confusion. "Is your birthday in June?"

"Yes."

"There were birthday cards too."

"No"—Lucy closed her eyes—"there weren't." She was trying to shut this information out.

"I'll try to find some proof for you. Brian was a good man. He was my mentor, and he was always kind." Sam's voice had softened.

Lucy didn't know what to say, but she didn't agree.

He glanced toward the kitchen. "Shall I get us a cup of tea? Would you like one? I make a very good brew, I promise."

She rubbed at her temples as Sam quickly took himself off to the kitchen. Had Brian really tried to be in touch with her? What did it mean if he had? And why hadn't she seen these alleged cards? It was ridiculous. Sam must be wrong. A reasonable voice in her head questioned why he would be, but she told herself to keep to the math. She didn't need to know the answer to everything. The truth was he had never contacted her.

Lucy wandered over to the shop counter. Barley was sleeping behind it on a round pillow in the sunshine. He opened his eyes for a minute just to acknowledge that it was her but didn't move from his spot. Lucy reached for a big blue binder resting by the cash register that she guessed must contain the business accounts. Surely there would be computer files too? Simple, straightforward factual stuff that she could understand. The stuff her mom said she was good at.

After a few minutes, Sam returned from the kitchen. She noted in the most neutral way possible the pleasant sight of a tea tray with two floral-patterned Emma Bridgewater mugs being carried in his lean muscular arms. He set down the tray. The tea looked rich but with the ideal amount of milk swirled in. She lifted the mug and took a sip. "Thank you. It's very good."

He pulled up a stool to the other side of the counter. "You know," he began slowly, "it's surreal to be up at the register with you. I keep expecting your dad to be up here. It's hard for me to understand that he's really gone."

"When I arrived yesterday, I had a weird feeling that he'd somehow be here," she admitted.

"He would have never wanted to upset you." Sam glanced toward the children's corner.

"Let's not talk about it. Tell me about the business." After she took another sip of the tea, she nodded toward the binder. "Is that all the paperwork?"

"Yes, I put everything in there."

"What about a computer?"

"Right under here." He reached for a laptop on a shelf below the countertop. "I recommend you look at it all…"

"Fine." She pulled the overstuffed binder toward her and opened it.

"Lucy? Before you get into the numbers, do you mind if I show you around the place a bit more?"

She turned to look at him. "What, are the numbers bad?"

His eyes widened. "No, no, I just want you to see the place first before we discuss the details."

Lucy took another sip of her tea. "Details are what I want to focus on."

"It might help if you look at the property," he said. "You'll see how much of it is currently being used by the bookshop."

Was she being unreasonable? "Okay. I do want to see the whole operation here."

It became awkwardly quiet between them. Maybe she shouldn't have used that word "operation" for this charming bookshop. She concentrated on finishing her cup of tea.

After a moment, Sam set down his mug. "Let me show you the main floor first. There's a small kitchen in the back where I make tea and coffee. Then we've got one other room on the main floor. It's Brian's studio." He paused. "His apartment is upstairs. Let me show you the whole layout." Barley watched him as he got up, probably evaluating whether Sam was going to take him on a walk. "We aren't a particularly big bookshop but we do have a lot of loyal customers."

"The shop isn't in debt or anything?" Lucy was reluctant to leave the binder.

"No. Brian would never let that happen. But you do know that most bookshops operate on a very thin edge of profit, right?"

She frowned. She hadn't ever thought about it. She only knew that she loved bookstores—or bookshops. She stood to follow Sam. They walked past the children's section and into a narrow hallway, where there was a bathroom for customers, and a door that separated the bookshop from the rest of the building.

Sam opened it. "We also keep our supplies and backstock in the room to the right, but what I really want is for you to see Brian's studio." Sam had stepped into the room on the left. He flipped the light switch, though he didn't need to because the late afternoon sunshine was streaming in. "The studio," he said, his voice full of pride.

The ample-sized room was filled with light. Big windows filled the south and west walls. *What a great place to shoot photos*, she thought, before stopping herself.

Sam began sliding out frame after frame of colorful printed

illustrations from a shelving unit along the wall. "I thought you'd want to see these."

She approached to take in the beautiful ink illustrations with sweeping lines and vintage colors. There were landscapes with boats and cottages that looked like they were from children's books, and small sketches of a dog and a ball. Each illustration was vibrant, with reds, yellows, and blues, but stylish and elegant too.

Brian's signature was located at the bottom corner of one of the prints. She stepped closer. It was slanted and each letter contained a flourish. A flourish she recognized because it was hers, her signature. She felt chills run up her back. "Do you have other samples of Brian's writing?"

Sam stared at her for a moment and then went to the desk at the front of the room. He surveyed the surface and selected a sheet of paper containing a list. He handed it to her.

She scanned through the note. It was as if she herself had written it. Their handwriting was identical. Same angle, same flourish on the a's and e's. Not that she had any doubt, but this was confirmation at another level that she was Brian's daughter.

"I can see him here at this desk." Sam's voice interrupted her revelation. "He could spend hours selecting the right color or researching the location of a scene for one of the books he was working on."

"His illustrations are wonderful. I had no idea." She was still gazing at the swoops and swirls of his lines.

Suddenly Sam's words came out fast. "I miss him, Lucy. I miss his laughter. If only you could have heard his hearty laugh. He should have had so many more years with us." The words had seemed to gush out of him, before he stopped and walked to the window. Lucy picked up a sketch while allowing him some privacy.

Sam gazed out toward the countryside. "It just feels like he's away on holiday."

"What happened, Sam? No one has really told me." She leaned against the edge of Brian's desk.

Sam seemed to be focused on a tall tree outside. "I was in the shop, he was in here. I heard Barley bark, and I ran in. I thought he had fainted. There was blood on his forehead. I didn't know. I called 999 and then I got freaked out that it wasn't only a fall, so I tried pressing on his chest. Giving him mouth-to-mouth. I called his name, I called it over and over again." Lucy saw him take a deep breath. "It didn't work. It was a heart attack. I couldn't save him."

He kept staring out the window. "I had noticed things, but I didn't pay enough attention to them. That he hadn't been as energetic in the couple of weeks before. I thought it was a cold. I should have told him to go see the doctor. Maybe if I had done something earlier I could have kept him alive."

"Oh," she sighed. She knew how those thoughts would rub at him over and over again. She'd thought them with Paul. She still felt that same kind of regret, but now she tried to let it go. She understood maybe he needed to confess to her. "Sam, I'm so sorry. I didn't realize when I asked for the details that you had actually been there with him. I'm sure you did all you could."

Sam frowned. "He shouldn't have died."

Lucy leaned against the edge of the desk and echoed his words in a whisper. "He shouldn't have."

With a friend, this might have been an appropriate time for a hug, but Lucy barely knew Sam. She ran through different expressions of consolation through her mind, philosophy about death, her own experience with it, and rejected them all.

She wondered if Sam had family in the area for support. Outside the window, a group of little brown birds caught her eyes as they flitted around a tall tree and swooped down to the grass again.

She mumbled out loud, "I forgot how it aches constantly right after you lose someone."

"You lost someone too?"

"My father." She paused and saw him look puzzled. "My step-father," she amended.

"Does it get better?"

"I don't believe he's coming back anymore."

"Every day seems wrong. I don't want to let the connection go."

"Maybe the memorial will help," Lucy said, even though she wasn't so sure about that either.

"It feels too soon. Like Brian should be invited."

"Memorials are for the rest of you to be with each other."

"I guess."

They stayed silent until Barley started barking at a bird that flew too close to the window.

Sam shook his head. "I should show you the upstairs," he said in a flat voice.

She was tired. The sunshine on the chairs outside beckoned to her. But she nodded. She knew it had to be done. Back in the hallway, Sam opened a simple white door. They went up a set of tan carpeted stairs leading up to the apartment.

On the landing there was a small antique table with a bouquet of dried-out flowers on it. To the left, a cozy living room met her eyes. The walls were done in a sage green, but the curtains and cushions were in muted reds. A brown leather couch covered with a plaid blanket nestled in between side tables, piled with books and reading lamps. Every surface was covered with stacks of magazines and more books. Against the wall was a sink, small fridge, and an oven. It was a comfortable jumble. The hallway led past a bathroom and then they came to the closed bedroom door. Sam stopped there.

Brian's room. He indicated that she should go first. Her hand hovered over the handle of the door. She turned the knob slowly, holding her breath. It clicked open. The rest of the place had been public, but this was Brian's most private space. The room was dark and still. She heard her own footsteps tap against the wood floor. The green curtains were thick and pulled shut against the windows.

She gently opened the heavy drapes, watching dust fill the beams of sunlight.

With a better look around the room in the daylight, she started to breathe easier. There was nothing scary here. This was simply a man's bedroom. He wasn't actually here. She was okay. A few years before, Lucy had gone through all of her stepfather's things. She felt a familiar mantle of responsibility settle around her chest. At least she didn't recognize Brian's shirts, or know a special suit he used to wear. As she told herself again, this was just a man's bedroom.

Sam stood just inside the door waiting for her. In the center of the room was a plain bed with a quilt done in squares of gray ticking.

There was a mug on the nightstand next to the bed. Lucy approached and saw with a shock that there was a dried coffee stain in the bottom. A nearby clay jar was filled with exotic-looking Japanese marker pens. She knew them. Had the same ones saved at home.

"He loved that kind of pen," Sam offered quietly. "And those Moleskine journals. There are photo albums too." He sighed. "I haven't been able to come in here since...before."

Stacked along the top of the nightstand was a collection of black sketch journals. She leaned closer and saw there were years written on each of the bindings. She scanned to see if her year, the year she was born, 1991, was in there. But these only began in the later nineties. He must have started them after he left Seattle. Still, she felt a strong urge to read them, and to see his hand-writing again.

She cast her eye over to a dresser on the other side of the bed. A pair of black canvas sneakers were tucked in below it. She bit her lip. She had been wrong. This wasn't a cold survey of clothes and furniture. The things in here had meaning. A kind of sacredness. These were Brian's shoes. Somehow they made her think of Mr. Rogers's sneakers from the children's TV show.

On the top of the dresser was a collection of framed photos. She recognized one of herself and reached for it. It was a school photo, in a tiny silver frame worn to bronze on the sides from being held. Against her will, she had an uncomfortable urge to cry. Then a few tears burst out of her. She quickly brushed them away from the corner of her eye, hoping that Sam hadn't seen. There she was in her pink T-shirt with the drawing of a cat on it, the one that she had worn almost every day in third grade. It completely surprised her that he had this picture, because he had left long before that day.

Lucy wiped at her eyes again and took a deep breath. She looked over the other things on the dresser top. Drawings that she had done in fifth grade. Even a clipping from when she was in the Fourth of July parade in sixth grade. Had her mother sent these?

Lucy sat down on the side of the bed. She reached for the picture of herself again. She hadn't realized that visiting Brian would be this confusing. How could he have these things and never contact her? She couldn't reconcile her feelings.

Sam shifted in the doorway. "Look, I know this is a lot. Would you like to go for a walk? I should take Barley out."

She glanced out the window to the sunlight and green trees. It was so dark in Brian's room. Still, had she done enough at the bookshop for the first day? What about the accounting? A headache had formed along the back of her neck and head. She suspected that the jet lag would not help her evaluate the book-keeping right now.

Sam moved forward to take the coffee cup from the night-stand. This had been an exhausting afternoon, but his presence somehow managed to calm her. "Is it a long walk?"

"How about we take a quick walk around the village? I'll drop you back off at Flora's in fifteen minutes."

"Okay, then. I think fresh air is a great idea."

Barley was exceptionally happy with this arrangement. Lucy saw that he waited patiently to get his leash on but after Sam securely snapped it shut, he pulled for the door. She was almost as happy as Barley to get outside. After all, she was in England. It was late summer. It was even as Henry James praised, a summer afternoon. The most beautiful two words in the English language, he claimed. And as she passed under the fragrant rose-covered doorway and onto the walkway, she felt herself relax. Sam pointed to the businesses up the street. "Beena's tea shop is the one with the striped awning on the corner. And right across the street from us is Matthew's florist shop. He's a great guy. He's part of the friends' business group too. You'll meet him at the memorial."

The florist shop was painted in a soft green. Brightly colored hanging plants and a big selection of healthy green-leaved plants in modern white planters filled the curved window. A potted lemon tree was right outside the door and propped up beside it a board with the message "Welcome happy plant people!" scrawled in chalk.

"This town is extremely charming."

Sam nodded. "The best kept secret in the West Country."

Lucy was trying to get her bearings. "So, the bookshop is one of the last shops on this road."

"Right, the butcher and deli are all in the center of the village. Down here we only have the B&B, florist, empty storefront, and us. And then beyond our section is the river and the playing field. And up the road a bit is our tourist attraction, the famous Symonds Gardens—"

"Where Brian wrote his first children's book," she interrupted.

"Yes, you've got it," he said proudly, meeting her eyes with a smile, and Lucy felt an irrational flush of satisfaction at his approval.

Barley pulled them toward the plantings around Hollyhock B&B. He was sniffing diligently at the stones lining the low fence around the property.

"Did you grow up around here?"

"Ha! No," he laughed, then catching her surprised expression, added, "Sorry, it's just that most people know right away from my accent. I'm from Liverpool. I came here with my mum when I was in secondary school. My parents had split up. She had always worked in gardening, she has a knack with plants and she knew she could get a job at a large commercial plant grower in the area, so we moved here."

"You stayed after high school?"

"Brian encouraged me to go to university. I did, but I kept working for him on weekends and eventually I took over the bookshop while he continued to concentrate on his illustrations."

They crossed the street. Just past the florist shop they veered to the right and took a small road past a row of cheerful newer cottages before heading toward a large grassy field. "The river is right there," Sam said.

"I'm not used to a river running through town. Seattle has some lakes and Puget Sound." They walked along a flattened grass path toward extraordinarily big trees with limbs reaching gently toward the river. Barley pushed his nose into every tall clump of grass. Then he rolled on the ground. His delight made her laugh. Lucy stretched out her arms and breathed in the air. "Barley seems happy."

"He is. He's a great dog." Sam smiled at her. "Brian loved him. Do you have any pets?"

She shook her head. "I never had one, since I'm at the store all the time."

"You said last night that you run a mattress shop, right? Do you like it?"

Lucy brushed the hair away from her face. "What I like best is being at the warehouse where the mattresses are made. It is so calming there."

He nodded. "I feel that way about the bookshop."

That shut her up. Lucy had no idea how to respond without talking about the future of the bookshop. How could she tell him her plans when they would surely put Baslow's Books in jeopardy?

After a pause in their stroll, while Barley put his paws into the cooling water, they turned around and walked back to the road. Far off in the distance, Lucy could see a church with a square top. Even farther beyond that the hills rolled forward with fields of grass and a grove of trees. She could pinch herself. This world was so different from her own home. "Did Brian walk Barley?"

"Yes, every day. They had their routes and this was one of them. It's been an adjustment for Barley too, but having him with me has made things seem more normal." Sam called out to Barley, "You tolerate me all right, don't you, Barley?"

They stopped outside of the B&B. Barley sat on Lucy's feet and looked up endearingly for a treat. Sam dug into his pocket. "What? I thought you liked me?"

They laughed and Barley switched to Sam's feet once he spotted the treat coming. She wished they could stay laughing like this but since they were back in view of the bookshop, Lucy felt she needed to at least say something more specific about her schedule for the week. "Thank you for showing me around today. I know we didn't get to the financial details yet but I learned a lot. I'd like to go over them tomorrow and make up some plans."

He looked down at her. "I worried whether you would like the shop. But you do, right?"

"Yes, I love it," she said. That part was simple.

"Baslow's is such a special place." He looked so happy at her response. Lucy thought again of Maura's gag order and rejected it. Sam deserved to know she had to sell. She took a breath. Better to rip off the bandage now. "I have to tell you something."

"Sam, is that you?"

A woman with sandy hair, red lips, and smokey-lined green eyes strode up to Sam. She moved in and gave him an intimate greeting. Kisses on either side of his cheeks. A hug that lasted longer than normal. He looked a bit embarrassed with a flush that appeared over his cheekbones. "Deborah. You're back."

After they embraced, Sam put his hands in his pockets. Barley looked up for a pet, but Deborah ignored him.

"Yes, I flew in yesterday. I was so sorry to hear the news. I texted you. But I didn't hear back?" A slight frown moved over her face. "I've been free all day." Her tone was critical.

"I'm sorry. It's been a busy time." He turned abruptly to Lucy. "Lucy, this is Deborah, the tour director at Symonds House. And this is Lucy, Brian's daughter."

Immediately Deborah's flirtatious look changed to one of somberness. "Oh my goodness. It is so good to meet you. I'm so sorry for your loss. Brian was a dear friend to Symonds House."

"Thank you. I'm looking forward to going there."

"Oh, of course. He must have talked to you about it, it being the setting of his book and all. Please come by soon. Brian was beloved to us." She turned to Sam and brightened her voice. "I expect to see you sooner rather than later?" She reached her arms out to him.

"You'll come to the memorial?"

"You won't be free before that?" Deborah's mouth tightened.

He winced. "I'm booked with meetings to plan the event."

She seemed to deflate a bit. "Of course. I'll see you at the gathering then."

She swiftly reached toward him, got in a side kiss, and whispered something that made Sam smile.

Lucy felt distinctly uncomfortable.

"Nice to meet you." Deborah said goodbye firmly and walked off toward the shops up the street.

Sam watched her go. With the ease of their earlier conversation broken, Lucy opened the gate to Hollyhock B&B and prepared to say a short goodbye.

Flora appeared at the window and opened it wide. "Hello, good to see you back, Lucy. Hi, Sam," she called out to him. He was still standing at the gate.

"Flora, how are you? Barley and I will be off now."

"You took good care of Lucy today?"

Lucy looked over to Sam and smiled. "Yes, we got a lot done."

"There's more to do tomorrow," he said. "I'll be at the shop in the morning."

She shook her head. "I'm sorry. I'm meeting Maura in the morning so it will have to be in the afternoon."

His eyebrows rose slightly before he nodded. "Okay. Just come by when you can." Then he waved and headed off. She watched him talking to Barley as they went toward the bookshop, Barley's head tilted up as if he was listening. They had a sweet bond.

Flora pressed her hands against her apron. "Dinner is cooking. It'll be about forty-five minutes. Want to join me in the kitchen while I stir the pasta?"

Lucy was tempted by the rich smells scenting the air but she shook her head reluctantly. "I'd better check my emails first."

Upstairs, she settled into the cozy armchair and scanned through emails until she spotted a note from Nina.

Hi Lucy, hope you are having a wonderful time. Just wanted to let you know that things are good. But I did notice a package came in when I was up in the office this morning. It was a thick certified mail envelope from Sleep Bold. Don't know what that means, but I thought I'd let you know. Please send me news of your trip so far!

Lucy frowned. A certified mail package could be important. She reached for her phone to call Aaron when she heard Flora calling to her from the bottom of the stairs. She quickly wrote a few sentences back to Nina and promised to write more later.

It turned out the couple from breakfast were joining her for dinner too. Although Lucy was a little disappointed she didn't get a chance to talk with Flora personally that evening, she was glad to have a chance to slip upstairs after eating. She hoped to have some time after her call to be alone and to take a long bath in some fragrant bubbles from a local shop.

Lucy pulled the curtains shut in her room and hopped onto the bed. Then she dialed Aaron's number.

In a few seconds, she heard Aaron's voice. "Hi, sis. How's England?"

She sat up in bed while tucking a big pillow behind her. "Hi, I was going to call you. It's beautiful here."

"Are you eating crumpets and drinking tea?"

"Why, yes I am, love," she teased back in a fake accent.

There was a pause, before he asked, "How has it been, meeting your family?"

"There isn't really any actual family. It was just Brian. But the people here are like Brian's chosen family. The villagers have been very nice." She took a quick breath. "I've met his wife."

"Not too weird?"

She laughed, surprised how grateful she was to be able to talk about it with him. "She's fine but 'weird' is a good word for all of this. The trip is happening so quickly that I don't have time to reflect on anything. And with Brian, it is like trying to meet a ghost. One that everyone has a different opinion about. So yeah, it's been strange."

"You'll be back this weekend, though, right?"

"I'm flying out Saturday."

"Good. I don't want you to get stuck over there."

"Aaron. I've only been here one full day so far. But I've seen the location and it really is a nice place. I think if we do it right, we can sell it for top dollar." She left out the part that the profit would be divided by three now. Aaron didn't need to know about Sam right away.

"How soon can you put it on the market?"

"This week. I will have this wrapped up before I fly home." She felt certain it was true.

"And how soon to sell it? That's the more crucial information here."

"Maura, Brian's wife, says that she has a few buyers in mind already."

"Is there any money that you can get immediately?"

"Maybe? I haven't looked at the bookshop profits yet. There could be some artwork money. But the property is good, Aaron. You will have your new branding soon enough, if you're patient."

He coughed. "I was patient all last year. Now I've made a promise to Serena to be a good husband and I'm committed to providing for my share. I've got to be sure Wellslept will turn a profit."

Lucy was surprised by the tone of Aaron's voice. He was so serious.

"Okay, I'll get some figures later tomorrow. That's when we meet the real estate agents."

"Let me know what you come up with. Everything matters now."

"Aaron, is there anything new with Wellslept?" She hoped her question sounded natural.

"Yes." His voice was more cautious now. "I got a new offer from Sleep Bold."

"For what?"

He sighed. "For a job, Lucy."

Lucy clenched the phone in her hand. "What? First they want to buy us out and now they want to hire you?"

"Is it so hard to believe that they would want to hire me?"

"No, of course not, but why would they do that?"

"Because they're moving their entire headquarters here to Seattle in the spring and they want someone familiar with the area and market."

"Oh, well, you aren't familiar with their kind of products." Lucy wanted to dissuade him from even considering it.

"Not so fast. They are really beginning their move into the eco-conscious market. They want a bigger line and presence. I have to admit I'm attracted by their energy."

Lucy felt tension creep into her shoulders and neck. What she had seen at the Sleep Bold store was a misleading marketing strategy, not good energy. "But you can't leave us. What would Mom and I do without you at Wellslept?" she heard herself wail.

"I'm only listening to their offer. I haven't committed to anything." He paused. "Honestly, I don't want to be a new employee. I'm still pushing for a merger."

"Then please don't promise them anything yet. I'm getting the money. Promise me you won't commit to anything?"

"I won't promise them anything, okay? Not until you get home at least."

With that assurance, she said goodbye and hung up. She noticed that her shoulders had lifted up to her ears. The call with Aaron had brought everything into focus. She'd had a day to relax and now she couldn't waste another minute.

$\mathcal{T}$he next morning as Lucy stepped from the stairs to the hallway, she spotted Flora rushing out of the kitchen balancing a tray of toast and a French press cafetiere full of coffee. Lucy followed her into the breakfast room and chose to sit by the window at the same table as the day before.

"Hi, Lucy. Coffee or tea? Grandad's not feeling good today, so I'm on coffee and kitchen duty." Flora gestured with the cafetiere and the metal tray of toast tipped dangerously toward the floor. Lucy saw there was a new man sitting at one of the tables and the older couple at another.

"Tea, please, but can I give you a hand?"

"No, no, that's okay," Flora said, but immediately she stumbled and, in her attempt to save the toast, the French press slipped out of her hands and shattered on the floor.

"Oh, no. I'm so sorry everyone." Flora's face flushed red and she set the toast down lightly on the table. Lucy righted the toast tray more securely while Flora ran into the kitchen. She reappeared with a broom, just as the smell of something burning reached Lucy's nose. This wasn't good at all. Lucy met Flora's eyes. "I'll sweep up, and you do the cooking."

Lucy grabbed the broom and started sweeping up the glass pieces into a tray. The couple glanced over and then left their table. But the other guest got up to help himself to a piece of toast. "I'm glad I already got my cup of coffee. I guess the early bird really does get the worm." He glanced at her with an engaging smile.

Lucy smiled back. "That was good timing." He was wearing a blue polo shirt and dark jeans.

He bit into the toast. "I wonder if she makes the bread?"

Lucy finished sweeping the wet liquid, coffee grounds, and glass into the tray. "I'm sure she did. Don't eat all the toast, I'll be back for a piece." She grinned at him.

She found Flora bent over the sink, an abandoned and burnt frittata next to her. Flora straightened up and Lucy could see tears had made a trail down her cheek. "I'm sorry, Lucy. I don't do well when Grandad isn't feeling his best."

"That's okay. We're all okay. And you saved the toast."

Flora took a shuddering post-tears breath. "Yep, I saved the toast." She lowered her voice. "Did the Jensens leave?"

"The older couple? I saw them get up. But the other guest is still in there."

Flora's voice got wobbly. "I wanted to impress them. They're from a travel magazine and we need a good review."

"Oh, I'm sorry. The other guest seemed happy enough."

"He's some kind of a developer, I think."

Lucy perked up. "Real estate?"

"I don't know."

Lucy turned around and headed toward the dining hall.

She hesitated at the doorway. She didn't want to talk to the wrong person about the bookshop. But he had spotted her and smiled again.

"Hi, I'm Lucy Baslow."

"Nice to meet you, I'm Geoff Scott."

Lucy took a breath. "Flora told me you're a developer and I thought I'd ask...Do you buy properties in the area?"

He tilted his head. "Are you selling?" he said with a grin.

She hesitated, but only for a second. "Yes. I've recently become part owner in the bookshop next door."

"Sit down and let's talk."

She felt her heart hammering as she took a seat.

He leaned back and smiled. "I'm in the area for a wedding, but I'd be happy to help. I develop commercial properties for manufacturing businesses, mostly. However, I might know someone that would be interested. I already noticed that little gravel car park next to the bookshop when I drove up. Do you own that as well?"

"Yes," she said cautiously. "Of course, I don't want to do something that would change the character of the area."

"Understood." He reached for his wallet. "Here's my card. I'll take a quick look at it before my event today."

Lucy reached into her purse and handed him her card in return. "I'm from Seattle. But you can email me."

His eyebrows lifted. "Seattle? Wakeby is more cosmopolitan than I expected."

Her phone buzzed and she got up. "I'm sorry. I've got to go."

Flora passed her on the way back into the breakfast room. "Are you leaving? I've got fresh coffee."

Lucy glanced at her watch. "Sorry, but I'm off for a big day."

She heard Geoff heartily accept another cup as she slipped out the door.

Maura was waiting for her out in front of the B&B. This time along with her big sunglasses, she'd tied a colorful scarf in her hair. Lucy felt somewhat plain, with her proper round-neck white silk blouse matched with a pair of black pants. She had thought the outfit would help her send the message to the agents that she was serious about finding a buyer. Lucy opened the front car door and slid into another cloud of Maura's perfume.

"Good morning, Lucy. I don't know what I'll do when you're gone. This is beginning to be a nice habit, starting the morning off together."

"Well, hopefully you'll be gone too, on your way to London."

"I'm going up there Wednesday to look at apartments." She smiled broadly. Lucy noticed how white her teeth were.

"So, remind me—who are we seeing today?"

"Three agents; two locals and one with offices here and in London."

"A Londoner?"

"Yes, I think it's a good idea to have someone on board who has connections to larger companies that might want to relocate into the countryside."

"Well, guess what? I've got someone like that already." Lucy handed over Geoff's card.

Maura examined it. "Looks promising. Maybe we can skip a few steps, if he's interested."

Maura pulled out of the driveway. "We're going to Bath first, then we'll try some agents in Frome, not too far from here."

"Great."

The roads were clear, and Lucy liked watching as the green hills whizzed by. Again, they drove into Bath. They parked in the same lot by the church and walked through the old town to a grand curving building with black tiles in the entryway.

Once inside the heavy doors, a different style emerged. This office wasn't all beige like Sappworth & Higgins. Here, an industrial staircase led to an office done in white marble. Maura pushed her way through the glass door.

After a moment, they were ushered into an office with light icy-blue furniture and shown to their seats. Adele Alberg sat across from Lucy and Maura wearing a white silk dress and cream blazer. Lucy thought she was the epitome of what they called an English rose, with a soft pink blush in her cheeks and wide gray eyes.

After welcoming them, she got down to business. "I've been taking a look at your property. Wakeby is one of a cluster of villages that often gets recommended for people moving out of London." She handed out a few sheets of paper with details of properties for sale. "These are some listings available now."

Lucy and Maura looked them over. A quick glance at the numbers told Lucy their property had worth, if not the numbers she was used to seeing in Seattle. Plus, she had to divide the total price by three. If she was doing the exchange right, it looked like she could be putting nearly three hundred thousand dollars into the mattress business. It filled her with a bubbly warmth. Aaron would have to be pacified. She was sure it would be enough to slow him down, at least.

Then Adele pulled up pictures of Baslow's Books on her screen. "These are the photos that you sent me, Maura." Lucy winced. They were all dark and wintery.

"Do you have any specific buyers in mind?" Maura interrupted.

"Yes, I do. There's a developer who has been looking for a place to build new homes in the region and I think they might be completely interested in the charming location, right in the village center."

"I guess they would plan to incorporate the old building into the design?" Lucy said. "I've seen that done a lot in Seattle."

Adele blinked and looked at Maura. "It's freestanding, correct?"

Maura nodded.

Adele continued, "Since it stands alone, and is not part of an existing block of buildings, it would be very easy to remove to make way for the new development."

Lucy stared hard at Adele. "Remove it?"

Adele delicately raised her eyebrows. "That's just one option.

Who can say? There are other ideas, of course. With the proper tidying up, it might be a good spot for a restaurant, for instance. But I understood you were in a hurry, and the developer I'm thinking of could be of instant gratification to everyone."

She looked thoughtfully at Lucy and continued. "I believe the plot itself has more value than the building."

Maura leaned forward. "Sounds promising."

"Either way, it needs to be readied to be shown." Adele selected a piece of paper and pushed it toward Lucy with her manicured nails. "My recommendations are that the entrance be scrubbed, windows shined, wooden exterior repainted, and the pavement swept before I send a photographer out. That bush in the front reminds me of spider webs, especially now that we're coming into autumn. Ideally it would be removed. The interiors need even more sprucing up. From your photos, Maura, that yellow paint color behind the register is particularly off-putting, and the cracked green tile at the entrance should be ripped up or covered with something nicer. I think a black cement would be more modern. Finally the chair and books should be removed from the window. The photos need to represent a blank slate."

Lucy swallowed hard.

Maura looked at her with a supportive smile.

It was business. She needed the money. "I guess we could look into it."

Adele smiled like she already knew they would say yes to her requests. "Ladies, I'd like to represent you. I've got a solid base of clients locally as well as in London and they can provide you with references if you wish."

"Thank you, Adele. We'll let you know as soon as possible. We do want to move fast," Maura asserted.

They shook hands, took their personalized presentation folders, and emerged back into the normal world.

After a short drive south, they arrived in a village a little smaller than Wakeby. The second agent was friendly, but Lucy found the strong smell of cigarette smoke emanating from him and the bits of food clinging to his beard hard details to ignore.

His office was a mess of papers and his vast collection of rubber band balls added to her concern. He promised them a speedy sale and hinted that he had a buyer interested already. Lucy had to adjust her expectations when she heard that an auto tire seller might want to go in.

Once back in the car, Maura laughed out loud. "Okay, he was not what I expected. Sorry, Lucy."

"A big difference from Adele's," Lucy agreed.

"The next two are known for their great staging so I doubt we'll see any more rubber band balls," Maura said as she pulled them onto the main road leading out of town. About thirty minutes later they entered the town of Frome. There were shops along several streets, and Maura found parking easily.

The couple who ran this agency met them at a café at the top of a very narrow cobblestone street in the busy town. They enjoyed crepes and coffees at the cozy bistro while hearing about the way the agents thought they could style the business. There was talk of flowerpots, benches, pillows, and even a fake lamp post that they would put out front. They suggested that the business could go to a hair stylist, home decor shop, or a restaurant.

Maura interrupted again. "But do you have anyone you think you could tap right now to come look at the property?"

The man, Neal, nodded enthusiastically. "Of course, we'll have a party there and invite all the agents in the area to attend." He leaned closer. "This is a little naughty, but vape shops are looking for good locations, and we could go down that route as well."

Lucy blanched at the thought of a smoke shop with its strong aromatics next to Flora's sweet B&B.

The woman, Tiffy, nodded. "Don't forget the grooming business, Neal. We have a client that would absolutely love, love, love the location. Our cat-groomer-and-boarding expert has a thriving chain business called Petty's."

Lucy found herself nodding back. The idea of losing the bookshop to a pet groomer felt better than the idea of the building being sold only for destruction. That suggestion had made her feel sick. A cat grooming place was much more gentle.

"We need a buyer for the whole building. We're not talking about leasing, you know," Maura reminded them.

Tiffy and Neal reassured her that they completely understood.

Maura put her hands in her lap. "Wonderful. In that case, we'll get back to you by tomorrow."

As they walked back to the car through streets with cobble-stones and happy shoppers, Lucy and Maura easily dismissed working with the man with the smoking habit.

Lucy felt comfortable with Tiffy and Neal. "I can already see an animal grooming spa there. I like that."

Maura frowned. "Look, Lucy, I know that the idea of turning the business into a housing development doesn't sound as nice, but Adele is the only agent that had a really lucrative buyer in mind. Despite what Tiffy said, I'm pretty sure an animal grooming shop doesn't have the funds to buy the building. Adele is a professional. That's what we need."

"But a housing development sounds too drastic for such a small village." Lucy swallowed. She knew that really attractive developments were rare; the ugly ones sprouted up only too often in Seattle.

Maura brought out Adele's brochure from her purse as they waited to cross the street. "It isn't what I'd call a small village. And if Adele found a client for us, we wouldn't be the ones building it. That's up to the zoning laws. We'd just be the catalyst. You know, this kind of change is happening all over England. The thing is, I do think that Adele will want to sell it. She's a shark. She can find the grooming salon client as well as Tiffy and Neal. We both need real money. We both will be leaving and never coming back. And"—she paused—"Brian wanted us to benefit. He didn't live in the village all his life. He didn't give the property to the village. He gave it to us."

"I think Sam wants to keep the bookshop going," Lucy reminded Maura.

"We need to be firm with him. You and I are selling. He can't win. I'm certain he can't afford an attorney, but he could delay the whole thing." Maura sighed. "It would be just like him."

She stopped to look at Lucy. "I want you to work on him. He needs to know why you need to sell. He certainly won't listen to me. So it's up to you to convince him. Spend time with him. Soften him up."

Lucy groaned. This wasn't her plan—to trick someone. "I don't think he softens."

"I bet he'd like the profit as much as we would. Find out what he really wants. Maybe we can negotiate with him." Maura unlocked the car door for Lucy. "We need to get this done now. I want us signed this week with Adele, and then you're off to Seattle with something completed."

Maura was right about that. Lucy didn't have much time.

"You are very focused."

Maura looked out the windshield into the street and started the car up. "I know what I want."

"And so do I," Lucy replied, remembering the talk she had had with Aaron. "I'll talk to Sam." *In an honest way*, she thought. Surely then he would understand.

Maura smiled. "Fantastic."

They drove along the motorway with the top of the car down. It was early afternoon and the sun was out. Lucy watched the fields stretch out on either side of the car. Not too long after Maura turned in the direction that would take them toward Wakeby, the hedgerows around the side of the road became charmingly overgrown. Lucy wanted to reach out and pluck a leaf from the bushes as they drove by.

"Maura, I need to talk to you about all the stuff in Brian's rooms and his studio. It's on my list to go through his belongings. Are any of the things yours?"

Maura tilted her head. "Some of the kitchen things might be. But I took most of my things out of there at least a year ago."

"So I can clear out Brian's personal things, right? Just take it all to the Goodwill?"

"What's a Goodwill?"

"A place to donate old stuff."

"Right, there's a charity shop nearby called Goodman's. The churches will take things too."

"I think I'll leave the furniture in there. To leave it styled for a new buyer."

Maura looked skeptical.

"A new buyer might not be a developer," Lucy said, guessing why she wasn't responding.

"It's a lot of junk. We should hire a company to do it."

Lucy winced at the thought of someone ripping apart the beautiful rooms. "There isn't that much upstairs. I have four more days. I can do a lot in that time and maybe we can hire a company to remove the rest after I'm gone."

"Or it just gets professionally cleaned out now."

"No." Lucy was surprised she felt such resistance to the idea of the place being empty. Despite Adele's plan, she hoped the building would stay intact. "Not with the memorial coming up."

"Oh, that's right."

Maura pulled into the alley to let Lucy out.

"Get Sam to agree to the sale. Tell him we need to close down the bookshop after the memorial."

After Maura drove away, Lucy stayed for a minute across the street looking toward Baslow's Books. Sure, it could use a little sprucing up. The rose at the door was a tangle of blooming color and it could do with being trimmed, but she completely rejected the idea that the rose needed to be removed. And take away the books in the window? Seriously, it was as if Maura and Adele didn't read books and hated coziness. Lucy was certain Adele wasn't thinking big enough about who could love it.

As if to prove the point, as she crossed the street she realized the store was filled with shoppers. She was curious to see such a big group inside and walked in to see several women who looked to be in their late eighties and possibly nineties going through the books. Sam was up at the register joking with a few senior couples wearing sensible shoes and raincoats. She noticed that he had them all laughing. She hadn't seen him looking so comfortable and relaxed before. It made her want to join in.

Near the entrance, a man lifted a book and smiled at her. "Could you tell me if this book is his latest? I can't see the small print." She quickly realized that this gentleman thought that she worked at the bookshop. It was probably her white blouse making her look like an employee. She picked the book up to find that the name of the author was Sam Burke. She flipped to the back to see the author's photo. It really was him. The very same Sam, now standing up at the register, was posed in a gray shirt with his hand on his chin in front of a wall of books.

She looked up at him. He continued to ring up books for the line of customers. How interesting. Sam was an author. He hadn't said a word about it. The book had an attractive cover. The title read *A Death in Hampstead*. A Victorian crime novel. That must have been why he was pleased she read historical mysteries. She cracked it open and spotted the date of publication. "It says here this one is from last year. Have you read it?"

He chuckled. "Oh no, this isn't for me. But my daughter loves Sam's books, so I thought I'd get her the latest."

"Sam would know for sure."

"I know, but he's up there surrounded by the young ladies."

Young? She hadn't seen any young ladies. Glancing up at the counter, she saw that indeed Sam was now smiling and ringing up books for two stylishly dressed younger women who seemed to be hanging on his every word. Lucy realized that they weren't all over eighty in here.

She looked again and saw what they saw. He was different from the guys she was normally drawn to. He seemed completely at ease in the shop and was kind to the customers. She loved the way he wore his shirtsleeves pushed up past his wrists. Hip enough, with his Converse sneakers. Smart enough obviously to work in a bookshop, and now he was an author too. She saw him look up from the ladies, to catch her eye for a minute. Had she cataloged that he was handsome too? She felt her cheeks flush, hoping he couldn't read her mind. He nodded at her before turning away to take a book from the next person in line.

She glanced back down at the book in her hand, searched the stacks for his name, and found two more books. "I can't see when these ones came out. We'd better ask."

"Miss, can you tell me where the loo is?"

She looked from the gentleman to a tall, distinguished woman wearing a bright orange Pucci-patterned caftan dress and leaning on a cane. "Of course, it's down the hallway on the right."

The woman, who Lucy thought sounded like Julia Child with her rich, low voice, peered toward the back. "I've got all these books I want to buy. I've been unable to resist them, but they are too heavy for me. Would you mind carrying them?"

Lucy glanced back at the man she'd been helping, wondering who she should assist first. The gentleman took Sam's books from her hands. "That's all right, dear, I'll go up to the counter myself. You help Fran."

"Bathrooms are this way." She reached for the tower of books and the woman gave her a grateful glance.

"Lovely. I'm an avid reader. We register once a month to come on this bus tour and I plan out all my book purchases in advance. But I found even more I must have." She laughed.

"Where else do you go on the tour?" Lucy asked as they inched toward the back of the store.

"We're from Bath. This time we took a route that circled up until we reached Avebury. We did a tour of the mounds, that's Avebury, you know, and some of us just like to look at the gift shops, and then we stop in Wakeby for lunch and more shopping. After that, we're all ready to head home again."

"That sounds wonderful."

"Are you American?"

"Yes, I'm here visiting."

"Where from?"

"Seattle," Lucy said with a lilt in her voice, not knowing if this woman would know where it was.

"Boeing is there, I seem to recall."

Lucy smiled, thinking that there were quite a few other companies she could've mentioned.

"How do you like it here?"

Lucy felt surprised by the question. "It's beautiful."

"You must be Brian's daughter. I see a hint of him in you."

"Yes, I've come to"—she was going to say "sort things out" but changed her mind—"to go to the memorial."

"Good for you. And it must be a balm for everyone that you're here. Like a part of Brian has returned."

Lucy hadn't thought of it that way—that her being in Wakeby might be a comfort for the others.

One of the young women who had been talking to Sam rang a little bell. Fran frowned and tucked herself into the bathroom. "Don't let them leave without me. Tell them that Fran is coming," she said before shutting the door.

"Of course," Lucy said, strangely charmed at how quickly she'd become a store employee. Fran definitely had a decent margin of time before the bus left. Several people were still lined up to finish purchasing books. Eventually, as the store started to empty out, Lucy walked up to the desk with Fran's heavy stack—she was apparently interested in thick historical romances—and set them on the counter. A young woman with long blond hair and a high voice was talking with Sam.

"Excuse me, I just wanted to let you know that Fran's in the bathroom."

The young administrator looked at her with irritation. "We won't leave her." She turned back to Sam. "So, will you be free then?"

"I'm waiting to see what happens."

"Come to our party. We'd love to see you. Maybe you'll connect with a job there."

He nodded. "Maybe."

She reached into her purse and pulled out a card. "This is my number. The party is at 9 p.m."

He took it and swiftly put it in his back pocket. "Thanks, Poppy."

Her answer was a pleased grin that abruptly changed to a scowl when she saw that Lucy was still hovering nearby. Poppy rang her bell again and shooed a small group of people talking by the bay window out the door. "Time to go." She walked over to the bathroom door just as Fran lumbered out. "You know we want to avoid the traffic, Fran."

"Of course," she said obediently, while shooting Lucy a sneaky look behind Poppy's back.

Fran turned to Lucy after Poppy had stepped out the front door. "That woman is the worst hurrier I've ever seen. Personally, I've learned that the best things in life are worth waiting for, like me." She had a big hearty laugh at that. "Here are the books I need." She spoke more quietly to Sam. "Sorry about Brian, dear."

After she paid at the counter, Lucy walked with her to the door. To Lucy she said, "Despite the circumstances, I hope you enjoy your stay here in England. Traveling can change your life. I highly recommend it."

Lucy loved Fran's bright personality. She wasn't sure she'd ever met anyone like her. "Thanks, Fran. It was nice to meet you."

The older woman stepped through the doorway slowly. "You too. See you next time, Sam."

He had followed them to the door and actually winked at Fran. Lucy felt charmed by the way he seemed to enjoy this group.

Lucy shut the door. "They were nice. Your customers."

"They're such avid readers. Helping them select books is often the best part of my month," Sam said, picking up a few books that needed to be reshelved.

"Do they come regularly then?"

"I've got several groups that stop by on a monthly basis. Fran is a character. She was once a secretary for the Mountbatten family. She has lots of stories."

"Wow." Lucy paused, hesitating. "Sam, I saw your books. I didn't know you were a writer."

He stopped straightening the shelves and she saw a flush develop along his cheekbones. He looked down at his hands while he spoke. "Brian encouraged me to try writing once I had devoured the mystery section. I sold my first manuscript a few years ago."

"They look really good." She smiled. "I'd like to read one," she said, then worried if she should have said she'd like to read them all. She'd never met an author before and wasn't sure how to talk about their work.

"Mr. Hayden mentioned you were helping him. Every time he's here I have to stop him from buying books he's purchased before." Sam grinned. He reached over to a haphazard pile of books sitting on the countertop and pushed one toward her. "Here you go. This is actually my first. Mr. Hayden got it mixed up."

"What do I owe you?" Lucy reached for her purse.

He shook his head and made a face. "Nothing. It's a gift."

"Thank you. I can't wait to read it."

"There's another book you need." He walked over to the children's section—which she wouldn't refer to as Lucia's Corner, even in her thoughts.

Sam bent down, pulled out a hardcover book, and showed it to her. "*The Gardener's Cat.*"

"My father's book." She resisted reaching out to take it, a little afraid of what she would find in the story.

"We have all of his books, but this one is where you should start."

He held it out and she had no option but to take it. He left her standing there and went to the door to turn over the sign. "A good sales day means we're free to close early. We should walk up to the garden today."

"I'd like to, but we need to go over the accounting. Also, I need to go through Brian's things. Maybe we could do that together. We haven't discussed the future of the bookshop yet, and I've only got a few more days here."

"Barley could really use a walk." He gave Barley a meaningful look. In response, Barley lifted his head and gazed at her soulfully. "Symonds closes early on Tuesdays. You'll get to see the garden without the tourists. I should have mentioned it earlier." He stood up and grabbed the keys from the counter. That noise really caught Barley's attention.

She felt her impatience rising. "Sam. There is still so much on my list to get done." It was barely three o'clock and she wanted to achieve something today.

"I'll help you with everything on your list."

"Now?"

"Tomorrow."

She looked him up and down. "Not good enough."

"We can plan things while we walk. Tell me what you need done. The shop is closed tomorrow for the memorial. We can get through a lot then," he offered.

She sighed. "Is it a long walk?"

"No, it's only at the far end of the village."

"Brian's book is really set there?" She looked down at the book in her hands. The cover art of a walled garden was exquisite.

He tilted his head. "Yes. The whole place is stunning. There's a stately manor house where they hold weddings. They've got a restaurant too. American tourists love it." Now he was teasing her.

Barley, tired of waiting, barked.

"Yes, you are coming too."

"So you're both in this together, I see." She reached down to pat Barley's wiry curls.

Lucy weighed her feelings. If Sam helped with the cleanup it would go much faster. "I guess it will feel good to stretch my legs for a bit. I'm used to riding a bike around."

Sam got on Barley's leash. "Consider this your grand tour of Wakeby. You can get to know our customers and our village."

On the way to the famous Symonds gardens, they passed the florist's and a dress shop. Sam pointed to Beena's tea shop. "If you come back here in the winter, you can sample Beena's incredible hot chocolate chai combination."

"I'd love that." She had to tell him soon she wouldn't be back.

"That must be Evangeline's wine shop," Lucy said, noting the rows of wine bottles, candles and blue-and-white-striped pillows in the window.

"Yes, and next door to that is where your dad and I often went for dinner, the White Hare pub. You should try their brandy plum tart with ice cream."

A beautiful woman wearing a long white dress came out of the pub carrying a woven wicker basket filled with cosmos flowers. Lucy thought she looked like a character out of some romantic French movie. She smiled at them before heading up the street with her dog. "Who is that?"

"She's new around here. I think she's a big-name artist or photographer. We do have culture and interesting people in our village, you know." He grinned at her. Lucy again noted the difference between the way that Sam and Maura thought about Wakeby.

On the left side of the road a tall hedge had sprung up.

"Now here is where you'll get the best fish and chips." He pointed to an isolated row of cottages across the road to the right.

"Which one is the restaurant?"

"The one with two chimneys and the little car park. Beyond that, that next little white one, that's your granny's old cottage."

She looked at him in shock. She had not thought about having a granny, grandma or any other elderly relative. "She's not still…?"

"Alive?" He shook his head firmly. "No, she passed away years ago. But I think you might have a great-aunt still living. Lucy, this is where your family actually comes from. Didn't you realize that?" He looked at her quizzically.

Lucy found it was hard to breathe. "Is my great-aunt here?"

"No, she's in Scotland. We get Christmas cards from there."

"Has anyone tried to contact her about Brian?"

He closed his eyes. "There's been so many things to do. Maybe you could write to her?"

Lucy felt a fluttering in her heart. To write to her great-aunt, a living relative of hers, stretched her mind. "I could do that." At least she hoped she could.

Lucy looked up at him. "So, my granny," she tried out the unfamiliar word, "lived here in Wakeby?"

"She died pretty young, when Brian was my age, I think. Your mother, she didn't tell you anything about Brian's family?"

Lucy frowned. "My mother didn't want me to have anything to do with my father. I don't know anything about him except from what Maura has told me."

Sam looked toward the little cottage. "I'll show you where Brian kept some of your family photos when we get back, and his address book." He paused. "And I'll take you to the family plot at the cemetery."

She hesitated at the thought of visiting a cemetery. "Oh, you don't have to do that."

He didn't reply, but the set of his mouth gave her the idea that he was planning on it.

They continued a little farther and soon left the cottages and village behind. Sam indicated they follow a plain grassy path that led from the road to the hedge. "And we're here."

She looked around. They were not standing at an entrance to anything. There was only the same tall green hedge going along the side of the road.

Barley started pulling at his leash toward a faint trail that seemed to disappear as it reached the hedge.

"What do we do now?"

Sam smiled. "Go through this hedge."

"Are we supposed to go this way?"

"If you're in the know, yes."

"And you are?"

He smiled more mysteriously. "Your father was given special permission to come whenever he wanted. I think that should extend to you."

He lifted the branches aside, and she saw there was a tunnel through the greenery and an opening. She brushed past him, aware of his strong arms holding the boughs away from her, then ducked her head into the narrow space and climbed over low tree limbs until she stepped out the other side and into a fairy tale.

Far off in the distance, an incredibly beautiful warm-colored stone manor house stood settled at the bottom of a gentle hill above wide stone steps. Lucy wondered how it was possible that this was all here, hidden from the road. The land seemed to have expanded and, glancing around her, there was no sight of the village anywhere, only lush green hills in the distance and benches set out in various places along a path that led to the grand stairway.

Sam caught her expression and smiled at her as they left the hedge and stepped onto the gravel path. "Impressive, eh?" He directed Barley to the right. "We'll go the roundabout way so you can see the small gardens first before we end up at your father's favorite spot."

The path they were on drew them away from the lawns and into an enclosed area blooming with purple salvias and yellow daylilies with a large carved water fountain at its center.

"It's so peaceful here," Lucy murmured in a low voice, not wanting to disturb all the natural sounds.

"Even when there are tourists, it's a nice place to visit. The restaurant is on the other side of the manor so this area stays fairly quiet. The gardens are large enough for everyone."

Barley seemed to sniff out something in the leafy ground covers flanking a colorful riot of dahlias, sedums, and alstroemerias. He pulled Sam and Lucy along the enclosed path and then under a stone portico. Once out of the formal gardens, she saw a row of benches dotting the large grass lawns. They had the place to themselves. It was like they had stepped into another time. Her black pants and blouse suddenly didn't seem as appropriate as a dress would be.

They walked for a while before arriving a few feet from the back of the manor house. "You'll love the garden that Brian wrote about." A little way from the house was a tall hedge wall. The top of the hedge was trimmed into a row of diamond shapes. They walked along the hedge until they reached the corner where it connected with a stone wall.

Sam stopped abruptly. The rounded wooden door in the wall that led into the garden was shut. A note on the door said the garden was reserved for an event. Sam frowned while trying the handle. "I can't believe this. You have to see it. Maybe we can get in over the hedge."

"It's okay. I'm already impressed."

"No, you have to see inside. I want you to see it for Brian. He tried to come here every Tuesday. Said it helped him think of new ideas."

They walked around the perimeter. He tried to find a gap in the thick topiary, but it was futile.

"*The Gardener's Cat.* It was set right in there?"

"Yes, children still come here asking about the cat," Sam said, still pulling at the hedge. "I believe they sell cat stuffed toys here, if you want one."

Lucy eyed Sam grasping at the greenery. Maybe the stone wall along the other side could be scaled. She had noticed a robust wisteria climbing up its side. It would not be a very ladylike move to climb a wall, but...

"Hey, I bet if you could give me a boost over there I can get a footing on that wall and take a peek." Climbing walls and trees was just the kind of thing that she and Aaron did when they were kids.

They moved closer to the wall. Sam glanced around them, then obligingly cupped his hands and Lucy stepped into them. She scrambled to put her foot on an outcropping of stone, stretched up, and grabbed a sturdy wisteria branch. Success.

Here was a view straight out of *The Secret Garden.* "Oh, it's beautiful."

In the middle of the garden was a bed of intricate knot-shaped boxwood with tall gaura flowers bursting out of its formal shape. The late afternoon sun was just resting on the airy tops of their red-and-white flowers. Summer daphne odora, white nicotiana, and miniature roses gathered together at the base of a small topiary of a sleeping cat. Against the far back corner two barely visible wooden benches nestled next to ornate planters filled with overflowing butterfly bushes, their purple spires creating a kind of private spot. For a second, Lucy thought she saw an older man sitting on the bench reading a book. Embarrassed, she looked away quickly. Drawn back to the garden, she blinked and looked again. The bench was empty. Her breath caught in her throat. A second later she detected a flash of someone approaching from around the outside of the garden. She let go of the branch and jumped back down to the ground. "Let's go. Someone's coming," she whispered.

Their feet made awkwardly loud crunching sounds as they quickly ran away along the gravel path. Barley was out front pulling Sam back toward the locals' exit. After they reached the fountain, Sam stopped and laughed. "I believe we're safe. That was a fast escape. You kept a good pace."

She laughed with him. She had felt like a kid running through the garden. "It was worth the peek. It was a little jewel box in there. This whole place is truly magical." She gazed around the fountain to the long bed of colorful petunias and purple asters that went on for what seemed like forever. She shook off the vision of the older man. "I can see why Brian was inspired here. Thanks for bringing me."

Barley pulled at the leash to sniff at the base of a tall echinacea plant as they strolled toward the exit.

"I should have made sure the garden wasn't rented for the evening." Sam sounded regretful.

"It's okay. I saw it, thanks to your boost."

"Not for long enough. And not so you could smell it. It's meant to be aromatic as well."

"That's okay," she said, feeling frustrated with his stubbornness.

He shook his head. "We'll have to come again. It was one of your dad's favorite places. It's important you read the book and experience the garden."

"Sam, I appreciate you trying, but you can't make him matter to me." Lucy regretted her choice of words the minute they were out of her mouth.

"Brian was someone we all cared about. He should matter to you." His face tightened. Was he judging her?

"Explain it to me, Sam. Why didn't this great guy ever come back to Seattle? Why leave my mother and me to struggle by ourselves? I can't get my head around this version of Brian that you all have here in England, versus the one I've grown up with."

Sam put his hands in his pockets and looked to the ground. "Could it be that it wasn't Brian's fault you didn't hear from him?"

She frowned. "What are you saying?"

Sam lifted his head to look at her. "Did your mum want you to be in contact with him?"

Lucy stared back. "No, I'm pretty sure she didn't. But I don't think that meant she was hiding things from me." She paused. There was a chance. Her mom had been so angry. "At least, I didn't think so. I had no idea about the cards you mentioned."

She looked at him, a stranger to her, awkwardly trying to tell her about her own father. Even that wasn't right.

Sam cleared his throat. "Look, my parents were terrible with each other. Screaming, angry craziness. I don't know the details of what happened between yours. Brian was a good guy here with us. He really was. He was exceptional. He may not have had contact with you, Lucy, but I'm certain that he put your name on the wall and sent you birthday cards because he loved you."

At first, she wanted to argue some more. Sam was staring at her, his eyes intent on her, his face filled with determination. Then she had a new thought. She let a little laugh escape. "So you really think it comes down to the fact that all parents are basically bat-shit crazy? You're saying none of us can escape them."

A smile played on his lips. "It's my best argument."

She swallowed. "Fine. I misspoke before. Of course Brian does matter to me. It's just I didn't expect any of this." She sighed. "I feel very confused."

"Brian was the most productive I'd seen him in these last few years. I believe that he'd finally found what made him happy. I'm sure he always felt bad about what happened to your mum and you, but I know that he loved his quiet creative life here in Wakeby. He took immense pride in the bookshop." Sam shrugged. "The main thing is that you're here, and that you have the chance to get to know who Brian was, and how important the bookshop is."

She kicked at the gravel below her feet. It was time to tell him her real plans. She hated him not knowing. "You mentioned visiting the cemetery. Maybe there'll be time after we get everything done and signed."

"Signed?" he echoed.

Lucy suppressed a gulp. She had to get everything out in the open. She nodded while looking straight into his eyes. "Signed to be sold."

Sam stood blocking the path toward the way out. "If you're talking about selling the bookshop, then there is something I want you to know." His eyes widened. "The village needs Baslow's. The whole county needs Baslow's. It brings in tourists from the gardens. There aren't that many bookshops to choose from out here. We can't sell. The three of us must find a way to keep it going. I was going to tell you this before I even knew I was going to be an inheritor."

She chose her words carefully. "Maura wants to move on," she said gently.

"Okay, but you aren't Maura. You're a Baslow. That's what this"—he waved his hand at the gardens—"is all about. We can buy her out together."

Lucy got very quiet and it seemed like the garden became still as well. "I don't have the money to do that."

He looked closely at her as if he was hoping she wasn't telling the truth. "I thought since you were from Seattle with your own business, you would have the kind of funds to buy her out."

She clenched her hands together. "Sam, you got it wrong. My

business at home is in trouble. I have to act fast to save it. That's why I came here. My brother was threatening to leave the company only this morning. I really need the money. I'm sorry, Sam. The bookshop is wonderful. But if I don't get money from this, then I lose my own business. And break a promise I made to my stepfather."

The lines in his forehead creased and he shook his head as if he was trying to shoo away the thought. "But I can't close the bookshop. I'll have to find a way to buy you both out. The village needs it. I can't do that to Brian." His anguished-sounding voice broke off.

Lucy felt terrible and stuck. She didn't have a choice.

When he began to speak again, he sounded determined. "I know you were out with Maura this morning. At least promise me you won't make any permanent decisions without letting me know first. I need to stay informed."

"Okay." She nodded. "I promise. But Sam, you should know it's my goal to have it ready for the market before I leave. We went to see real estate agents today. That's what we were doing."

He let out a long breath. After a while he said, "What does getting ready for the market entail?"

"Getting the place cleaned up. Arranging for repairs. Getting Brian's personal things packed up. Picking a real estate agent. Getting papers signed. Readying the business to close. I just won't be able to come back so it all has to be done now." She felt upset going through the list. It sounded so final to say out loud that the bookshop needed to close.

"When do you leave?"

"Saturday."

Sam gave her a look like she was crazy. "For one, I don't think that getting an agent is the only avenue for us. Maura is thinking too narrowly." He looked down at the ground for a minute then back at her. "There's a lot more for all of us to consider before we blithely sign off on the shop," he said in an irritated tone.

He briskly led them back to the exit. As Lucy weaved her way through the laurel branches each one resumed their place and the secret world of the garden was erased from view. A big white delivery truck drove by leaving them in a cloud of exhaust. It was as if those beautiful gardens just beyond the hedge were not even there.

Sam didn't say much on the walk back. She tried to act natural but she felt awkward. She asked him a few questions about the memorial while trudging along the side of the road. He answered in short sentences. She worried that he was going to delay the whole thing like Maura had predicted. At least he knew the truth. She could not save the bookshop.

Flora was plumping up the cushions on the couch when Lucy walked in, having said a brief goodbye to Sam.

"Hi, Lucy. You okay?"

"Oh, it's been another long day. I don't think I got enough done and I guess I'm tired." Lucy wondered how much the disappointing talk between her and Sam showed on her face.

"How about a cup of tea? I've just put the kettle on. We can have tea while I cook. It's chicken in a cream sauce on the menu. Oh, and it's just you tonight, so we can eat in here if you'd like."

Lucy considered going up to her room but the lure of caffeine was impossible to resist. She told herself it would help her stay awake, which would mean she could make more plans. "I'd love to."

"All right then, normal tea? Or green?" Flora walked over to the cozy gray enamel stove.

"Thank you. I'd love a cup of English breakfast." Lucy looked around the kitchen. Everything felt clean and fresh. It seemed like ages had passed since her first evening here. "These wood countertops are so nice."

"Grandad is very good at building things, and we redid this

kitchen a few years ago. I had to pay him with his favorite chocolates from France, but he finished it so beautifully."

"How is he doing?"

"Oh, he's up and he's had his lunch and feeling better." Lucy
watched Flora pour a little hot water into the blue enamelware
teapot, and then swish it out. "He sometimes feels very poorly. He
calls his stomach upsets a part of old age, but I don't like it even if
the doctor says he is fine. Dinner won't be very spicy tonight,
hope that's okay?" She dried her hands on a tea towel that read
"Wiltshire" before putting two plump spoonfuls of loose tea into
the teapot followed by more hot water, popping on a knit tea
cozy, and carrying it over to the little kitchen table.

"Everything you make is good so no worries about tonight."

Flora briskly moved to her china cabinet and brought out two
delicate teacups painted with dainty yellow flowers and topped
with gold rims as well as a little milk jug with a darling purple
pansy painted on the front.

"Except the burnt frittata." She giggled a little while she set
them on the counter and Lucy settled into a cushioned bar chair.
"I hope you like your tea strong. I've put in several scoops."

"I'm on a roll today. The stronger the better. I'm fighting a
headache."

"Tea will help. I'll get you a glass of water too." Flora went
over to the sink. "Did you get a chance to see our village today?"

"Maura and I went to meet some people this morning and
Sam and I went to Symonds this afternoon. It was amazing." Lucy
was careful not to reveal where she'd been with Maura.

"Did you meet some estate agents?" Flora asked casually.

Lucy squirmed.

Flora glanced at her. "One of them has left a phone message
for you."

"We're just putting out feelers at this point."

Flora looked shy for a minute. Then determined. She reached
over to briefly touch Lucy's arm. "Is there any chance you might

keep it running? Baslow's, I mean? It is so nice to have a book-shop next door."

Was this the moment that Maura had warned her about? Would her answer be turned into local gossip?

Lucy appreciated what Flora was asking, but shook her head. "I have a family business at home that I run. I don't see how I could also do it here." She added, "But nothing is decided. I don't know what Maura's plans are or how Sam might figure into it, of course."

"Maura is involved with the bookshop plans?"

Lucy nodded.

Flora lowered her voice before speaking again. "I don't mean anything by it, but Brian and Maura had been separated for a long time. A lot of water under that bridge. I'm just a little surprised."

Lucy felt she needed to defend Maura. "She's been helpful to me."

"And Sam is part of it too?" Flora asked.

"Yep, we are all inheritors."

Flora's eyes widened. "All inheritors," she echoed. "A three-way split."

Oops, Lucy thought. Perhaps she had already said too much.

"That's great. I'm so happy to hear it. Sam is a good guy. And great at running the shop."

That certainly wasn't what Maura had said, Lucy reflected.

Flora paused to catch her breath. "There's one thing I think I should tell you. Sam was the one who arranged and paid for your dad's burial. I just thought you should know about that."

"Thanks, Flora," Lucy said thoughtfully. Sam was complicated. A little like her father. A different reputation depending on who you talked to. Lucy slowly sipped the rich brown tea out of her cup while being careful not to drink down any of the loose tea leaves. She wasn't used to those being in her cup.

Mr. Emery walked in, wearing a thick tweedy sweater despite the mild fall afternoon.

Flora lifted the pot. "Would you like a little, Grandad?"

"Yes, please. Are you going to read Lucy's tea leaves, Flora?"

"No, I wasn't going to alarm her with the tea leaves just yet."

Mr. Emery smiled at Lucy. "Flora will read your fortune. She's very good, you know."

Flora laughed. "I'm good at seeing patterns and I learned from my granny what the little symbols are."

"Well, I'm game." It was a good distraction from talking about the bookshop, and Lucy was secretly delighted. She knew that Nina would love to hear about a tea-leaf reading. "What do I do?"

"Drink up all the tea and then turn the cup three times."

Lucy held the footed china cup carefully and watched the painted yellow flowers spin around in the palm of her hand as she turned it. After the proper three turns, Lucy handed over her cup.

Flora carefully considered it from all different sides. She winked at Lucy. "To me, it all looks good. You certainly are surrounded by many people. See this?" She pointed her finger at a clump toward the rim of the cup.

Lucy saw a blotch of leaves with one a little farther apart.

"I think of this as a message." She paused. "Yes, you'll be getting an important letter." She looked up impishly. "Ada is having us all sign a card to be presented to you at the memorial, so maybe that's it."

Lucy closed her eyes. "Oh no. It's not necessary to do anything for me."

"Don't worry. It's not really about you. Ada is the one who likes to be the star at all of our local events."

Lucy remembered Ada's brightly colored polka-dotted raincoat and how she was quick to talk to Lucy. She and Flora shared a grin. "I think I can see that."

Flora turned the cup around, considering the leaves. "There is something happening here. People are waving at you. I'm not sure if it's goodbye or hello."

A buzzer rang out from the kitchen. Flora jumped up. "Oh dear, I've forgotten to check the chicken."

It wasn't long before Flora had their dinner on the table in the cozy kitchen. Lucy saw how she took care to present the dinner on the most darling green plates. A sweet pea bouquet had been arranged on the table and each napkin had been ironed. While they ate, Mr. Emery and Flora told her more about the village.

"Has your family always had the B&B?" Lucy asked.

Flora smiled and looked at her grandad. "Yes, my granny loved running it."

"Do your parents help with the B&B too?" Lucy thought it was a big job for just one young woman.

Flora's hand hovered over the platter of chicken. "My mum died when I was very young. My dad"—she glanced at Mr. Emery —"he remarried and has a whole other family. Grandad and Granny really raised me. So it's mostly just us now. And Russell." The bloom reentered her face.

"Who's Russell?" Lucy was trying not to conjure up a Jack Russell terrier in her mind.

"Russell is my boyfriend. He lives in Edinburgh at the moment. He's at university." Flora passed the platter to her grandad.

The kitchen was quiet except for the sounds of their knives and forks.

"What does Russell do?" Lucy asked, enjoying the happiness on Flora's face.

"He's studying to be a geologist." She giggled. "Actually I was worried that meant he'd travel the world while I was here in Wakeby, but he's assured me there is plenty for him to do right here, which is good because I love running the B&B." She took a sip of water. "Have you always known you would be a businessperson?"

Lucy felt her face grow hot. Was that what she was? "No... well, maybe." Lucy considered letting that be the end of it, but she couldn't lie without feeling guilty later, so she kept talking. "I didn't really know that I was going to work in our family business. I studied photography in college, but when my stepfather got sick, it became important that I step in and help our company."

Flora's smile broadened. "I was curious if you shared Brian's artistic nature. He was such a wonderful illustrator. I would love to see your photos."

"I don't have much time for photography anymore." She quickly diverted from the question. "I should say, this dish is so good."

Flora smiled more widely. "Thank you. We are serious about food at Hollyhock Cottage."

She wanted to ask Mr. Emery about her grandmother. She was sure he would know something about her. It was something she was working up to when there was a knock at the door. Flora jumped up to answer it and, alone with Mr. Emery, Lucy took the opportunity to ask the question.

"Mr. Emery, did you know my grandmother?"

He smiled and leaned forward. "Yes, I did. Mary-Ann Peach was a good woman. Very proud of Brian. She felt that moving to America would give him a chance to get ahead."

"Do you think she knew about me?"

"Now, I suppose she did."

Lucy swallowed.

"I can't speak for her with certainty, but Mary-Ann always wanted to help others. She seemed to know everyone. It would have made her very happy to know she had a grandchild. I never heard her speak of you but if she knew, then I imagine she thought about you a lot."

Lucy sighed. Was this another loss due to her parents' craziness?

After a few minutes, Flora came back into the dining room.

She reached out to put a couple of books, one of them a large hardcover picture book, on the edge of the table. "That was Sam. He brought these for you, Lucy."

It was Brian's picture book and, on top, Sam's paperback.

Lucy wondered if this meant Sam was offering her a gesture of goodwill after their awkward discussion about the bookshop. "Thank you. Sam showed me my father's book earlier today but I haven't had a chance to look at it yet."

"You haven't read it ever?" Flora didn't hide her disbelief.

"Nope." She sighed. It was one more thing separating her real experience of Brian from the people who lived here.

"Well, I think you'll like it. And also Sam's book. He's usually shy about sharing his books with newcomers. I guess he must like you." Flora grinned mischievously.

"I think he had to tell me, after a customer pointed it out to me at the shop." Lucy laughed.

"Maybe it will give you a chance to know them both better." Flora smoothed her hands on her apron. "Can I get you anything else? A glass of wine, maybe?"

Lucy thought about her big day tomorrow. "No, that's okay. It was really wonderful. Thank you."

Lucy went upstairs and sat down on her bed. Then her phone buzzed. The text was from her mom, instructing her to come home. *I hope by now you've discovered that there isn't any money to be found there. I know Brian. I don't believe people change. Especially drinkers. Aaron has just told me you are sharing the inheritance. Not surprised. You shouldn't be either. It's time to come back.*

Lucy couldn't believe it. Her mom had broken her disapproving silence to send her a disapproving text. Lucy was just about to set up her phone so it wouldn't disturb her while she slept when it buzzed a second time.

Her mom again? She reluctantly lifted it back up. Red and purple hearts and red rose flower emojis filled the screen. This text was from Bruce. *I'm thinking of you. You've already been gone too long for my liking.*

She was grateful for his much nicer message. Had she responded to his last email? She rapidly texted him back, *Four more days.* Her finger hesitated over the heart emojis. She decided on a string of green and yellow hearts and green plants. She hit send and set the phone where she could see it. Bruce responded right away with a text that read, *How's London?* Lucy frowned—hadn't she told him she was staying in a village? She was considering sending him a reply when he texted a picture of Big Ben and a sleep-face emoji. She sighed. She'd explain it all later. Sent a thumbs-up, then a blowing-kiss emoji, tapped the do-not-disturb button, and put it down on the bedside table.

She rolled her shoulders, dimmed the light, and reached for Brian's book. The pages were wide, as this was a book written for children.

As she opened it to the first page of the story, she relished the feel of the thick, smooth pages under her fingers. Many tiny pencil strokes had created a picture of a kitten sitting in the kitchen window of a big crumbly castle. The kitten was watching a gardener tend to row after row of identical boxwoods. It was apparent the gardener was always alone. People walked right past him and the gardens on the way to the castle.

One day the cat danced on the windowsill and caught the eye of a little girl staying at the castle. Lucy recognized Symonds Manor from the illustrations. The girl came to follow the cat into a big walled garden where the gardener was pruning a boxwood. The gardener was pleased to have a visitor, so he did something unusual. He pruned the boxwood into the shape of the cute cat. Lucy noted that it was the same as the topiary she had seen in the garden at Symonds. The little girl clapped her hands in delight. She told her brother and they both came back the next day to see the cat and the old man.

On the next page he created a bird from a yew hedge, and for the boy he made a rhododendron resemble a poodle. They all thought a topiary parade of animals would look smashing. The gardener was inspired. The long row of boxwoods became a procession of deer and rabbits, balls and diamonds. It wasn't long before children came from far and wide to see the amazing shapes. The walkway to the castle was transformed into a whimsical menagerie. By the last page, the gardener wasn't lonely anymore and the laughter of the children delighted him and the cat every day.

Her father's drawings were spectacular, stylish, and magical at the same time. She wanted to step inside them, to sit there peacefully on the garden bench in the sunshine amid the woodland creatures. Instead, she sat on the bed gazing at the book until she felt her head nodding.

For a moment, she was there, feeling comforted by the garden animals all around her, and a calm presence beside her.

Brian, she thought sometime much later as she woke in the middle of the night, the book having fallen from her chest to the bed next to her, *why have you put me in this position? I don't know what to do.* Nina had said to just be herself, but even that was proving difficult because she had suddenly become a different version of herself. One with a family history, new friends, and the responsibility of a bookshop.

8

The following morning Lucy was early to the breakfast room. There was no sign of either the older couple or the developer.

Lucy had dressed casually in her jeans, a T-shirt, and scarf. It felt so much better to be less formal. She sat at the table by the window, lifted her cup of tea, and gazed out at the garden. She could get used to this view.

Despite her late-night misgivings, Lucy was determined to get an early start. Cleaning the shop and clearing away Brian's items would at least be the easiest things to cross off her to-do list.

Halfway through breakfast Flora came in to check on her.

"Good morning, Flora. I think I'll start today by getting some supplies to tidy up the bookshop. Would Ada's be the place for Windex and paper towels?"

"Yes, she ought to have everything. Though Windex is a brand I've never heard of. You probably mean Windolene? A spray for the window?"

"Yes, that's what I'm looking for. Is there anything I can get you?"

Flora thought for a moment and then shook her head. "No,

thanks. But have a great walk through our village. You'll find Ada's all the way up on the right."

Right after breakfast, Lucy headed outside. The flower shop across the street was open. A middle-aged man wearing a waxed cotton coat, corduroy trousers, and worn leather loafers stepped out to his entrance with a watering can and waved at her. She called out a cheerful "Hello," while guessing he was the owner of the shop that Sam had mentioned.

Once around the small roundabout, she entered Wakeby's main shopping street. It was bustling with people. The morning sun was shining brightly and the streets were busy with mothers pushing strollers and children not yet old enough for school. Lavender and rosemary filled stone planters outside of the stores. Lucy paused when she arrived at Beena's tea shop. A menu on the wall of the café offered sandwiches, shortbread, and English breakfast tea. Lucy made a mental note to find time to try it out when she noticed someone inside was waving vigorously at her.

It was Beena herself. Lucy smiled and made her way to the door. As she entered big glass canisters filled with bright green, yellow, and pink hard candies caught her eye. The smell that met her nose was a blend of chocolate and sugary jelly beans, with a hint of buttery caramel. It was heaven. This wasn't just a café, it was a candy store. Along the back wall, her eyes drank in the crowded shelves of teacups, teapots, and little bowls. Tea towels, jams and chutneys, the hard kind of placemats, and quilted tea cozies all called out to her. This café shop was irresistible. This was where she would find a present for Nina. And for Aaron. Even her mom. She might as well do it now.

Beena was wearing a pale blue apron over a coral blouse and jeans. She pulled the glasses that rested on the top of her head onto the bridge of her nose. She had a lovely smile that spread across her face. "Lucy." She came around from the counter and gave her a hug. "This is an unexpected delight."

"Your place is wonderful."

"Are you needing some breakfast?"

"No, Flora has been taking great care of that. Would you mind helping me get a few bags of candy? I want to bring some home for my family."

"In that case, you must try this clotted cream fudge," Beena said with a playful grin. She handed a sample to Lucy.

She popped the fudge into her mouth. Her taste buds flooded with a salty sweetness and her tongue registered the granular feeling of the sugar. After she savored the caramel bite, she nodded vigorously. "I'll take those for sure."

Beena was helpful, but Lucy caught Beena looking at her, more frequently than would be usual. In a few minutes she had selected a bag of butter mints, blackcurrant and licorice hard candies, a bag of butterscotch toffees, and something called Coltsfoot Rock. Beena kept adding little treats until Lucy had to beg her to stop. When Lucy caught her looking at her again, Beena blushed.

"I'm sorry, dear, but I keep seeing flashes of Brian in you. I've been missing him, you see, so it's hard not to." Her cheeks flushed deeper, tinting her brown skin a rosy hue. "Hard not to look for him."

Lucy struggled to find something appropriate to say.

Beena held up her finger. "I have a surprise for you."

She pulled out an ample box of Snickers bars. "I used to get these in for Brian. He said you loved this kind."

"I do love Snickers," Lucy said, wondering how he knew these things about her.

"Little bites of America, he called them. I'm planning on bringing them to the memorial. He would have been so happy to see you here. It makes me sad and happy." She was smiling, but tears filled her eyes until her smile began to wobble.

Lucy put down her things, stepped around the counter, and gave her another hug. It struck her that she was starting to feel differently about her role as Brian's daughter. She was getting better at it. It wasn't so much how she felt about Brian that was changing, but her appreciation for the kindness of the people of Wakeby.

Beena blinked and wiped her eyes. "You're a good daughter, I can tell. You must be a great help to your family back home."

"Thank you. It's been an adjustment to come here. And learn about my father."

"Anything you want to know, I'd be happy to answer. I think out of all of us here in Wakeby, I'm the one that has known him the longest."

Lucy hesitated, but her mother's text was fresh in her mind, and Beena had been so kind. "Beena, I do have a question. It's a little awkward to ask."

"Yes? That's okay."

"Was my father an alcoholic?" She bit her lip, regretting how rude it sounded.

Beena widened her eyes but didn't shy away from speaking. She came out from around the counter and beckoned Lucy to sit down across from her at a little table. "It's how I met your father, actually. He had just moved here and we met at the closest AA meeting, in a town nearby. Those days seem like a lifetime ago. He and I shared that struggle between us. My husband had just left me, one I had gone against my entire family to marry. I had no one. My family nearly disowned me and I couldn't find a way out for a while. Eventually the meetings helped. Brian's work helped him. And running my shop in this village helps me. I feel I belong here, due mostly to the way Brian created the tone of community in our business group."

Lucy dropped her eyes to the table. It was the second time she heard of Brian's effort to bring the village shopkeepers together. Another positive. "I'm sorry to ask like that, but my mother hasn't told me much about Brian, and what she did tell me wasn't very nice."

Beena nodded. "It's okay. When Brian came here, he made a real effort to change his entire life. I think he succeeded. He might have made some mistakes along the way, but overdrinking wasn't one of them."

"Was he a responsible person? Choosing to be an artist doesn't seem like a stable career." Lucy continued to cringe inside, knowing everything she was saying sounded so judgmental.

Beena smoothed her gray hair back before resting her hands in her lap. "I know it might appear that way from the outside. But you didn't know him. He was very organized. He loved to share and teach others. He worked on each contract with the various publishing houses very professionally and he put that money back into the bookshop. It's true that his aunt left him the building and that made it easier for him to make his business finally be profitable. The property gave him a toehold to build from. But he was the one that took that gift and made it into something for all of us."

Lucy's eyes pricked with tears. "Thank you. It means a lot that I know this. I'm lucky to have met you."

Beena smiled at her. "I'm so glad to have met you too, Lucy. Brian was special to me." She reached out to pat Lucy's hand. "Even though we are now missing one of us, we have to keep doing our best as we get through this."

Lucy paused, thinking of her stepfather. "It can take a long time."

Beena nodded. "One day at a time."

The door opened and a mom with a toddler in hand and pushing a baby in a stroller came in. Beena stood up. "Lucy, would you like a cup of hot chocolate or a piece of shortbread while I attend to these little ones?"

Lucy laughed, "I don't dare. I'll be hyper from all the sugar."

She left with promises to see Beena again soon, feeling lighter and happier that she had trusted Beena to ask about Brian, and had received thoughtful answers.

The shop right next door was Evangeline's. As Lucy walked past she noticed the shop was dark and the cute sign hanging on the door read "Ferme." So she strode up the street looking for Ada's shop. She knew she had arrived when she got to the store with windows covered in posters announcing sales on toilet paper and garden gloves. This store was twice as wide as the other places on the street. Lucy entered through a sliding glass door and saw Mr. Cowcroft sitting behind the counter. He was watching a loud TV, but immediately turned the volume down when he saw her. "Welcome, Lucy," he said in a hearty voice.

"Hello, Mr. Cowcroft. Could you point me to the paper towels?"

"Kitchen towels are down the aisle behind you."

She made her way around the shelves and put the paper towels, a mini spray can of black paint, and a small pair of garden clippers all into a plastic orange basket.

Lucy was rounding the corner of the garden aisle when a door opened at the back of the store and Ada popped out. "Lucia, how do you do?"

Lucy smiled in return. Hadn't she told Ada her name was Lucy? "Hello, how are you?"

"Busy as always." Ada peeked into her basket. "Can I help you with anything?"

"I've offered to clean up things at the bookshop."

"Is the bookshop going on the market then?" Ada had moved so close to her that Lucy could see Ada's makeup had settled into the furrows in her forehead and traces of lipstick feathered away from the edges of her lips.

She hadn't expected the question to be put so plainly. Lucy blinked. "Uh, no, we haven't gotten that far yet. I'm just tidying up for the memorial and packing away some of my father's personal stuff."

"Is that so? Because we don't need you to repaint for the memorial." Ada spoke with a sharp voice while peering into her basket.

Lucy sputtered in surprise. "Oh, well, um, you're probably right. For now, how about window cleaner?"

"Follow me."

Ada led her over to the cleaning products. "Lucy, I don't want to pry, but I heard you were visiting estate agents. Understandably, this has made me concerned."

Lucy felt her face flush. How did Ada know that?

"I want you to know that there are rules about doing building work in Wakeby."

"There are?" Lucy quickly put a bottle of Windolene in her basket.

Ada's eyes narrowed. "Yes, and, if it were to be put on sale, as the lead parish councilor of Wakeby, I'd expect to be informed before that decision was made."

"Oh." Lucy seriously regretted coming to the local store for her supplies. She hadn't realized that Ada would be so nosy. She decided to play dumb. "This is all very new to me."

Ada clucked. "I assume you understand that Wakeby is a special place. We don't want anything that could disturb our delicate balance. One bad egg could affect the whole basket."

"Of course." Lucy decided she was done shopping at Ada's forever.

Mr. Cowcroft was up at the counter. He looked surprised when Ada nudged him aside to ring up everything Lucy had in her basket. Lucy had hoped that Ada wouldn't see the telltale garbage bags and work gloves at the bottom and get even more agitated, but she was clearly out of luck as Ada ran each item through the scanner and placed them into a plastic bag excruciatingly slowly. "The bag is an extra charge." She paused to stare at

Lucy. "We've been in business for thirty years and consider our shop to be the cornerstone in Wakeby. I can't imagine any other general store business going in, for instance. Or a bakery. It wouldn't be suitable."

Ada waved her thick arm, and Lucy realized that a bakery adjoined the grocery store. "Oh, do you own both businesses?"

"Yes. We are very invested in Wakeby, you see."

"Right. I see."

"Just put your credit card in here," Mr. Cowcroft added kindly while pointing out the machine was ready.

Ada's voice softened. "Brian loved it here, you know. Honoring his memory is deeply important for everyone." She looked hard at Lucy. "He especially wouldn't want Wakeby to change."

Ada reached under the counter and pulled out a bag. "If you're really getting ready for the memorial, then here are some decorations I've gathered. You can put these up."

Lucy accepted it. "Thank you." As soon as Mr. Cowcroft gave her the receipt, Lucy reached for her things, managing a nod in his direction before leaving as fast as she could.

Now she knew why Maura had warned her to keep quiet. Ada didn't miss a thing.

Sam opened the door to the bookshop as Lucy walked up. "Hello. First time I've seen you in the morning."

His eyes looked a bit puffy and his reddish hair was still damp and tousled. He had a mug of coffee in his hand. After their last conversation about the bookshop she was relieved he was acting normal and didn't seem too disappointed. She smiled, wanting to keep the lighter feeling between them. "Good morning. I'm planning to get a lot done today."

"We've got a full day. I didn't forget that I promised to help you. For now, I'm trying to relocate our book tables for the memorial tonight. This caffeine is the first step." He took a sip.

"Will the bookshop be big enough?" Lucy wondered.

"It will work, and there will be extra room in the garden and on the walkway outfront."

He looked at the bags in her hand. "You've been to Beena's. And Ada's." He seemed to zero in on the garden clippers peeking out from one of the bags. "What are those?"

"Clippers for the front entry," she said.

"Not for the rose." Sam's voice was low.

"It's just a little cleanup so people can get in the door."

He frowned. "No. Brian loved that rose. There's no reason to touch it."

"It catches on people's clothes. We need the place to look cared for. Especially when so many people are coming to the memorial."

"What they expect is to see it looking the same as when he died. His place. His rose. His shop."

She stopped herself from saying that things had already changed. She knew saying that would hurt him. Instead she pulled out the other cleaning supplies. "How about I clean windows then?"

"Fine. I'll get out the mop after I get the tables moved. Might as well do the floors."

Lucy watched him walk back to the counter. While Sam restocked some books and shoved tables against walls, Lucy looked in the bag that Ada had supplied. Black streamers and black balloons were tucked into the bottom. Lucy groaned. Black definitely seemed the wrong message. It wasn't a dark-humor-themed birthday party. Did streamers even belong at a memorial? She placed the bag of decorations by the sink in the back kitchen and went to the sidewalk outside of the bookshop.

After spraying and wiping down the big window in the front, she moved on to scrubbing down all the paint and stone that surrounded the window. With a stepladder she was even able to wipe away the dust and grime that had settled on the Baslow's Books sign. It was very satisfying. Finally, Lucy wiped her hands on her last dry towel and went through the now shiny front door. She had left Sam inside to mop.

As she walked in, she frowned. The bookshop looked bare without its tables. The floor was definitely dusty. Barley was there, sleeping in the sunlight under the window, but it was clear Sam hadn't done any mopping in the bookshop. She couldn't see him at all. She strode into the back kitchen. The bucket was in the same place. That's when she saw the studio door was ajar. She walked quickly toward it and opened it. Sam was there, holding the mop and looking out the window.

"I don't want to do this."

She walked closer to him. "The mopping?"

"The memorial. I don't want to talk about Brian with people. I don't want to say a final goodbye."

"I don't think it works like that," she said quietly. "I will always feel connected to my stepfather."

"How?"

"When I work in the office, I think of him there with me. Sometimes I reread the emails he sent me. I keep the gifts he gave me. I am doing things he would know about. I do things I think he would approve of. I keep his favorite flowers growing in our parking lot." Lucy's voice had lowered to a whisper. "I never fail to think about him."

"I've been writing something for the memorial. But it feels flat." He turned to her. "What you're talking about seems more real than saying a bunch of words."

Lucy looked up at him. "We need the words, Sam. That's your gift. You're the writer. I'm sure other things will emerge to keep Brian close."

Sam's shoulders dropped a little. "I guess the village is coming whether I want them to or not."

"It will be nicer with a clean floor as well," she said, and then when he met her eyes, she offered him a light smile.

"Fine. I'll mop. But Lucy, no streamers."

"I agree. And those aren't from me. Ada gave me that bag of stuff." She followed him into the kitchen. "Do you have any Christmas tree lights?"

"Fairy lights?"

"What about if I put some up in the window? It's nicer than streamers and black balloons."

He nodded. "Sure, that will look good. They're in the shed."

She stopped him then, as he went toward the door. "It will be okay tonight. In my experience, memorials have a shape and then they are done. Weeks and months later when everyone expects the grief to be over, but it isn't, that's what's unexpected. That's what goes on too long."

"Did that happen to you?" he asked.

Lucy thought about how much she still missed Paul. "You know, I have a friend named Nina, and she knew my dad. We talk about him and that helps." She looked up at him. "I think you'll be okay because of your friends in Wakeby."

He gave her a brief nod. "Thanks." He shifted on his feet. "Okay, back to the list. Fairy lights then mopping," he said to her as he and Barley went out the back door.

Lucy wandered back into the bookshop. She longed to grab a book from the shelves, settle into the armchair, and just read the day away. She found herself drawn to the mystery shelf where Sam's books were stored. While she waited for Sam, her eyes rested on the satisfying order of the books stacked on the shelves. In each book was a possibility of joy: a magical place to visit, a hero or heroine to meet, or a new friend to make. With grief, books allowed a chance to revisit a story you once shared with the person you had lost. She didn't know what books Brian had loved. Paul had loved hard-boiled detective and noir mysteries. Walter Mosley and Curt Colbert were favorites of his. Her eyes scanned the shelves easily spotting other favorites. The Elizabeth Goudge books were near the middle of the shelves close to the Gabaldons. Down at the bottom by her feet were the Oscar Wildes, the Laura Ingalls Wilders, and at the very top of the bookcase were the Chimamanda Ngozi Adichies and the Austens.

But there was something more. It was not just books that made a bookshop feel so right. This one was special. This one had welcomed her in. It was quiet. It was small. Was it the warm tone of the wooden floors and bookshelves? Was it the armchair at the entrance? Was it Barley? She shook her head. Whatever it was, when she was in this bookshop, she felt lifted up.

Sam arrived with a box of stringed lights that turned into a mess of tangles when she tried to extract just one. He sat down next to her and they worked together to untangle them. Hanging the white fairy lights was much easier once they were separated. She found that there were hooks already secured into the walls around the front window. While she connected them together, Sam mopped the entire store and then left to get them some lunch from up the street.

Once she had the lights up and plugged in, Lucy unlocked the front door and went out to assess the overall look through the window. She didn't want it to look like the Christmas holidays. Maybe candles would have been better, but how good could candles be in a shop full of books? Once through the door, though, she nodded in relief and satisfaction. It was magical the way the lights dipped and twinkled in many layers across the window. As she ducked under the roses in the doorway on her way back in, she realized it would be the perfect time to trim a few leaves off, especially since Sam had gone up the street. She found the pair of clippers and came back out. She stood looking at it for a moment, vowing to be careful, and then knew what to do.

Quickly, to get it done before Sam came back to object again, she cut off the trailing wisps that were catching on her clothes and hair, and then started off at an angle to let the bush still hang over the doorway a bit. She cleaned up the bottom of the rose by pruning back some of the leaves there. The only problem was that when she went to cut off one long cane, it got stuck on another, so she had to cut it too. Her heart started to beat in anxiety. She glanced up the sidewalk. He wasn't coming yet. Losing the bigger canes made the upper part of the rose fall over too much. She cut each stem that was left hanging haphazardly. She swallowed hard. Had she pruned it too much?

She wanted to call Flora, but she knew Flora was probably slaving over thirteen kinds of cookies for the memorial. So she stepped back to get a bigger view. Then she stepped back even farther and decided to cross the street. From across the road she looked at the shop and caught her breath.

The rose was still lovely. It curled around the doorway like a delicately arched eyebrow. The lights in the window added a warm feeling. Above the window, the gold lettering of "Baslow's Books" now shined bright against the black paint of the sign. There was a pile of pink roses and branches on the sidewalk, but she would drag them to the backyard. Overall it looked like a picture from a romantic Pinterest board.

She felt all warm inside, proud of the work she had done and proud of the bookshop. She had to admit, being a Baslow meant something. She wanted to remember the bookshop like this, glowing in the sunshine. If only she could keep it. Somehow, own it from afar. But of course, that would be impossible.

She spotted Sam walking down the street. His eyes seemed to widen as he saw the discarded rose stems on the sidewalk. He rushed up to the door and stood still, frowning deeply as he observed her pruning job. He strode right into the shop and shut the door firmly. He didn't even look at the window. She took a deep breath. It appeared he wasn't very happy with her work.

After Lucy had pulled the branches to the back garden, she

cut an armful of pink roses in various stages of bloom. She came in through the back door just as Sam was boiling the kettle.

He spun around. "You butchered it. I can't believe you did that."

"I was trying to make it look nice. People need to be able to get in the doorway."

"It looks like a poodle," he said angrily and walked away from her.

"It's called pruning. And I've got these roses to put in a bouquet, if you have a vase." She called after him, making her voice sound confident. If the rose did die, she would feel unimaginably, horribly bad.

"Under the sink," he muttered.

She tiptoed around Sam during the next few hours. Generally following the list that Adele had suggested, Lucy swept and scrubbed the tiles at the entrance and dusted the shelves. She couldn't see what the problem was with the yellow interior paint. It seemed like a happy color to her. A few hours after lunch, Sam walked up to her with a piece of paper in his hand. "Listen, I guess the rose looks tolerable."

"I'm sorry. It wasn't as easy to trim it as I thought. I did cut off more than I wanted to."

He shuffled from one foot to another then handed her the paper. "Will you take a look at this? It's my speech for tonight."

"Me? I'm not a writer."

"You are my audience. I'd like to hear what you think," he said simply.

She took it outside and sat on the back steps. His speech started out with a predictable formal sort of history, but as soon as she read the details Sam had included from Brian's life she was completely drawn in. Sam's last words referenced her idea of finding ways to keep Brian's spirit going even after he was gone.

Lucy put the piece of paper down. She watched as a gentle breeze lifted the leaves on the tall tree behind the shed. Bright light dazzled and shifted through the branches. Maybe she had forgotten her own lesson with Paul. While she had kept Paul's memory alive through Wellslept, she had forgotten what Paul used to tell her, about all the fun and beauty life had to offer. She'd been good at holding on to his presence at work, but she hadn't spent much time at all celebrating the way he had lived or the things that he loved. Maybe it was because she tried to pretend he wasn't gone. Even on his birthday, they had failed to have a cake or go kayaking on the lake. She recognized a pattern to act out of fear rather than joy. She was staring out at the sunlight when Sam walked out to sit with her.

"Is it okay?"

She nodded at him. "Yes, it's wonderful. It's the kind of lesson that sometimes people can forget. The brightness, you know. We spend so much time feeling sad instead. It made me realize I've been guilty of moping more than celebrating my stepfather."

Sam sat down next to her and looked out at the tree in the backyard. "You've mentioned him before. Tell me about him."

The bookshop was quiet and they were alone. "He loved excursions, jumping in the car just to do silly things like play mini golf, hire pedal boats, or visit fruit stands. In the winter, we never missed a drive to look at the holiday lights. And he'd make popcorn for home movies. He was enthusiastic about each of our interests. For Aaron, my brother, they spent hours together playing *Call of Duty* and *Grand Theft Auto*. For me, he bought me a beautiful camera and went with me to search out the best shots." She sighed. "I normally think about the business as where I connect with him most. But maybe that isn't the whole story."

"How long has it been?"

"Five years."

"A long and short amount of time." He paused. "I've never been on a pedal boat."

"Come to Seattle and I'll take you," Lucy said, before she realized that was the remotest possibility ever.

"London might be easier." Sam grinned.

The bells rang at the bookshop door. Sam stood up and called out his welcome. Lucy followed him back in to see Flora walk in at the same time with a bag of supplies slung over her shoulder. Flora clapped her hands at the beauty of the window showcasing the bountiful rose bouquet of open pink blooms reaching toward the twinkling lights. Soon, Lucy was swept into discussions about where people would stand and where the refreshments would go. Sam worked around them, replacing light bulbs that had worn out and straightening the bookshelves.

In the late afternoon, Lucy snuck away up the street to the village's only dress shop. She had slowly become aware that her blue blazer would seem too formal for the memorial, her skirt too tailored, and her black pants too boring. She needed something gracious and something that would show her respect for the event. Lucy was hoping that specific "something" would be in stock here. As she opened the door, a shopgirl wearing a cute vintage-style crop top and a pair of very distressed jeans looked up from her phone. "Welcome to Frolics and Frocks."

Lucy blinked. Had she said frolics and frogs? "Hi, I'm looking for a dress."

"Is this for the memorial tonight?"

"Yes, and it would be good if I could also wear it for a wedding party back home."

"Yours?"

"No, actually my brother is getting married."

"Hmm. We've got two dresses that might work for you." The girl looked her up and down. "You a ten?"

"I'm an eight," Lucy proudly declared.

"Where?"

"All over."

"No, I mean, you're an American, right?"

"Yes."

"Then you'll be a ten here."

Lucy felt defeated at that. The girl went to the rack in the back of the store and grabbed a mini dress in shimmering yellow with puffed sleeves, and a vibrant blue sheath with a low-cut neck and straps of fabric webbing in the back.

Lucy kept herself from rejecting both of the dresses outright. These were more decorated and more colorful than her normal style. The girl pulled back the curtain on the dressing room. "There hasn't been a wedding around here for a while. Some people thought that Sam would get married to his girlfriend, but that didn't work out."

Lucy blinked. "Sam at the bookshop? To, uh, Deborah?" She knew she shouldn't pry for information and yet she was curious.

"Yeah, that was a train wreck because of her family. Anyway, you're Lucy, right?"

"Yes." Lucy was still very interested in this gossip about Sam.

"Sorry about your dad."

"Thanks. Did you know him?"

"Not that much. I know Sam better," she said, and Lucy suddenly wondered if this girl had a thing for Sam.

"We have hats and fascinators too, you know."

"I don't think I'll be needing something that formal."

"Suit yourself."

After stepping into the dressing room, Lucy wriggled out of her skirt and into the first dress. The puffed sleeves made her shoulders look like they belonged to a football player. So it would have to be the bright blue tank one. It slipped on easily as it was made out of a heavy silk-like viscose. The V shape in front was so low that the band of her bra was showing but otherwise it looked good. She tied the belt around her waist. It looked pretty flattering actually. She could pair her ballet flats with this. It was a change from her navy sweaters and skirts. It looked like the kind of dress that she could wear anywhere and look nice, useful for packing in a suitcase, as long as she could pin the opening shut. She shook her head. She wouldn't be traveling after this trip. It would be back to home and work. A feeling of gloom settled into her chest. Of course the only traveling she would be doing would be for mattress industry conventions. The last one was in Cincinnati.

"How's it going?"

Lucy pulled up her jeans underneath the dress, stepped around the curtain, and walked into the room.

The girl looked astonished. "Wow. That actually looks really sexy on you. I wouldn't wear jeans with it though. Or sneakers. Or those…what you're wearing. We've got some block heels that would go."

Lucy wanted to protest that she wasn't planning on wearing her sneakers.

"And you'll want a different bra. We've got stick-on cups or a camisole."

"I thought I'd just button up my sweater over the front."

The girl looked at her with her mouth pinched into a disbelieving frown. She sighed. "Try a demi camisole." She walked off, presumably to find the tank-style bra.

A second later, the girl handed her a pair of low heels and a pretty cream-colored half camisole that had a built-in bra. "This should work."

Lucy pulled it on, slipped the dress over her head a second time, this time with the shoes, and stepped out to the mirror again. She looked softer and younger. The shoes elongated her legs and forced her to stand up straight.

The shopgirl glanced up from the register. "Should I make up a receipt for the dress, shoes, and cami then?"

It was on the tip of her tongue to say she'd take the dress only, but suddenly Lucy imagined herself, for some reason, out to dinner with Sam. "Yes, all three."

Back in her jeans and T-shirt for her Wednesday scheduled

outfit, she wavered a bit when she saw the cost on the receipt, knowing it would be even more in dollars than in pounds. The girl was pulling out a tray of jewelry. Lucy felt herself wanting to roll her eyes. She wasn't there for earrings. But the ones the girl pulled out were pretty beaded ones that could have been from Anthropologie. She laid them on the glass countertop.

"What do you think about these earrings? They're a perfect match."

Lucy agreed that they were lovely, but she didn't need a pair of earrings. "No, I think I'll pass on those."

"Suit yourself."

As she closed the shop door with her bag in hand, she almost stumbled straight into Ada. "Oh, hello, Ada. I'm sorry, I didn't see you there."

Ada's soft, round face was accented with very big earrings and her glasses had darkened in response to the afternoon sunshine. "I've been looking for you. I've arranged for the champagne, apple juice, and hors d'oeuvres for the party tonight." Ada glanced at her shop bag. "Did you get a dress for the event?"

Lucy hesitated. "Do you think this would be okay for tonight?"

Ada peeked into the bag. "Of course, that looks acceptable. Hopefully you are putting it with something black." She leaned in closer. Lucy could see her lipstick had rubbed off onto her teeth. "Will Maura be in attendance, do you know?"

Lucy shook her head. "I think she said she was going to London?"

Ada pursed her lips. "Typical. Well, I have supper to do before we get ready. Come along, Daisy." Ada pulled her dog up the street toward her store.

9

_____

That night, as Lucy slipped into her new dress and pulled her black sweater over her shoulders, she hoped the event would go easily for her new friends. Lucy remembered her brooch from Paul. The simple gold rose looked perfect pinned to her sweater. She brushed her hair and swiped on a tinted lip gloss and hoped she hadn't made a mistake with the bold color of the dress before she went next door.

Lucy found Flora in the back office of the bookshop. Her hair was pulled up in a bun with a few romantic curls escaping around her temples and she wore a fitted denim shirt dress with floral platform sandals. "Ooh, you look nice."

"You do too."

Flora grinned widely. "My boyfriend is coming tonight." She pointed to a box on the kitchen table. "Could you hand me those?"

Lucy saw Flora was tucking a few small bottles of apple juice into the refrigerator. She handed the bottles over, glad to spot that the refrigerator was already full of wine. Flora handed her a platter to carry out. Some early birds had already arrived and were talking in groups at the front of the bookshop. There was a little hush, she felt, as she walked behind Flora to place the first platters of baked treats down.

Lucy felt shy, knowing she would be on display to the whole village tonight. For now, she took the easy way out and followed Flora back into the kitchen. "I'll help you in here."

"Oh no, I'm fine. Go ahead and mingle." Trays of food were lined up in an orderly fashion on the table, covered with cling wrap.

She reluctantly turned back toward the bookshop, hoping to see Evangeline or Beena, when she heard her name called. "Lucia."

Mr. Cowcroft was beckoning her over to a small table. As she walked closer, she saw that a large photo had been put up on the wall. It was a black-and-white portrait of Brian. She felt a deep internal recognition.

Big serious eyes, a hint of a smile. This was him, looking up from his office chair with a steady gaze. A person you wanted to know. Lucy felt stunned by the recognition of that look. She remembered it. A wisp of a memory tugged at her but fled as Mr. Cowcroft asked her a question.

"Does this seem right?" The photo was hanging a bit catty-wampus and he adjusted it to the left.

"Yes, I think that's good. It's wonderful." She blinked quickly. He had brought a box full of photos as well as the portrait, and she walked over to look more closely.

Lucy saw a part of the life of her father she didn't know. Many of the photos were of him at the bookshop doing readings. There was one of him reading to a group of children at a library. There were a few of him and Maura, and one also of him with Sam, behind the counter.

He had aged considerably from the picture of him she normally carried around in her mind. She always thought of him from the early 1990s. In these more current photos, gray had crept into his hair, and he was wearing glasses that slipped down his nose. She seemed to have his brow, his eyes, his hair, and those freckles.

Mr. Cowcroft spoke. "You look lovely, my dear. How are you doing?"

Lucy smiled. "I'm okay, thank you. The photos are really a gift, Mr. Cowcroft."

"I'm glad you like them. I was thinking of you when I selected which pictures to bring."

Flora appeared beside them and set down a plate of hors d'oeuvres. "You've done a nice job of gathering these of Brian." Flora's voice began to waver just as the door opened.

Beena and Evangeline had arrived. They rushed in to surround her and Flora with hugs. Beena set down two red-and-white-striped bowls filled with candy—Theo's chocolates in one and Snickers bars in the other—with a little placard explaining that they were Brian's American favorites. She stayed close to Lucy's side as Evangeline went to deliver several wine bottles to the kitchen area. Beena whispered to Lucy, "We are here for each other, aren't we? To celebrate Brian, but to help each other get over his loss."

Evangeline rejoined them. "How are you holding up?"

"I'm okay." Lucy said this at the exact same time as Beena.

"How are you?" Lucy remembered to ask.

"Good, good. Okay," Evangeline managed to respond and then she laughed. "I guess we're all okay, but not great—more like confused." She touched the corner of her eye. "I admit I am looking for Brian to show up so we can talk about all this."

Beena pointed to the roses in the vase to the left of the photos. "They smell wonderful in here. Are they from the front entry?"

Lucy sighed. "Yes, but Sam doesn't approve."

"Sam is a little tender tonight I think," Beena said.

Lucy scanned the room. "Where is he?"

"We saw him outside greeting people."

Lucy turned to look. He had changed into his pressed gray

dress shirt and black trousers. She saw Deborah standing by his side, gazing up at him. Lucy looked away quickly, surprised to find she was disappointed that Deborah had come.

The room became warmer as more and more people arrived, but with Beena, Evangeline, and Flora around her, she didn't feel afraid of all the strangers anymore. There were several middle-grade students in the crowd. They were part of a choir that would be singing. One parent had touched her on the shoulder and mentioned that all the kids in the village loved the bookshop and Brian. She found the mom's words comforting. It was a much less lonely affair than at Paul's memorial. During that event, Lucy had been thrust into the role of host when her mom had collapsed on the couch earlier in the day. She had shaken hands with so many people she didn't know, and even with Nina there to hand out refreshments, it hadn't felt like anything more than a trial of endurance.

"Attention, attention. I'd like your attention." Ada stood between the cashier desk and a beautiful arrangement of trailing flowers on a large stand. She rang a little bell and spoke into a microphone. "We're here tonight to honor our friend Brian Baslow. In the back we are collecting funds for a plaque for the roundabout. I want Brian's name to be commemorated here in Wakeby forever. Please donate. Now the choir from St. Basil's church is here to sing a song, and then we've asked Sam to begin with a few words."

Lucy scanned the room for Sam. He was inside now and his face looked serious, pale, and determined. Deborah was still by his side.

A small group of kids shuffled to the front. The choir director, a bearded man in his thirties, came up to the front of the room with his guitar. Lucy was surprised to recognize the song. It was "Hallelujah" by Leonard Cohen. They sang in soft voices and Lucy let the music wash over her as she stared at the photos, and over at the empty dog bed. Apparently, Barley hadn't been invited for the ceremony. Beena glanced her way and patted her arm. Finally, her gaze came to rest on Sam again.

When the choir stopped singing, Sam walked up to the microphone and retrieved a familiar piece of paper. "Firstly, I'd like to thank the students for their performance. It was just beautiful. Secondly, thank you all for coming." He cleared his throat. "Brian was born and grew up in Wiltshire. He moved to America in his early twenties where he met Lucy's mum and moved to Seattle, where she was born. He was an artist all his life. He won contests at school but it was in Seattle he found a name for himself illustrating for a famous record label, before coming to London to pursue his career illustrating covers for top-tier rock-and-roll bands. When the music industry changed, Brian came to Wakeby."

Sam's voice deepened. "Brian was ready to try something new. He began to work on children's books. *The Gardener's Cat* took off and he collaborated on many more. As you know, the bookshop grew out of this work and Brian became a pillar in our community."

Sam looked up from his notes. "He helped many people in a quiet way. He made donations, would always get the raffle ticket, and found extra for people who might have needed it. He hired me..." His voice became gravelly, and Lucy held her breath, hoping he'd get through this. She found herself feeling his sadness and heard some sniffling in the crowd. Sam quickly said, "And believed in me." The man in front of her dabbed at his eyes.

Sam coughed then kept going, his voice slowly regaining its strength. "There is no way to fill the space he has left. But I think the way to honor him is to live our best lives. That's what he would have wanted. Not for us to feel bad. Think of the happiness he would feel knowing that we were succeeding at the lives we wanted. I think of the joy he took in finding just the right color for his illustrations and just the right book for every one of you. When I think of how he was unfailingly kind to people and supportive of their dreams, it makes me want to be that way. He always had the highest opinion of us. The only way to bear the fact that he is gone is to be the kind of people that he believed we could be."

The room was silent. Sam muttered "Thank you" and left the stage to go stand at the back near the door. People around her murmured thank-yous to Sam and patted his back as he passed.

Ada stepped back up to the mic. "Thank you, Sam. That's what we are here for after all, to celebrate Brian's life, to gather as a community, and to extend the legacy of the bookshop."

She paused. "And now I'd like to have Gail Gerkin up to discuss the reason why this building has always been important to the history of Wakeby."

Evangeline drew in her breath. Lucy caught Flora's eye. She had a sour look on her face.

Gail had her hair pulled up into a bun and wore a brown sweater and brown skirt. "I'm Ms. Gerkin, the parish secretary and historian. Not many of you are old enough to remember, but there has been a shop at this location for my whole life. Of course, we know the village has been here since before the 1400s when the quarries drew people here. But in more recent times, before it was a bookshop, Mrs. Kerr and her husband ran a very respectable shop. It did a very good business from the 1930s until the 1980s. Many of us have wonderful Christmas memories of visiting Mrs. Kerr and sampling her cherry cordial.

"Before that, it was a construction office for the architect Archibald Knares and a home to their family." While Gail looked down at her notes, Lucy wondered if she was going to go back through the course of history until they all found out King Arthur had stayed at the location. At least this speech was giving her a chance to dry her eyes.

"Of course, Brian continued on in his aunt Mrs. Kerr's footsteps by establishing this wonderful shop in the 2000s. Bookshops are vital to the fabric of our region. This bookshop enjoys a protected spot as the very last building before the river and bridge, so its site is essential to Wakeby's character." Lucy noticed Gail's tone of voice had suddenly changed from droning to one of sharpness. She started to sweat as Gail looked directly at her. "The people of Wakeby village would never let the character of this land change. New ideas and developments do not interest us. We let the guiding hand of the past determine our future." She opened her eyes wide and stared down at the people in the room.

Once it was evident that she had concluded her speech there was some reluctant clapping.

Ada accepted the mic back from Gail. "Thank you, Gail, for your historical tribute. And now a word from Lucy, Brian's daughter."

Lucy looked up at Ada, not understanding.

Ada waved the microphone. "Where is she? Come on up, Lucy."

Lucy felt the people around her start to look at her. Ada had lied. She pressed her lips together and accepted that she would have to say something. She walked up to the microphone and felt the brightness of the lights and the closeness of the room. What was it Maura had told her to say? She couldn't remember. She looked out trying to find Flora's face but couldn't see her.

Instead she found Sam's steady eyes on her.

She took a wavering breath and began while talking to only him. "Wakeby is such a special place. A kind town that cared deeply for Brian, my father." She took another breath to try to steady her nerves. "I have seen this care for him every day that I've been here and know that he was lucky to live here. I am grateful to know that my father lived a well-loved, good life among you." Her heart was beating like a drum in her ears.

She turned to the rest of the room. "Ms. Gerkin is right. The bookshop is very special."

"Don't sell it then," someone called out. Lucy felt her whole body flush with heat. Had Ada spread the word about the real estate agents and then ambushed her up here? Sweat trickled down her arms.

She returned to Sam's gaze, afraid to look away from his face and into the scary crowd. There was something in the way he nodded at her in encouragement that made her want to cry all of a sudden. "I would like to personally thank Sam for making the bookshop so special and I'd like to thank Ada and Flora and all the others for making this event so special." She'd used the word "special" twice. She cringed but just kept going. "Please give them a round of applause for creating this beautiful evening." She was done and moved away from the mic, away through the people, and back to the safe harbor by Beena and Evangeline. She felt her clothes sticking to her. Beena made room for her next to the counter. Evangeline gave her an encouraging look.

Ada returned back to the mic. Her voice boomed into the microphone. "Flora, are you there?"

There was a pause and Flora walked into the crowd with several bottles on a tray. "Gordy and I have provided champagne for everyone. I'd like to lead a toast to Brian."

Ada went on to tell the group about a time when Brian was supposed to turn up at a local fair to read a book he had illustrated but when he arrived, he had brought the author, a musician, and a balloon artist as well. There had been so many balloons that even Ada brought one home that day. "The balloon even looked like our dog Daisy." Ada smiled. For a brief moment, Ada seemed far away, caught in a happy memory. Then she seemed to shake it off. She raised her glass. "Brian was a special friend to all of us. Let's drink to Brian's long-lasting legacy in our village." Once Ada stopped speaking, Lucy was relieved to raise her glass along with everyone else. Before there was a second round, Lucy decided to escape to the backyard. She needed some air.

She whispered to Beena where she was going. Around her people were raising their glasses and drinking again. She nodded at the happy crowd as she pressed on through. She had got as far as the bathroom before she was stopped by an older couple with angry looks on their faces.

"Is it true you're selling the bookshop to a developer?" a woman with dyed orange hair and extremely white Keds sneakers asked.

"No, no," Lucy objected quickly, pushing down the raw anger she felt at Ada for starting this problem. "We haven't made plans yet."

The man looked down at her past his bulbous nose. "Out for a quick buck, are you?"

"No, that's not what's happening." Lucy spoke a little louder, not only because she thought he might be hard of hearing.

A young woman wearing a blazer and a ponytail rushed up to her. "Hello, could I talk with you?"

Lucy moved toward the hallway, pleased to get away from the older couple. "Sure."

Instead of following her lead, the woman stepped in between Lucy and the exit. "I want to know how you felt about the fact that the town historian is suggesting the property should not be developed."

Lucy frowned. "Do I know you?"

"I'm Zoey Otis. I write for the *Salisbury Journal*."

"A newspaper?" *Oh, no*, she thought desperately.

"Yes. I was just covering the memorial, but it seems there is a bigger story here." Her young face was lit up with something like hungry anticipation. "What are your plans for the bookshop?"

Lucy noticed that now more people were tuning into their conversation. She felt her face flush hotter. "There is nothing happening here."

"As an American, do you have any rights to sell in the first place? And I'd add, do you have the ability to know what is right for this community?"

"This is a memorial. For Brian Baslow." Lucy stared at this

woman with her probing eyes and sensed a sea of hard faces around her. Up near the podium, she saw that Ada had paused with her glass in her hand to gawk at the reporter. Flora was now at the front of the shop having an animated conversation with a young man. Flora couldn't save her.

Lucy looked back at the reporter. "Of course I care about the community. And this event is for my father." She tried to leave but was blocked by the older couple still standing in the hallway. She felt cold and thought she might faint. She kept backing up but the reporter pressed closer.

"How much money will you make by selling it?"

Her head felt woozy. She glanced up to see Sam approaching with an empty platter. He saw her face and looked at the reporter. A scowl formed.

He strode up to her. "Zoey, back off or leave. This is not the place."

"But you were the one…"

Sam met Lucy's eyes. She felt her face drain of its remaining color. Had Sam invited this reporter? He stepped in front of her, blocking her access to Lucy. "Zoey, I am asking you to stop."

Lucy didn't wait to find out what else Zoey was going to say. She understood that while Zoey was turned away from her, she could slip away. She stepped assertively past the older couple, brushing against the woman's beaded sweater, and headed directly out to the backyard. She saw a group of teenagers there already. Where could she go?

The hollyhocks caught her eye from Flora's yard. She let herself in through the side gate. She could hear the teenagers laughing at something. Probably her. She stumbled toward the stone bench set under the arbor and sat down. Her head was swimming, but the bench was solid beneath her.

She wrapped her arms around herself. What was Lucy of Wellslept Mattresses doing here in a 300-year-old building with a group of strangers celebrating a man she had barely known? She was tempted to step away, far, far away.

She looked up at the sky with its purple clouds unfurling against the darkening blue of the late-summer nightfall. An evening bee was still buzzing in one of the hollyhock blossoms lining the back fence. After a long time had passed, she felt her heart slow down. But she was still left with the question. *What am I doing here?* She thought that she could clean up the bookshop, get the accounts settled, and clear out any personal belongings of her father. But that was all on paper. She rolled her eyes at herself for being so naive. Everything here was just as complicated as her life at home. Here, she'd begun to appreciate the bookshop, the village, and the people. They weren't flat numbers on paper. Settling for just any buyer for this place wouldn't be the right way to get money. She knew it, but it was very easy to say while sitting out under an English sky on a September evening—while at home, Wellslept needed her to find a way to save it too. She was in a mess. She put her hands on her head.

"Lucy, are you back here?"

She looked up to see Sam coming through the gate. The top buttons of his shirt were undone and his sleeves were rolled up.

"Did you invite that reporter to the memorial?" she said.

He frowned. "You were ambushed. I didn't know Zoey would do that." He met her eyes, ran a hand through his hair. "I did invite her. I thought she would do a tribute story to Brian. I want to save the bookshop, but I would never do anything hurtful to get it. I want to apologize to you." His eyes were shadowed. She thought he looked drained.

She took a deep breath. "It was so shocking to feel that anger from that couple and the person that yelled at me."

"It was wrong, but they feel powerless." He looked into her eyes.

"What do they think I can do?"

"Stop rushing into things. Help me find a solution."

"I want to."

He reached out his hand to her. She took it and was sad when he let it go once she was on her feet.

"Would you come join us? It's just friends left inside now. I promise." He smiled encouragingly.

She nodded, then followed him back to the bookshop.

Flora called out from the back office area, "Sam, did you find Lucy?"

Evangeline and Beena came from the bookshop into the kitchen, where Mr. Emery was sitting at the table.

Lucy moved past him into the now wildly messy kitchen. "I'm here. Whoa. What happened?"

"Many, many toasts to Brian," Evangeline replied.

"Oh, Lucy." Flora set a bouquet of flowers down and came around to give Lucy a hug. "I'm so sorry that whole thing happened. I'm sorry I didn't have a chance to come find you. Are you okay now? By the way, this is my boyfriend, Russell."

A young guy with close-cropped hair and freckles, wearing a black sweater and pressed gray pants, leaned forward and shook hands with Lucy. "Pleased to meet you."

"Glad to meet you too." Lucy smiled and then turned back and looked into Flora's eyes. She wanted to express her approval about Russell, but instead she said, "I'm okay, I just had to get some air."

Beena glanced at the others. "Lucy, while you were gone, we were talking. Sam explained to us that you need money for your business at home."

Sam met her eyes. "I hope that was okay."

"We'd like to help find a good buyer for the shop or even"— Beena glanced at Evangeline—"help buy the shop ourselves."

Could they do it? Buy it themselves? Lucy looked around at their caring faces, surprised at the wonderful idea and thankful that they were still supporting her now that they knew about her finances. "Thank you. I'm sorry that I can't save it."

Flora nodded. "We all have businesses. We understand."

"What are you thinking? Is there something I can do to help?"

Evangeline brightened up. "We'll try to raise the money among ourselves."

"We also want to see if anyone we know would buy it outright," Beena added.

Lucy hesitated. "The real estate agent put the total price at nine hundred thousand pounds."

Beena started coughing. "That much?"

Flora reached out to touch Lucy's arm. "I'm sorry to ask this, but what if we got enough money to buy out Maura first?"

An odd nauseous feeling stole over her. She couldn't say yes. She knew each one of them was looking at her in a kind of desperation. "I don't know."

Sam cleared his throat. "Let her think on it."

She wanted to leave it at that. She wanted to keep the smiles strong on the faces of her new friends, but the thought of Well-slept turning into a Sleep Bold kept her from doing so. She would support their efforts. She wanted the right buyer, but she had to think of home. "Listen, I'll support everything you have in mind, but I have to at least have it on the market before I leave. Of course I don't want to sell the bookshop to the wrong people. But I've promised my family in Seattle that I'll come back having taken action toward saving our business. I can't budge on that. I'm really sorry." She finished speaking and waited for the smiles on their faces to fade.

"That's good enough for me," Sam said quickly, before he disappeared into the studio then reemerged with a special bottle of whisky. He poured a little into the remaining plastic cups and passed them around. "A toast to saving the bookshop together."

"To new beginnings," Evangeline said.

"To Brian," Beena said, lifting her cup of sparkling water.

"And to Lucy," Flora said.

Lucy was certain the whole bottle of Scotch would be gone by the time they finished toasting one another. As soon as she could, she raised her glass. "To my Wakeby friends." As she said it, she felt it was true, and hoped it would stay that way when the shop sold.

Sam turned to Flora. "So Flora, are any of your biscuits left?"

She laughed out loud. Lucy loved the bright sound of Flora's laugh. "I do have a secret stash for the cleanup crew, which appears to be us. Can you reach the canister I hid on the top shelf?"

He jumped to attention and reached for a tall can with a blue stripe. "Shortbread," he said happily as he lifted off the top and handed it to Lucy.

Lucy took one and devoured its solid buttery goodness. "Flora, you really are talented."

Sam nodded. "That's what I've been telling her."

"I think you're all just hungry and tipsy."

"Not enough," Sam said and reached for the bottle again.

After Sam agreed to set up a website called "Saving Baslow's Books" and Evangeline invited them all to her house for dinner and to plan further, Beena and Evangeline called it a night, leaving after a flurry of hugs.

Suddenly it was just Mr. Emery, who was nodding off in the chair, Flora, Russell, Sam, and Lucy.

There were plastic cups on every surface. Lucy started to gather them.

"You don't have to clean it all up," Sam said.

"Yes, I do. I want it to look good again for tomorrow..." She had been going to say "when Maura comes by" but stopped before finishing the sentence.

Flora looked at them. She spoke softly. "Even though we have new plans, I still feel sad that this evening's over. Like we have to get back to regular life now without Brian."

Sam poured them each another shot of whisky. "One more cheers to Brian then." He walked over to the record player in the studio and put on some music. "Let's not go back to the future. Let's enjoy the past a little more."

Lucy groaned a little when she heard his choice. "'Louie, Louie' by the Wailers?"

"It's the Paul Revere and the Raiders version. Brian liked to play this one before he put on the Sonics version and then go on to play Mudhoney and Nirvana records. Shall we rock out? Do a grunge tribute?"

Flora smiled ruefully. "Sorry, guys, but I've got to get to bed. Breakfast at the B&B comes no matter how much I've slept. And then Russell and I have plans to go to Bath for the afternoon."

Lucy walked up to her and gave her another hug. "Thank you, Flora. I feel so lucky you are right next door, and I know Brian must have felt that way too. And also, you don't have to make my breakfast if I'm the only guest."

Flora hefted up her baskets and smiled. "We've got a sweet family tonight plus you. Come on, Grandad."

Mr. Emery had fallen asleep in the kitchen chair and woke slowly before standing up very carefully. Sam and Russell helped them carry all the trays back next door.

While Sam was gone, Lucy ran around picking up leftover napkins and dropped flower petals. She hoped their plan to find a buyer would work. She looked up at Brian's photo. His gaze didn't waver. "Was this what you wanted?" she asked quietly.

Sam returned from Flora's through the front entrance. He flipped the sign to read "Closed." For some reason her stomach tightened a little. It was just the two of them.

"I'll clean up the rest."

"Thanks, Sam, but it won't take long if we both work together."

"You get to take those photos with you. Gordy left them for you. He's a good guy." Sam spoke the words with a hint of a slur in his voice as he went around turning off lights and picking up bits of cake from the floor.

"All these photos? I don't know where they'd go."

"On the wall?" He smiled while he walked over to get the broom. Then he turned away to sloppily pick up the sweepings and put them into the garbage can.

He looked up at the clock. It was already after one. "Most of this is cleaned up now. I'll do the dishes in the morning."

"Before…"

"Before the meeting with Maura, I know. She called me." He pulled on his coat. "I like the way the shop looks right now. In fact, I'd say it improved the day you got here."

Lucy let the compliment pleasantly wash over her before dismissing it, putting it down to the alcohol. She replied neutrally, "It does look pretty with the twinkle lights. It probably looks wonderful in the winter holidays."

He raised his eyebrows. "How about every six months you take a holiday here? You could come see it yourself."

"Sam. That line of thinking won't work." She wished he would stop proposing ideas that required her to be the downer every time.

"Why not? If we get an investor, I think it could be the start of an amazing business model."

"I can't be part of this."

He wagged his finger at her. "Lucy. You will always be a part of this. You are a Baslow. Don't you get it?"

She hadn't thought of her connection to Wakeby like that before. Even without the bookshop being a bookshop, she was now a part of the history of Wakeby. "I never thought of it that way." A silence fell between them.

"One more thing to do." Sam switched off the lights in the front window, then jingled his keys in his pocket. The room fell into a soft darkness, lit only by streetlights. She opened the door to step outside. "I guess I'd better say good night so I can be up for our meeting."

He locked the door behind her, then turned around and stared at her. "Wait."

She swallowed. They were standing so close. She loved the way he was looking at her now. Calm strength radiated from him. He moved even closer and touched her hair. "A leaf. A leaf from the rose has fallen into your hair." She reached up to echo his touch. Their fingers brushed against each other. The space between them narrowed for a long moment. She was afraid to move, to breathe. His eyes darkened and he looked like he wanted to say something more, but he abruptly turned toward the sidewalk. "Good night, Lucy."

"Good night, Sam," she said, her voice suddenly breathless.

The next morning, Lucy opted for two cups of Flora's coffee. Today's blueberry scones were perfection, and nothing was spilled on the floor by Flora. There was a family with two little toddlers running around the breakfast room dropping random bits of cereal, but apart from them it was just Lucy. Flora herself was cheerful as always, but there were shadows under her eyes. Lucy felt certain she had the same ones under her own.

She'd wanted to talk again with Sam before Maura arrived but there was no time. She'd received a long email from Bruce the night before. His obvious feelings for her made her feel guilty enough to respond before the rest of the day got going. He mentioned that Lucy's mother had roped him into more wedding duties and how he couldn't wait to take her out sailing on his partner's vintage Chris-Craft speedboat. She wrote to him about the gardens and the river and tried to muster up enthusiasm for their wedding duties. She paused to gaze out the window at Flora's garden. That life felt very far away. It was filled with stress and she didn't want to think about it. Each day here she felt such freedom from her mother's expectations. And maybe from Bruce's too.

Lucy sent her reply to Bruce and finished up her cup of coffee. Maura met her outside Flora's front door before they walked next door to meet Sam. "How did it go last night? Did you convince him to sign?"

"No. The memorial was super intense. In fact, there's been a change in plans."

Maura looked so stern at this that Lucy decided to distract her from the real news with the story of Ms. Gerkin's talk and the presence of the reporter. Maura scowled furiously. "I hate this place."

They walked around the back. The bookshop was closed for the morning and they were meeting in the kitchen area. Lucy walked in first and saw that Sam wasn't there yet. The dishes were still in the sink and there was a garbage can overflowing with napkins.

Maura shook her head. "I think it has gotten dirtier in here since we left. He's such a slob."

Lucy glanced at the floor where some dried petals and leaves had fallen back out of the bin, but she didn't really think of that as dirt. "No, these are leftovers from last night."

Lucy put on the kettle. Maura pulled a pen out of her purse and took a seat at the table. "Have you had a chance to box anything up? Or discuss what to do with all the stock?"

"No." Lucy was relieved when Sam walked in and saved her from saying more. She hadn't even begun to think about that.

"Oh, good. I really need that cup of tea today." Sam looked terrible. His hair was sticking out funny and his voice was very low and rough.

He nodded at Maura and brushed past Lucy to reach for the big teapot. She waited for him to meet her eyes or say hello to her, but he didn't. Instead he filled the teapot with six fat bags of tea. Lucy widened her eyes but didn't comment.

Maura was getting out the folder of materials from the real estate agent and placed a copy on the table for Sam.

She was just starting to talk when the kettle began its whistle. Sam moved away to turn it off. He filled up the pot and set it down heavily in the middle of the table.

Maura grabbed at her stack of papers. "Careful."

A tense silence followed. Lucy felt obliged to say something. "This is so nice. We never have tea like this back home."

"Starbucks all the way then?" Sam asked.

"Honestly, yes." She somehow felt that if she kept talking she could fill up the awkwardness. "But we have Vivace's and Victrola too. There are lots of amazing roasterias in…"

Maura interrupted. "Look, Sam. Lucy and I are ready to sell this property. We want to keep it simple. And that requires that you go along with our vision."

"Why don't you at least hear what Lucy and I have in mind?" His voice sounded positive.

Maura turned to stare accusingly at Lucy. Lucy shrugged awkwardly.

He calmly poured the tea into a large ceramic beer stein. Probably the only clean cup left in the cabinet. "I'm getting the message that you want to get a profit out of this property. But you can get that without selling it. A first suggestion is that this space could be rented as a party place or a classroom. Or it could be developed to bring in more customers. The space could stay the same, but the bookshop could expand its revenue."

"I'm going to stop you right there, Sam," Maura interjected. "I've talked to a few estate agents. They think the property could bring in close to a million pounds. Split three ways, that would give each of us enough to invest in our own dreams. You know I don't want any solution where I'm tied to anyone else."

"How much do you need?"

Maura frowned. "Are you saying you could buy me out?"

He moved his head ever so slightly. "Do you know how much you would need? I might have an investor."

Maura raised her eyebrows. "Four hundred thousand pounds."

Lucy knew Maura was putting her cut higher than even Adele suggested.

Sam scoffed. "But is that what you need?"

"I don't have time for this." Maura rolled her eyes. "I've got the agent's number right in my phone and I'm planning on calling them today to put the place on the market. She has some real interest already. So unless you can make"—she put her hands up into quote marks—"'an investor' appear by tomorrow, we are moving ahead."

"I'm working on that..."

Maura blinked. "What?"

"Last night, a few of us agreed to have a go at raising enough money to buy you and Lucy out. We also agreed to put some effort into finding an investor. I want a say in who buys the bookshop."

"You are delaying the whole process."

"I'm not delaying." Sam's face was flushed. "You're lucky that I'm not working with Ada to block the whole thing."

"How do I know that you're not? You used to be a thief. Why should I trust you?"

Sam's cheeks flushed a dark mottled color. "Maura," he said in a sharp, hurt voice.

Maura looked at Lucy. "You should know the truth about him."

He spoke quietly. "Do you really want to dredge up the past in front of Lucy now?"

"Pfft," Maura made a disgusted sound. She directed her comments to Lucy. "He thinks he can rattle me because he knows that I had an affair while I was with Brian. Give up on that one,

Sam. I am human and that's all it was. I wasn't arrested for anything."

Lucy sat there in shock at both of their dirty laundry being aired. She didn't know where to look, but it wasn't up at either of them.

"Brian never stopped believing in you, Maura, but he was a saint and I am not." Sam took the flyer with Adele's face on it and wrinkled it up in his fist. Then he stood up. He didn't look at Lucy or at Maura. He walked into the bookshop and shut the connecting door between them.

Maura sat there fuming. "How stupid can you get? You have made a titanic mistake in listening to him. You're supposed to be working with me. Did you forget how much you need the money? Did you forget your duty to your family business?"

Maura's words resulted in a stab of fear that Lucy felt in her gut. Had she made a mistake listening to Sam and the villagers? Was she gambling with Wellslept's future? "No, I'm not forgetting. I just want to give Sam a chance for a happy ending here."

"I wasn't lying. Sam was caught stealing in this very village a few years ago. He'll do anything. We may have to evict him." Maura put her head in her hands. "This will have to go to court," she wailed, while picking up her phone to start scrolling through different contacts.

Lucy recognized this as an overreaction. It was a similar move to the kind her mom often made. "Maura. Hold on." Maura would blow this thing right into a court case if Lucy didn't control her. "Nothing is happening. It's just a lot of mean things being said." Lucy found herself almost wishing she was dealing with her brother and mother rather than these two. She wanted to direct a glare at Brian. But his photo was in the other room.

She picked up Adele's now-wrinkled flyer and smoothed it out on the table. "There isn't any reason why we shouldn't go ahead with getting all the paperwork ready to sign with Adele. I've just agreed to let the ladies in the village try to find a buyer that is more suitable. I told them and Sam that we wouldn't sign the paperwork until I had to leave. They've got a couple of days to get the word out, that's all."

Maura's mouth twisted into a disapproving frown. "I feared you would be drawn into the kind of insulated rural friendships these people have here in the village. But they aren't all they say they are. Beena flirted with Brian all the time. Evangeline couldn't hold down a career anywhere else, and Flora's father went into bankruptcy a few years ago. Only her grandfather's pension is keeping them going. They are lying to you about life here." Maura nodded toward Flora's B&B, then glanced up at Lucy with distrust and lowered her voice to a hiss. "Oh, and Lucy, don't be caught up by Sam's ability to charm women. He's slept with most of the women in this village. So if he comes on to you, know that it is only about having leverage over the bookshop. And"—she paused, her sharp eyes on Lucy—"has he even shown you the bookkeeping for this place? I'd guess you're saving a nonprofit charity. It will be out of business in one year without Brian here."

Lucy wanted to strike back at Maura. How could she say those things? At least she had a smooth response for the talk about Sam, because she'd been telling herself the same thing. "Sam has a girlfriend up at Symonds. So don't worry about me, Maura. There are only two days left of my stay here. I'm sure I'll be safe from his charms." Lucy spoke very calmly as she stood up.

"Really? Because I'm getting a bad feeling. The kind of feeling that requires a lawyer." Maura shook her head in disgust, put on her sunglasses, and walked directly out the back door, not bothering to close it behind her.

After Maura had left, Lucy aimlessly opened the top of the teapot. It was still warm. A wet clump of teabags sat slumped against the ceramic wall.

Was Maura right about all of this? Had she been taken in? Was she falling into a trap set by Brian? She closed her eyes and remembered how she felt holding the Jane Austen book in her hand when she'd first arrived. She thought about the warmth of the people at the memorial. She opened her eyes. There had to be another side to each story Maura told. At least she hoped there was.

After gathering some of the papers together, she made her way into the bookshop. "Sam? Maura said some terrible things in there."

He stood for a second longer and then walked over to the chair in the window. "What did she say?"

Lucy felt an embarrassed heat flush across her throat and cheeks. "After you left, she said things about Flora, Beena, and about Evangeline."

He looked down at his hands. "Well, I can tell you about myself. It was ten years ago. I was in my last year of school when my cousin came with my aunt and uncle to visit my mum. My cousin was very silly, and she stole something from Ada's shop. Ada caught us. My cousin couldn't afford to get into trouble one more time. Her father was a brute. So I said I did it."

He laughed ruefully. "Believe it or not Ada called in the police. Afterward, my mum dealt with me and I worked for Ada for one very long summer. Maura argued relentlessly to Brian that he shouldn't offer me the job here." He glanced around the bookshop. "You see why I am so indebted to Brian. I'm lucky Brian believed in me."

Lucy had half expected a story like this.

"You can ask the others to tell you more, but each slander that she made is only that." He looked gravely at her. "The people are good here. Not perfect maybe, but good."

The bookshop's phone rang and Sam went to get it. As he talked, Lucy heard his voice lighten and lighten.

She rolled her shoulders and shook her head, trying to shake the morning out of her mind. If there was something to find out about Sam, she was certain that Flora would have told her already.

Lucy decided to get back on track with her to-do list, but as she was getting her phone out of her bag, a rambunctious group of preschoolers showed up. Returning from his phone call, Sam welcomed them in and soon was on the floor, showing the kids books about bugs. She saw he was a sunnier person with a toddler by his side, pointing at the book he had started reading to them. She caught an expression of gentleness on the child's face looking up at Sam that was mirrored in his own. Lucy caught herself wishing for that moment the night before, when he had looked at her so intently.

After a flurry of children's books purchases including one of her father's books, it was just the two of them in the shop again.

"So how long can you really stay?" Sam asked.

"What do you mean?"

"Can you stay a few days longer?"

She swallowed. "I don't think so."

"You were going to leave on Saturday, I know, but I got a call earlier that might change everything."

"What? Who?"

Sam smiled widely. "An old friend of Brian's. A wealthy friend. He's going to be in the area and wants to meet us."

"Us?"

"I told him you were here. I told him you're desperate to find an investor for your father's bookshop."

She looked at him cautiously. "I am."

Sam went over to his computer to pull up a Google search for a guy named Tedd Ives. "He was immediately interested. He could be the one, Lucy. He owns several BMW dealerships in the region and he's always liked Brian. But he can't be here until Saturday night."

"My brother is getting married the following weekend."

"It could mean everything." Sam reached down and scooped

up Barley in his arms. "Could you deny this pup his bookshop?" Barley regarded her with his cute round eyes.

"I don't want to."

"Then stay."

Sam looked so earnest and excited by the call.

"You think this guy is really interested?"

"Yeah, I do. And he wants to meet you. Something about Brian and the grunge years and Seattle. Whatever it is, I don't care, as long as he invests in us."

He was looking at her with sincere hope in his eyes. She wanted to help. She smiled. "Okay. I'll see if I can stay."

Lucy stepped out to the backyard to call Aaron. She took a minute to look warily at the horse chestnuts that were still fully ensconced in their green spiky casings before sitting down beneath the tree.

"Lucy? Hey, how is it going?"

"I'm good here. How are the wedding plans going?"

"They're going great. I'm getting to know Serena's family extremely well."

"That okay?"

"Yeah. It's really nice to be part of a big family, just different."

"We never had that. Ours keeps getting smaller."

"How about you? You getting a bigger family yet?"

She laughed a little. "Barely. But that's not why I'm calling. I wanted to know if anything big has happened at home...because I need a few more days here."

"I've sent feelers out to all the companies that you and I agreed upon, and a few others. I've got a phone call scheduled with the president of Mattress Revival on Friday and a luncheon with the vice president of Sleepsy Fields on Monday. I thought you might be at that one with me."

"Sleepsy Fields? Not them."

"Look, I'm talking to everyone. Trying to create some buzz."

He sounded like he was listening to her. She would have to

trust that he knew what he was doing, at least until she got home. "Okay, but do you need me for any of the wedding stuff?"

"Hold on, let me get up the calendar."

She looked up into the big green leaves above her. She hadn't even thought to check their joint calendar, something she would do every day at home. It was a little embarrassing that she had put Wellslept so far out of her mind that she'd forgotten.

"Okay, there's a dress fitting for Tuesday. That's pretty important. We do the practice rehearsal on Thursday. You'd better be home by then or Mom will absolutely freak out, but I say stay there if you can get some money. Those bills aren't going to pay themselves without some quick action. I don't want anything to go to collections."

Aaron was catastrophizing again but Lucy tried to stay neutral. "Of course, I don't want that to happen either. Just give me until Sunday or Monday, and I'll know more."

"Okay...and Lucy? Bruce says hello."

"Nice, thanks," she said nonchalantly. Did Aaron know about them?

"We've been talking a lot over the past few days. Bruce has got a lot of great ideas about our business. I feel like all the training I went to last spring has really set me up well. I know the business theories he's talking about well enough to have a real discussion with him. We may be brewing up a pretty good idea."

"Okay, but don't get too far down the road on this. I'll be home soon."

He sighed, loud enough for her to hear it all the way in Wakeby. "Of course, Lucy. Keep your foot on the brakes at all times. Isn't that your motto?"

She tried to be diplomatic. "It's smart advice."

"For some of us."

"Well, expect me back home by Monday night." The other way out of arguing with him was to hang up quickly.

"All right. See you then, sis, and be ready to roll."

She loved Aaron but he was so determined she was afraid he wasn't thinking clearly. She frowned after hanging the phone up and walked back into the bookshop. Sam was up at the counter, working on the fundraising website.

"I'll stay until Sunday or Monday if I can change my flight."

Sam smiled and exclaimed, "Excellent. Tedd is going to take us out to the restaurant at Symonds Manor."

"What's it like?" Lucy wondered immediately if Deborah would be there.

"It's a very posh restaurant. You could wear that dress again."

"From last night?"

"Yes. It suits you." He grinned quickly in the way she'd grown to enjoy. Then he looked down at his computer. "So, what do you think of this?"

She walked over to look, feeling a glow from his compliment. On the screen she saw the webpage he was putting up. It was, for lack of a better word, ugly. Or clinical? She tried not to let her opinion seep into her tone of voice. "Interesting layout, but…"

"But?"

"Don't you have any better photos of the bookshop?"

"There's this one. And the one from a few years ago when we had the new sign made."

Lucy sighed. "I see the photos show the place. But they aren't, you know, warm." She thought back to the other day when the bookshop had been gleaming in the sunlight.

"Here is Evangeline's website. I thought I'd just follow her template."

Lucy leaned in to look at the website for Evangeline's wine shop and wrinkled her nose. The photos showed the whole shop from one poorly lit view.

"Isn't there a photographer that you use in this area? I remember you saying that lady in town was a photographer."

"Well, I think she does big stuff for companies in London.

Locally, we all call Jeremy. He works out of Salisbury. Does mostly corporate shots. We all use him around here."

Lucy reached toward the computer and Sam slid over. She typed in the website for Wellslept. "This is more what I expected."

The website had changed over the years, but the photos showed the shop in warm lighting. There were close-ups of linens and long shots of the mattresses in a line. She particularly loved the shots of the warehouse with the light streaming in from the overhead windows. She felt a pang of homesickness.

"This is your place?"

She nodded.

"Your website looks very professional. How much did you pay for it?"

She squirmed a little in the chair. "Not much."

He looked at her. "Really? Seattle doesn't charge much for websites?"

She paused and decided she'd tell him. "I took the photos and designed the site."

His eyebrows rose. "Oh, you did it? Now I feel embarrassed by my attempt here."

"No, it's good."

"Will you help me do this? Take some photos?"

Why did she say anything in the first place? Could she do it? She looked down at her hands. It would be different to take photos here. But she couldn't not help. The photographer they were using didn't tell a story, didn't bring the viewer in, didn't make you feel anything. And she could do it on her phone though wishing now for the camera that Paul gave her. She looked up at him. "Okay, I'll take some shots for you."

"Do you need lighting? We've got some lamps."

"Wait, Sam, I will take the photos—but not now. Now, I want to look at the business."

"But shouldn't we get the webpage updated as soon as possible?"

She felt a sweat come over her. Was he delaying again? She forced herself to respond. "Okay. I'll do one hour and get you a few easy photos. Establishing shots will have to wait until tomorrow morning when the light is perfect. But for now, I can do a few beauty shots of books for you."

"For us."

She looked up. "Okay, for us, for Wakeby. And then we talk shop."

Her reward was his grin. "Great."

Without even thinking it over, she knew exactly where she wanted to start. It was as if her creative brain had been waiting for an opportunity to burst out. "I need the tea tray and two mugs of tea, please. Make it hot, I'll need to see steam."

He leaped up and went into the kitchen.

She had a plan for the armchair in the window. While he put on the kettle, she made a stack of cream-colored books to sit on the armchair. These shots would create a feeling of comfort. She wanted to hug herself. She knew the photos would look amazing. She limited herself to two shots of the book stack. Once the tea arrived, she took several shots to capture steam drifting up from the teacups.

She followed up with a few photos of the brightly colored beanbags in the children's book area. She also wanted a good one of the doorway. She couldn't resist standing at the door and shooting into the shop, but those shots didn't look right. Too bright. It finally worked when she stepped outside the shop, focused on the rose at the door, and got the bookshop in the background. Barley was happy to sit in the doorway for a handful of biscuits and those pictures of him with his little brown eyes looking up at her with the bookshop right behind him were probably the best of all. She flipped through them on her phone. They were like candy. Each one lit her up.

While Sam was in the back office making phone calls, Lucy took a look at the website he had been creating. He had chosen an easy template. She transferred her photos over and put them in. Would he think it was too pretty? She quickly looked at a few websites that she knew were successful. It gave her the courage to place her photos on the page. She'd need a shot from the street in the morning to put at the top of the page.

Sam came back carrying a stack of books.

"Stop, don't move."

She walked around in front of him. He was wearing a white button-up shirt that clung to his chest. He had rolled up the sleeves, showing his strong forearms. The light was perfect coming in from the window. She could see a light reddish stubble covering his jaw. He was looking at her suspiciously. "Angle yourself a little to the right." She lifted her phone.

He frowned. "I don't need to be on the website."

She wanted the photo. He was so attractive. She knew the photo would be like catnip to any woman looking at the website. Clearly it wasn't just for her. "I'm the photographer. Now cradle those books in your hands and look down at them like they're the newest Louise Penny release."

He sighed, then did as she asked.

She adjusted the camera, trying to get it to reflect exactly how she saw him. She wanted to show how the light revealed the way his shirt fit perfectly into the waistband of his jeans, the gleam on his belt, his hands in focus holding on to the stack of books.

Then, even if she didn't need it, she took one of his face. He noticed the change in her position and grinned. She caught that too, before he started to protest and turn away. "Enough."

She surrendered. "Okay. I'm done."

"I came in to see how you were doing on the website, not to model." He looked toward the computer, the stack of books now gripped tightly.

Wordlessly, she spun the laptop around and Sam leaned down to look at it. She'd chosen one color to be the theme. It was the same light blue trim as the windows of the shop. "These are, you know, what I could get done with my phone. And I didn't have a set of filters."

He quickly looked up, staring at her in surprise. "These are good, Lucy. Really, really good. I didn't know you could do this. They draw you in. That's the most important part. To show the place is open and friendly and full of books."

She nodded quickly, warmed by his tone of voice, even though it was hard to accept the compliment for work that seemed easy to her. "Thank you."

"This is better than I thought possible." He was still marveling.

Lucy wanted to keep basking in the relief that he liked what she'd done. She was itching to look at the pictures she had just got of him. Yet neither of those things would move them forward on her to-do list. She cleared her throat. "It's time to talk financials."

Sam glanced at Barley, as if the dog might save him. But Barley was sleeping soundly with his head tucked into his chest on his little pillow. "Okay, we might as well."

Sam opened up a few files on the computer and handed it to her. She scanned the data in each of the spreadsheets. She felt her body become cold.

She looked up. "How do you survive on this salary?"

She watched a flush along his neck become a little blotchy. "It's not uncommon for a bookshop to take in only a small profit." He paused for a moment, took a breath, "I supplement this with my book income. It's still not a lot." he paused. "Brian supported his income with his illustration royalties. If there was a tight month for us, Brian would also supplement the bookshop from those royalties. We do all right during the holidays and that gets us into the next year."

She took a deep breath. How could she criticize when she had done it herself? The deeper issue was that the bookshop by itself was not a highly lucrative business. It was a business that supported Brian and Sam in a part-time capacity.

"How much do you think Brian was making in royalties from his books then?"

"He told me once. About thirty-five thousand pounds a year from royalties. And that was because he had so many. But the first one earned him the most, I think."

"Was he working on one"—she hesitated—"before he died?"

Sam looked down, and then up at her. "Yes. He was." He reached for his phone. "I should have given you his agent's number earlier but here it is." He texted it to her.

"Thanks."

"He lived a comfortable life, Lucy. Not as fancy as Maura would probably have liked but he was rich, you know, in friends and books and doing what he loved to do."

She nodded. Brian had been different from Paul. Paul had stayed in Seattle and worked with his parents' company for his whole life. Brian had traveled and had a creative career.

"The book business is not an easy one. We only get forty percent profit on the books. I'm sorry, Lucy."

"How long can you keep it running? Without Brian's help."

His face lost its animation. He looked down at his hands. "With the inventory we have, I think I could stretch it through the Christmas holidays. Then we'd have a month or two more."

"But there would come a time that you wouldn't be able to make a profit."

He nodded.

"And after, you would return the unsold books."

"Yes."

"And sell the furniture, I suppose."

"Yes."

"My father's artwork would need to be saved or donated or sold."

Sam objected, done agreeing with the sad picture she was painting. "Or we could *not* sell the business or the building."

Lucy was about to tell him to face reality when the door

opened.

Flora walked in with her boyfriend, Russell. "I just wanted to let you know we're taking off for our drive to Bath, Lucy." She looked up at Sam. "Could you check in on my grandad? I'll be home by nine, but I just wanted to make sure he was okay."

"Of course." Sam's voice didn't give any indication of the hard discussion they'd been having.

The door swung open just behind Russell and this time Barley jumped up and began to bark.

"Lucia, is that you?"

Lucy's heart sank. It was Ada and another woman: the historian from last night's memorial, who was carrying a basket full of paper flyers.

Ada clapped her hands. "I'm so glad we ran into all of you. I want you to formally meet my friend, Gail. Of course, you all heard her wonderful talk last night."

"What can I do for you?" Lucy said in her most professional voice.

"Gail is the head of the historical preservation group at the parish," Ada added unnecessarily.

The woman pushed her brown-rimmed glasses up on her nose and fixed Lucy with an unfriendly stare. "I've been made aware that you are selling the Baslow building."

Lucy stood taller. "We aren't doing that—"

Gail interrupted, "Our organization is active in maintaining the culture of our villages."

"Okay," Lucy said, playing along.

"Our data has revealed that the building is over three hundred years old. I am planning on submitting an email to our group. I can have over a hundred people here on a weekend to stop any unwanted parties from buying the building."

Once again Maura's warning about not letting the information about selling the bookshop get spread around came back to her. She now knew she'd better choose her words carefully. "We want the business to continue to be a bookshop. In fact, I believe that Sam would be happy to continue to run the bookshop."

The woman's mouth grew even firmer. "I understand there is a buyer interested from a development group."

How the heck did this woman know about the developer she met? "Isn't it allowed for us to sell the property to whomever we wish?"

The woman shook back her dull brown hair in such indignation that it was almost comical. "Not to a *developer*," Gail spat. "Not to any industry. Not to a Londoner or someone undesirable." Gail narrowed her stare.

Lucy widened her own eyes. "What?" What did she mean by undesirable? Was she making a xenophobic statement?

Ada quickly added, "No bakeries or grocers."

Gail looked Lucy in the eye. "This is not a warning. This is real. We will preserve the building at all costs. Tell Maura what we have said. She's the one that will be here to deal with it after you've gone back to America."

Lucy had an idea. "What kind of business would you accept?"

"Pardon?"

"Well, I get that you don't want a developer. I don't either. But is there a kind of business that would be okay, if it wasn't a bookshop?" She glanced apologetically up at Sam.

Gail glared at her. "A proper kind of shop with proper owners would be acceptable."

"What does that mean?" Lucy feared what Gail thought was proper.

"Something British," she offered, as if it was obvious. "Clothing, sewing shop, restaurant, homewares, a garden shop."

"A coffee place?" Sam asked.

"No. We have the bakery for that," Ada warned.

"And Beena's teashop, of course," Gail added.

"A community center?" Lucy wondered.

"We already have one."

"Dog grooming?"

"I suppose."

"A crafting space?"

"A what?"

"A place to learn crafts, like wreath making, floral arranging, journaling, photography, with the books and materials in stock to make it lucrative." Lucy was surprised she had somehow put photography in there.

Ada shrugged. "As long as it didn't sell pastries."

"Do you have an art school wanting to buy the property?" Gail's voice was mocking.

Lucy sighed. "No."

Gail straightened her posture, which allowed her to look down her nose at them. "I think our message is clear."

She lumbered past Lucy and frowned at her. "Maura couldn't have found a better partner than you. Poor Brian." She glanced up at the photo of Brian still on the wall. "Good afternoon, Sam, Flora."

"Wait. Would either of you want to invest in the bookshop?" Lucy pushed through her feelings about Ada and Gail. "Or become a partner?" Her voice came out high-pitched and squeaky. She definitely hadn't run this by Sam.

Ada turned back to look at her in surprise. "Oh, well…"

Lucy felt her heart thudding rapidly against her chest. "We're trying to find investors, or people who can donate."

"I'm not sure an investment would be appropriate," Ada spluttered.

Once they were out the door, Lucy apologized to Sam. "I'm sorry I just blurted that out. I know you probably don't want Ada involved."

He heaved a sigh of relief. "You had me picturing a kind of future I had never thought of. In fact, I'm not sure if Ada being a co-owner would be a worse choice than just moving on." He rubbed his eyes.

Flora walked over to Lucy and put a hand on her arm. "They're the bullies of Wakeby. Try not to let them influence you."

"I didn't realize how quickly news could get around about the real estate agents."

Flora's cheeks flashed a bright red. "I might have told Ada where you were the other day. And about our developer guest. I'm really sorry."

Lucy closed her eyes. Flora was young. "It's okay. Ada seems impossible to brush off."

Sam looked up at them. "I can't tell if Ada just doesn't want a café to compete with her bakery or if she actually cares about Wakeby. A café would work here along with the books. Flora could make her award-winning pastries for us."

"Ooh, Ada wouldn't like that," Flora murmured.

Russell spoke up. "Tell Lucy about your award-winning galette, Flora."

She glanced indulgently at Russell before turning to Lucy. "I worked for Ada when I was a teenager, basically we've all done a stint in her shops. At her bakery she has a very rigid sense of what is acceptable. Nothing French, nothing with unusual fruits, and nothing but enriched white flour." She raised her eyebrows. "I once tried to make a wheat galette with a fig and pear filling and she about had a heart attack. She threw it in the bin."

Flora raised her hands. "I didn't make anything unusual for a long time after that." She turned to look at Sam. "Brian was the one who asked me to make something special for the book club he was hosting. I made that same galette. He loved it. So I entered it into a contest. My recipe won a national contest. All thanks to Brian."

"Figs and pears together. I'd love to try it." Lucy turned to Sam as well. "I also love the combination of cafés and bookshops. That's a great idea."

He tilted his head. "So was your idea. If we could make a go of doing readings and hosting classes in the back, we might bring in more income."

"I love notebooks and cards, and you could carry more of them," Flora added.

"Unfortunately, none of these ideas solve our immediate problem of buying out Lucy and Maura," Sam said.

Flora sighed, her big eyes full of concern.

"Lucy and I plan to meet with an investor Saturday night for dinner at Symonds. So don't worry yet."

"A dinner together," Flora said. The smile returned to her face. Lucy noted the calculating gleam in her eyes. She suspected thoughts of matchmaking were flitting through her mind. Lucy was grateful she hadn't confided in Flora about her appreciation of Sam.

"Oh yeah. I'll be staying one more night, if that's okay?"

"It's more than okay."

Russell glanced at his watch. "We've got to get going, Flora."

She hugged Lucy and waved goodbye to Sam and Barley. "Okay. See you later."

After Flora and Russell left Lucy felt Sam looking at her. She smiled. "What?"

"Those were really good ideas for the bookshop. For some reason, we never thought to offer classes."

"Everyone around here is so creative. I'm sure you could do really well."

"You're a talented photographer and a clever business owner. Why didn't you tell us those things the first night we met you?"

"Because I'm not. You guys just don't have a good photographer around here."

He shook his head. "Sorry, but those photos are proof that you've got the Baslow eye."

Lucy groaned and shook her head. He had said it lightly so she could shake it off, but inside she felt pleased.

He caught her gaze then jumped up from the counter and

shut his computer. "Want to go for a walk? I've got to take Barley out."

"Now? Where? To Symonds?"

"No," he said quickly, his voice dropping in volume. "How about the cemetery?"

She tried not to wince. "How about somewhere else? I want to see it, I do," she said, when she saw that he didn't seem convinced, "but maybe tomorrow?"

"We can go by Beena's house instead. She lets me walk Barley through her yard on the way down to the river. It's close."

"Well…" She paused.

"We can talk business as we walk."

Lucy agreed, because she thought it might be easier to talk about Sam's future away from the shop.

Sam got Barley on his leash and led them both toward the river, the same way Lucy had walked when she had first met Ada and Gordy. This time, as she traveled over the stone bridge, she tried to see the small river below, but the banks were full of tall grasses and it was hard to determine its size. Sam crossed the bridge without a comment but she thought it was special the way the river wound itself through Wakeby. Once across the bridge, they started down a narrow lane with tall bushes on either side. The little path led past a stone house with a white portico at the entrance. "Beena doesn't mind that we come here," Sam said, "and it's one of my favorite spots to walk with Barley."

They took a well-worn gravel path that turned to dirt and ended up on the side of a grassy bank with a single bench beside a tall tree. Lucy stretched out her arms in the dappled light. The river below them rippled lazily along and quietly reflected the leafy green tree that stood beside it.

Sam sat down on the bench and she perched next to him on the wooden slats. He let Barley off the leash, who immediately ran down to the water.

"Sam, you are obviously good at selling books. If things don't work out…" She winced, "Have you considered working at a bookshop somewhere else?"

His face darkened. "I've considered it. It would probably mean moving to a city to find an independent bookshop like ours. Plus, I need to be able to write. Bookshop salaries aren't that much but if I get enough books written, hopefully they will pay off."

"You'd take Barley with you? I never asked before, but are you okay with adopting him?"

"Yes. Barley is welcome at my flat. My landlady understands."

"Is there any other reason to stay in this area?" She said it before she could stop herself. She wanted to know if he'd talk about Deborah.

Sam turned to her. Seemed to be considering his answer. Suddenly Barley emerged from the river barking like crazy. An angrily honking goose was barreling up the bank and targeted on reaching Barley. Sam yelled, "Come, Barley, come."

Instead of obeying, Barley was intently focused on the goose, running around it, darting toward it. Soon there were more geese, running faster than one would think possible with their webbed feet. The geese were taller than Barley. Barley fled into the river. Sam disappeared over the bank, and Lucy ran down to the edge. She was afraid of the large beaks of the birds. She knew it would hurt to get pecked by one. Barley yelped as a goose got his tail and Sam waded into the river, grabbed on to Barley, swung his arm toward the most aggressive of the geese, and strode out of the water with Barley tucked next to his chest, goose-free, white shirt wet and clinging to his skin, one arm still free to ward off the geese.

Lucy had to catch her breath. Sam walked up to the bench to get Barley's leash and directly snapped it on. With Sam's flushed cheeks and the now-wet shirt revealing a fit torso, she couldn't help but to wonder to herself how she had ended up working with a handsome bookseller and author with a great British accent. He used an exasperated but gentle tone of voice while he chided Barley. Lucy hoped that Sam was still as sincere about adopting Barley after getting dunked in the river. Barley and Sam seemed to shake themselves off in unison.

"Are you both all right?"

"Yes." He peered at Barley, carefully pressing on his fur. "He seems fine. Maybe we ought to head back so I can switch out of this."

"Sure." *Not at all visualizing that,* she thought.

They followed the path, crossed back over the bridge and were nearing the bookshop when Barley started pulling and barking. There were two men standing around the doorway to the shop.

Sam strode up. "We're not open right now."

The man saw Lucy. It was Geoff from the B&B. "Lucy, good to see you."

He turned to Sam. "I'm Geoff Scott. I work for Highlands Development Company. Lucy told me about the property a few days ago. Just thought I'd come here with my partner and look around a bit. I take it that it isn't on the market yet?"

Lucy felt so exposed and embarrassed that Sam was probably now thinking she called in the developer that Gail had mentioned. "No, it's not on the market. You said you'd email me?"

"Your partner, Maura called and said it would be fine to come by." Geoff shared a glance with the other man. "This is Peter. We work together. After a quick walk around the other day, I thought it was worth a look-see. We've looked at it online and are prepared to make an offer."

"Nice to meet you. A perfect spot, close to the river and main shopping," Peter said approvingly.

Sam's shirt was damp and rumpled, his hands scraped from the run-in with the geese, and his hair mussed. He hardly looked like the picture of a savvy businessman. "You were mistaken. We don't want a developer coming in here."

Geoff looked only at Lucy. "I understood from your partner that you need to sell."

Lucy tried to speak in a confident voice. "There are three of us that own it. This is our other owner, Sam Burke."

Sam wasn't shaking hands. He stared hard at them despite his hair hanging into his eyes and wet shirttails.

"Aha. Could we come in?"

Sam hesitated, while holding on tight to Barley's leash. He looked to Lucy, his eyes meeting hers. She tried to assure him that it was up to him whether to let them in. After a moment, he reached into his pocket, unlocked the bookshop, and the men followed them in. Sam took a defensive position behind the cash register as the men walked around the shop. She noticed they weren't looking at the books or displays.

Lucy hovered near Sam, trying to convey without words that she hadn't invited this invasion.

Geoff spoke first. "Like I said, this is a unique property. One ripe for our new open farmer's market concept. We manage several outdoor shopping malls and a location like this would serve us very well for a particular client. Our building would be sustainable and feature grass-grazed roofing. We'd like to make an offer before it goes on the market. We have an authorized amount that we are willing to suggest. No bidding, no extra fees, just a straight-up honest proposition."

Peter removed a sheet of paper from his briefcase and placed it on the counter. "One million."

Lucy couldn't believe it. It was over the amount that they had hoped for. A vision of Wellslept swam before her eyes. A completely remodeled, healthy, vital Wellslept Mattresses. A triumphant expression on her face as she went to tell her mother and brother. But immediately the vision wavered and spoiled, when she thought of what would happen to Baslow's.

"Your plans don't include the building? You would tear this building down?"

Sam took one look at her and left the room. She felt guilty and ashamed.

"This is an ideal location for us, but the value is in the entire lot and nearby riverbank for the outdoor dining we would offer." Geoff stood patiently by.

"How long do we have to decide?" she asked him, while hating the stunned sound of her voice, and the impression she was giving that it was he who was in charge.

Peter nodded. "Your partner, Maura told us that you'd be making a decision in a few days. This amount is only available before it goes on the market." He now produced a folder with a lot more papers. "You'll want to review these."

Geoff stuck out his hand. "Take a moment to think about what it could mean to you and then call us. I'm available anytime to answer your questions."

"Have you told Maura?"

"Haven't reached her yet. I'll be following up with an email. I'll expect to hear from you all very soon." He emphasized the word *all* and glanced toward the door that Sam had disappeared through.

Lucy looked down at the paper. Had she really got the number right? It still said a million pounds. She nodded.

Geoff and Peter shook her hand again and walked confidently out the door. She saw them walk into the parking lot next to the building and wander around for a few minutes, pointing at the trees and talking together.

Lucy wasn't surprised when she got a call on her phone from Maura shortly after.

"Hi, Maura. They've come by––"

"Have you seen the paper?" Maura interrupted.

"No? The newspaper?" Lucy was immensely glad of the distraction.

"There's a write-up about the memorial. Lucy, it is not good for us."

"Is it online?"

"I think so."

Lucy ran over to the counter and clicked on the computer screen.

Maura's voice began to drone out the headline, "'Memorial for Beloved Bookshop Owner Overshadowed by Talk of Development.'"

"Really? Seriously? This is not good. And it's a lie. It wasn't like that."

"I know you mentioned the memorial, but you didn't talk about this."

"I didn't think the reporter would do this. Are there quotes?" Lucy scanned the article.

"Yes, one from Ada and one from the parish historian."

Lucy groaned. "I had no idea."

"Not a surprise to me. I warned you about her and I was so right."

"I'm sorry."

"This had better not scare off buyers. In fact, I want Sam to sign now. We have to get Adele working on the sale. In case this blows up even more."

Lucy realized that Maura didn't know about Geoff Scott's offer yet. She made a quick and terrible decision to not tell her. "We need until the weekend, Maura."

"We?"

"I told Sam I'd go with him to meet his possible investor. Sam said he owns a bunch of successful BMW sales locations, so he has the money."

"Doesn't sound like a bookshop buyer."

Lucy shook her head. Why was Maura so negative? "We're still meeting him. And then we'll meet you on Sunday if it all doesn't work."

"Adele and I can be there at 9 a.m."

"Great. My train is at noon, so as long as we're done before then…"

"Of course we will be. It only takes a few signatures to do it."

Lucy held the phone away from her head for a minute after Maura hung up. *What have I done here?* She needed time to think.

She found Sam in the storeroom, wearing a dry gray T-shirt and sorting books. "Maura called."

He didn't turn around.

"Maura called and I didn't tell her about the offer. I told her that we were meeting with your guy. They'll send her an email anyway but I can't control that."

He shook his head. "It shouldn't require a decision. You told me you'd wait until we found the right buyer."

Her heart constricted. "I did. I'm not changing my mind."

He didn't reply.

She was tired of talking to his back. "I'm going upstairs to sort through stuff. Do you want any of Brian's clothes?"

"No. Thank you for doing that. I should have done it but…" He hesitated and turned to face her.

Lucy stopped and met his eyes. She saw the pain in them. "I know. It's okay. You shouldn't have to do this alone."

"Are you sure you want to?"

She wanted to be useful. She wanted to feel like something was completed. And she wanted to help Sam. "Yes. I will do this."

His eyes held hers for longer than necessary. "Thank you, Lucy. This is all so damn complicated and I wish it wasn't."

Lucy spent the rest of the afternoon taking things out of drawers and sorting through socks, shirts, and pants. There were plain cotton button-up shirts and grunge band T-shirts. She recognized a few names like Nirvana, Mudhoney, Gas Huffer, and Feast. There were ties and scarves. She ran her hand along a nubby green wool one and, after hesitating, she put it aside for herself. There would always be room in her suitcase for scarves. She stopped after the dresser was empty and the bed was covered with neatly folded piles of clothing. The room was quiet and comforting. It helped to hear Sam in the shop below talking to a customer. She thought about calling Geoff back. There had to be a way to reason with them. To tell them they didn't need to tear down the bookshop. She went to get the folder and read through everything. It was clear they wanted to build shops and restaurants. Why not incorporate a bookshop? Wouldn't that work? Would it still be Baslow's in a different building? Immediately, her mind asked, *Without the rose?*

Wakeby could still have its bookshop and, in Seattle, a newly remodeled Wellslept could buzz with customers. For a minute, she tried to envision a new bookshop. She couldn't come up with anything but a boring standard-issue bookshop devoid of personality. Oh, how she wanted to accept the idea and go home with the money, but she knew that for it to be Baslow's, it had to be right here with the old floorboards, armchair, and big windows.

It was past six when Lucy finally left Brian's room. All Brian's clothes were separated out for charity. She'd been avoiding the notebooks, which Sam had told her were hers to take. Those she put into bags with the intent to ship them home to Seattle. She'd also put in a call to Brian's book agent, but hadn't heard back.

With Flora still out with Russell, Mr. Emery and Lucy had a quiet dinner of warmed-up curry. Every few minutes she checked her phone, but Maura didn't call and Geoff didn't email. At 10 p.m., her phone indicated she did have an email. It was from Tedd Ives, the possible investor. He was delighted to be meeting her and Sam on Saturday. He told her that he had been very sad to hear of the passing of her father. He wanted to do anything he could to help her. Lucy read the words over again. She felt a great sense of relief settle in her chest. "Anything to help her" sounded really good. Perhaps things would be okay.

10

*E*arly Friday morning Lucy finished her breakfast with a sense of gratitude. There were only two more breakfasts like this left before she had to leave. The toast and jams continued to delight her every morning. Even when the black-currant jam was replaced by blueberry, she still loved every bite. After she said good morning to Mr. Emery and a tired but cheerful Flora, Lucy looked over the list on her phone. She had to take more shots of the bookshop. Also, she had this last full weekday to get a hold of the book agent and finish her sorting of Brian's personal effects.

That morning, Lucy started with an exterior photo shoot. Up above, the sky was filled with wispy white clouds and she knew today was going to be a perfect September day. She was strangely buzzing with happy energy. The morning light dancing across Baslow's exterior gave the building warmth and depth. The street was quiet except for the sound of birds high up in the trees. She set up her shot from across the street and waved hello to Matthew as he began watering his hanging planters. Long shots weren't her area of expertise, and she needed a real camera to do the picture justice, but for now, she would call it good enough. The bookshop didn't need any help anyway, she thought. The charming blue trim and gleaming windows spoke for themselves. After moving up and down the street, Lucy got the shot she wanted. It felt so good to be doing this again. She'd forgotten the delicious tension between the vision in her mind and her ability to make it happen. She'd forgotten the joy she felt after getting something just right. She crossed back to Baslow's, stopped at a newly opened rose bloom, and breathed deeply. "You're in the shot too," she whispered to its petals.

Satisfied with the photos, she went inside to upload them onto the computer. As Sam became busy with customers, Lucy retreated upstairs to Brian's apartment to set a long line of garbage bags along the upstairs hallway for Sam to take the nearest donation place. The empty rooms looked like they were waiting for something to happen. Lucy had saved the pens in Brian's room. After uncapping one of them, she sat for a very long time on the gray armchair in the bedroom window before finally writing a brief, halting letter to her great-aunt.

By the end of the day she had switched into her sweater set and skirt and prepared to go up to Evangeline's house for dinner. She closed the door of her room and came down the stairs. Outside on the street, Flora was loading a few baskets of food into the B&B's car. Sam was talking with Mr. Emery.

As Flora arranged the items, Matthew came running across the street with a gigantic bouquet of roses. "Lucy Baslow, you must have a very besotted friend in Seattle because he ordered all of my red roses for your bouquet."

Lucy blinked. "For me?" She lifted them to smell before realizing they were the hot house variety. She wanted to sink inside herself. "What am I going to do with these?"

"Bring them to the party?" Mr. Emery suggested.

She felt unreasonably embarrassed to look at Sam. She hadn't told him or anyone she had a boyfriend. She wasn't sure that

Bruce technically was a boyfriend. She sighed. "Yes, that's a good idea."

"Aren't you going to read the card?" Sam asked in a very casual tone.

She reached in, pulled out a simple card, and read it silently.

You said four days and now it's six. Missing you, babe.

"How romantic, it must be from someone special," Flora teased.

Lucy blushed, feeling Sam's eyes on her. "Just an old friend."

With a little arranging, everyone fit into the car. Lucy and Sam were squeezed tightly into the back seat with Barley on Sam's lap and the bouquet between them. Lucy was highly aware of Sam's shoulders pressed next to hers while trying to ignore the roses poking at her neck.

As they set off for dinner, Flora said, "You'll love Evangeline's house, Lucy. She lives near Symonds. It's a small cottage but it has a great big garden for us all to sit in. I love it there, and I hope that maybe Russell and I will eventually end up in a place like it." She sighed.

"Maybe so," Mr. Emery said as he drove them along narrow winding roads bordered by white wildflowers, offering glimpses of long stretches of yellowing grass. Lucy heard the humor in his voice as well as the love for Flora. She hoped Russell was worthy of her.

As they rounded a country lane overflowing with little pink and white flowers, a corner of a chimney became visible, then the rest of the house. They rode up on a dirt lane between hedges and parked by an unpainted picket fence next to a cottage that's entryway was nearly completely covered with leafy green vines.

Lucy was just lifting out a basket from what she was now calling the boot when another car sped up the drive and screeched to a halt. Maura got out and strode up to Lucy in a total huff.

"Lucy, I want to speak with you right now."

Lucy put down the basket. "How did you know I was here?"

"They used to have the book club here on Friday nights so when I saw the bookshop, tea shop, and B&B closed, I just knew."

Lucy had only one objective and that was to get Maura out of earshot of everyone else. She didn't want to ruin the party with a scene. But Maura didn't follow her lead. "Don't try to run away from me. We have an offer, you know we have an offer, and you didn't mention it."

"I wasn't sure how I felt."

Maura scoffed at her. "Not sure? One million pounds and you aren't sure. We need to take this deal now. Please tell me that you aren't so foolish that you would let this kind of opportunity go by? Please tell me that you haven't imagined the good it could do for your own business that you professed that you needed to save just a few days ago. This isn't just a kindness for the village anymore. This is a serious life-changing offer. Tell me you get this."

Lucy stood like a deer in headlights, shaken and wordless. Sam and Barley came to stand beside her.

"I have the paperwork in my car." Maura quickly walked toward her convertible and pulled out the folder. "It's simple. We sign it, and everything is taken care of."

"No." Lucy found her voice. "It's not simple. They're developers. I read the paperwork. They don't want the building."

"The building? You hadn't even seen it before this week in your whole life. Your father isn't worth it, you know. I don't know why he left us this mess to clean up. I can see you've been brainwashed by them but you don't have to fix a screwed-up situation that he created." She scowled at Sam.

"Maura. Stop this," Sam interjected in a low, angry voice.

Pain seared through her at hearing Maura talk about Brian

that way. Lucy recognized the words her mother might have said. Old shame emerged that she was supposed to feel because she was his daughter. Lucy stared at Maura. "I didn't know Brian. But I do know something about him. I know that he would not want a shopping center to replace the bookshop."

"So what? We wait around for months while this deal goes away? We drown in the costs of maintaining this building for the thanks of whom?" She shook the paper at Lucy.

Lucy stood up tall. "We are raising money and we are speaking with an investor. If nothing comes of it, we're hiring Adele. You said yourself she would find us a buyer."

"I didn't know you'd be putting restrictions on who was good enough to buy it."

"Well, I am," Lucy said, speaking through her fear with every word. She was not forgetting Wellslept. She was terrified she was making a mistake. She was also terrified that signing with Geoff Scott would be a bigger mistake.

"You will be talking with my attorney," Maura spat at her and got into her car. She backed up, spinning her tires.

Sam quickly turned to Lucy. "Are you okay?"

She shook her head. She felt a distinct need to vomit.

He put his arms around her. Barley sat on her feet. Lucy gave in to the comfort of being held by him. After a minute, he said, "So dinner with me tomorrow night is still on then."

She looked up at him and laughed, then really looked at him, holding her. Here was a man she could love. The thought shocked her very much.

"Lucy, what is going on?" Evangeline opened her front door. The entire gang poured out to surround her. Lucy stepped quickly away from Sam, who awkwardly tugged on Barley's leash.

She looked into their kind faces. "There's been an offer on the bookshop. A developer wants to put an open market and restaurant there but doesn't want the building."

"For how much?" Beena asked quietly.

"A million," Sam said.

She saw the surprise and then worry settle into Beena's eyes.

"I told Maura I wouldn't accept." Just saying it brought another twinge of fear to her own chest. She attempted to ignore it.

Evangeline moved forward to hug Lucy. "Thank you for caring about Wakeby, Lucy. Please come into the garden. Let's have dinner. Nothing has changed. We're still going to save the bookshop together."

Lucy followed Evangeline up a side walkway thick with blooming pink anemones. They entered the back of the property with a view of the rolling hills beyond. A grand old tree stood alone sheltering the backyard. Under its branches, a wooden table with a white tablecloth was set up. Lucy was still stunned from her encounter with Maura. She watched as Evangeline took the roses from Bruce and stuck them in a white clay pitcher, which immediately made them seem less formal. She came back a second later and plonked a large glass of pink wine down in front of Lucy. "Here, I think it's time for wine, don't you?"

Lucy downed a good portion of the rosé while Flora unloaded a tall cake decorated with scalloped puffs of frosting, sugar-studded strawberries, blueberries, raspberries, and edible violet flowers. They all oohed and ahhed. It was a sensationally beautiful cake that demanded to be photographed. Lucy felt herself return to calmness. She longed to preserve the moment, to take photos of all of it, the table, the fields, the lace on Evangeline's dress. She reached for her phone. It would be for Nina, she told herself as she took a quick photo of the cake, before Flora took it inside the house to be kept safe from mischievous dogs.

"Beena is inside assembling her salad and I'm making a lovely trout. I have more wine, of course." Evangeline smiled at Lucy.

The trout was cooked to a moist tender flakiness. Beena's salad was a surprise medley of freshly picked blackberries, spinach, and goat's cheese. Everyone took a piece of French bread and spread it with local butter. They sat under the tree and filled themselves. Lucy looked out to the fields beyond while the others talked around her. September had never felt like this. Within this circle of friends, she felt supported. Even Maura's words didn't move her away from this feeling of belonging. Normally, she'd be stressing out in a Pavlovian back-to-school way and returning to the routines that would get the store through the winter. But here, September was still in the fullness of summer—or at least that's the way it felt, overlooking the golden-tinted green fields with a glass of wine in her hand.

A place at the table had been saved for Brian. Instead of food Evangeline had placed a candle there. It flickered silently while they ate. Sam sat next to Lucy with his arm outstretched across the back of his chair, and Barley had stationed himself between them. Barley frequently looked up at her, watching the bread carefully in case she should drop a crumb. It was hard not to drop an extra few when those big brown eyes were on her.

Sam had already mentioned to the group that they would be meeting an investor tomorrow night. Beena reported that she had written emails to her friends who loved to read and they all discussed whether an official GoFundMe for the bookshop might work along with the bookshop website.

Flora stood up. She went to get the cake with Sam's help. Once it was set on the table she decorated it with candles. "Tonight, I want to make a suggestion. Let's all make a wish for the future, something that Brian would want for us, and blow out the candles."

"But we're not singing 'Happy Birthday,' right?" Sam asked with a grin.

"Right. I'll count one-two-three, and then we'll all blow them out together."

Mr. Emery chuckled. "Let's not hear any more questions, Sam. I'm ready for a taste of this cake."

Flora lit the candles on the cake and once she had them going, said, "One, two, three...wish!"

Lucy thought quickly and said, "I wish for this feeling of peace to last forever, for the bookshop and for Wellslept to survive," surprising herself with the order of priorities, before taking a big breath and blowing out the candle in front of her on the cake.

About an hour later, Lucy and Sam were washing the dishes in Evangeline's kitchen. Lucy handed scraped plates to Sam and he scrubbed and rinsed them in the dishwater. They were laughing with Beena, because she had brought each of them more Snickers bars. The cake had been so good that Lucy didn't want to have anything else. What could possibly follow a moist white cake with sugar-dipped fruit on top?

"Beena, are you trying to send us all to the dentist?" Sam put the candy bar in his pocket and refused to eat it now.

Flora had bit into hers right away. "No one is worrying about the dentist today, Sam."

"I didn't want to compete with your beautiful cake, Flora, so I saved them for the washing up," Beena responded. Lucy was wondering when was the last time she'd been in a group of friends like this, teasing each other.

"The cake was so beautiful." Evangeline paused to chew her bar. "Lucy, did you take a photo of it?"

"I did. Nothing fancy, just a quick picture."

"Your photos for the website are so good, did you all get to see them?" Evangeline asked.

"Amazingly well done, didn't I tell you that, Lucy?" Sam said, catching her eye and grinning.

Lucy felt distracted by his long glance and her hot-feeling face and as she handed Sam the last platter it slipped from her hands. They both reached for it and Sam brushed his hand against hers. She kept her face calm and smiling, but her heart wouldn't stop pounding. She tried to cover it up by talking. "It's easy to take photos here. Every place has a pretty view or charming moment to capture." She said quickly, "In fact, I'm surprised that you don't offer retreats at your place, Flora. Lure in the city folk that are dreaming of escapes like this."

Mr. Emery walked into the kitchen, with Barley following him. "What's this?"

"Lucy was just proposing we offer retreats."

He looked puzzled.

"I mean like a spa weekend or a cooking retreat. You could teach the participants, Flora. Or create your own cookbook and sell it as a Hollyhock Cottage cookbook."

Flora's eyes filled with tears. "My own cookbook."

Beena set down her dishtowel to give Flora a hug. "We've been telling her that for a few years now. Maybe she'll listen to you."

"I can totally see it, Flora."

"Remember I told you that Brian had bought me cookbooks?"

Lucy nodded.

"He suggested the same thing. I haven't been confident enough to attempt it."

Lucy wiped her hands on her jeans. "Well, I agree with..." She paused to choose how to refer to him and settled on not saying her father but instead his name. "With Brian. You should start with that cake and think of the favorite dishes of the people who stay with you."

Evangeline chanted, "Do it, do it!" Beena and Sam joined in.

Flora laughed a little. "Okay, I think I will."

"We can light a candle on a piece of cake again for you to wish on," Sam suggested.

"That won't be necessary." Flora rolled her eyes at him and Lucy thought again at how she loved being with this group of friends. She wondered how she'd feel in a few days when she'd have to leave them all behind.

---

he following day Lucy got back to her list of final to-dos. After breakfast, she borrowed a stamp from Flora before walking up the street to the post office to solemnly put the letter to her great-aunt into a sturdy red postbox. On the way back, she said a cheerful good morning to Matthew, the florist who was out watering his plants, and then pulled open the door to the bookshop. Sam was busy in the back, so she got to her next task, emailing herself all the financial documents from the business. She sent an email to Nina promising tea and candy. She checked her calendar for any new wedding tasks. Upstairs, she put mementos in boxes with her Seattle address. Sam had promised to ship Brian's notebooks to her.

Lucy wandered back into the shop looking for packing tape. Sam was at the counter staring at the computer with a frown of concentration on his face. She went over to the counter and found the tape. From there she glanced at Lucia's book corner. It didn't make her angry now. There was a dust ball on the floor just in front of one of the bean bags and she kneeled down to pick it up. In the stacks, a copy of *The Gardener's Cat* caught her eye. She reached down to pull it out. Instead of reading it though, a different story filled her mind. *One day, a long time ago, a father left. The mother and her daughter survived. He wrote her letters and he brought her here. It wasn't her fault about any of it.* She really tried to believe it.

Brian was a man who lived his life and left her a bookshop. And a chance to meet some wonderful people. That was it. She wasn't blazing angry anymore. It felt like something else. Maybe it was just regret.

She shut the book and sat up. "Sam?"

He grunted.

"Let's go out."

He looked reluctant and glanced back at the computer. "We haven't had enough of a response to our GoFundMe and I want to make sure I respond to every comment."

"It's my last full day and you promised we'd visit the cemetery."

"Now?"

"Yes, now. I'll go to Flora's and see if she'll pack us a lunch."

She saw acceptance of her idea steal over him. "I have been wanting you to see it before you go…"

She finished his sentence, "Home? It seems so weird that I'm already leaving."

"Life is strange," he muttered. He shut the computer and smiled. "You up for a bike ride? The cemetery is an easy few miles."

"Sure, I'd like that."

"Okay, I'll get the bikes out then."

Lucy unlatched the gate out the back of the bookshop and walked into Flora's garden. Tiny purple asters had started to bloom all along the walkway.

She found Flora inside the B&B working in the kitchen with a pile of recipes strewn about. She had on an apron and was vigorously stirring something in a green glass bowl.

"What's happening here?"

"I took your advice. I'm going to put my recipes into a proper cookbook."

Lucy clapped her hands together. "That's wonderful. I'd love to own a copy."

Flora looked up at her with an impish grin. "You're going to be my photographer. I've seen your photos and I want you to do my book."

"Oh, what a dream that would be." Immediately an image formed in her mind about how the book could look. The thought of Wellslept and Aaron overshadowed her vision. "I'll be too busy in Seattle to do it justice. When I'm at home, I'm really busy."

Flora changed her expression and wiped her hands on her apron. Lucy saw another side to Flora. The one that was capable of running an entire B&B. "I insist that you be involved. I need someone creative like you on board. I'll start by emailing you to test my recipes."

Lucy hesitated, hearing her mom's voice telling her that she wasn't really a good cook. "I'm no good in the kitchen, Flora."

"I won't take no for an answer." Flora raised her eyebrows and tucked a dog-eared recipe card into a worn cookbook. "So, what's up?"

Lucy smiled shyly. "I wondered if you could help me pack some food. We're going on a bike ride." She paused. "We're going to visit the cemetery."

"Oh, I'm so glad you're going to go for a visit." She walked around the counter and swept Lucy into a hug. Then she reached for a basket out of the cupboard. She moved back to the refrigerator. "I've got the perfect plowman's lunch for you."

She placed a half round of bread, a wedge of cheese, and a small glass jar of homemade apple chutney all into the basket. Then she reached for some grapes. She pressed carefully on the red skin. "Yes, I think these are ready." She reached for a thermos. "You'll want lemonade." She looked sharply at Lucy. "Unless you want wine for a more romantic picnic?"

Lucy blushed. "No, I don't think this is like that."

"Why not? Were those flowers really from a boyfriend?"

The red roses. Lucy paused to think. Bruce matched a girl she didn't feel like here. "I did just start seeing someone in Seattle."

"If he's not your official boyfriend, then I think you should be open to having fun with Sam. I saw him with his arms around you last night after Maura walked off."

Lucy thought of that hug and how her heart warmed around him. She thought of his eyes when he looked at her the other night. She also thought of Deborah and that brought her back to reality.

"But is he single? Maura said he dates lots of girls."

Flora looked thoughtful. "I don't know about Deborah. I couldn't tell the other night if they were back together or not. But I can tell you he's not a ladies' man or anything. Maura just doesn't like him."

"Well, the other small problem is that I'm leaving."

"But not today."

Lucy laughed. "Flora, you are an incurable romantic. I am leaving tomorrow, so no wine."

"Okay. And Lucy?"

She looked up at Flora's serious tone of voice.

"I've been wanting to tell you that we will still be a town of readers and writers, no matter what happens tonight or tomorrow after you sign the papers. You're our friend now so I won't be blaming you, whatever happens."

Flora had stated Lucy's fears out loud and forgiven her in advance. Lucy reached out and gave Flora a tight hug. While her arms were still around her, she made a confession. "It means a lot for you to say that. I can't seem to save the bookshop any more than I can save my own business."

"Ah, Lucy, you've been putting yourself under too much pressure. It shouldn't be up to just you. That's why I don't think that it's fair that you have to be the one that decides for all of us. As long as you do the best you can, that's all that matters. I'll understand and I think that Beena and Evangeline will too."

Flora smiled and stood up straight. "Besides, Grandad says that Wakeby will always be a special place. He says it's in our village's DNA."

"I hope he's right."

Flora sniffed the air. "I think tonight's pudding is almost done."

"I'll get out of your hair now. Thanks for the darling lunch."

Lucy picked up the basket and headed toward the back door through the breakfast room, each table still topped with its own flower. Today it was daisies. She stopped, her hand on the doorknob. "Flora?"

Flora looked up.

"Can I take some daisies with me?"

She nodded. "Yes, do! There are cutters by the bench outside, and I think you should also bring the roses from the bookshop."

Lucy closed her eyes. "I should have thought of that. It will be perfect."

When Sam saw her carrying the basket, his eyes widened. "Flora has worked her magic." Sam already had a backpack for their water bottles and as he worked at getting the basket attached to her bike she ran upstairs and pulled on some shorts. A quick glance in the mirror made her grab her skirt and put it on over the shorts. She felt more like Audrey Hepburn that way. She grabbed the roses from their vase and bundled them into a tea towel that she found in Brian's kitchen. When she emerged from the shop, Sam had the bikes ready. She placed all the flowers into the front basket with an ironic smile. Riding a bike with flowers in her basket was beginning to be a thing of hers.

It wasn't long after they set off before the road became

narrow, and Lucy had to keep reminding herself to stick to the left side of the road. At first there were moderate-sized houses with Volvos parked in their driveways. Then they left the homes behind and there were large grassy fields on either side. Mostly the road rose up at a gentle incline but sometimes it dipped and they'd enter a cooling shady tunnel made by leafy branches.

She followed Sam past the last small house and then saw for herself a little weathered sign secured to a stone wall. They had arrived at the cemetery.

Sam got off his bike and led the way in through the plain entrance. There was a paved path for cars and they pushed their bikes along it. The graveyard was framed by a green hedge and beyond it was a vast view of the valley below. Lucy listened to the sound of the birds cawing in the distance. The dark red leaves in the nearby cherry trees gently swayed in the wind.

They parked their bikes. Lucy removed the flowers from the bike basket and carried them in her arms as she followed Sam across the grass and along a row of gravestones. The grass was unevenly cut as they made their way past some very old headstones. She passed stones that were so worn that the words had disappeared. There were tall stones with crosses cut into them and others that had stone vines carved around dates from the 1860s. There was a newer one with gold lettering and a pixelated black-and-white picture slowly fading in the sun. She approached to see if it was Brian but was relieved that it wasn't. She hoped he had something simple.

Sam stopped. She looked down. The name "Brian Whitman Baslow" was carved into a plain flat stone of black granite. Sam frowned and then bent down to wipe it clean of dust and grass. "Here it is. Brian's final resting place."

Lucy bent down to her knees to place the flowers. "It's beautiful, Sam."

"I'll meet you back at the bikes." His voice sounded husky.

She whispered back, "Thank you."

Soon she was all alone with the dead. Yet there was so much life around her. The wind in the trees, bees buzzing, and far off, the sounds of birds. She turned her attention to the inscribed letters. Brian Whitman Baslow.

She spoke to the grave. "It's me, Lucy."

She paused. "I'm glad I came, Brian." Suddenly she had to sit down on the dry grass. There was another word forming in her mind. The word was "Daddy." It felt oddly shaped in her mouth. But before Paul had come along, all that time she had had a daddy. That's what she called him as a child, even though he had gone. She had called him that to herself, because when she asked her mother about Daddy, her mother always got a sad look on her face, and sometimes a look of anger.

When Paul and her mother had married, it felt safe for Lucy to be angry as well. Lucy gazed at the pink roses and white daisies lying against the granite stone. She hadn't thought about herself as a child for so long. She'd thought she'd left those days behind. She could not say if her memories were actually real, but more that she had a relationship with him in her mind. Someone who she might talk to in her thoughts on hard days after school and when she was alone in the apartment waiting for her mother to come home. This was the man she was talking to now.

It felt weird speaking her thoughts out loud. But she needed to say one more thing. "Brian, I'm sorry I didn't find you earlier. You matter to me and I will never forget you." She patted the stone gently. It was warm from the sun.

She got up and something caught her eye. She hadn't even noticed the gravestone next to Brian's. The sun was glinting off some carved stone roses. She read the looping letters. Mary-Ann Peach Baslow. Her grandmother. It had to be. She swallowed. She read the years. 1919–1995.

This was her family. A part of her belonged to them. Brian had surely been here to visit his mother's gravestone. And now she was here as well. She reached back toward Brian's grave and took a few roses and placed them on her stone. *There, she thought. Your granddaughter has come to visit.*

She shook her head. Tried to take it all in. Gave in and reached in her bag and took a picture. When would she ever be back here? She turned around, went back, and took another photo of Brian's grave. Her feet refused to leave. It felt like this grassy, peaceful buzzing of bees and birds singing would go on forever. She took a video. Finally, she had to go. What more could she do or say? There was no end to the stillness in a graveyard. Brian and Mary-Ann weren't going to talk back to her.

She made her way out to the bikes. Sam was leaning on the crumbly stone wall that surrounded the entrance to the cemetery. He had laid out their late lunch on an old bench just next to it. "You okay?"

Lucy nodded. She sat down on the bench. "It is, I don't know, it's like seeing the headstones makes everything more real. Sometimes I'm surprised to know that I'm really connected to Brian and to the Baslows. That a part of me definitively comes from here. Belongs here. That still amazes me."

"This has been a big trip for you. Meeting us all and having to learn so much." Sam passed her the butter for their bread. "I want you to know I'm grateful to you."

"Why?"

"For coming here today for instance. Also for encouraging Flora last night. We all love her and worry about her being alone if her grandfather dies. And for taking those beautiful photos of the bookshop. You must keep taking photos. It's your thing."

"Do you really think so?" Lucy asked.

"Yes. I see it lights you up. There was happiness written all over your face when you were working."

"I do love it. I don't see how I could do it, though. How do you do it? Keep writing?"

"I have to do it. Writers are my heroes. It's who I am and I've accepted that. Of course, your dad's encouragement was priceless to me."

"But I'm not good like you, I mean, you're published. There are tons of photographers."

"How many photographers do you know personally? Working at the bookshop, I've had a chance to meet many writers. I met more in London when I started going to conferences. It sort of demystified what a writer was. I started to feel like I wasn't a nobody writing nothing. I started to feel like I belonged. Maybe it's that I grew to see myself as one of them. Didn't you get that through your university?"

"School," Lucy groaned. "I mean it was good, but the stakes seemed so high back then. We were expected to graduate and get into galleries right away. And I quit. I didn't think I should keep going when I wasn't a natural talent anyway, and I was needed somewhere else where I could make a massive difference. Helping keep Wellslept going is real work."

Sam shifted on the bench, stretching out his long legs. "Writing is real work. So is photography. We do it for ourselves, sure, but Brian taught me to think about the work as being for others too. Like someone needs to read what I'm writing. Even if it's just for a little escape into Victorian England. You know, the writing itself isn't always fun. I resist sitting down to write a lot, but I always keep in mind that it's what I'd do even if I couldn't sell the books."

"When do you do it, the writing?"

"In the morning. We rarely open before ten and sometimes it's eleven. Brian and I both followed the principle of working in the morning on our creative stuff and then keeping to the business in the afternoon. For so long, it was ideal." He spoke wistfully.

"We'll just have to get Tedd Ives to see that the bookshop has to stay open. So you can keep writing the way you like to."

"If you think you can convince him, I'll agree with whatever you say tonight." He looked at her with an optimistic grin.

She laughed. "I think we'll be more successful if we both convince him."

Sam picked up the thermos and poured out the lemonade into plastic cups. "She thought of everything."

"Flora suggested wine, and now I wish I had said yes," Lucy said, curious to how he would respond.

He glanced up at her, meeting her eyes. "Wine might have made it perfect, except that we have to go out tonight." He smiled and looked away. Lucy wondered if he was just being nice. Maybe he was just a nice guy. Maybe he was just missing her father and saw a little of him in her. It was futile to entertain thoughts of him anyway, she chided herself. Absolutely futile.

They ate in silence, while around them a breeze gently blew through the branches above. At one point a lone car drove by and somewhere a dog barked.

"When I think of Paul, I think of the big weeping willow trees where he is buried, and when I think of Brian, I'll think of these grassy fields and the sunshine."

Sam nodded before he looked reluctantly at his phone. "I'm truly sorry we can't stay longer. We need to get back on our bikes soon. I've got to get Barley out for his walk and prepare the bookshop for Tedd's inspection before we go tonight." He tilted his head. "Ready?"

She nodded, feeling grateful that, even if the day had to end, there was still a whole evening left. "Ready."

Back at the bookshop, Sam put away their bikes. "Tedd will meet us at seven at Symonds. I hope they still have the outdoor seating set up."

"Doesn't he want to come here to the bookshop?"

Sam's smile faltered. "I suggested it, but he insisted that he would buy us dinner and get to know us first. So, we will insist he comes here after we eat, okay, partner?"

"Okay."

Lucy glanced at her watch. "I'll switch up my clothes and meet you in thirty minutes. Are we driving?"

"No, we can walk. But I want to swing by my flat and drop off Barley. Will you come with me?"

"Of course."

While Sam took Barley out for a brief walk, Lucy pulled on her dress. She brushed her teeth, added fresh lipstick and blush. She put on her blazer over her shoulders then fluffed up her hair. She checked herself in the long mirror back in the bedroom.

Oops. It was Lucy from the mattress convention. Too professional. Too done. She heard Aaron's voice in her head. *Don't be so formal. Be approachable.* Wasn't that what she wanted? She took off the blazer, grabbed her scarf, and tied it around her waist. She popped her cardigan over the dress and smiled. They were walking so it had to be the ballerina flats, but they looked fine. She looked like a confident version of herself. She was going to sell this Tedd Ives on the bookshop. She would convince him of the sound investment. She and Sam would convince him together.

Sam's eyes widened and he grinned as he saw her. "You look great. Tedd will be impressed."

"That's the plan. Impress and invest," she said happily, pleased with the compliment.

"We're going to do this tonight. I can feel it," he said as he held open the door for her.

Sam didn't live far away. They walked up a drive and entered a small basement apartment in a bigger house. The apartment was lined with books. There was a tan couch. A forlorn-looking fig tree. On the floor, a round dog pillow rested on a simple gray rug. Sam had been in a suit jacket at the memorial. Tonight, he wore a white button-down shirt with fresh gray jeans. He looked great.

Once they'd dropped off Barley, they continued with their walk.

"Tell me more about this guy," Lucy asked.

"Tedd is a person who likes to collect interesting things and people. Brian fit into that category quite well. I guess they met years ago when Brian was working in the music industry."

"Why do you think he'll want to buy out the bookshop?"

"Maybe he needs a hobby? I mean he's rich, and why not become even more quirky by owning a bookshop?"

"I understand there are bookshops in Winchester and Salisbury," Lucy countered by repeating what Maura had told her.

"Too far away, and not as nice as ours. Ours is the best and the only one that has its own children's section named after you."

"Stop it," she warned him with a look. "You know I don't love it being named after me."

He raised his eyebrows. They walked up through the town. Lucy noticed that the deli was still open and a group of kids was hanging about the entrance. One of them nodded at Sam. He said hello. When they went by the deli, the shopkeeper waved at them. They waved back. She got a sense of belonging. The boost of happy energy from feeling welcomed lightened her step.

"I just love this village," Lucy said.

"Maura isn't happy here, but you feel it, don't you? It's not just the location," Sam went on. "It's finding people like your father, and like Evangeline and Beena. Flora, her grandad. Not all villages around here have a personality, but Wakeby has always felt like a positive place to me."

Lucy wondered if she could be happy in a place like Wakeby. The bookshop was Sam's thing, but the studio, she could see herself there. She could see working with Flora too. That she would really love. If she lived here.

The houses gradually spaced out with grassy fields between them. They had fallen silent together while they walked. The light was hazy pink in the sky and shadows of night grew longer under the trees. "Are we going to slip in through the hedge?" Lucy wasn't sure she wanted to climb through the laurel wearing her dress.

"Just once more. I think the walled garden should be open. I was hoping we could duck in before we meet Tedd."

She had to smile. Sam was determined to get her into that garden. "Okay."

Sam held the branches steady while she carefully stepped over the lower limbs of the laurel.

Far off, the windows of the manor house were glowing like warm beacons. They moved quickly along the darkened gravel pathways until they neared the manor house.

They reached the walled garden. The topiary hedge walls of the garden stood tall. But this time the wooden door was ajar. He smiled at her and nudged it open. "We're in luck."

He reached out his hand and drew her into the walled garden. Shadows from the trees and hedges shaded the garden in purples and blues. The benches toward the back were barely visible. Only the white flowers remained glowing around them. She breathed in the most heavenly floral scents. "I've never been anywhere like this."

"Brian loved it here. I wish you could have come with him. But at least you've had a chance to enjoy it now."

Lucy was drawn to a great planter near the brick wall filled with white flowers. "It's so beautiful. What is it I'm smelling?" Jasmine, she was sure of, followed by nicotiana and some other elusive scent.

She turned to Sam. He stood in the shadow right behind her. He leaned closer to smell the white flowers draping down the wall right above her head. He closed his eyes to breathe in the scent. When he opened them, he didn't back away. "It's impractical at best to tell you, but I can't help myself. You look so lovely tonight…" His voice trailed off.

She stared up into his eyes. She swayed toward him, deciding she was not going against nature in a garden in England. Without hesitation, he bent to kiss her lips. She kissed him back. It started out as the lightest of kisses but then it lasted and deepened and drew her to him completely.

She looked up at him, stunned. At first he stared back at her, eyes dreamy, but she saw the surprise steal over his features.

He took a step away from her. "I'm sorry. I guess I was caught up in the moment."

She reached out and touched his arm. "A kiss for good luck." She tried to minimize the earth-shaking feeling of his kiss.

He bent his head, his skin coloring red up to the roots of his hair, and turned quickly to the arched doorway. "That's right. A little luck is welcome tonight."

Lucy was grateful the path was deeply shadowed as they wordlessly walked up to the manor house. She was also grateful for the normal sounds of the gravel crunching under their feet. She kept sneaking glances at him. Had that kiss happened? Did he truly like her?

They walked around to the front of the house so they could enter the restaurant. She saw a round circular driveway lined with boxwoods leading up to an entrance portico. Something about the entrance struck her as familiar. A vast manicured lawn was split in half by a path that led from the parking area to the restaurant entrance. At the far end of the house, she could see people sitting at tables and holding cocktails on a large airy terrace. She glanced at Sam then and caught his smile for courage. He seemed to be back to his ordinary self. She straightened her posture. Together they went up the stone stairs toward the umbrellas.

Sam spotted Tedd sitting at a table with a view of the gardens below. "Tedd," he said and extended his hand.

Tedd stood up. He had grown out gray hair, which just touched his shoulders. She guessed that must have been blond at one point. He wore all black and his clothes were nicely fitted. He had the look of an aging wealthy rock star. Tedd wore a gold signet ring that she noticed as they shook hands.

"Sam, so sorry for your loss." Tedd looked from Sam to Lucy. "And you must be dear Brian's daughter, Lucy. What a pleasure to meet you. You are positively glowing."

He sandwiched her hands in his, and she kept smiling through the unique greeting. "Thank you. It's nice to meet you too."

"An American, correct?"

"I am. From Seattle," she added.

"How wonderful. I have a few business contacts there. Come sit by me." Lucy caught Sam's eye for a moment, wondering if Tedd was always this friendly. "Your father was a Renaissance man. He had so many talents and a passion for music. That's what we originally bonded over, did you know that?"

"No, I guess that makes sense though."

"He made all those posters and other work for the music rags in the eighties. This was before the children's books, you know. I was a label rep in those days and I looked him up and hired him on the spot to create work for our label." Tedd laughed. "We shared some great times. I even have some of our record album work framed in my showroom lobby."

"Wow, that's wonderful."

A waiter showed up to take their drink orders.

The men looked at her. Lucy knew just what to order while seated outside at an English country house. "A Pimm's, please."

The men seemed to agree on G and Ts and soon all was going well. There was a lot of talk about Sam and his books, how he was using the internet to sell them, and the return on his advertisements. Tedd seemed to be very interested in profit margins and turning advertising into sales. She was surprised that Sam seemed just as eager to talk about email marketing and running ads for his mysteries. She hadn't known about this side of him.

She tried to concentrate while replaying the secret kiss in her mind.

"And what do you do, Lucy?"

"I'm the president of an artisan mattress company." That was easy. It was her automatic response.

Tedd's eyes widened. "I've been just thinking about investing in one of those."

Now she was listening. "Who?"

"Have you heard of Yonder?"

She shook her head.

"They deliver mattresses to your home after you order them online. It's amazingly profitable. Do you have that model?"

She frowned. "No, we're still a mom-and-pop kind of place. Been there for forty-nine years." She felt the pride in her voice.

Tedd looked at her and tilted his head. "Yet there is so much excitement in the internet shopping arena, don't you agree?"

"That's what my brother has been telling me."

"Best to get out in front of industry disruptors, I say. I learned that one the hard way."

The waiter arrived with their drinks. They all smiled and Tedd raised a toast. "To Brian and his legacy." Lucy raised her glass. Filled with slices of cucumber, strawberries, and orange floating in an amber-colored liquid, her drink couldn't be more appropriate for a late summer evening.

Tedd looked at Lucy for a long moment. "Regarding business, I'd recommend developing a product that can be delivered. I think it's a very intriguing model. Companies that can deliver may well put local stores out of business. Just as, I'm sure you both know, the internet has had that effect on bookshops."

Finally, he had brought up the bookshop. Lucy looked to Sam, hoping he had a positive way to spin everything.

Sam caught her look and gave her the slightest of winks. "That's why Baslow's is so unique. Brian and I had a plan to incorporate online purchases. We wanted to provide the best kind of hybrid experience."

Lucy wondered when he had come up with that idea. The waiter reappeared inconveniently and they all ordered.

"I'll have that steak but no carbs." Tedd smiled. "And would you mind not bringing me any bread?" He looked at them and laughed. "I've decided that if the Dukan diet is good enough for the Middletons, it's good enough for me."

Tedd handed back the menu. "Now, Sam, you were saying?"

Sam started to pitch the bookshop again. "Brian and I were looking into how to sell books through a subscription box just before he died. We thought it would be a way to reach customers that couldn't come as often to the actual bookshop."

Tedd stroked his chin. "Really? Subscription boxes. My wife buys those."

"Baslow's isn't just a bookshop either," Sam went on. "I'm sure you know that Brian had his wonderful art studio in the back of the building and that space has unlimited possibilities."

Lucy jumped in. "The added space has the capability to work as an event space, a classroom, and even a café. It would work as a community-based place where people could come to learn how to craft, for instance, or we could even host author readings there."

Sam interjected, "That's also where a computer bay could be located. I'd like us to be a place to support writers. We even have a B&B next door where we can get baked goods to supplement retreats. So if you were to invest, it would become a full-service modern bookshop."

Tedd perked up at that. "I like that idea. I really do. Something I'm interested in is space for a performance stage. Can you see the back studio with a small stage built-in?"

"The garden in the back is pretty big, if an outdoor performance space is needed," Lucy added, suddenly worrying that

Tedd's vision was for a rock music club. "And there's room for parking along the side lot."

"Great. I'm glad you've thought of everything." He smiled. "Why don't we go down there after dinner to take a look? I haven't been there for a few years and my memory is hazy about the size of the location."

Lucy met Sam's eyes. This seemed to be going very well. As the sky became more black than blue and the patio lights took over, they continued to talk, namely about Tedd's plans to visit Morocco and the impact of the new economy for BMW sales. Lucy hoped they would get going to the village before it got too dark to enjoy the bookshop and its shiny new look.

Just as she was starting to relax, Tedd asked another question while wiping his hands with the fabric napkin. "So, Lucy, you won't be staying permanently in Wakeby, is that right?"

She awkwardly swallowed the last of her creamed peas. "No, I can't. I have to return to Seattle."

"So it is only Sam."

"Maura, the other inheritor, has other plans as well," Sam added.

Tedd stroked his chin. "Oh, so Maura is involved too. I met her of course, when Brian married her."

"Not for long. She's moving to London," Sam quickly said.

Their plates were removed.

"Excuse me, I hope you are having a delicious meal."

Lucy looked up to see Deborah standing there in a green vest over a white blouse and pants. Lucy stiffened.

"I'm the events coordinator here and I wanted to welcome you to Symonds Gardens formally." Deborah's face was flushed.

Tedd straightened up in his chair and spoke in a warm tone. "It's been a delightful meal. I haven't been here in several years."

"Then welcome back. Sam is a regular. In fact, if I could borrow Sam for a few minutes, I'd appreciate it."

Lucy looked for any response from Sam. He was gracious as he murmured to Tedd, "Excuse me."

After they left, Tedd smiled at Lucy. "That was serendipitous. I've been wanting to speak with you privately all evening."

"Oh?"

"I have something to confess." He sighed. "We were close friends, Brian and I, back then. I'm afraid I had a hand in Brian staying in England instead of returning to America."

Startled, Lucy stared at him. "How could you be involved?"

"He was doing so well, you see, but he refused to set down roots here, like get a flat or commit to any jobs longer than a few months. I was signing bands and had a ton of work. Together we were doing really well. I'd get him the jobs and he'd do the work. He was even getting work for major bands. He'd already done work for Sub Pop in Seattle so it was easy to attract the attention of British bands here. I was getting calls from bands getting worldwide attention." He gestured with his hands. "Big names. It would have been insane to go back right when he was blowing up here. And we were having so much fun. So when your mum sent him an ultimatum letter, I hid it."

Lucy must have looked as shocked as she felt.

He held up his hand. "Just for a week or two, while he finished a really good job with the *NME*, a music magazine. But by the time I gave it to him she was incredibly angry and wouldn't change her mind. She told him she didn't want him to come back."

"You hid her letter for two weeks?" Lucy felt a combination of anger and frustration. Anger at Tedd and frustration with her mom. "Did you try to contact her yourself? To help him explain?"

Tedd winced. "Look, I was twenty-eight at the time and not all that mature. Frankly, I was happy that Brian was staying. I regret now that I didn't take the time to think a little more about you. Or even about Celia having to raise you without him. I only thought about the work we could do."

"Did Brian even try to change her mind?"

"Oh yes," he huffed, "of course he did. He sent multiple letters. He called her for days, and they once had such a loud argument over the phone that the downstairs neighbors mentioned it to me. But after a while, he seemed to give up."

"Why didn't he physically fly home?"

"I don't know. Like I said, he seemed to give up. It was even hard for me to get him to be enthusiastic about the work. And then, too soon, the industry changed. Analog artists needed to become digital. The contacts we had with the bands at the time were great, but their influence started to wane. Pop music had a second go at the charts. All that innovative new wave and grunge music took a back seat. I got married and went into the car business. Brian was invited to visit with his aunt. He decided to stay here in Wakeby. He began to do the children's stories. We stopped being London scenesters. It happens to the best of us."

"That's why you warned me about industry disruptors? You've been through it?"

He glanced at her. "A sharp lady. Yes, that's why. I never want to be left behind again. I don't like things to go pear-shaped around me. I don't like needing to hunt for scraps. I guess Brian wasn't as averse to risk or to scraping by."

"With the bookshop, you mean?"

He nodded and took a sip of his G and T.

"I don't think the bookshop is a risk."

"Books are part of an antiquated industry." He wagged his finger at her. "And there's always a risk when an owner dies."

That stung.

"Actually I think you'll find that the hunger for good stories is evergreen," Sam said, arriving back at the table with a high flush around his cheeks. He settled into his chair and took a big gulp of his drink.

He didn't meet Lucy's eyes so she sat there wondering what had gone on between him and Deborah. She felt her heart sink.

Then told herself to stop thinking that way. She was leaving, and Deborah was not.

Tedd turned to him. "Sam, now that you're back, I thought I'd mention that I saw in the newspaper some talk about the potential of turning Brian's land into a development property."

Lucy's heart sunk even further. She had really hoped Tedd hadn't seen the article from the memorial. "We're not considering that as an option. We haven't even hired a real-estate agent yet."

"Ah, but I presume you will be doing that soon."

She met Sam's eyes, willing him not to mention the offer on the table.

Sam seemed to collect himself. "If we don't find an angel investor such as yourself, we will need to look for an appropriate buyer. It's a jewel of a place. To raze it for development would be the ultimate insult to everything Baslow's and Wakeby is becoming known for."

Tedd raised his eyebrows. "Oh, and what is that?"

Lucy jumped in on the response to this one. "A popular destination for Londoners wanting a weekend getaway. Ever since I arrived, I've been surprised at how special the village is. I think more people would come if they knew it was here. I've even thought that with the B&B next door we could bring in designers and advertisers from London to do product shoots in the bookshop studio, and they could stay right next door." It had gushed out of her mouth. Perhaps due to the second Pimm's that had arrived.

"We?" Tedd queried. "Do you still want to be involved?"

She shook her head and tried to mask her mistake with a smile. "No, not me. I didn't mean that. But I see so much potential in it. Maybe Flora and Sam could consider it."

Sam nodded but she suspected he was just trying to be positive. She'd never mentioned that particular idea to him.

Tedd looked at Sam. "Sam, what is your commitment to this

shop? You're a writer as well, I understand. Which of these things will get your full commitment?"

Sam leaned forward. "I cannot imagine a better place to commit to than the bookshop. From the minute I open the shop, I feel happy. I feel like I belong, being surrounded by books. I can work hard all day and still come away feeling inspired to write. I love it there."

Lucy quelled a lump in her throat. It hurt to think that his joy in the bookshop could be coming to an end.

Tedd raised a hand. "I see that, but if there are adjustments, like a café going in and designers, students, and tourists providing traffic, you will become much more busy. In order to make the shop attractive to investors, it would need to make a decent profit. I always figured for Brian and you it was a labor of love, but not a money-maker."

Sam spoke cautiously. "It was enough for Brian to maintain his lifestyle."

"Yes, and I see that you would be happy with that too. But I want my personal investments to work for me. A two-thirds investment as you proposed on the phone would mean I'd expect a healthy return. If I put my name on a bookshop, it becomes part of my brand. People would expect an experience like the one they have when they walk into one of our showrooms. You would be the personal extension of my brand, Sam. What do you think of that?"

Sam's eyes widened and his tongue seemed to have frozen. Lucy was afraid he'd blow it by being too honest.

Lucy spoke up. "Sam is foremost a professional bookseller so he would have you covered. What else are you looking for in an opportunity, Tedd?"

"You know I'm a successful businessman. I've also collected many things in my travels and pursuits. I'd like to think that if I purchased a bookshop, it would reflect all my interests. In fact, that's why I want to confirm the square footage in this place."

Tedd pushed away from the table and hailed the waiter. "I think we're done."

He smiled at Lucy. "Let me drive you into town. The both of you."

She let her purse rest in her lap. "Thank you, Tedd, it was a wonderful dinner."

Tedd reached for his car keys and smiled at her. "You're welcome. Now let's see this bookshop."

12

"Y̶ou'll love riding in the convertible on a night like this," Tedd said as he unlocked the shiny black BMW with the top down.

The car smelled brand new and the leather was buttery soft. Lucy leaned back to look at the treetops as they passed overhead. A heavy beat was playing loudly out of the speakers. Tedd had chosen Nirvana to celebrate her hometown, and as he sang along with music in the open car, it felt like Tedd might be in a good enough mood to say yes to the shop. Lucy was aware of Sam sitting behind her, and she shared a quick grin with him as Tedd turned up the music as they went through another tunnel of trees.

The village looked as charming as ever and she was so pumped that she didn't see the garbage scattered around the front of the shop, or the words scrawled on the sidewalk outside the door until Tedd was parking right in front of them.

In drippy red spray-painted letters, read the words "Wakeby First." Her heart clenched. She felt like she'd been punched in the gut. Someone was trying to make the place look like a dump. She got out of the car and moved past the banana peels, crinkled newspapers, and eggshells to shoo away the bird that was trying to peck at a paper bag full of who knows what wadded up in the corner.

Sam leaped out of the car. "What has happened here?"

She looked past Sam to Tedd, whose smile had been replaced by a tight frown. "Tedd, when we left, this sidewalk was immaculate. Someone has played a prank on us." She called it a prank to soften the shock she felt. Really, it was an assault.

Sam was madly trying to pick the garbage up and she glanced around the street, wondering if someone was watching them and getting a good laugh.

"Please ignore this and come inside." With suddenly shaky hands, she opened the door. She was relieved that nothing had been damaged inside. The window was still lit by fairy lights and the inside looked warm and comforting as ever. Tedd walked in behind her and closed the door firmly. He looked around the store, nodding. "This is like I remember it."

He was immediately drawn over to the table with the photos of Brian and stood before it. Sam came in from the back entrance, having presumably got rid of most of the loose garbage, and walked over to join him. They spoke in low voices about Brian.

Lucy called over. "Whisky?"

They both nodded. She made her way into the back office, reached into the cabinet, and got out three glasses. She had realized by now that whisky was the answer to everything here. She put the glasses and bottle on a tray and set it in the studio. She thought that Tedd might feel more nostalgic if they had their drink surrounded by Brian's work. The guys joined her at Brian's desk. In silence they knocked their glasses together. Tedd walked over to the area where Brian's illustrations sat stacked against each other. "May I?"

He flipped through them until he found one of Brian's most romantic drawings. It was of two lovers on a sailboat. The woman was leaning on the railing looking into the sea and the man was looking at her. The lines of the boat had a swirling vintage effect and the deep blues and rust oranges of the sky behind them captured a moment in time. "See, this is what I was telling you, Sam. Brian was an expert at this kind of stylistic image. Those swoops there. The control over the lettering. He was unique."

After a few minutes, he leaned the stack back up against the wall. "Amazing body of work."

Lucy caught Sam's eye. Was Tedd feeling good enough to do more than admire Brian's work?

Tedd finished his drink. Lucy hesitated, "Do you want another, or an ice water?"

"A water would be grand. Let's see the rest of the place."

Sam met her eyes. "I'll take him on the tour."

They went outside to admire the outside space first. She could hear them talking about whether the shed could be removed, and a stage put in its place. Lucy honestly couldn't imagine anything larger or louder than a string quartet being able to perform in the long but narrow yard. Next, Sam and Tedd came inside to look at the upstairs apartment.

Lucy thought about how it could work if Tedd did say yes. The bookshop would be taken care of. She would go home with enough money to satisfy Aaron. It felt odd to think of herself as suddenly done with this place. She felt a sudden emptiness; a chapter closed. This past week had been such an immersion. But it was not about her. Tedd would be a great solution.

They were looking out at the main street from the landing. She was about to go up when she heard Tedd ask, "How's she taking it?"

"She's doing fine. I've been trying to get her to understand more about Brian so she can see how important this place is."

"Does she have the funds to save it herself?"

"She says she doesn't. But it isn't about that anymore. I just think that if she realizes how important Brian was, she'll understand the value of the bookshop. Maura will sell to anyone. I don't want to see this place torn down."

"Unfortunately"—Tedd looked out toward the window—"this is a great setting for a group of townhouses."

Lucy about died. She hurried up the stairs with the water. "Here you go."

The men startled a little.

They made their way around the upper apartment and back down to the bookshop. Tedd returned to the spot in front of the display honoring Brian. "Well, kids. This was a fun night but now that I'm here, I see that I couldn't transform this place into what I was envisioning. It just isn't spacious enough for the museum and concert space I have in my mind's eye."

Lucy found her voice. "Wouldn't you like to invest in it as just a bookshop then?"

He cocked his head to one side. "I have one rule that I follow. If I don't personally feel a spark of energy, I don't do it. I don't have enough time left to engage in things that aren't fully my passion and, frankly, I'm not much of a reader." He smiled ruefully. "But don't give up. This place is special. If you can see yourself here in five to ten years, Sam, then I'm confident something will work out."

"Are you sure, Tedd? It would mean so much to me to know it was in good hands," Lucy said, trying to hide the desperate sound to her voice. "Would you consider making a donation to our GoFundMe?"

"You know what I will do, Lucy?" He paused while looking around again. "I'll see about getting some of Brian's artwork together from the nineties. I'm feeling an urge to take a look at those old promotional pieces again anyway. Maybe they're worth something."

"Thanks, Tedd. Appreciate your time." Sam moved forward, and Lucy was amazed that he was able to act with such composure after hearing Tedd's rejection. Sam reached out his hand and they shook firmly. Tedd turned to Lucy and shook her hand too.

He glanced toward Brian's photo a final time and nodded his head. "Cheers, mate."

Then he stepped out the door, walking delicately past a broken eggshell on the way to his car.

Lucy and Sam waited silently until the car had pulled away. She was afraid to look at his face. When Sam spoke, his voice was flat. "It's easy to be confident when you're someone like Tedd Ives."

"Did he even want to buy it in the first place?"

Sam shrugged. "I don't know. He wants a kind of museum bookshop. He told me he thought he'd like to display some cars." He swung his hands wide. "Welcome to the museum of car parts." He walked over to the register. "Here are some nice headlights."

Lucy could tell he was upset.

He turned to look at her. "I thought I'd be fine with some kind of half museum, half bookshop. But I'm not. I'm definitely not fine with anything changing. But it doesn't matter what I'm fine with. I know you're leaving, and I'll sign the papers tomorrow, Lucy. Whatever ones you want to sign. It's time to move on."

She walked up to him and briefly put her hand on his shoulder. "I'm sorry. Maybe the GoFundMe will help."

He seemed to shake off his angst. "I haven't looked all evening."

Lucy held her breath as Sam booted up the computer. The light from the screen flickered on and she hoped that the numbers would be encouraging. She was wishing for some tiny bit of happy news. Something to chase the gloominess from Sam's face. The screen loaded and they both saw it. No change at all.

He pressed the screen shut. "Would you help me clean up outside? I want the bookshop to look beautiful as long as it can. I don't want that sign to be there on the pavement in the morning."

"Of course," Lucy said lightly, despite the deep heaviness in her chest.

"What a perfectly wrong ending to this strange night," he said with a sigh as he strode toward the supplies. "I'll get the bucket and soap."

Outside in the quiet night, Lucy swept up the few remaining food scraps into the garbage while Sam got on his hands and knees to scrub at the sidewalk. It was late.

"Was it those kids we saw earlier, do you think?" she asked. "They knew we were gone from the shop."

He scrubbed the soap into pink-tinted suds. "Could be. Though I think someone else encouraged them to do it."

"Like Ada?"

"I don't know. Maybe it was Gail."

"The historian?"

"Who knows what pent-up anger she might have?"

Lucy wanted to smile, to lighten the moment, but nothing could do that. "I think it was Ada. Or even Maura, angry at us."

"Whoever it is, at least we'll get this taken care of before anyone sees it."

"Only if they didn't post it on social media already."

His shoulders slumped. "I forgot about that possibility."

Sam was able to scrape away at the paint, so it became more of a light stain than clear words. She filled the bucket again and again with water until they had rinsed the sidewalk clear. She even dried it with a towel. And she recleaned the window after discovering that the broken eggs had been cracked against the glass. Finally, she threw the last of the paper towels into a garbage bag. Once they were done, she waited outside under the rose while Sam turned out the lights and locked the door. There was no traffic at this hour.

"Adele will be here at 9 a.m.," she said in a sad voice.

"Okay." He was far away in his thoughts.

"Sam?" She opened her arms. He stepped into them, pulling her close in the dark. The ache at having lost Tedd's investment was eased by his arms around her. She dared to rest her head against his chest and breathe in the scent of his clothes.

After a long moment, he gently stepped back. "Lucy, I'm sorry I kissed you earlier. You're leaving tomorrow, and I know you've got someone in Seattle." Before she could say anything he whispered, "See you tomorrow," then turned quickly away.

Her heart ached. She wanted to run after him, but he had been so firm, and every word had been true.

She watched him head toward the bridge until he had become a mere shadow, before she turned to enter the B&B. Lucy rapped the knocker as gently as she could.

Flora opened the door, took one look at her face, and drew her into a hug.

Lucy tossed and turned all night, finally giving up at six in the morning. She slipped out of bed to pull open the curtains. The birds had begun singing in the misty morning light. Shadows still clung to the trees in the distance. But there was a promise of sun in the sky. She could smell a slight hint of cinnamon in the air. *Flora must be baking something delicious.* Across the street, there was a truck at the florist's with an early delivery. She loved it here. The little village humming together to start the day. An image of the view out the window of Wellslept flashed into her mind. Their street was busy with traffic, and somewhat uncared for. People zoomed by in cars going to other places. Hardy weeds survived in the cracks of concrete. She closed her eyes to shut out the image. It was too stressful to imagine.

There had to be a way to keep this moment alive. She reached for her phone and opened the camera. In a frenzy, she took pictures of her room, of the window, and of the flowers on the bureau. Out the window, she saw Sam walking along the road with Barley. She held her breath, hoping he'd stay in the frame, and took a picture.

At 8:45 a.m., Lucy stood looking out the bookshop window, waiting for Maura and Adele to arrive. She'd spent the early morning getting ready for her trip home. Her stomach felt sick. Her beloved breakfast sat heavy in her stomach. She'd planned to have a walk around the town and say goodbye to everyone after the meeting, but Maura and Adele didn't show up on time. Twenty minutes late, Maura texted that they were both held up in traffic.

At nearly eleven, Maura drove up and parked outside the bookshop. Sam had been pacing around with dark bags under his eyes. Her own stomach was tight with pure dread. Lucy kept telling herself that it wasn't over. That the right owner would be found. Maybe even the GoFundMe would raise enough money to buy her out. When Maura walked in with Adele, Lucy tried to remain positive.

Adele was wearing a white blazer with a big enamel necklace and matching tailored pants. She reached out her hand to Sam. He shook it briefly and welcomed her formally to the bookshop. Lucy wondered if Adele saw the same thing in Sam that she did. She probably read him as a bit scruffy and lacking in ambition, since he was the kind of guy to choose to work in a bookshop. Lucy saw the serious, attractive, and kind guy that they all loved around here. They walked into the kitchen area after taking a quick peek into the studio. "Ah, this could be a fine jewelry shop, or even a bank."

After a small hesitation, Adele pulled out a chair at the kitchen table. Maybe she had thought they had a conference table back here. She retrieved three gold folders with white edges from her cognac-toned tote bag. Maura sat down and eagerly pulled the folder toward her.

As Adele reached again into her bag, Maura whipped out a pen from hers. "Where do I sign?"

"There are several pages. Initial everywhere I've marked with Post-its, please, and sign your name on this last page."

She directed a look to Sam. "Can you give me an idea of the general cost of utilities?"

He answered her in brief sentences.

When Maura passed the document over to her, Lucy hesitated. "Adele, you can see how charming it is here. Do you have any leads for bookshop buyers?"

She looked sideways through her long lashes at Lucy. "You can count on me to reach the largest number of buyers possible through our network. I'll have the best photography taken to represent this site. We'll price it correctly and I'm sure the right buyer will find this place irresistible."

"You don't think we should close the bookshop then?"

"No, not if you want to encourage a shop owner to buy it."

She turned to Sam. "I assume you'll be able to continue working here until a buyer is found?"

He looked at Lucy and nodded slightly. They'd looked at the finances and determined that the bookshop was safe through December.

Lucy reached for the pen. "To confirm, we can reject any offer we all don't approve and take it off the market if we want to?"

Maura growled, "Get on with it, Lucy."

"Yes, that's right." Adele seemed calm, except, perhaps, for a faint twitching near her left eye.

Sam didn't hesitate. He brusquely signed his signature. "Anything else?"

"We're not done yet." Adele pulled out another set of documents to sign. "Each of you needs to initial all the pages. Since you're the person working here, Sam, I'll also need all your contact information."

He quickly wrote his numbers down.

Lucy felt a knot in her shoulders begin to form after she glanced at her watch for the second time. This was taking much longer than she had anticipated.

"Here are yours to sign, Lucy." She started to vigorously sign her name. If they got it all done in the next half hour, she'd still have time to walk around Wakeby before she had to leave.

Then Adele had a question about the lock system they used. Maura wanted to know whether Adele thought the outside needed any extra gardening done. Lucy fumed while she waited for Adele's response. She wanted this to go faster, not to talk about shrubbery.

Finally, Adele collected all the papers back into her golden folders. She smoothed her hair back. "I must see the flat upstairs, the garden, and the adjacent car park."

Lucy glanced at her watch for the third time.

"I can take you around," Sam said. "Why don't you go ahead, Lucy? I know you need to see Flora. I think if you leave now, you'll have enough time to get your stuff and go." His thoughtfulness brought a lump to her throat. It was all happening too fast. She hadn't planned to rush away without a proper goodbye. She realized too late that she was going to have to try hard not to cry. "Okay, yeah, you're right. Thank you."

Adele responded, even though Lucy hadn't been speaking to her. "Thank you, Lucy. I want you to know I'll move as quickly as I can on this. I know you all want this to be resolved. I'd ask that each of you keep quiet about any pending sales or interest. I don't want to scare off any potential buyer. Even a small bookshop buyer might be alarmed by any neighborhood antagonism."

Lucy replied, "Of course." She wondered if Adele knew the extent of the resistance. This morning the shop looked just as it always did, unless you knew where to look on the sidewalk.

Maura gathered her purse. "Are you catching the two o'clock train?"

Lucy nodded.

"Then I'd better drop you off at the train station. Is your stuff next door?"

Lucy nodded again. Was this it? She'd have to say goodbye to Sam now? In front of them? She sighed. Walked up to Sam. "I'll have to call you about the bookshop. We'll have to stay in touch." Her eyes were welling with tears but so far she'd managed not to spill any.

"Wait, you should take these." He reached under the counter and took out a cellophane envelope holding what looked to be photographs inside.

"Thanks," she whispered.

He held her eyes for the longest moment.

Barley jumped up from his pillow and came over to her. She knelt down to pet him. "Oh, Barley, how did you know I have to leave?"

Sam moved forward to take Barley. "Have a safe trip, Lucy." His voice was thick and low.

She couldn't look at him. She tore herself away.

"Adele?" Lucy paused, with her hand on the shop door. "If we do find a bookshop buyer, please have them keep Sam on as manager." Lucy knew she sounded sappy, but she wanted to make sure Adele was aware that Sam would want to keep running it.

Adele smiled and spoke smoothly to Sam. "Of course. I'll do my best."

"How soon will it take for the property to go live?" Maura asked.

Adele glanced at Maura. "I'd say no more than six days."

Lucy walked through the door. Overhead, a bird flew out of the rosebush.

. . .

Lucy burst into the B&B and grabbed her suitcase and tote bag. She brought them down the stairs in a rush. Flora had heard her and met her at the door. She pressed a bundle of cinnamon and pear scones into her hands.

"Oh, Flora, thank you." Lucy gave her a good squeeze of a hug. "You've been such a good friend to me. I so appreciate you welcoming me here."

"I'm the one who has had fun getting to know you, Lucy. But I'm sure we'll keep in touch. The tea leaves say so." She grinned.

Lucy hugged her a little tighter. Her throat got choked up and a few tears ran down her face. She didn't see how there would be any need for her to return.

Flora looked back at her through her own water-filled eyes, her smile going sideways. "Promise to keep in touch."

Lucy swallowed the lump in her throat along with the feeling that it would be futile since she wasn't coming back. "I promise."

A tear leaked out of Flora's eyes and down her face. "No, I mean it, Lucy. I need you to keep me going on this cookbook project. You're going to be making my recipes."

Lucy brushed away a tear. "Okay, I really will." No need to tell Flora the sad state of her kitchen.

"Good. I don't want to have to come to Seattle to get you to cook."

"You'll tell Evangeline and Beena and your grandad goodbye for me, right? Maura is driving me to the train."

"Of course." Flora stood waving at the door until Lucy let herself out through the gate.

Maura brought her car around and Lucy lifted her now even heavier suitcase into the back seat.

As soon as Lucy shut the passenger door, Maura pressed her foot to the gas. They flew by Baslow's Books. Lucy, who had hoped for a leisurely last look, instead took a brief disjointed glance at the shop, the sign, and the rose before Maura accelerated out of town.

"This will happen quickly now." Maura smiled smugly. "You came to the right choice, Lucy. Remember, there is no use trying to save something that you aren't a part of." She drove so fast that the road up to the train station was already in front of them. Maura deftly pulled into a parking spot out in front. Maura handed Lucy her tote from the front seat and leaned in for an air kiss. "You can expect to hear some good news from me in a few days, I bet. I'm certain that I can even get Geoff to remake an offer on the property."

"Okay, Maura. Thank you for the ride." Lucy pulled her suitcase close as Maura jauntily waved goodbye. She figured it wasn't worth arguing with Maura now. She watched as Maura's car disappeared in a spray of gravel.

Lucy took a deep, shuddering breath. What was next? She showed her ticket to the attendant. By the time she pulled her luggage to the cement platform, the signs were indicating the train was approaching.

There was nothing for it. She was expected home. She boarded the train, sat down in a worn seat, and painfully watched Wakeby disappear behind her.

13

She made it to Heathrow within a couple of hours. Settling into her seat on the plane had been her end goal and, after a straightforward nine-hour flight, getting through customs on the other end took the rest of her energy. She hardly knew her name by the time she slipped into the town car from the taxi company that Wellslept always used.

Lucy leaned against the car window. Home again. A few miles from the airport the city of Seattle rose up against the gray sky. Tall skyscrapers arched around Puget Sound as the freeway tucked itself below the grass slopes of Beacon and Capitol Hill.

All she wanted was to get to her apartment and then get into bed. Once home, she shed her clothes. There was no food in her apartment except one slightly squishy apple. She managed to order and eat half a pizza before crawling into her pajamas.

The next time she opened her eyes the morning light was coming in through her window. It seemed all wrong. She stretched and opened her eyes. It was wrong. There were no English touches, no smells of baking. Her bedroom was as she had left it. Four walls all done in beige. No artwork. A random upholstered chair holding all her clothes. There was no velvet couch, bunny-patterned curtains, or sounds of birds chirping. After stumbling into the kitchen to make some tea, which brought on longings for Wakeby so wistful Lucy wanted to double over in misery, she opened her suitcase and started to remove her clothes. They had retained a little of the smell of England on them. She thought of Flora again. And the comfort of Flora's home.

When her mom sold the family house, Lucy had taken everything she couldn't bear to part with. Her mom had made her so mad, filling her condo with everything new. Lucy dragged home vintage bedside tables and her parents' wedding china. The quilts that her grandparents owned. The books that they read, even the embroidered pillowcases they slept on. She had stored it all in her extra guest bedroom, in the linen closet, and in her own room. When she thought of those boxes now, she felt like they had become objects again, not heirlooms. Things in boxes didn't make a home. She hadn't experienced what a real home looked like in a long time. Flora's space was clear, and she loved the things in her home. Her plates, linens, and teacups were in use. The lovely garden was in use. Lucy discovered a longing to have her own garden. She closed her eyes just to conjure up the vision of the hollyhocks in Flora's yard and the neatness of her kitchen. To try to feel the difference before it faded away.

At the washing machine, she paused. Would she wash away a part of herself by cleaning her clothes from England? She shook her head at the crazy thought. But still she felt a pang as she pushed the button to start the cycle. She had liked Lucy in Wakeby. She was lighter and filled with purpose. Could she be that person here?

Aaron had told her he wanted to meet at Wellslept. At 7 a.m. the sun was just rising over the mountains in the east as she left the apartment. It wasn't the prettiest of mornings, because as soon as the sun crested, it got lost behind a thick layer of clouds.

But the gray day wouldn't stop her. She got on her bicycle and headed up past the hairstylists and accountants' offices. She saw their mushroom-shaped building ahead in the distance. That was her place. But then she crossed the street and gasped. Right across from Wellslept was a gigantic reader board sign advertising a new neighbor, the up-and-coming business, Mattress Roundup. The sign was impossible to ignore. This neighborhood was a jumble of apartments near the lake and a few stores. But the grasping ugliness of Mattress Roundup threw the balance far away from charming.

A new problem struck her as she approached the Wellslept building. How had she never noticed how grimy the paint was becoming on the exterior? There were three dead plants in the entranceway and one light bulb had burned out. Why hadn't Aaron fixed that? She got out the key and let herself into the showroom.

As she walked in, her foot caught in a hole in the carpet. She didn't remember there being a hole there before. How had she not recognized how old-fashioned the brass bed frames really were? Also, now you couldn't look out the window without seeing the gigantic ugly Mattress Roundup sign. She went over to furiously pull down the paper blinds. That only released a torrent of dust and, on second thought, made it too dark in the showroom. "We'll have to get new blinds or something," she grumbled to herself while her confidence wavered. Maybe she'd make a list.

That only reminded her of the bookshop. She looked out the window at the new construction. She had thought sometime last night that she could fix up Wellslept just like the bookshop. But she was wrong. It would cost real money to be able to make it look as fresh. At least thirty thousand to repaint the building. New carpet, new shades, new bed frames, new internal paint job. A remodel would take two hundred thousand or more. Somehow, she just hadn't seen before how tired the place was. She knew then, concretely, even with a possible influx from the sale in Wakeby, it wouldn't be enough.

She went directly into her office. Stumbled in the door. Here was Paul's desk. There was the corner she'd read books in as a tween while waiting for Paul to finish some paperwork, before taking her out for a chocolate shake at Dick's Drive-In. In the top drawer of the desk was his ruler, measuring tape, pen collection, extra tie. She wanted this room to calm her. To steady her. To make her feel safe and strong like he was beside her encouraging her. This was the chair he had sat in. How had he made tough decisions? There must have been a few, after his parents died.

She turned on her computer to take a look at the sales results for the week she was gone. She swallowed. One sale. A king-size Oak, but still it wasn't enough. She looked at Paul's photo. "I didn't get the money, Paul." She spoke out loud. "Things are going to change." Her voice was flat, desperate.

A used Subaru station wagon pulled into the parking lot. She was surprised when she saw her brother getting out of it. What happened to the BMW? She pressed her cool fingers under her eyes, smoothing away the tears.

Aaron entered the hallway and she looked at him quizzically. "What's up with that car?"

He laughed. "All part of getting married."

"Really? I never thought you'd drive a station wagon."

He shrugged. "A lot has changed for me."

"I like the new you," she said lightly.

He paused, looking Lucy over. "You've changed too. No blazer for once. Come upstairs. I just want to get a fresh cup of coffee before we start."

She felt a rush of anxiety as she followed him up to the break room. She took in the worn carpeted steps on her way to the second floor. As she passed the display of bunk beds on the left she kept seeing even more that needed to be done. So, in the kitchen, she tried not to look where the chair legs had worn white scrapes into the linoleum floor. Aaron started getting out the ground coffee.

"While you were gone, we got an offer from Sleepy Fields. We could be absorbed there as one of their lines of mattresses."

Lucy crossed her arms. "I hate them."

Aaron laughed. "I kind of do too. They scent all their products with artificial fragrance. I had to take a shower to get rid of the perfume smell after I visited their offices." He filled the machine with water and pushed the start button. He turned around casually. "So, there is another possibility. A good one."

"What's that?"

"Bruce and I have been doing a lot of talking since you've been gone."

Bruce. She reached for the mugs. "You mentioned that before."

"He wants to invest in us."

"I thought he was in high-tech startups?"

A flash of annoyance went across Aaron's face. "Bruce loves the idea of selling mattresses through an e-commerce platform."

"People buying their mattresses online?" Lucy echoed, thinking suddenly of Tedd Ives.

Aaron's jaw tightened. "It's a great idea."

"I can't imagine what the shipping costs would be on just the Willow alone."

He cleared his throat. "It won't be the Willow. We'll design a special Wellslept mattress that can be sold and shipped easily."

"Wellslept mattresses aren't stuff and fluff." A familiar urge to fight with him rose up in her.

"I know. I also know that with this one online mattress, we can make enough revenue to support our other lines. And move into the future." His voice was full of hope and confidence.

Lucy leaned against the counter, considering. "Bruce thinks we're worth investing in? He didn't mention it to me." The thought of the rose bouquet he had sent made her uneasy. Should she confess to Aaron about dating Bruce again? Was Bruce doing this just for her? Her stomach tightened.

Aaron found the creamer and set it down next to the coffeepot. "He likes the idea of our artisan approach. We won't be the first to try it, but we will be the most natural choice, like always."

She knew the look on Aaron's face. The one that said that he was already sold on the idea. "How would the investment work? Would this be a new company? And do we keep our name?"

"It will be an acquisition. They buy us, but in the agreement, we remain the president and chief product officer of Wellslept. We continue to direct the growth and message of Wellslept, but we operate under the umbrella of E-Investments West."

"And Mom, what role does she have?"

"Well, that's interesting. Do you know that our Instagram account has been blowing up? Some influencer bought one of her coverlets and we've been getting a lot of interest and requests for her work."

Lucy gawked at him. Could it have been her college rival Amanda?

Before she could ask, Aaron continued. "There haven't been enough orders to save the company, in case you were wondering. But enough that Bruce is considering supporting Mom in a side project for her bedding designs."

Lucy glanced at him. He did seem confident. She liked the hope on Aaron's face. She'd seen it when he announced he was getting married, and now she was seeing it again. It seemed the old Aaron she remembered from before Paul died was still in there.

"What part will you do?" Lucy asked, and then wondered what role she would have.

Aaron smiled. "I'm going to work in expanding our markets nationally. I'll establish our branding with Bruce as well as conceptualize our new products. He's going to have me study some of the other businesses they've launched."

"And me? Have you got a job for me?" She smiled, teasing him.

"Of course. You'll be my copresident, overseeing the whole thing—oh, and traveling with Bruce to conventions."

"What if people don't like them? What about returns? I don't know, Aaron. We could end up losing everything."

He cleared his throat. "I looked at the books again. Even with our history, Lucy, or the money that you'll eventually get, we are not going to be able to survive with a competitor that is freaking right across the road from us." He raised his voice at that. "We have to evolve."

"It's just such a big change for us. Wellslept is our identity."

"Hey, Wellslept is not my identity. I'm Aaron Welland. I'm a part-owner in a mattress company. I'm a designer, marketer, and a salesperson. I'm a fiancé. And soon a…" He stopped talking very abruptly.

Lucy took his sudden pause as an opportunity to jump in. "You're also a son. Would Dad want this?"

Aaron looked up at her. "I discovered something while you were gone. Did you know Dad really loved woodworking?"

She frowned. That was an odd thing to bring up. "Yeah. I remember it was his hobby."

"He loved his hobby more than Wellslept."

"No." She frowned. Where did Aaron get that idea? "Paul loved Wellslept. He loved it here."

"That's not what I found out. Dad wasn't only Mr. Mattress. He had other things he cared about. Other things he wanted to do."

"How do you know?"

"I found some stuff while I was looking for their old wedding photos. I found some letters too."

Now she was all attention. "Letters? What did they look like?"

But Aaron was still on a mission to convince her about Paul. "Did you know he helped found a woodworking collective in the eighties? Sounded like he wished he'd had the chance to do more."

The day in the bookshop came back to her. Had Sam been right about letters after all? "Aaron, these letters...Mom let you look at them?"

He made an awkward noncommittal noise. "She doesn't know I got into them. They were kind of hidden under the photo albums. The point is that Dad had a bigger life than just Well-slept. I think he would have liked us going in this modern direction."

"Well, he wouldn't like to see us get squashed by Sleep Bold or Mattress Roundup. That I agree on."

She sat for a minute thinking of how she and Aaron would still be working together and how that part would make Paul happy. "Okay, let's talk to Bruce."

"Maybe you could meet him yourself later today?" Aaron walked over and gave her a hug.

"Today? Whoa. I've barely got home. Don't you want to come?"

He laughed. "You have no idea how busy I am. You do realize I'm getting married on Saturday, right? You visit him. Serena and I have wedding stuff to do."

"Okay," Lucy said reluctantly.

He smiled at her in response, lit up with what she imagined were visions of mattresses in boxes.

"That's right, Mom." Lucy had been on the phone for at least thirty minutes, trying to pin her mom down on what exactly she was supposed to do for the prewedding party. Because she was waiting for a phone call from a European fabric distributor, her mom wanted Lucy to drive all over town picking up table linens and wedding gifts and a custom order of macarons in a full rainbow spectrum. Celia had not mentioned England even once. It was as if Lucy hadn't left. It was on the tip of Lucy's tongue to ask about the letters, but she kept stalling. Her mom was just about to hang up when she remembered the weird comment that Aaron had made about Paul and woodworking. That she could ask about.

"Mom, there's one more thing. I'm trying to figure something out."

"Oh, really?" Her mom seemed happy now that all the pink and white balloons would be ordered.

"Did Paul really want to do woodworking and not Wellslept?"

"Oh, honey. That was a long time ago."

"Did he ever say anything about a career in woodworking?"

"I don't think so. I don't think it was that important to him. Just a hobby."

"Oh." She was strangely disappointed. What did she want Paul's hobby to mean anyway?

"Why are you asking me this?"

"I hadn't realized that Paul had a creative outlet." Lucy didn't know how to explain what she was even asking.

"You've always been a reliable girl. We both felt that was your best trait."

"Who?"

"Paul and I." Celia paused. "Add rosé wine to the shopping list, Lucy."

Lucy's cell phone vibrated. She felt a moment of happiness, hoping that someone in Wakeby might be contacting her. She glanced down at the screen. *Bruce free at 3:30.* Aaron had somehow set up a meeting already.

"I'd like you to add limes to the list as well, darling, and bring them to my condo. You know where I keep the extra key."

"Limes," Lucy muttered, adding it to the list.

After running several of her mom's errands, Lucy had a quick drive-through lunch from one of the larger Starbucks coffee shops in the area before getting on the bridge to take her over

Lake Washington. Once in downtown Bellevue, it took several minutes circling the buildings in the small downtown area to find where she should park the truck. E-Investment West headquarters was in a tall building with an unremarkable courtyard. She strode into the drab corporate lobby feeling anxious. When the elevator door opened to the twelfth floor it was like she was in a whole different building. As she stepped out onto modern cement floors, a swooping bent wood reception desk met her eye. On it, a vase of fresh orange and pink gerbera daisies sat perkily on top of the counter. A young man looked up from a computer screen. "Hallo."

"Hi, I'm here to see Bruce Larson."

He looked at the screen and nodded. "Are you Ms. Welland?"

"Baslow. Welland." Lucy blurted then paused. "I mean I go by both."

"Great. I'll let him know."

She sat down in the lobby on an orange leather bench. Seeing Bruce again would be nice, she told herself. He walked into the room and looked around until he spotted her. He was wearing a dark blue sateen shirt tucked into blue jeans and no socks with his black loafers. She'd forgotten how fit he was. She was surprised to see him wearing thick-rimmed glasses.

"Lucy. Great to see you." He reached in for a hug and held her a beat too long. He stepped back and waved his hand toward the hall. "Come in. Let's talk about this joint-venture idea Aaron and I have been batting around."

Bruce led her past the reception desk and into a warmly lit hallway with blond wood doors.

Once inside his office he pulled her to him. "Hey, you," he whispered to the top of her head. Lucy tried to feel a sense of homecoming in his arms. He held her face and kissed her deeply.

"Lucy, don't ever go away again. I've missed you."

He paused and waited. She figured out he was waiting for her to say the same thing. "I missed you too," she whispered into his shoulder. "I had such an amazing trip. You should have seen the village where I—"

"Come see what we've got planned. This is where we've been setting up shop. I don't know if Aaron told you, but I've been in direct-to-consumer businesses since college and I have never been more excited for an industry disruption like the one we've been talking about."

"Okay," she said cautiously. She thought he'd ask a little about her trip before launching into business.

"Can I get you a cup of coffee?" He gestured toward a cute Keurig-type machine.

"No, thanks." She didn't want any extra caffeine in case it made her more stressed than she was feeling already. "Let's just get into this big idea you guys have." A window behind Bruce's desk looked out beyond the freeway and toward the Cascade Mountains.

He raised his eyebrows. "Hey, maybe it's selfish, but I really want to work with Aaron. He's a great guy. When we stumbled upon this distribution idea, the both of us got so excited."

"What makes you think that an e-mattress is going to work?"

He grinned. "The success of Amazon. It's the way I myself want to shop. But what's great is that Wellslept mattresses come with more than a nod to sustainability. You already have access to the producers of those kinds of healthy materials. Aaron and I have hammered most of the details out. We figure an e-mattress by Wellslept would be made with bio-engineered foam, no phthalates, no dyes. Your mom's designs on the covers are genius and fresh. They already telegraph a modern, clean look. We simply have to develop an eco-design that can be shipped in a box."

"So, you are talking foam. How long do you expect those mattresses to last?"

He opened his hands wide. "Lucy, I don't want to develop a crappy product. It will be the best we all can make."

"What if the idea doesn't change the industry? What happens to Wellslept?"

"I know this is a big leap, but there are already a few companies in the game and early numbers say they are doing very well. But none of them have Wellslept's commitment to health, so that's our edge." He leaned back in his chair. "Reputation is what you guys are bringing to the table. Our company will bring the innovation expertise to make the product fly out the door." He nodded toward the hallway. "My partners love me, but at the end of the day, they have to believe in the product as much as I do before we take on a company. We are all on board with this one."

"Are you committed to keeping our other lines going?"

"We have to be careful with that, you see."

Lucy braced herself. "What do you mean?"

Bruce reached for his computer. He tapped on the screen. "Let's talk about it this way. You guys offer what? Twenty-two different styles?"

She shook her head. "Twenty-five. With customizable options that can take it up to thirty."

"You know Sealy mattresses? They offer hundreds of options." He paused. "Here's my take on product lines. I believe that modern consumers only want one or possibly two choices, max."

"What?" Lucy thought of all the different types of backs and preferences people had about their sleeping experience.

"Data from our testers reveal the best successes come with the simplest buying structure. People don't want that kind of brain-crushing choice and they don't want to go into a showroom to be bullied into buying something by a group of salespeople."

She felt anger at his echoing the common misperception about salespeople. "That doesn't happen at Wellslept."

He arched his eyebrows. "Come on. It's the nature of your business."

"Not like the other places. We have nice people working for us. We have relationships with our customers."

"Millennial and Gen Z customers don't want that experience anymore. They don't want a person in a suit to walk them around a showroom. And who has time to drive around anyway? In Seattle traffic?"

"Weekends?"

"Still a hard sell to get customers to drive to you, since you only have one location." He looked up at her. "There is a reason to maintain the showroom. It gives us weight, a significance. After all, Wellslept has been in business for…"

"Forty-nine years," Lucy completed the sentence. They shared a smile.

"So, yes. The showroom stays, but there need to be changes with that too. I don't want to overwhelm you, but there will be precise changes in every way. Remodeling and rebranding."

"For instance…?" Lucy felt Bruce was considering a tidal wave of changes.

"Your brand is too homespun. Your product photos are great, but the website design isn't modern enough. Your marketing is too wide. The copywriting is too verbose."

He continued. "Partner with us and we will provide Wellslept with all the tools to compete in this modern marketplace. It's what we do. Aaron insists you and he be co-presidents. Aaron is in charge of new product development. Your mom also gets the budget to develop the line of bedding we will offer. I do need to say here that we will not offer more than one or two sheet set styles, so we will need to discuss some restrictions with your mom. Happily, she's already getting buzz on her personal work. The four of us approve the new mattress and Aaron and I redesign and represent the marketing and the e-commerce platform."

"And the warehouse? Where will the new mattresses be made?"

He sighed. "I'm sorry. This can't be done on an artisan scale. We need to be able to go big for the e-mattresses. Like I said before, we will need to cull the lines." He paused. "Any other questions?"

Lucy's heart was beating hard. This discussion had her way out in the middle of a frozen lake, and she couldn't go back. She was already out there balancing on the thin ice. "So, what you're saying is we will not need the warehouse. We will remodel the showroom. We will create a new mattress to sell. What is the part that is still Wellslept?" She swallowed the bitter feeling that prompted her reaction, urging herself to be open, to remain open. "If everything looks different and feels different, I'm not sure where that is?" She tried to keep her tone light but failed.

He looked at her face and softened. "Wellslept is you and Aaron. Wellslept is the weight of your experience. It's the story that we tell about your family. It is in the same commitment to sustainable high-quality sleep mattresses that you've always had. I know it's scary, but you have to step out there, make the change, and believe in yourselves if you want to excel."

She looked down at her hands, then up at Bruce. He had it too, an eager look. Maybe she would get that look too. After she took it all in. "It is a big change to think of Wellslept differently, but if the industry is going to be disrupted anyway, then I'm glad we're having this talk."

"Excellent. I guess the next step is to have a sit-down with our legal team." He smiled. "And we also have a wedding coming up."

Lucy stared at him for a minute, confused if he meant them together, until she realized he was talking about Aaron. "Oh, right. Yes. Bridesmaid duties." She grabbed her purse and pushed back her chair.

"I'm thrilled to be part of the wedding. Looking forward to the rehearsal dinner in, what, only two days now. I'm also hosting a bachelor party for Aaron."

He paused at the conference room door, blocking her way. "Dinner tonight?"

"Uh, how about tomorrow?"

He looked crestfallen. Lucy swallowed, feeling guilty. "I'm really tired. Jet lag, you know."

"Sure. I mean, I guess we'll be seeing each other all week but..." He reached for her and drew her close again. "I'll just have to top up on a little more of you right now then." Between the coat rack and a filing cabinet, he kissed her again.

She tried to feel romantic, but all she could think of was limes and paper plates and mattresses in boxes. Bruce gave her butt a squeeze before he opened the door. "Rest up, babe. See you tomorrow."

"Bye." She turned toward the wrong direction, and then turned again to get back to the corporate elevators.

Once she got back into her car, she slumped against the steering wheel. It was all happening so quickly. Bruce was so sweet, why couldn't she feel excited to see him? She should have made sure he wasn't doing the mattress thing only because he liked her. She winced. And then there were the massive changes he proposed for Wellslept.

She wasn't ready to go grocery shopping yet. She would go to the warehouse. Her beloved warehouse.

Lake Washington was choppy with waves as she drove over the bridge to get back to Seattle. The freeway took her through a long tunnel on the Seattle side of the lake, and then she popped over Beacon Hill to descend into the industrial but tree-lined area where the warehouse was located. The way into the parking lot was blocked with construction signs. Already the old building across from the warehouse that she always had assumed would be there was surrounded by aluminum fences and keep-out signs. Lucy circled around the back of the warehouse and parked in the loading zone.

Lucy hopped out of the car and walked up the ramp to the warehouse. The comforting smell of the fresh wood normally calmed her but today it just brought tears to her eyes. She emerged past the mattresses and into the main room like a lost soul. Nina looked up from her computer. "Lucy, you're back. How are you?"

When Nina opened her arms for a hug, Lucy gladly reciprocated and held on a little too long.

"Are you okay?"

Lucy blinked tears out of her eyes. Her throat was choked up. "Yes, it's good to be home."

Nina hesitated. "Shall I get the kettle going?"

A few more tears leaked out just at the thought of tea. They walked into the main work area and Lucy pulled up a stool next to the counter, taking a breath to calm herself. She tried to redirect the conversation. She opened her bag and brought out the amply-filled crumpled paper bag from Beena's shop.

Nina accepted it and peered inside. Golden toffees packaged into a paper British phone box rested on top of a wild assortment of hard candies. Hidden down farther in the bag the special kind of tea that Flora used and a small book from the bookshop nestled together.

Nina clapped her hands. "Oh, this is so perfect. I love everything. And this book, *Gardens of Southern England*, looks so interesting. Thank you."

Lucy cracked open the book. "A garden I visited is in here." She found the pictures of Symonds. Was it only two days ago? She could sense the peace that came with the long walking paths stretching out before her. She could almost feel Sam by her side. But that hurt, so she quickly pointed at the manor house. "They have weddings there, and this walled garden is where my father set his book."

Nina scooted closer to Lucy to look at the pictures. "It looks like the quintessential English garden. Wow, how lucky you are."

Lucy got out her phone. "I did take some pictures."

Nina clapped her hands and reached for her phone. "Wonderful, I knew you'd find some inspiration there." Nina scrolled through and then stopped. "These are stunning. Each one seems to tell a story."

"It was easy. The place is full of iconic views."

"It's not just the place. You have a good feel for the imagery."

"The pace of life is so different too." Lucy didn't want to dwell on the joy she had felt taking them.

"Wait, who is this?" Nina had a gleam in her eye.

Lucy felt her cheeks warm ever so slightly. It was the picture of Sam holding the books in the bookshop. He looked amazing. Those blue eyes, messy hair, handsome, fit, and smiling at her. "That's Sam."

Nina raised her eyebrows. "And you were going to leave out the part where you met a cute guy?"

"It's complicated. Sam is the third inheritor."

"Really? And he's single?"

Lucy's cheeks had accelerated to burning hot. "Yes. He's single. I think."

"And he has an accent?"

Lucy laughed. "Yes."

"A good kisser?"

Lucy's cheeks flushed. She peeked at Nina through her hands. "Yes."

Nina's eyes were wide open. Her laugh was full of delight. "Lucy, nice! And now?"

Lucy shook her head. "And now nothing. I live here. He's losing the bookshop and will probably have to move out of Wakeby."

"What a hard situation."

Lucy felt the air leave her. Her shoulders drooped. "I haven't heard from him. But Flora has already emailed me. She's my friend from the B&B. She wants to hire me as a photographer for her cookbook."

"She sounds lovely. You've got to go back. Visit them again."

Lucy rejected that idea. "I can't. I'm about to be busier than ever. My purpose is here." Even as she said it, she heard her own voice fall flat. Lucy patted the table and looked around the warehouse. Lucy seized the moment to ask Nina the question that had been bothering her. "Nina, can I ask you something about Paul?"

The kettle had begun its slow but insistent whine. Nina jumped up to pull it off the burner. She dropped three tea bags into the teapot and filled it to the brim with water.

"What's that?"

"Do you ever remember Paul wanting to do his woodworking as more than a hobby?"

Nina raised her eyebrows. "That's an interesting question. Paul told me that as a teenager he was happiest when he was working on a whittling project. He loved to carve things."

Nina checked the steep, then poured a little milk into each cup and handed one to Lucy. "Cheers."

Lucy took a sip and was surprised when her eyes filled. The scent of the tea was light and fragrant. This was the B&B in a cup. "Aaron said Paul didn't really want to work in the mattress business. That he was good at woodworking and design."

Nina looked out at the open room before turning back to Lucy. "You know, the family expected that Paul would take over the business. That was natural to them. Paul knew that. I think he hoped for a while that he might be able to have two careers." She paused to take a sip of tea.

"I always thought he loved running Wellslept."

Nina looked more carefully at Lucy. "To tell the truth, Paul spent more time down here at the warehouse than he specifically needed to over the years. He'd work on his personal projects instead of what he was supposed to be doing back at the office, you know. But I never said anything."

"I didn't realize how much he liked woodworking."

"He devoted a lot of time to it before he met your mother. Afterward, I think he delighted in your mother's creativity. He

287

was a bit of a shadow artist. He supported me as well, allowing me to work around my crafting classes."

She smiled. "But it wasn't all supporting us. Paul did get a few of his pieces in that wood design shop and became part of their collective. I don't know if it's still there of course, but in the eighties, it was a real honor to be shown there."

Lucy was trying to wrap her mind around this. "He was good at running the business."

"Yes, he was. Paul was a good man. You know, when he was in the hospital, I brought him some of his pieces that he had made."

"How did that go?"

"We had a good laugh about the old days." Nina paused. "He said that those days in the warehouse had been precious to him. I've always kept the pieces he was working on." She smiled at Lucy. "I think he was delighted that you, also, were artistic."

"But he did the responsible thing. He kept up the business."

"Yes, but he also didn't have a degree or the internet. He was an only child. His parents were still alive and expected his participation. The business was thriving and he fell in love with your mother. And you. That certainly made him happy. The most happy."

"Do you have any of his carvings here?"

Nina shook her head. "I have a few at home. I'll bring them in to show you."

Lucy nodded. She finished her tea. There were no leaves in the bottom. No messages. "We've had an offer for the business. It's from my friend and Aaron's friend too. He has a plan to turn us into an e-commerce business. Given the choices, I think it's the best move for Wellslept."

"Tell me about it." Nina gave Lucy her full attention, leaning forward in her chair.

"Bruce and Aaron have hatched a plan to sell mattresses online. They want to develop a style that can be shipped in a box."

Lucy's stomach tightened as she waited for Nina's reaction.

Nina kept a steady gaze on Lucy. "I looked over those numbers when you came last. I think I've known for a while now that things are going to change, one way or the other."

"Before I left, I didn't understand the amount of money that would be needed to save Wellslept."

Nina smiled. "It's funny actually. Wellslept might leap into the future right past those brick and mortar stores."

Lucy felt a jab of anger. Nina wasn't responding like she'd thought she would. "I don't think it's funny. I don't have to choose to sell to Bruce." She felt tearful. In reality, she knew there was no staying the same now that Mattress Roundup was moving in across the street.

"I'm sorry. I didn't mean to be flippant. I know this isn't what you wanted." Nina paused for a moment. "By the way, I've been offered a teaching position."

"What? Where?"

"At a private art school on Capitol Hill. Modern weaving is making a big comeback."

"Oh, wow." Was Nina saying that she was leaving already? That she was already jumping ship?

"I wasn't sure about taking it, but maybe this is the right time."

"So you haven't accepted it."

"Not yet."

"I don't think we should give up completely on...Paul. You could still help here."

Nina patted Lucy's hand. "I know it seems like keeping the business open keeps a little bit of Paul alive too. I know this is so hard to accept, but he isn't in Wellslept. I believe he loved you and Aaron more than anything. More than Wellslept."

"He did love us," Lucy conceded, suddenly more tired and achy than she'd been since arriving home. Lucy felt herself getting angry. "I'm the most horrible person to let it change like this."

Nina sighed. "Lucy, when was the last time you googled sleep habits?"

Lucy had to laugh. "I know what you're saying, but I never liked it like that. I just loved it for being a special place. I don't totally love the mattress business."

Nina closed her eyes. When she opened them, she gazed directly at Lucy. "I know this sounds harsh, but Wellslept is a little like your wubby. A place where you feel safe. You are too special for a safe life, Lucy. You've got to shine."

"I think I'll lose him," Lucy said, her fear out in the open.

"He will still be in here," Nina said, touching her own chest. "You don't need Wellslept for that."

"Maybe," Lucy whispered, feeling even more mixed up than before. Like there was so much noise coming at her that she couldn't hear any one thing.

She decided to switch topics. "Let's go over any unpaid shipment bills before I leave."

After a review of the latest shipments and inventory, Lucy briefly hugged Nina goodbye and went out to the car. She didn't feel any better. Instead, she felt worse. Nina hadn't helped her. She had basically said that she was okay with moving on. It felt like a betrayal.

Lucy arrived back at Wellslept determined to make sure Bruce's numbers were for real. He had made some crazy claims about the industry. She went first to an e-commerce mattress website. It was very clean and simple and the first thing she saw was a video. It was basically telling her how the mattress industry made money off of commissions.

Next she went to Amazon and looked at mattresses. She was astonished at the number of reviews. If each one of those represented a buyer, then these brands were doing much better than Wellslept.

She looked at the screen again. This time she took Wellslept's data back over the last five years. The numbers got smaller and smaller. She opened up her bank statements. They had been putting off so many things for when the money would come again. She had never thought to question whether the money would actually come. If Bruce was right, maybe the money wasn't going to ever come. She snapped the top of her laptop closed and began to pace around. There was no going back. Each pathway to save Wellslept ended with a change.

At close to six, she left. Her mother had mentioned she'd be out for a walk and dinner with a friend and Lucy wanted to get into her apartment before she got home. After a quick trip to the grocery store for the limes and everything else, she drove over to Kirkland and parked in the little lot. There was a boat launch next to the building and as she shut the car door, she could smell a heady mix of grass, boat fuel, and lake water that came from Lake Washington just a few feet away. The condo had a retro-modern feel because it really was from the fifties. With its open stairway and bamboo plants, the place reminded her of vintage Hawaiian hotels. She walked up the staircase to the first level with two heavy bags of groceries, grateful her mom wasn't on the top floor. It was quiet inside and, calling out, she checked that her mom wasn't home yet. Lucy knew she had to seize the moment.

Reflections of the last sunbeams of the day on the lake outside danced across her mom's living room walls. The sun wasn't due to set for another half hour. Her mom's apartment felt like an Anthropologie store, enhanced with the same Blue Capri tropical candle smell floating in the air that the store used. Her pride and joy was an Anthro sofa sewn in a colorful denim patchwork with sequins embedded in the fabric. "Dramatic" had always been a good way to describe her mother. As she walked past, she saw the couch was covered with wedding magazines.

Lucy brought the party groceries to the kitchen and put everything away. Outside the big windows she saw many boats on the lake. Days like this were still warm enough to fill the beaches along the shore with picnickers.

After checking her mom wasn't just driving up, she made her way to the guest bedroom. She heard the furnace behind her turn on and a truck drive by outside, but apart from that the entire apartment was still. She swallowed. Behind the mirrored closet doors was the box she was searching for. She was certain the letters were in there.

It took her a few tries, but she finally uncovered the box with the photo albums. Just underneath those, she gently pulled out a file of airmail letters and postcards. She took the file over to the guest bed and sunk into the cushions. What she discovered was a stack of sealed, unopened letters and cards from Brian. Sam had been completely right. She forced herself to open up the first envelope, and unfold the deep creases of the paper inside.

Dear Lucy,

Happy Birthday! I'm writing to tell you that I am the proud owner of a bookshop. I've had so many requests for me to carry children's books that I've opened up a little business.

Love,

Dad

Dear Lucy,

Happy Birthday! The bookshop is growing. I have been busy illustrating books and have a new one to do about a group of hedgehogs.

Love,

Dad

. . .

Dear Lucy,

Happy Birthday! I've got great news. I'm getting remarried. I've told Maura all about you. I hope you can come. You are always welcome here.

Love,

Dad

She flipped through unopened Christmas cards as well. Each one left her stunned and shocked. She lay back on the teal blue pillowcases and listened to the boats going by. There was only one more letter to read. The last one.

This one had been opened. She slid it out slowly, feeling chills run through her body. The top page was a letter from Paul.

Dear Brian,

I hope you are well. I'm forced to admit that I may not have many letters left in me, so I wanted to let you know that Lucy is doing well. While I haven't broached the topic with her, I'm certain that she would respond if you tried contacting her again at our work address. After all these years, I believe that even Celia might be willing to accept your presence into Lucy's life.

Like I feared, Lucy did leave college. She has nobly come to help me with Wellslept. Lucy has shadowed me these past months and I'm confident she can keep the business going until it is time to let it come to its natural end. I'm trying to convey to her that I want the business to sustain her and Aaron and keep them secure until they are ready to commence their own careers.

. . .

I've told Lucy this but I don't think she is listening. She is determined that I will get better. She won't listen to anything that indicates it isn't true. I'm afraid that both her mother and I supported her in this kind of thinking. But the doctors at the hospital are not giving me that same latitude.

So I sign off with the urgent suggestion that you help Lucy see her way to returning to school to further her interests. I'm worried she might become stuck here. She doesn't deserve a life like that. I want her to thrive. If you can see a way to support her in that, I'd appreciate it beyond words. She and her brother are the very jewels of life. I'll try to talk to her about you Brian so she can begin to know that there are many of us who care for her and when one goes, there will always be others. I hope this letter isn't too morbid, and that we continue our long and valued correspondence.

Paul

Lucy put her hand to her mouth. She scanned her memory for any discussion where Paul had mentioned Brian, but all she could think about was the softness of the blue flannel shirt he wore and the way his bony wrists stuck out when she took his hands. She sat for a long time before she reached for the next part of the letter. The second letter was stapled to the first. In the fading light, she flipped over the page and struggled to read Brian's familiar handwriting.

Dear Lucy,

You've been on my mind since I had a little spell with my health last month. I have always imagined you coming to visit me, so I hadn't written a letter like this. It's only because I've been a bit concerned about my health that I thought it might be a good idea to make sure I'd laid things out in words. Maybe you don't even care, but it's okay. A letter goes both ways. I am getting it and the letter from Paul sent to you in the mail today.

To you, I want to give all my love. I've tried to follow you from afar. I read the Seattle Times *online. I've wanted to be aware of your world. Your mother, she didn't feel that way. So I've been at a distance. I have always regretted my decision to leave Seattle. When I left, I always thought I was coming back. But one day, I realized that I wasn't. One day, your mother wrote to say she was getting remarried.*

You know what happened next? I got a letter from Paul Welland. Yes, your stepfather contacted me. He was very kind. He wrote to say that he would take care of you. I trusted him. Over the years, he would mail me things about you. When he got sick, I wanted to come to meet him. But it happened too fast. He told me that you offered to step in while he was sick. He was so proud and grateful. He also told me that he expected that you would want to meet me one day. He told me that you were talented. And he gave me an idea that if I left you the bookshop, you might use the proceeds to strike out on your own, when the time was right.

I've wondered so much about you. How you grew up, if you didn't like the taste of melons, if you'd got my big feet, even. How your laugh sounded. But I stayed true to my respect of your mother's wishes. Should you ever want to contact me, I am always ready.

. . .

Your great-aunt Claire, she doesn't like melons either. You look a little like her, actually. And me too. If you meet me, you'll see. I have a good life. Trying at times, but good. You are welcome to come anytime to visit me.

Love to you, always,
Dad

Her eyes flooded with tears. She pressed them shut to stay in that moment with her two dads. After a while, she traced the words with her finger that Brian had written in his wonderful stylistic handwriting. Then she read Paul's letter again and felt her chest clench, her sobs release. She felt so very grateful to Brian to have one more piece of Paul.

She sunk deeper into the pillows. When she promised Paul to keep the family business secure, she had meant it for forever. He had been more realistic than her. It didn't have to be forever. She thought that he cared about his parents' legacy. But his letter was focused on her and Aaron's future. He had wanted her to thrive. What did "thriving" mean? That was a very active word. She felt exhausted from trying to keep the business thriving.

She hadn't given much thought to her own life. When it came down to it, had any of them been thriving since Paul died? She thought that making sacrifices for the business was what made his death bearable. But what if security wasn't the highest priority? What if the legacy that Paul wanted to leave for them wasn't being safe? What if it was to be able to have the choice to thrive?

She sat there as the ache in her chest lessened a bit. Could she try something new? She could at least help Aaron. She knew what he wanted. The sun had sunk beyond the hills across the lake already. The shadows had grown longer and she hadn't turned on a lamp. The wires of her bra pressed against her chest. Her toes got cold.

"Lucy, are you here?" her mom's voice called from the door.

Lucy jumped up from the guest bed, tucked the bundle of letters into her purse, and shoved the box back into the closet. She straightened her T-shirt, wiped her face, and emerged from the bedroom. "Yes, I'm back here, looking for decorations we can use."

Her mom met her in the living room, flipped on the lights, set her heavy tote onto the floor, and sat down on a kitchen stool. She gazed at her with a disapproving eye. "You look tired."

"It's this darn jet lag," Lucy said.

"I've bought you a few things to wear. A dress for our brunch and another for the wedding."

"Oh, I've already got one for the wedding."

"Don't be ridiculous. I've found one that will look great on you."

"I guess I could look at it."

"The wedding photos will last a lifetime, so we can't rely on your judgment about this."

Sam liked it, Lucy thought, warmed by the memory.

"Who?"

Had she said that out loud? "Never mind."

14

The wedding was three days later. There had been a wedding shower, and a bachelorette party. Lucy had barely been home, as she was required at every event. Bruce had been frequently by her side and had truly been a lifesaver for her. Without his relaxed personality and sense of humor, she wasn't sure how she could have endured the Welland Bridal experience. With Aaron and Serena, they were becoming a tight-knit group.

The morning of the wedding, on her way to the joint makeup session with the bridesmaids, Lucy stopped by Wellslept to make sure the signs were up to announce they were closed for the day.

As she neared the shop entrance, Lucy saw a brown paper package was stuck halfway between the glass door and the outdoors. Retrieving it, Lucy saw it was from England. She opened it with excitement. Out of the padded envelope, nestled inside some tissue paper, she drew a pair of beaded earrings, perfectly matched to her dress from Wakeby. There was also a tiny note in Sam's handwriting.

Wanted to give these to you on that last day.

Hope you get them before the wedding. You'll look beautiful. Sam.

Sam. He hadn't forgotten her. She swallowed, aching with a surprising, deep longing. She turned around, drove back to her apartment. Took off the greige dress her mother had insisted upon and put on the blue one. This wasn't a formal wedding with all the bridesmaids in the same dress. As long as she wore the coordinating wedding sash, Lucy was allowed to choose any dress she liked. Suddenly she wasn't fading into the background. Suddenly she looked different. Lucy stared at herself quizzically in the hall mirror trying to identify the feeling. After a moment, she had it. She looked vibrant. Like a woman who valued herself.

Along with a straw wedding hat—also a requirement—she was determined to wear the pin from Paul. The rosette looked elegant enough for the wedding. She loved the idea that Paul would be represented. She poked the pin through the heavy fabric and then stood back to admire the look. Finally, she put on her new earrings. The little beads twinkled, sparkled, and reflected light. She felt like she was wearing a delicious secret. A froth of happiness bubbled just below her skin. She would have to call to thank him.

As soon as she drove up to Serena's family's house, she got a text from Serena begging her to come find her. Lucy found the little room where the ladies could finish getting ready.

Serena pulled her in through the door. "Oh, good, I'm so glad you're here, Lucy. My sisters are still getting their hair done and I think there's something wrong. The dress feels so tight, I'm a little worried that I might faint."

"Okay, just sit down and I'll call my mom, she can fix it for you. Or, wait, maybe I can tie it differently so that you can breathe better?"

"No, don't call your mom," Serena said dramatically.

"Fine, let's try rewrapping the ties in the back, but if I unravel it, it might make it harder to put back again."

"That's okay, I just don't want to think about it. I want to be relaxed and happy."

"Okay, I'll do it." Lucy first undid the attached silk ribbon that was wrapped around Serena's waist. "If I undo all these ties, we can unbundle you."

Lucy held her breath as she unraveled the fabric ties holding the folds of the dress around Serena's waist. Serena's stomach was rounder than she had ever noticed before. Lucy looked up to meet her eyes.

Serena followed her glance. Her face had gone pale. "Aaron and I have a secret."

Lucy dropped her voice to a whisper. "Is it what I think?"

Serena nodded.

"How far along?"

"Eleven weeks. We found out for sure right before Labor Day weekend." Serena was biting her lip and watching Lucy.

Lucy suddenly felt she understood a lot more about Aaron's behavior recently. And about Aaron's used Subaru. She felt a giggle escape. "Am I going to be an auntie?" She squeezed Serena's hand. "That's wonderful news."

Serena smiled broadly but raised her other hand. "Thank you, but, Lucy, it is still a secret. At least for today."

"Okay, you got it. I know nothing." Lucy stood back considering, while still mulling over the exciting news. "Let me fix you up. I'll just go like this and loosely cross this tie over here and make a bow in the back."

She rewrapped Serena in the white gauze and it looked fine, but when she stepped away she saw that the tie in the back stuck out like a child had done it. Serena was twisting around to see herself in the mirror. "It looks like I have a key stuck into the back of the dress, like a wind-up doll."

Lucy giggled again. "Yeah, that's not the right look."

Lucy knew what she was going to do. She took Paul's pin off her dress. "Here. I'll just pin your ties together and it will look great and relaxed."

"But that's yours."

"It's okay. It's something borrowed, right?" She felt her voice going husky. She knew that Paul would have been happy that the brooch would save Aaron's bride's dress. She quickly undid it from her dress and slid the pin's backing through the fabric. The clasp behind the metal rose held the silk ties perfectly and the brooch looked like it belonged to the dress. "It looks beautiful."

"What will you do?"

"I'll be fine, I have these earrings."

"I love your dress and those are so pretty, I've never seen them before."

"They're from England," Lucy said softly, reaching up to touch their delicate strands.

The sound of laughing and squealing met their ears. Lucy could tell that the sisters had arrived. Serena looked up. "Thanks, Lucy, for everything. You've made becoming a part of your family so much easier."

"Serena, we are the lucky ones."

Suddenly Serena's father started yelling that it was time to go. He'd rented a minivan to drive them over to the church. Lucy wanted to groan when she saw that she was expected to sit in the back of the van next to Serena's younger siblings. She thought it was typical that she was still considered one of the kids. It was just the way the seating was, but she couldn't help to feel that this would also be her place once Serena and Aaron had their own children. She tried to put those thoughts out of her mind. Today she would be a good helper. And at least she had her mom to shepherd around.

But when she got to the wedding, she saw that her mom had an older attractive man hovering around her. They were laughing and her mother had a flush about her cheeks that Lucy hadn't seen for ages. Her mother had mentioned that Serena had several handsome uncles. Was this one of the uncles she'd been talking about? Lucy couldn't seem to catch her mom's eye.

When she finally did get her attention, her mom had looked very cross when she registered Lucy wearing her blue dress, whispering, "Why did you choose to wear this bright"—she looked her up and down—"getup?"

"I feel good in it."

"But beige complements you," Celia hissed.

Lucy ignored her and soon she was busy with wedding duties. After doing her part to hug Aaron's friends and welcome distant relatives, she joined the sisters in the wedding processional.

The wedding became a series of special moments. There was the moment she saw Aaron at the front of the church with a short haircut and tux. When she first saw him, she thought she was going to cry. He suddenly resembled Paul in a way she hadn't noticed before. The tiny moment when she saw Aaron put his hand on Serena's back as she arrived down the aisle to stand next to him. There was the big moment when Serena and Aaron said their vows. A moment after the vows as the jubilant sound of the entire church clapping filled the room. All of it was beautiful.

During the reception she took her seat at the family table. Lucy was glad to see Serena's parents laughing together as they ate their meal and posed for impromptu pictures. She knew that Serena had to talk them into a quicker ceremony than they would have traditionally wanted. All around her the wedding swirled but she felt detached. Her mom was seated next to Serena's aunt and they were deep in discussion about the beautiful Filipino noodle and pork dishes and the caramel sauce for the ice cream and the elegant white cake. After a while, Lucy decided to refresh her drink at the no-host bar.

Almost immediately Nina found Lucy. "I've got something to show you, but I didn't want to make your mom uncomfortable. Follow me."

Nina looked great. She wore black-framed glasses, her hair up in a chignon, and a dark green linen dress. They walked out the front door and stood in the entranceway beneath white tulle and fairy lights. "I brought something for you. Hold out your hand and close your eyes."

Lucy did as she was told, and Nina placed a tiny wood carving of a giraffe in her hands.

"Oh my gosh, is this one of Paul's?"

Nina smiled. "Yes. I thought of you the minute I found it. I knew you would treasure it."

Lucy held the little carving in her hand. She loved the long neck with lightly carved dots and its graceful body. It was no bigger than the palm of her hand but it had such character. She threw her arms around Nina. "I love it."

"He'll remind you to not be afraid to stick your neck out." Nina leaned in and matched her fierce hug. "I have some interesting news, Lucy. I decided to say yes to the teaching position." She gazed into Lucy's eyes solemnly. "Of course, I'll work with Bruce's employees on the development of the new mattress and write up documentation about our other styles. I think our secret mattress formulas will always be preserved. But I've decided this is my time to try out a new adventure."

Lucy's heart dropped. "We haven't signed anything yet. You don't have to leave us."

"I know. I just feel like my years with Wellslept are complete." She grinned impishly. "Whenever I've talked with Aaron, I can see how excited and lit up he is. About everything."

Lucy smiled. "Aaron really has grown up lately. I never would have predicted how thoughtful and smart he's become."

"Just as thoughtful and smart as his sister. I expect you'll have more time for your photos now. It's time for you to be excited too."

Lucy wasn't sure about that. They would be on a tight

schedule to bring their new mattress to the market. "Thank you." Lucy cradled the giraffe in her hands.

Nina stepped in close to Lucy. "It's not too late for you to change course. To stick your neck out and try something new."

"It is, though. I have to be here now. More than ever." Lucy thought of the baby that was coming.

"Hi, ladies." Bruce had wandered up to them. "I hope you don't mind, but I wanted to steal Lucy away. Aaron and Serena are going to have their first dance and I'm hoping to have a dance with Lucy."

Lucy shared a glance with Nina, who was smirking at her.

"I'm actually going to make my way out."

Lucy and Nina hugged again. Nina whispered into her ear, "Really think on having a life adventure, Lucy."

Nina winked as she turned to leave and Lucy followed Bruce back into the reception.

After Aaron and Serena danced, Bruce held out his hand. "You've been hard to track down tonight. Will you dance with me?"

"Of course."

Bruce was wearing an impeccably cut tux and amazing tie. He looked dashing. As they went out to the dance floor, he squeezed her hand. "I've wanted to hold you all night."

"It's been a bit of a whirlwind."

"Your dress is…colorful. At least I can always spot you in the crowd."

Lucy thought his comment made her feel a lot more like the sprawling giraffe than a princess as she held out her arms. "You look great. A tux is going the extra mile."

"Yeah, I get mine from an online rental company." He held her close and she let herself relax into his arms. He murmured, "You know, I've missed you. We should go dancing like this more often."

Lucy looked over his shoulder at Aaron and Serena. Maybe

this was what it was supposed to be like with two people working toward a professional goal, a team in action and a support that extended to love. She let herself imagine what it would be like. She saw family picnics and a house on the lake and her mother surrounded by grandchildren. It was a pretty picture.

Since the music was great, they hung out dancing and laughing with her brother. Serena had kicked off her shoes and looked so much more relaxed than Lucy had seen her previously. Bruce was funny and thoughtful all night. Of course he already knew everyone in her family and Serena's.

By the end of the night, after bubbles had been blown, toasts had been made, the wedding book signed, gifts distributed, and her mother on her way home with a relative, Lucy was feeling quite tipsy and tired. When Bruce suggested that for some fresh air, they take a walk down the street, to a little park with a view of the Seattle skyline that he insisted was most beautiful from this location, she agreed. They took a path through a playground and in a few minutes reached a setting with a view of the Seattle city lights.

Bruce pulled her close "To keep you warm," he said.

As they gazed out over the buildings and the water in the distance, Bruce began telling her about his plans for after the launch of the online commerce site. "It's going to be crazy during the launch so I'm so glad that Aaron got it done now." The blue water glittered in the distance and she could see a ferry boat traveling out to Bainbridge Island against the fading light in the sky.

"Got what done?" she said absentmindedly.

"Got married." He mused out loud, "Things are going to pick up now. We have to seal our dominance over the industry. Aaron and I will travel to New York and LA to get more investors. Can you just see it? We'll be featured in every local and national magazine for our innovations. Our company has a list of celebrity investors to cultivate and influencers to captivate. I expect us to be on panels at conferences, and in meetings to develop a global market as soon as the initial launch goes forward."

"So there won't be any downtime," Lucy said evenly.

"Nope, this is our life now. For each launch my company does, we ride a rocket ship. It will be wild and fun and hard work."

"I thought I might travel, every six months, to England. I might put on a retreat there," Lucy said, not sure what she was spinning out of her mouth.

Bruce swung his arm around her. "What? Back to England?" He chuckled. "That's not realistic for a company president, babe. We'll be promoting hard for a year."

He took her hands in his. "Are you having trouble making this change with Wellslept?"

"No, I've made peace with the new ideas for the company."

"Well, then, let those old situations go. Embrace your life running the new Wellslept."

Lucy let her fingers gently brush the giraffe in her dress pocket. She pointed toward the biggest building in Seattle. "Look how the light at the top of the building looks green against that orange sunset. I've always wanted to take a picture of it."

"I'd like an office at the top of that one," Bruce said, pointing at the largest building in the skyline, dark and sleek.

She gazed out across the city that reflected the last rays of light across the glass buildings. In contrast, the streets around them had darkened already. Bruce turned to face her. He lifted her chin and she waited for his kiss. His lips confidently touched hers and she kissed him back easily, but she felt like she was outside of herself. She tried again, but despite his more urgent kisses, she still felt unmoved. It had been this way all week, and she knew she couldn't put him off much longer.

He hesitated and lowered his voice to an intimate whisper.

"I want you to be my Laura to George, my Priscilla to Mark.

We'll take the business world by storm." He leaned in again, going for another kiss. "Would you like that?"

Lucy hyperventilated. Was he asking her to marry him?

He put his hand in her hair and his finger snagged on her earring.

It pulled. "Ouch."

He gazed at her. "I can put diamonds and pearls in those ears. You won't have to wear beads with me."

Lucy blinked several times, then stood back. "I, uh, I love these earrings."

Bruce raised his eyebrows, a smile still on his lips.

"Oh, Bruce," she sighed. "We haven't known each other for very long. As adults, I mean. I've had the best time hanging out with you during the wedding, you know, but I hope you haven't only decided to support Wellslept because you want me to be your Priscilla?" Lucy asked gently.

His eyes widened. "Oh, did you think I was asking something deep? I come on strong sometimes. No, I'm all for Wellslept in any capacity. I was carried away with the beauty of the day. It's only been a month since we've all reconnected, but it does feel like the best time, like you said. A beautiful day." He spewed out his answer, laughing huskily into the night air.

She echoed his laugh, but inside was experiencing a big sigh of relief that they had backed away from whatever he had meant. "I agree. It was a beautiful day."

Two days later, Lucy and Aaron were sitting at the conference table in Bruce's office. Aaron and Serena had postponed their honeymoon just to get all the contract details figured out before they packed their sunscreen and headed for Hawaii. Lucy had negotiated hard for three choices for customers. In front of her there was a sample mock-up video playing images of happy people dressed in white snuggling into their beds. Each image had an accompanying friendly description of its sustainability. The video illustrated how to pick a mattress in three easy steps. She and Nina had been in long productive conversations as well. They had settled on a healthy latex for their base material.

Bruce had coffee and apple cider donuts brought in to celebrate their contract signing. Celia was sitting beside her, showing Lucy her phone and exclaiming over all the new followers to her design account.

Bruce passed the documents over to them and provided them with folders that had the E-Investments West gerbera daisy motif. "Here we go." He read from the top sheet in the folder, "'A new chapter begins in Wellslept's historic life as an artisan mattress company. With nearly fifty years of experience mixed with the elegance of healthy modern design, Wellslept mattresses is where the customer is thought of first.'"

Aaron grinned. "Hey, that's great."

"First off, here's our production schedule. We've got to push to get this off the ground. My partners and I have made plans to launch by next January. Strap on your roller skates because we'll be locked in for at least the next five years."

Bruce pointed at Lucy. "We'll be unveiling it first at the big convention in Miami. Lucy will fly down there with me next week. We want to start promoting right away. I've booked us a seven-city tour. We need to hit the ground running. Lucy, you will have extra presentation and social media training from our consultant. A makeover to reflect the friendly Wellslept vibe. Everyone will know who you are. You'll have friends in every city when we're done."

"Friends in every city," she echoed. She thought of Wakeby. She thought of the tight weave of authentic friendship between the villagers there. She thought of the changes that would occur in Wakeby over five years. She thought of the bookshop.

Aaron signed. Her mother signed. Lucy's stomach became nauseous.

She excused herself to go to the bathroom. She entered the stainless-steel room and saw with surprise it was wallpapered with roses. No daisies in here, only art deco roses. Her heart raced. Roses growing up vines, roses on the hand towels, and rose soaps. Not to be completely old-fashioned, shiny Dyson hand dryers had also been installed on the walls. What was wrong with her? She didn't feel well. Her face was hot. There was a hard, uncomfortable feeling in her stomach. She stared at the wallpaper. She remembered the roses in Wakeby. Suddenly tears tightened her throat. She wanted roses. The kind that grew up the sides of bookshops.

Paul had said to thrive.

Could it be done? Change everything and go back to photography, and to Wakeby? She reached for her phone and pulled up the pictures of the bookshop. She remembered how easy it was to produce the shoot, how joyful she felt. She saw her photos of the rigid red roses on Evangeline's table. She lingered on the photo of Sam with the books and laughed when she looked at the photo she had taken of the sweet Barley under the rosebush at Baslow's. When would she see roses as president of Wellslept? She had heard Bruce say it loud and clear. There were many years in front of them, working to establish Wellslept in the e-commerce market. As copresident, she'd be fully in it. Fully in a life she didn't want. She knew she didn't want it. And if she didn't go back, Wakeby would grow and change without her. She shut her eyes, closed them tight. Trying not to see what was right in front of her. *Have a little adventure*, Nina had said. *Stick your neck out.*

Lucy fished the giraffe from her purse. "Is that what you're telling me?" she asked. "To stick my neck out?" She tried to become still. All she could think of was the thin paper of the letter where Paul had said he wanted his children to thrive. How could she? How could she turn away from Wellslept?

Thrive, he said. *You deserve to live.*

She opened her eyes. She took a shaky breath. Tried on what thriving felt like.

They were still sampling donuts when she returned. Her mom had her hands on a second donut and Aaron was smiling and holding a cup of coffee.

She took a deep breath and walked in. "I've had a change of heart. Aaron, I want you to be the sole president of Wellslept."

Her mom's mouth fell open, nearly ejecting the half-chewed pastry. "What?"

Lucy stayed standing. "I can't do it. Not as president. I'm happy to be involved with Wellslept, but I know Aaron will do better than me as a solo president. I've just realized that now is the time I should take to finish my degree. And there are quite a few things I want to start."

Bruce stood there with his eyes wide open.

Her mother frowned. "Is this really about a degree?"

Lucy didn't skip a beat. "I have a chance to work in photography. I never thought about pursuing it after Paul died, but I now realize that if I stay at Wellslept I will miss an extraordinary opportunity."

"You mean in England, don't you?" Her mother's eyes were piercing.

"Yes."

"I knew it," she cried out. "You are making the biggest mistake of your life. I've tolerated that trip back to England, but this just takes the cake. Don't you have any respect for this life we've created here?" She heard her mother's voice get tighter and Lucy felt the familiar need to calm her down.

She ignored it. Instead, she leaned into her anger. "Yes, of course I do. But why didn't you respect me? My life? I should have had access to the letters from Brian years ago. I should have had contact with him. All your secrecy stole a part of my life."

"Oh, for goodness' sake, I have no idea what pleasant dream

you think your life would have been like knowing Brian. He didn't support you when it counted and you know that."

Lucy raised her voice. "I would have liked the chance to come to that conclusion myself. All I have now is the letters he sent."

Her mother's face flushed. She clamped her mouth tight and looked away.

"That's right, I read them. I read them and read what Paul said too. Did you know he was corresponding with Brian?"

"I chose to disregard that impulse of Paul's."

Lucy took one look at her mom's indignant face. She didn't see an apology coming. "Look, I'll stay to help us transition to an e-corporation but after that I'm going to travel back to England and pursue my photography."

Her mom swiveled in her chair to face her. "After all your brother has done to get this merger going, are you really going to leave us high and dry? This is absolutely childish." She dropped her hands inadvertently rattling the china plate on the table. Her eyes bore into Lucy. "If you leave us, don't think that you'll ever be welcomed back to this family."

Lucy had not seen her mom this angry for a long time. A part of her wanted to back down, to agree to stay. She almost gave in, but her fingers brushed against the giraffe. She knew two things she had to keep to: one, she had to make her own decision and then be fully behind it; two, she could not control what her mom thought. She could not stop Brian from taking the job in England. She could not stop Tedd from not giving Brian her mother's letter. She could not fix the past and she couldn't stay trapped there.

"Mom, you can't be serious. Lucy is welcome back whenever she wants," Aaron said, finally getting a word in. He met Lucy's eyes. "I forgot you didn't finish your degree. But are you sure you want to go back to school now? Are you really sure about leaving Wellslept? It doesn't sound like you."

"My heart isn't in it the same way yours is." She found a smile. "I am sure about you and Bruce making the best decisions."

"Okay. I think you deserve to do something like this. To tell you the truth, I wondered how we were going to make this work with the both of us leading the company. Let's talk about it. Bruce?"

Bruce looked bewildered. But he nodded. "Whatever you need, Lucy. Aaron and I have a solid foundation. Celia, you're still in?"

Lucy's mother spoke sharply. "Of course I'm in."

Bruce leaned forward and set his hands firmly on the table. "Let's not get too ahead of ourselves. We still need to talk about costs, distribution, and our new roles. I'm going to need a new contract for you, Lucy." He looked thoughtful. "You'll remain in an advisory position during the transition and we'll revisit your role as we transfer into production strategy."

Lucy had no idea what he'd just said. She did feel guilty about springing her plans on him, so she nodded and agreed to meet with him later that evening.

As soon as she was alone, she made a call to—of all people— Tedd Ives. She wanted to know if he'd found a market for her father's old illustrations. She'd also had a funny tickle of a thought. She wondered if Tedd would like to invest in Wellslept.

Tedd called her back within the hour. He had indeed found an agent who contacted a gallery interested in representing both her father's grunge-era and children's illustration work, and when she told him about her plans to do photography, he mentioned a job he needed help with. When she told him about Wellslept, he commented, "Nice job being a disruptor, kiddo."

She was back in Bellevue by seven to meet with Bruce. She had suggested they meet at a cozy conveyor-belt sushi place but he insisted that she try out the sushi at the new hotel a few buildings away. She had to try their "amazing caterpillar rolls." She found him at the bar, the blue ceiling lights creating a kind of spaceship feeling around him.

"Hi, Bruce." She slid onto the bar stool next to him and they kissed.

"Hey, Lucy, you dropped quite a bomb on us today."

She stayed silent as the bartender set a large clay bottle and two small cups on the table between them. "Here is your sake."

"To us," Bruce said after he poured the warm sake to the brim of the small cups.

"To Wellslept," she echoed. "I, uh, I'm sorry about not talking to you about my feelings before blurting out my plans."

"You caught me off guard, Lucy. I even feel a little ambushed."

She winced. "Bruce, I'm sorry. I thought I could go through with it. I didn't plan on saying anything, but there's something there in England that I can't let go of. I want to give that side of myself a chance." She paused, stumbled over her words again. "When I realized how intense the launch of our products will be, I knew I'd not get back there for another year or five and I can't let that happen."

He sat there, sipping sake. "You're not interchangeable, you know. You will be needed to guide this through in some capacity. I am serious about your role in creating a strong foundation for Wellslept." He frowned. "I am serious about you too."

She took a long sip of sake. She felt crushed. Reached for his hand. "I'm so grateful to you. For all you've done for the company. For being my friend throughout the wedding." Had she used him? She winced, hoping not. "But I don't know where I'm going to be for a while."

Bruce stared at her and then pulled his hand away. "You want to break up with me too, not just Wellslept." He sounded resigned.

"Bruce, I don't think I'm really the best match for you. I don't think I can be a corporate life partner like you talked about."

"You don't have to be like that. But I thought we understood

313

each other. You've run your own company and kept it going. I admire that."

"But that isn't the true me. I was just surviving."

He looked confused. "Who is the true you?"

She wanted to say, *I don't know*, but she did have an idea. "I'm" —she swallowed—"I'm a photographer, Bruce. At least that's what I'm going to lean into when I get back to Wakeby."

"That was in London right?"

"No, Wakeby is my dad's village. It's in the countryside. I tried to tell you about it."

"I get this is what you're feeling now, but what if you're wrong? What if you're stumbling at the ten-yard line?"

"If I'm wrong, I'll come back. But if I don't go…" Lucy thought for a moment, and visualized cutting off her connection to Wakeby like firmly shutting the cover of a book. "If I don't try right now to follow my dream, I'll always regret it. I'm sorry, Bruce."

"I'm sorry too, Lucy Welland. I do not get it. But you get to be you." Then he grabbed the sake bottle and refilled his cup.

One week later, as her mother was planning her own trip to source fabric in Paris, after Aaron and Serena had departed to spend their honeymoon on a beach in Maui, Lucy had the Well-slept office to herself for the last time before the remodel began in earnest. She had agreed that the entire building be remodeled, even Paul's office. She parked the car and entered the hallway. The main showroom was already taped off with plastic as Bruce's company plans were to demolish and remodel the showroom area first.

As she headed along the entrance hallway to her old office, she noticed that a new photo had been added to the lineup of family pictures. She passed by the familiar ones. The first was a photo of Paul's parents holding hands on the sidewalk with a new Wellslept store just behind them. Later, a photo of her step-grandpa handing a pillow over to her stepgrandma and them laughing into the camera. One of her stepgrandpa with a bald head, her stepgrandma with her white hair permed into ringlets. Then, finally, one with only her stepgrandma bent and wrinkled, looking up with a smile to Paul. There was another with Paul in his big glasses from the eighties, and in the late nineties her mother appeared, tucked beside him with her frizzy hair.

She smiled, remembering how lucky she'd felt when Paul married her mother. A series of photos of her parents with very colorful backdrops conceived by her mother took her along the wall until the one where Paul was a little too thin. A little farther down past the ones of her and Aaron, she stopped in front of the last.

This wasn't what she expected she and Aaron would look like. She wasn't sure she recognized herself. They were laughing, and she definitely felt the love between them. But she looked buttoned up, pinched, and hollowed out. She stood next to Aaron with her shoulders raised up too high. She remembered how she was feeling that day. She'd been trying to convey professionalism and integrity to hide her real feelings of worry.

Lucy walked into her old office and looked at her own picture of Paul. She pulled it off the desk, intending to put it in a box to take with her. She sat at the desk he once used and sighed, her eyes filling with tears. "We've saved Wellslept, but not the way I thought," she said out loud. She removed the giraffe from her pocket.

"I trust Aaron will be okay. It's funny, but I believe Wellslept is a great gift for him. It's what he wants to do." She frowned and started again. "Before, when I imagined myself without Wellslept, I imagined myself lost and alone. Now I have a picture in my mind of what I could become if I let myself thrive, as you said. I met a friend, Flora, and we're going to do amazing things together. I have already made a summer pudding from her recipes and it actually tasted delicious. I have Brian's bookshop, I hope. And the Oak is doing well, and the Willow is too," she repeated to him as she had all the years since he died. She let a tear slip from her eyes and then another one.

Could she really leave? Would her stepfather know where she had gone? She had felt his love supporting her for so long. Would she feel his love so far away? Could she really stand alone on her own two feet?

As she took the calendar down, she changed the page to October, and her heart nearly leaped from her chest. There was a picture of a cozy armchair in front of a wall of bookcases and a ray of sun coming in from a west window. It was taken in a grand house somewhere on the east coast of the USA, but she saw the bookshop right through the picture. She laughed. Maybe Paul did know where she'd be going. Maybe his love was carrying her there.

She wiped away her tears as she opened her computer. She checked her accounts from the bank. A warm glow filled her heart. Her advance from the merger of Wellslept had arrived. After a recent discussion with Brian's agent, she had also agreed to sell several original sketches from *The Gardener's Cat*. The profits from those sales, along with her advance, would be enough to buy out Maura. It was not enough for her to buy the bookshop outright and be secure. Still, Lucy was now a consultant with E-Investments West and she would be paid regularly from that. Saving the money for a full buyout would take a lot more time. She rubbed her eyes, trying to clear it of the ghosts of the past. She looked at the giraffe, cradled in her hand.

Paul had given up his passion and he'd not lived long enough to return to it. She picked up the phone. Her heart started beating heavily. It was time.

"Hollyhock Cottage B&B, this is Flora."

"Hi, Flora, it's Lucy."

"Lucy! It's so good to hear your voice." Flora's voice lilted upward happily.

Lucy was relieved, because it made a difference how Flora was going to answer. "Would you have a room for me? Anything available next week?"

"Are you coming back? I can't wait to tell everyone," Flora exclaimed joyfully.

"Hold up, Flora. Can you keep this between you and me and your grandad?"

"A secret?"

"Just for a few days." Lucy hoped she could do it. Lucy had to cough to clear her throat. This next part was important. "Remember when we talked about doing those retreats and the cookbook and you said you'd like to and that it might be fun and all of that?"

"Yes."

"Would you still like me too? You don't have to of course, if you were just thinking about it, but I really want to try to make Wakeby a place to do that and I hope it's not a crazy idea."

"Lucy, I've thought about that conversation many times. I want to do it. I just haven't had the courage to try any of it out on my own."

Lucy let out the breath she had been holding. "We can do it together."

Flora laughed. "That's brilliant, Lucy, just brilliant."

"I am planning a—"

There was a knock at her office door. She looked up to see her mom standing there, leaning awkwardly against the frame of the door.

She decided to quickly wrap up her phone call to Flora. Although she knew it might be futile, she reminded Flora once more to keep her call a secret. After she hung up, she waved her mom in.

"I thought I'd find you here" her mom said as she strode in, her kimono-like jacket floating behind her.

Lucy wondered if that was a veiled insult, hinting that she was holding on to the past in Paul's old office.

"Yep. Just clearing out a few things," she responded with a look at her box of things to take.

Her mom brushed her curls away from her face. "When are you traveling back to England?"

"I've talked it over with Bruce and I've got some time next week that I can go, before I'm needed here again."

"Uh-huh." Her mom looked distinctly uncomfortable.

"Look if you are here to criticize my plans, I don't need to hear that."

"I'm not here for that. I'm here to offer you an olive branch or whatever."

"A what?"

"An olive branch." She sighed and looked away from Lucy. Her eyes seemed to find the picture of Paul that was sitting on the top of Lucy's box of things to take. "I wanted to say that I'm sorry about what I said at the Wellslept meeting. You are family to me for now and forever. I'm sorry for the way I handled things about Brian." She bit her lip. "At the time you were growing up, I wanted him out of our lives because I knew you would get hurt."

"I missed him," Lucy said simply.

"Yeah, I understand. I mean he chose to leave us. And then he thought he could have you love him anyway. He wanted to be a hero to you."

"That's not the whole story."

Celia raised her hand. One bangle slid down her arm. "I know that now. I even got an email from some guy named Tedd Ives telling me that just a few days ago. But honey, no matter how guilty or not guilty he was, what I'm trying to say is that I let my anger at Brian turn me into a bad parent. I let my feelings about him control the way I saw you. When you took responsibility for me and Aaron and the business, well, I thought I was being a good parent by making you tougher and teaching you to be sensible. I was a wild child and it didn't turn out. I thought I was providing you with a much better way to live. I was determined to keep you safe and sound."

Lucy saw that her mom was trying. She let down her guard a little. "You did keep me protected. The thing is that I'll be thirty years old pretty soon. So I need to give my dreams a shot before it's too late. I can't just stay safe anymore."

Her mom nodded. "I see that. I do want to point out that it is never too late to follow your dreams. The interest in my little coverlets is teaching me that."

Despite being glad for her mom, Lucy hoped that Celia didn't think Lucy ought to wait until she was in her late sixties to begin.

"I'd like to see them." Celia came around to the same side of her desk.

"See what?"

"I didn't get a chance to see your photos. Of the bookshop…" Her voice trailed off.

Lucy met her mom's eyes. She was serious. Lucy opened up her laptop and clicked on her photo file. The screen began filling with shots of the village, the postbox, the fields and stone fences and the bookshop. Lucy let her hand stop the photo scrolling right there. The one with the morning sunlight on the rose and the bookshop sign.

Celia cleared her throat. "That's quite good."

"Baslow's Books. That's where I'm going."

Celia kept looking at her screen. "No, I mean, your photos. They are very good, Lucy." She drew back to regard Lucy. Her voice was full and proud. "You have my eye for art."

Lucy smiled, enjoying the praise, although wishing her mom didn't sound so newly amazed about it. "How can I help it? It runs in the family."

· · ·

319

After a busy week, Lucy finally arrived at SeaTac, and the following day she stepped off the plane in London. She couldn't believe how the fears of arriving the first time felt so far away now. This time she was going home. She found the train to get her to Wakeby and after a comfortable train ride, was cheered immensely as she pulled into the village train depot. Mr. Emery picked her up again. She gave him a big hug when he emerged from the car.

"I imagine you want to tell Sam the good news."

She nodded, grateful that she had told Flora and Mr. Emery that she had secured enough funding to buy Maura out. He kindly took her luggage over to the B&B and left her standing on the sidewalk. Lucy gazed up in front of Baslow's Books and smiled. She loved it. She was surprised to see it so busy. But then she recognized the octogenarian component of the customers. It was their monthly visit.

When she walked in, she didn't see him at first. Her heart was beating rapidly. What if the words he said over a month ago weren't the truth? What if Maura had been right? What if Sam was back dating Deborah? She had told herself that if he was, it was still okay. This was about saving the bookshop and making her own way.

Fran lumbered over to her. "You still here?"

Lucy laughed, "Actually, I'm back."

"Good thing you came back. The shop is up for sale. It's terribly sad."

"I know. I've got a plan for that, I hope."

What if Sam wouldn't agree? What if he had moved on financially? She still didn't have enough to buy him out. She loved books but he was the bookseller. She worried, as she had worried for what felt like days now.

There was a movement behind the counter and she saw that Sam had been getting a package for one of the patrons. She quickly moved over while he was looking the other way. He was still looking down when he said, "How can I help you?"

"I'd like to buy this book...shop," she said.

He looked up and started. She saw his cheeks flush.

"Lucy, you're here." He seemed frozen, tightly gripping the book in his hands.

"I'm here."

He blinked. He waved at the elderly man standing next to her. "Watch the till for a minute, James, will you?"

He led her into the studio.

"How is this possible, Lucy?"

"I changed my position at Wellslept. The merger happened and I came into some buyout money. And last week, I finally got it." His face didn't change so she kept talking nervously. *Courage,* she told herself.

"It's not for the entire bookshop yet. I've only got enough to buy out Maura. But in a while, I can buy you out too. The main thing is that Maura has signed off on it. I had to agree to the highest price she imagined the bookshop could get but she finally agreed to her cut. She just wants to get on with her life."

"That's what I want too," Sam said.

"You do?" Her heart hurt. She had been wrong.

"Are you really planning to stay?" He didn't sound like he believed her.

She noticed he looked tired. She drank in the look of his skin, his eyes, his arms, his clothes. She wanted to stroke his cheek. "Yes, I am. I'm going to continue with my photography. I can work remotely for Wellslept. I've found someone nearby to study with. That photographer in town, actually, she offers mentorships. Plus, I'm going to help Flora too."

He looked...what was it? Troubled? She felt horrible. Had she made a mistake? She had wanted this to be a surprise, but perhaps he was angry with her. She hated the feeling, like she'd gone way too far, like she'd misread everything. Had he really just wanted to get on with his life?

She pulled the paperwork out of her bag. "This is it, you just have to sign here to take the bookshop off the market."

"I need to think for a minute." He walked toward the back of the room, his back to her.

She felt tears spring to her eyes. She set the paper down quietly and walked out the back door, then slipped into Flora's garden. She had so hoped that he would be happy about it, but maybe he'd already moved on.

She stood looking down at the cheerful burgundy chrysanthemums and purple asters planted in a row. She didn't feel their cheeriness at all. She heard the gate open and sensed that he was behind her.

"Lucy, you out here?"

"I'm in the garden."

He found her and sat beside her on the bench. "Lucy, I want to make you a proposal. After you'd gone, I tried to find another place to run a bookshop. I even hired an estate agent, but I couldn't find anywhere as special as this to run a bookshop. I've always loved books. I want to read them and I want to write them. I took this life for granted before. I don't want to let it go." He ran his hand through his hair absentmindedly. "What I'm trying to say is, I want to be your partner. I want to keep my ownership in the building. Don't plan to buy me out. We can co-own it. If you can trust me?"

She looked at him with her heart swelling.

He reached for her hands. "I know they say not to mix business with pleasure, but I think we'd be good at it. Look what we've already gone through."

"You're not with Deborah?" she squeaked.

"No, that ended the night we had dinner with Tedd Ives. You're not with the big bouquet guy?" he asked, warmly clasping her hands in his.

"No. That's done."

He suddenly looked lighter, his eyes bluer, his lips turning upward, and finally he leaned forward to whisper into her hair. "These past weeks have been miserable. I've missed you."

"I missed you too, terribly. Sam…" She drew back and stared into his eyes, now locked steadily on hers, then rushed to kiss him. She pulled back and, just to be sure he was real, she touched his cheekbones that she loved, the scruff on his cheeks, his hair, and then traced her fingers down to the collar of his shirt.

He reached up to touch her earrings, the earrings he had sent.

His face broke into a smile. "I knew you'd look beautiful in them." He pulled her into his arms. She put her head on his chest and listened to his steady heartbeat. He ran his hands along her hair and kept on holding her tight as the last summer bees buzzed around them, and the hollyhocks, now gone to seed, stood as noble sentinels gently swaying in the breeze. In fact, it wasn't until James called out for Sam from the back porch that Lucy remembered the bookshop needed its bookseller right away.

EPILOGUE

*F*ive weeks later, Lucy stood in front of the bookshop with the intention of getting a photo taken. This time, she was the photographer. She'd been wanting to take this photo ever since she'd arrived but other work had taken precedence. Other work that had her leaping out of bed each morning with an air of purpose. Her notebooks were filled with projects. Number one had been working with Flora on her cookbook. That had given her the confidence to take a job working with a friend of Beena's to showcase her homemade jewelry.

Tedd had brought her work too. It was harder to see the beauty in his BMW showroom, but she found it in closeups of a new blue metallic paint hugging the curves of next year's convertible. She had just finished the last of the photos for his office two days ago. And now the weather had decided to cooperate for the shoot she couldn't wait to do.

The morning fog had drifted away and they were enjoying a glorious rare sunny November day that still clung to the notion of fall. She had imagined the shot every day she'd been back in Seattle consulting for Wellslept. The idea of it had kept her moving forward day by day. After she set up the camera stand, she focused on her subjects. Sam swiftly picked up Barley and gave her a funny awkward smile.

"Just a step forward," she instructed. "Perfect."

She paused to enjoy how handsome they looked under the few brave roses still blooming. Even though they were deep into autumn, the roses hadn't quit. Some people said they had never seen such a year for roses. While she'd been gone, of course, Sam had not touched the vine at all. She took a deep breath and drew the scented air into her lungs. Above them, the Baslow's Books sign shined brightly in the sunlight.

She started the timer ticking and ran into the picture. She put her arm around Sam, and Barley lifted his nose into her shoulder. Sam looked down at her with a smile on his lips. She grinned up at him as the camera clicked quietly away.

* * *

THE END

COMING SOON...

Thank you so much for reading *The English Bookshop*. I hope you found it to be just the kind of comfort read you were looking for —and that you enjoyed it! If you liked *The English Bookshop*, please join my mailing list so I can keep you up-to-date on the gardens I'm exploring, the books I'm reading, and the recipes I'm trying as I write my next British-infused fiction, *The Jane Austen Road Trip*.

You'll find my newsletter sign-up at www.janiswildy.com

ACKNOWLEDGMENTS

First off, warmest thanks to you for reading my story! A great number of fantastic writers and friends got me to this point. I'm thrilled to be able to share them with you.

I want to especially acknowledge my writing mentor, Waverly Fitzgerald. From the very first novel classes I took with her in the 1990's, I felt welcomed by her into the world of writing. Waverly's insightful advice, passion for Britain, and companionship on this writer's journey gave me the strongest of foundations. Even though she passed away in 2019, I am still learning from her.

There is a special place in my heart full of appreciation for the Elliott Bay Bookstore in Seattle. A light open space filled with books, it's a place that has always made me feel inspired to be a writer. In fact, Waverly set up wonderful writing groups that met at the Elliott Bay Bookstore and I have many happy memories of our times at the bookstore café.

I want to thank my beloved friends in the Friday Writers Group: Linda Anderson, Rachel Bukey, Martha Crites, and Curt Colbert. To sit around a table with you and hear your writing is a delightful honor and privilege. It's even fun on Zoom.

Another group that Waverly established is the Friday Marketing Group. Also filled with supportive dynamic writers—Alice K. Boatwright, Jeffrey Briggs, Cecilia Aragorn, Charlotte Stuart, Luanne Brown, Martha Crites, and Robert Herold—who share the joys and quirks of marketing. I'm so grateful to learn from your endeavors.

Thanks of the greatest order go out to:

My developmental editor, Kim Kessler, who is a complete delight to work with.

My copy editor, Abby Parsons, who gave me so much confidence about my storyline.

My proofreader, Beth Attwood, who taught me a great deal about commas with positivity.

My sensitivity reader, Brittany Yost, who gave me a boost with her comments.

My cover designer, Leah Jacobs-Gordon, who is immensely talented and patient.

Professionals who inspired or mentored me from afar; Joanna Penn, Mark Dawson and James Blatch, Paul Teague, Jami Albright, Steve Henry, Ed Fotheringham, Marte Marie Forsberg, Brooke Castillo, Tonya Leigh, Jessica Brody, Blake Snyder, and Tim Grahl, Steven Pressfield, and Shawn Coyne.

Along the way, my dear friend, Sophie Ramsey, heard many iterations of the book. Having a friend that loves the BBC version of *Pride and Prejudice* as much as I do, has traveled with me to England, and listens to all my book ideas and enthusiasms is a relationship to be cherished!

Thank you to my friends, Wilma Angell and Penny Eachus, for the warm enduring sustenance of your friendship. Let the sisterhood flourish forever!

A bouquet of thanks goes to Rachel Bukey for being there with support and humor in a way that bookends my week and springboards me into the next. The time we spend planning and plotting is where the magic comes from. Writing isn't always easy but traveling through the writer's life (and to the Surrey Writers Conference) is a true pleasure with my FFGF.

I must also extend my thanks to Nancy Sackman for being one of my earliest writer buddies. Thanks also go to another early writing buddy, Angela Jane Fountas. Un grand merci goes to Reed Hutchinson for the gift of your talent and artistic mindset. Thanks to lovely friends Joan Engelmeyer, Tim Silbaugh, Juli Russell, and Ingrid Ricks. And to Elana Jassy, a special thank you for all the inspiring creative discussions we've shared over breakfast.

Extra thanks to Melissa Frondozo for your suggestions and to Eun-Gyong Lee for the gift of a book that helped at the last minute!

Many thanks go to my incredible beta reader: Marie-Therese Keegan.

Additional thanks go to Samir and Anya Manchanda for listening to all those writing podcasts in the car.

A debt of gratitude goes to my parents for installing in me a love of reading and an appreciation for their Canadian upbringing and traditions.

To my sister, Edwana Wildy, thank you for your great energy, sense of style, and humorous perspective. You and Eric keep me up-to-date. To Grace: thanks for sharing your drawings and stories with me.

Thank you to my mother-in-law, Estell Berteig, and the Berteig family, for your true support over the years.

Finally, to my husband Rolf, who has heard all the emerging storylines, the different podcasts, and new writing theories on my way to finishing this novel. To the man who supplies me with chutney and brandy butter, I couldn't be more grateful to you for your support! I'm so lucky to have you as the most wonderful creative role model and to Bryn, thank you for being a great listener who always has time to talk about marketing and entrepreneurship with me.

Lots of love to you.

IF YOU'D LIKE TO LEAVE A REVIEW...

... it would mean the world to me! The review can be as short as you like! One line can do it. The reviews really matter for how booksellers, algorithms and readers see the book. Thank you so much!

ABOUT THE AUTHOR

Janis Wildy is an author, an Anglophile and a lover of books that take her to beautiful settings. She loves planners, peonies and Pimm's Cup, although a dram of whisky or a cup of tea is always welcome. She lives in Seattle and welcomes emails at janis@janiswildy.com.

Made in the USA
Middletown, DE
30 November 2023

44060021R00203